KU-665-403

Bromley Libraries

30128 80539 591 3

Praise for Yoto Carnegie Medal nominated
The Song that Sings Us

'A magnificent adventure story.'

The Scotsman

'Career-crowning.'

***Observer* best children's books of the year**

'It balances the line between grief and wonder, hope and fear. I was chilled, heartbroken and felt reflected in it too, but the story, it is glorious and visionary with epic adventures and beautiful characters! I loved it so much.'

Dara McAnulty

'A gripping adventure that will set your heart racing and stir your soul. Utterly unputdownable, packed with unforgettable animal characters (humans included) … Vivid and original, this is a story for now.'

Helen Scales

'Beautiful. Heart-wrenching, gripping, strange and glorious. Jam-packed with brilliant characters and big ideas. Loved it! I am also now in love with a sea-faring tiger captain…'

Liz Hyder

'Beautiful, lyrical and fast paced. *The Song That Sings Us* is a story of our time. It parallels the urgency of the challenges we face to protect this world.'

Gill Lewis

'Wild, powerful and passionate, *The Song that Sings Us* is an extraordinary weaving of fierce action and tender poetry, a heart-wrenching yet hopeful symphony of the threads that connect all life on Earth.'

Sophie Anderson

'… a hyper-imaginative book, bringing to mind the complete works of Philip Pullman with their sprawling cast of animal familiars, Yan Martell's *Life of Pi* with which it shares a tiger on a boat – although this one has 'fur like fire and soot, whiskers like strands of white wire, green eyes like the aurora'.'

Jon Gower, *Nation Cymru*

'Captain Skrimsli!' the woman calls out over her shoulder, and the others take up the cry. 'Captain Skrimsli!' Even the rowers have stopped their singing now, and instead call out one word.

'Skrimsli! Skrimsli! Skrimsli.'

What does this mean? Is it an instruction that they need to follow?

Suddenly the cry of Skrimsli breaks down into cheers and the crew who line the gunwales step back. In their place is a huge tiger.

'Hold on tight!' the green-coated woman yells. 'The captain will get you aboard!'

From *The Song that Sings Us* by Nicola Davies
(Firefly 2021)

'Skrimsli was not a character I planned. He happened without me having to think about him first. And then he almost took over *The Song that Sings Us*, so it seemed a good idea to give him a story of his own, and to tell the history of how a tiger becomes a talking sea captain!'

Nicola Davies

Skrimsli

First published in 2023
by Firefly Press
25 Gabalfa Road, Llandaff North, Cardiff, CF14 2JJ
www.fireflypress.co.uk

Words © Nicola Davies 2023
Illustrations © Jackie Morris 2023

The author asserts her moral right to be identified as author in accordance with the
Copyright, Designs and Patent Act, 1988.

All rights reserved.
This book is sold subject to the condition that it shall not, by way of trade or
otherwise, be lent, re-sold, hired out or otherwise circulated without the publisher's
prior consent in any form, binding or cover other than that in which it is published
and without a similar condition including this condition being imposed on the
subsequent purchaser.

All characters in this publication are fictitious and any resemblance to real persons,
living or dead, is purely coincidental.

A CIP catalogue record of this book is available from
the British Library.

Print ISBN 978-1-913102-80-7
Ebook ISBN 978-1-913102-81-4

This book has been published with the support of
the Books Council of Wales.

Typeset by Elaine Sharples
Printed by CPI Group (UK) Ltd, Croydon, Surrey, CR0 4YY

Skrimsli

Nicola Davies

DEDICATION AND THANKS

This book is dedicated to everyone who struggles to
find a place where they truly belong.

With thanks (again) to my first audience: Jackie Morris,
Cathy Fisher and Molly Howell

And to my husband Dan Jones for ... everything

Who are you if you've never seen another face like yours?
Where do you belong if you don't know where your home is?
What do you call yourself when others call you 'freak'?
How can you be brave when you are full of fear?
Why would you choose purpose over love?

The tiger and the sturgeon and the owl are the keepers of the forest. Each must speak to each to keep the forest whole. But the owl, who speaks to both the river and the trees, is the greatest keeper of them all

Contents

1
Owl

Death and Birth

Night was Owl's time. He could move around the circus like a shadow, unseen and undisturbed. He could rest amongst the animal pens in the Menagerie Marquee, listening to the rumbling talk of the elephants and the comforting snores of the sloth bears. He could poke sticks into the little stove and cook whatever food he'd scavenged from the deserted mess tent. There was no one to gawp and jeer and call him a 'Freak of Nature: The Human Boy with the Face of an Owl!'

But tonight, Owl's peace was disturbed, because Narastikeri, the old tigress, was dying. Everyone in the circus came to take a look at her. Saldo and Zuta, the trapeze artists, were first, Zuta sobbing into a lace handkerchief. Old Galu Mak, the dog trainer came next and whispered to the tigress through the bars, 'You are crazy-pretty pussy cat, Madam.' The cooks and the stable hands, the wardrobe master and the maintenance ladies, the musicians and the master of provisions, all remembered the days when Narastikeri had been the star of every show. They all filed past, peered sadly at the withered creature panting on the dirty straw, and shook their heads.

Even the 'jantevas' – the roadies, whose job it was to lift and

1

carry and fix, and who treated everyone with contempt – piled out of their caravan and shuffled past to pay their respects. They clutched their caps in their big hands, mumbling like small boys at their auntie's funeral.

Everyone took Narastikeri's dying as a very bad omen. Another sign of the poor luck that had dogged the circus since they began this ill-fated tour. Majak's Marvellous Circus had been sent to the mountain provinces by the Nordsky Department of National Pride. But mountain people didn't like circuses and the weather had been harsher than anyone had expected, with heavy snow from October. The circus had ended up stranded in a small town, at the end of a broken train line, in a sea of snow. People talked of running away, but where was there to run to? Dalz and Tapis, the trick riders, had tried it two nights ago. They had vanished, with four of the best horses and a litter of beautiful hound pups that Galu Mak had planned to add to her act. Just this morning two of the horses had come back lame and spooked, without riders or pups.

'We're gonna die here in these damn mountains,' Galu Mak had said.

Narastikeri's procession of visitors continued. Owl watched them from his hiding place under the stack of benches behind the dying tigress' cage.

The last to make a visit were the boss himself, Kobret Majak, and his bear, Karu. Kobret was almost as big as his bear, a huge man with a face as hard as a cut diamond. Karu shuffled behind him, unkempt and dead-eyed, so much under Kobret's control as to have no real mind of his own. All the other animals drew back as Kobret and his bear passed by. They carried fear with them like a cloud.

In front of his audience Kobret Majak played the part of the jolly ringmaster. He claimed that kindness and reward were all he used to train his animals. But it was lies. Kobret possessed the power of Listening, the ability to tune into animals' minds. He liked to deny it because it had fallen out of favour with the Nordsky Government. But he had it alright and used it to force his way into the minds of animals, to implant pain and terror. That was how he made them do the tricks that made audiences gasp in wonder.

Listeners like Kobret could not enter human minds. So he used the claws and invincible strength of his slave, the bear Karu, to terrify the humans too. Animals and people only had to look at Kobret Majak and Karu to feel afraid.

Narastikeri was almost beyond Kobret's cruelty now. She closed her eyes and her belly heaved, trying to push out the cubs she'd carried for too short a time. It was obvious that she was slipping away, but Kobret showed no kindness or concern for the tigress who had been famous for her beauty and skill. As usual, all he thought about was money. He turned to Akit, the stable hand whose job it was to see to the care of the animals and growled.

'I paid a fortune to get her mated to that white tiger!' Kobret said. 'These cubs were supposed to pay my bills.'

Karu turned to Akit and bared his teeth. The man cowered.

'Narastikeri's old and sick, Boss,' Akit whispered. 'Maybe she shouldn't have been carrying no cubs.'

'How dare you criticise me?' Kobret roared. 'Don't you know how much money people will pay to pet a white tiger cub?'

3

Owl thought that Kobret would hit poor Akit, who raised an arm to protect himself.

'No, no, Boss. Course not.' Akit paused. Owl could see how much Narastikeri's state upset him: enough to risk Kobret's anger and Karu's claws. 'There is an animal healer in the town who we could ask for, Boss,' Akit suggested quietly.

'And what will *that* cost?' Kobret hissed. 'No. I'm not throwing good money after bad.'

'Could I have the key to her cage then, Boss?' Akit went on bravely. 'So I can make her a bit more comfortable?'

Kobret turned to the stable hand and poked him in the chest with one thick finger, while Karu stood close, snarling to back up his master.

'Comfortable? This is an *animal!* It is a mute, dumb *beast.* It'll be dead by morning, when I'll take the last bit of profit from it that I can: its skin. You have other work to do. Now get out, before Karu makes a meal of you!'

Karu stood up on his hind legs, towering over the man, who staggered backwards, then ran.

Kobret kicked the bars of the cage, cursed, and stalked out of the menagerie, grumbling and growling, just like his bear.

At last, apart from the usual sound of ropes and canvas arguing with the wind, it was quiet. The people had gone back to their cozy caravans to moan about this disastrous tour. The tears they cried over Narastikeri were partly shed for their own plight. Owl guessed that most of them had forgotten about the dying tigress the moment they'd left the tent.

Owl crept from his lair and sat looking through the bars at Narastikeri. Her fur was dirty and matted, and her breathing was irregular. Under her closed lids her eyeballs rolled. She gave a small growl of pain and bared her broken, yellow teeth. Years of Kobret's cruelty had made the old tigress mean, and Owl had always been afraid of her, but his heart hurt to see her suffering like this. So he shuffled closer, then closer still, until at last he could reach out a hand to touch her head. She flinched a little at first but then she let him stroke the stripes between her eyes.

Kobret kept the only key to the cage, so Owl could not get inside, but he gave what small help he could. He fetched clean rags and water and reached through the bars to clean her crusted eyes and drip water onto her lips. But he could do nothing to help the cubs. One by one, as the night went on, they appeared, each too small and weak to take a single breath. Narastikeri tried to lick them into life, but she was barely strong enough to lift her head. Owl's arms were too short to reach any of them – to clear their mouths and noses, or massage breath into the tiny bodies with their faint fuzz of pale fur.

The sixth cub was the last. It was not pale like the others, not one of the 'litter of beautiful white tiger cubs' that the Majak's had already advertised on posters all around the snowy town. This one was the colour of fire. But it too lay still and did not seem to breathe. Owl looked at it and wondered how something so bright could not be alive.

Narastikeri managed to open her eyes and look at her last, flame-coloured child. She let out a long, low moan and Owl felt her grief envelope him. How could she be comforted, he wondered. The only comfort he knew himself was to escape to the place he kept safe inside, the great green forest where he had been born. In his mind he could plunge into its greenness, not just a colour but a feeling of home, of peace and belonging. Its trees were huge, their branches reached to the sky, their roots spoke under the brown earth. He had lived in one of those great trees, in a shelter woven out of stems and twigs like a giant nest. Many creatures thrived there, bears and owls, tigers and wolves. Ancient fish, huge sturgeon, swam in the deepest pools of the slow rivers.

In that place Owl had not been a freak. He had fitted like an eye in its socket, or a leaf bursting from a bud. He remembered arms rocking him and whispering words:

'The tiger and the sturgeon and the owl are the keepers of the forest. Each must speak to each to keep the forest whole. But the owl, who speaks to both the river and the trees, is the greatest keeper of them all.'

Where was that forest now? Somewhere to the north was all he knew, because he had been stolen from it when he was so small. All he had to guide him was the name of his village, Bayuk Lazil, and the little wooden sturgeon on a string around his neck. He wrapped his fingers around it and whispered the words Bayuk Lazil like a spell. This was his route back to that place of green and belonging. Owl wished he could take Narastikeri with him, but he could not. Immersed in the comfort of his green home, Owl fell asleep.

He was woken by the shouts of the jantevas. It was light, the grey-blue light of a snowy landscape. In her cage, Narastikeri was quite still. The cage had been opened and the jantevas were swarming around her like eager maggots.

'Get out of the way, Freak Boy,' they told him. 'We got a dead tiger to skin and get rid of.'

Owl scuttled back to the safety of the stack of benches. Even in death the tigress was formidable; it still took five men to move her out of the tent to skin her in the open, then throw her remains into a waiting cart. The sixth was left behind to clean out the cage and to scoop the dead cubs into a sack. One by one they dropped like wetted lead, but as the big hand grabbed the last one, the orange cub, it squeaked. It was alive! Owl knew the man had heard it too.

'Leave the fire-coloured cub!' Owl called. 'Please!'

None of the other jantevas would have bothered to answer, but this was the one called Brack, who had a split in his lip. His brothers teased him and called him 'freak', the same word they used for Owl.

Brack shook his head. 'Orders!' he said. 'Orders.'

'Where will you take them?' Owl asked.

'Ground's too 'ard for burying,' Brack lisped in reply. 'Boss says drop 'em through the ice on the lake.'

He hurried away, with the sack over his shoulder.

Owl waited for the sound of the cart's wheels crunching over the snow before he moved. He didn't want the jantevas to see him. Then he hurried from the tent, turning his eyes from the bloody stain on the snow where the tigress had been skinned. Owl knew a short cut, a path the townspeople used, that ran from the perimeter fence around the circus, between the trees, down to the jetty at the lakeside. That would be where they'd take Narastikeri and her cubs. Owl ran along it, his short legs struggling through the snow, his arms flailing. But even his fastest pace was much too slow. By the time he had reached the lake, the jantevas were on their way back and their cart was empty. He was too late. A jagged hole in the ice showed black water where the bodies had been dumped. He lay down on the jetty and stared into the ice hole. Nothing. Narastikeri's body must have sunk straight to the bottom. He leaned further, trying to look through the blackness. There! There! His heart skipped; the sack had caught on something below the surface. He could see it still floating, almost within reach.

How long would a sickly newborn cub survive in ice-cold water? Not long. Heart racing, Owl wrenched a fallen branch from the snow-covered tangle of undergrowth and struggled with it to the jetty's end. He took two goes to hook the sack with the crooked, unwieldy thing. Then more long moments to loosen the knotted string that tied the neck of the sack. Finally, he reached inside and pulled out the fire-coloured cub.

It was a male, or would have been, but it was stone cold, still and limp. Owl sat down. He had thought himself hardened beyond crying, but tears came into his eyes now as the cub lay like a rag in his lap. Owl felt defeated, more beaten than ever before. Then he remembered something he'd once seen Galu Mak do with a newborn pup that hadn't breathed. She'd held the little creature by its back legs and swung it round. He remembered how the pup had spluttered into life. Owl stood up; he held the cub dangling by its back legs. It seemed so brutal, but he had to try. He swung the cub around his head. Water flew from its drenched coat and its small tail flopped about. He swung again. Once, twice. Nothing.

And then, on the third swing, a sound. A tiny, spluttering cough; a pink mouth opening to let out a noise more worthy of a mouse than of a tiger. Owl thought it was the most beautiful, important sound he'd ever heard. Owl rubbed the cub's fur to fluff it up, then put the cub inside his shirt, next to the warmth of his skin and began to trudge back up the snowy track towards the shelter of the Menagerie Marquee. As he walked, he felt warmth slowly spreading from his body to the cub's, but it was very still, only just alive. Owl realised that rescuing the cub was foolish if he couldn't find a way to feed it! However would he do that?

By the time he reached the menagerie, Owl had come up with no answers, and was beginning to feel defeated again until he saw that Taze was waiting for him at the entrance. Taze was the old hound who had belonged to the stunt riders Dalz and Tapis. The handsome pups they'd taken when they rode off into the night had been hers. She trotted up to Owl and pushed her nose into his shirt where the cub was hidden, as if she knew there was another baby that needed her help. In response, the cub squirmed and gave a demanding squeak, sensing the prospect of his first meal.

Owl scratched the soft place behind Taze's ears and she closed her eyes in pleasure.

'We will raise a tiger, you and me!' Owl whispered to her. The cub squeaked again: now that he had a chance, he seemed quite determined not to die. Suddenly Owl felt determined too; this cub *would* live and somehow Owl *would* protect him from Kobret's cruelty. As they walked in under the shelter of the canvas canopy, Owl found himself smiling with pure joy.

He was not alone anymore! A wild thought flew up from the green place inside the boy's heart, an impossible dream.

'We will find the green, you and I,' he told the cub. 'We will find my old home, where Owl and Tiger are the forest keepers.'

In answer the cub gnawed at his finger with its small toothless jaws.

'You are a monster!' Owl laughed and a word came to his lips from the language of that long-lost green place. 'Monster,' he said. 'Yes, *skrimsli*. Skrimsli! *That's* your name.'

2
Kal

Dark Stars

 Kal ran beside the horse, a flurry of snowflakes flecking face and body, hooves ringing on the frozen ground. Kal could smell the horse's fear: fear for himself and fear for his human companion.

'Run faster, Luja. Leave me behind,' Kal wanted to tell him. 'It's me they want, not you!' But Kal had never had the knack of entering a horse's mind; they had always understood each other well enough without that. In any case, Kal knew Luja would not go on alone.

The pursuers were not yet gaining on them. The wheels of their horseless chariots were no match for this rock-strewn ground. But a bullet had already grazed Kal's shoulder; it was just a matter of time before they grew close enough for another, more damaging shot. Long before nightfall gave them cover, the two assassins would be on them. Then Kal would be killed and maybe Luja too. Even if it drew more gunfire, riding was their only chance.

With the next running step, Kal placed a hand on Luja's shoulder, pushed off with the left foot and slung the right over Luja's warm flank. Low across the horse's neck, with the strands of his mane streaming, Kal felt the ripple of muscles beneath the horse's skin. In spite of their danger, there was that familiar surge of exultation that always flowed from Luja, as they leapt forward in a gallop that no other horse on earth could catch.

Bullets zipped around them, tearing the air with small ripping sounds. Luja's eyes showed white rims of fear yet, somehow, he found more speed. Soon the shots bit the turf behind his heels quite harmlessly.

Up ahead rose the sacred mountain, Tamen Haja: a huge ridge of rock, like the mane of a giant horse rising from the grassy plains. Its sides were cut by a hundred deep ravines made by a million years of spring meltwater. Kal had often run to that kingdom of rocks and streams to escape what other people wanted. *Do this! Go there! Be like this! Don't be like that!* Kal had pleased no one and fitted nowhere. On Tamen Haja there were only the demands of wind and water and sky.

One place was Kal's favourite refuge. The narrowest of gullies, cut where water had found a fault in the rock and widened it. There was a cave there that made a perfect hiding place. But how to reach it undetected by these two persistent followers? There was no cover between here on the plain and the slopes where the network of ravines began. The assassins would track their path easily. If only the snow would fall faster and hide them now! Instead, the sun dropped below the cloud and lit the plain with bright slanting light, illuminating everything in dazzling detail!

Dazzling! *Dazzling… That* was the answer.

'This way, Luja, into the sun!'

As if he'd understood Kal's words, Luja began to swerve,

galloping straight into the sunset. Kal glanced back and saw the assassins trying to shade their eyes from the glare. To them, horse and rider had now vanished into the blinding light. Kal urged Luja to go faster up the slope ahead, and then turned him at right angles to head behind a low ridge that ran all the way to the mountain. The pursuers would assume that they were still heading west. By the time the sunset faded, Luja and Kal would be covered by the grey bloom of dusk.

Warmth from the deep heart of the rock kept the pools in the gully bottom unfrozen year-round and started spring grass growing early. Luja sucked in the sweet water and cropped some tufts of grass. By the time they were picking their way up the side of ravine, the last light was fading from the sky. It took all Kal's skill and patience to help the horse navigate the narrow route and persuade him to stoop low enough to get inside the cave. But here they were at last hidden beneath a vaulted roof of rock. A fissure opened to the rear of the cave, a crooked crack that led to open air three hundred feet above. This made a chimney that would guide their smoke up to where the air moved swiftly, whisking away any tell-tale plume. Kal had been visiting this secret spot for years and always left a little store of sticks and kindling tucked away on a rocky ledge where damp couldn't reach. Kal's fingers found these now in the dark, and the flint and steel wrapped in oiled cloth. Friendly flames sprang up and yellow light filled the cave.

A dark patch of blood stained Kal's shirt sleeve which peeled away to reveal a scratch half a finger long across the muscle at the top of the arm. Luja stretched over to snuffle at it with his soft nose, ears back.

13

'It's fine,' Kal told him. 'It's not bleeding.'

Luja snuffled again.

'It's already scabbing over,' Kal reassured him. 'I'll bind it with a strip of cloth. It'll be fine.' Kal tore a strip from the hem of the shirt and bound the wound tight.

'There! See?'

Finally, the horse ceased his inspection and curled his legs beneath him like a cat soaking up the warmth from the fire. Kal shuffled closer to him. Everything about Luja was a comfort: his size, his warmth, his smell. Kal breathed it all in and the dam that had held back the horror of the day crumbled. Kal's whole body shook as the memory replayed.

Kal and Luja had been travelling to Talo Numikalo, the ancient sanctuary of the Horse people, where Kal had been raised. Kal was the child of a Herring father and a Horse mother: a wild man who vanished back to sea and a nomadic shaman who left as soon as Kal was weaned. No one had wanted Kal, a dark little creature who cried easily and snarled readily. Like a troublesome parcel, Kal had been passed between various outposts of Herring people family. And when that didn't work, Kal was sent to Talo.

Talo Numikalo was part monastery, part refuge. It was an ordered community of people and their horses, all with deep knowledge of the Sea of Grass. Kal had rebelled against its calm routines and quiet duties because rebellion was a habit, a strategy for self-protection. But the Talo residents had better things to do than scold and punish an awkward child. They let Kal be and watched at a distance to see what would happen. What happened was that Kal found horses and loved them.

Horses never asked for or expected anything, they just accepted. Kal understood them without thinking. Left free, and alone except for the horses, Kal thrived. Talo became the nearest Kal had to 'home'.

Talo was an ageing community, as few young people now wanted to know the secrets of the Sea of Grass, the medicinal properties of its thousand plants, or how the land and ocean worked together to keep the grass sea lush and green. They didn't even want to know the old way of working with the sea's beautiful wild horses; nowadays people preferred the easy force of metal bits and leather bridles. So the Talo community was awash with old knowledge with nowhere to go, and some of it flowed into Kal in spite of the instinct to resist.

When Kal left childhood behind and became a person strong enough to haul a lobster pot or a creel of herring, Father's relatives decided that the 'troublesome parcel' could at last be of some use. So Kal was only free to spend time at Talo between the end of winter fishing and the start of spring planting.

It was a long journey from the Herring people to their old friends. Kal and Luja had begun in the afternoon of the previous day and travelled through the night with few rests. The weather was still cold. Kal was glad of the cap of felted wool and the padded yellow coat that the Herring relatives found so outrageous: gifts from Kal's last visit to the Talo community.

The final part of the journey passed quickly, because Luja wanted to run and was happy to carry Kal on his back. The Grass Sea had streamed around them, coming to life at last after the long winter, even though snow still lay in a few shaded hollows. Flocks of small birds swarmed over its surface, huge yellow bees buzzed among the earliest flowers and arrow-shaped formations of cranes called above, as they headed north.

Kal and Luja played their usual games. The horse would turn to nip at Kal's feet, which was Kal's cue to swing feet and legs to the other side. Luja would give a little buck as he sped along; this was the cue to slide under Luja's belly and cling there, head almost hitting the ground as it rushed beneath them. Best of all was when Kal stood on the horse's back as he galloped, arms spread wide as if they were wings that could carry them away.

It was joyous to return to Talo after the winter of rough sea, hauling nets in the dark and taking baskets of fish to market in various rickety little carts. As usual, Kal had been scolded for everything: hair, clothes, behaviour, life prospects, ideas, speech. It was like being a bush constantly attacked by pruning; there was never any way to grow. Riding over the grassy plain, Kal was so busy soaking up the sense of freedom that the smear of smoke over the low thatched buildings went unnoticed. Only when Luja gave a low whicker of alarm and voices reached them on the wind, did Kal see that something was very, very wrong. Luja snorted, ears flat, nostrils wide, sucking information from the air. Kal slid from his back, down into the grass and crouched low to peer between his legs.

Snow had begun to fall in swift spurts, like the whisk of a curtain across the scene. Still, Kal could see enough to be filled with horror. Flames leapt through the roofs of the buildings.

16

Horses screeched in terror, wheeled around and fled, vanishing into the smoke. The people were not so lucky. Talo Numikalo residents ran to escape the fire and were calmly struck down by two identical attackers. They were tall and slender, dressed in close-fitting garments and dark face masks. They moved with precision, more like machines than humans. Each carried foreign weapons, long guns slung over their shoulders that caught the light. But they did not use these; instead, they picked off the fleeing Talo residents with Erem crossbows and finished them off with clubs that fishermen used to kill big fish.

None of the Talo people fought back; they were healers, artisans and shamans, not warriors. They could not resist these killers who were so expert, so coldly calm. Any survivors who managed to evade the first round of slaughter were pursued by the two killers in their small horseless carriages.

Kal was close enough to recognise some people through the shifting veils of snow. Nurmi, who had tried to teach Kal to make healing teas from a hundred different plants when all Kal wanted to do was run with the horses; Puun, who showed how flatbread was made in smooth wide rounds, though Kal had only managed to burn it; Yurti and Laiden who had introduced Kal to Luja as a newborn foal.

At last, the screaming stopped. There was no one left to scream. But the killers had more to do. They dragged two bodies from one of the horseless chariots. These were dressed in the waxed overalls and peaked caps that every Herring person wore to sea. They gave one body a crossbow and the other a club, then positioned the bodies carefully. Kal realised that they were trying to make it look as if these Herring men had attacked Talo and had been slaughtered in return. The killers stood looking at the carnage as if over a well-ploughed field. Then they greeted each other with a strange little gesture, a kind of hand-flapping wave, the sort of thing two children might do: twins with a secret language of words and signs.

That was when they noticed Luja and Kal, half hidden in the grass. Only the crack of the rifle shot and the wetness of the blood had woken Kal from the trance of horror. Just in time, Kal and Luja had turned and run.

The fire in the cave glowed warm but still Kal shivered. But for the lucky glare of the setting sun, they would be lying now with snowflakes settling on their open eyes. Kal drew closer to Luja, breathing to match his steady breaths until there was enough peace to be able to think. Somewhere in the terrible images that crowded Kal's mind there were clues, information.

Who were the attackers? Who would gain by killing a bunch of old Horse folk. And why did they want to make it look as if Herring people had done the killing? One thing was certain and that was that they were not thieves or madmen. Killing was their business. Kal shivered; professional assassins would not give up. They might be creeping through the night now, this minute. Hiding alone in a cave was wrong. Kal and Luja must return to where they were just one horse and rider among many. Perhaps they could find out what was going on, what all this meant.

As soon as the moon rose, Kal doused the fire and roused the dozing Luja, who was reluctant to leave the warm cave and go back into the chilly night. Kal whispered in the horse's ear, words of nonsense and affection and his temper was soon restored.

They picked their way along the river and paused at dawn to rest a little. Kal scanned the ravine and listened: there was nothing to hear but water and the morning cries of birds; nothing to see but rocks and branches, scraps of sky and Luja's pale coat gleaming in the early light. That coat! *Milk white with stars made from darkness* was how Yurti always described it. *There's no horse like him in all of Erem.* The assassins would spot it from a mile away.

There were still some fruits left on the mayoban bushes that grew in thickets by the flowing water. Kal gathered them and rubbed them into Luja's coat. Their dark brown juice changed him into just another grubby, dark horse. Luja snuffed at the smell of the juice in disapproval.

'We need to be disguised,' Kal told him.

The yellow coat and tall felted cap were just as distinctive, of course. Kal shoved the coat deep into a crack between two rocks. The felt cap sank in the river and with it the ribbon that tied Kal's long braid. Kal peered at the reflection in the pool, a wary face and a cloud of dark hair. As unfamiliar as always but at least now it would not match what the killers had seen.

They would head for Turgu, the main port of Erem, where there were ships and crews from Nordsky, Rumyc, Danet and even further; both Herring and Horse people came there to buy and trade.

'We'll hide in that crowd,' Kal told Luja. 'We'll find Havvity. She'll know what's going on.'

Saying Havvity's name out loud took away a little of the horror of the previous day. Havvity was the closest thing to a real sister that Kal had: not a blood relative but the niece of Kal's father's first wife, Meghu. In spite of the fact that Meghu hated Kal as 'the child of that horse witch', Havvity and Kal had grown close. Havvity was sure and steady, always kind when Kal was tormented by dark moods and self-doubt. But since the unplanned appearance of Roko, Havvity's baby son, Kal had repaid a little of the debt of her kindness, by defending her from Meghu's cruel disapproval. This and the rush of fierce protective love that Kal felt for Roko had brought the two young people close.

Kal pushed away the thought that the pursuit of the two assassins might force a flight beyond the borders of Erem, far from Havvity and Roko. For now, the horror that they'd witnessed and what it meant could be buried in the beat of Luja's hooves.

At sunrise on the second day they reached the low plateau of short, horse-grazed turf that tilted gently towards the sea at Turgu.

'Now my friend,' Kal whispered to Luja, 'run like the wind!' Tired and hungry though he was, Luja broke into the loping canter that he could sustain for miles. Blue sky showed between the clouds and small herds of wild horses dotted the green. Luja sniffed the air to gather their news. It seemed impossible that anything really bad could happen in such a place.

But as they entered Turgu, Kal knew at once that something was wrong. The air crackled with fear. The busy, cheerful clatter of the town was gone, replaced with silence and the banging of doors. Householders were covering their windows in weatherboards, as if a great storm was on its way. In the market square, stall holders were packing up, tight lipped and unsmiling, and shops were drawing down their blinds. Kal managed to buy a loaf from a baker as he shut his door and stood in the shadow of a tethering tree to share it with Luja and watch what was happening. Horse people were all leaving town in a hurry, horses, ponies and carts clattering over the cobbles in their haste. All around, black looks flew from Herring to Horse and back.

A Nordsky horseless chariot, like a big green fish-box on wheels, came into the square. It coughed black smoke from a pipe in its rear and something growled under the lid at its front. It was like the chariots that the assassins had used, but uglier. The driver steered the thing slowly up the road, while a man stood up in the back with a megaphone. He wore a black uniform with a red symbol on its collar. Two Nordsky soldiers in green uniforms walked beside the chariot with rifles ready, staring left to right as if they'd like to shoot everything they saw. Megaphone man repeated his message over and over again.

'Attention all citizens. Turgu is now under the command of Military Forces. You have nothing to fear. We will restore order, control the conflict and prevent war. We order all Horse people to move out of the town at once. Herring residents must keep off the streets. Stay in your homes. Remain calm.'

What conflict? What war? The green uniforms were Nordsky army, who always found some excuse to flex their muscles in Erem. But who was the one in black? He spoke with a Rumyc accent. Why could Nordskys and Rumycs tell Erem people what to do? A cold bubble of fear burst in Kal's belly; would Roko and Havvity be safe in a town at war?

21

Following behind the chariot was a Herring boy in a waxed sea-coat, with a hammer, a bag of nails and a pile of small posters in a bag slung over his shoulder. Every few yards he stopped to pin a poster to any wall that would hold a nail. The boy nailed one to the door close to Kal and Luja. He glanced nervously at Kal and gave a quick smile.

'Always liked Horses me,' he said. 'But there's them 'ere what doesn't, right now. I'd make myself scarce if I was you. Sharpish!'

As the boy moved on up the street Kal read the poster he had put up.

Wanted for Murder at East Cove
Rider 15-17 years. Male, wearing traditional
Horse headdress and yellow coat.
Pale horse with distinctive spotted pattern.
Reward offered for information leading to capture
Reports to Commander Lazit,
Automator Forces, Turgu Garrison

Kal's heart froze. Wanted for *murder?* East Cove folk were Kal's father's people. They had never been kind, but Kal didn't want any of them dead! What was happening? How was the world unravelling so fast? Fear spread through Kal's body now, like ice crystals blossoming across a windowpane. Kal grabbed the poster from the nail and scrunched it into a pocket.

'Come on, Luja,' Kal breathed. 'We need to get off the street. We need to find Havvity.' Kal darted down the alleyway that led to the Black Fish Café, where Havvity worked for her Aunty Meghu. Luja's hooves scraped and echoed on the cobbles and the Black Fish sign swayed a little, announcing '*the cafe that never closes*'. But it *was* closed. Kal knocked on the door. A small window, two floors above the cafe opened and Meghu popped her head out. Kal hoped she hadn't seen the posters.

'Oh, it's you and your stinking beast!' she cried. 'Go away!'

'Is Havvity in?' Kal called. 'How is Roko?'

'Like you care!' Meghu snarled. 'Haven't you heard? Your lot killed everyone in East Cove who wasn't at sea last night. Go away!' The window slammed shut.

Everyone in East Cove? Not a murder but a massacre! Just like Talo. Someone wanted to set Horse against Herring and Herring against Horse with lies. Kal pulled the poster out and looked at it.

Wanted for murder…

Rider 15–17 years. Male, wearing traditional Horse headdress and yellow coat.

This lie did two jobs: it blamed the killing of Herring people on a Horse; and it silenced the one person who knew the truth. Kal saw now exactly why the assassins had given chase!

Luja's hooves made nervous clopping sounds on the cobbles. His ears swirled, picking up the sound of running boots and angry voices just before Kal did. At the end of the alley, an old man appeared pulling at the bridle of a mouse-coloured pony. The creature was lame in its right hind foot. The man was terrified. The shouts grew louder. The man tried to get the pony into the alley, but they were suddenly surrounded by a mob of Herrings, men and women. The Herrings carried objects that had come easily to hand: a rolling pin, a walking stick, a butter pat, even a wooden doll to use as weapons. Ordinary objects and ordinary people turned to evil.

23

Kal and Luja fled down the alley as the mob advanced. But the road beyond was filled with rows of marching soldiers, each black uniform carrying the symbol of a red fist closing around the earth. Kal and Luja were trapped.

A hand landed on Kal's shoulder and Kal spun round in terror. It was Havvity with little Roko in her arms. Havvity's sweet open face was clouded with fear, but Roko took his thumb from his mouth and grinned.

'Kawwyy!' he exclaimed, his version of Kal's name, and tried to wriggle from his mother's arms into Kal's.

'Not now, Roko love,' Kal said. 'In a minute!'

Luja wickered softly and snuffled his nose into the child's hair.

'This way. Quickly.' Havvity pulled Kal and Luja into a stone arch and through groaning stable doors to a small, covered courtyard. She pushed the doors shut just as the Herring mob came round the bend.

Kal and Havvity stood very close with Roko sandwiched between them, eyes locked over the top of the child's small head. Havvity's expression softened at last, and her eyes said *hello, good to see you.* Kal put a finger to Roko's lips.

'Shhhh, shhh.'

'Shhh,' Roko whispered back, thinking this was a game, until the shouts of the mob grew louder and more frightening, and he buried his face in his mother's coat.

They all held their breath until, at last, the shouts retreated towards the square. Rain spattered on the roof above them in the sudden quiet.

Roko plugged his mouth with a thumb once more and leant sleepily into his mother's arms.

'I'm so glad to see you, Kal!'

'And I you!' Kal said.

'I feared you were dead, Kal, killed with all our kin at East Cove.' Havvity's lips trembled. 'And now today those posters. What's going on?'

'I hoped you'd tell me!' Kal breathed. 'I left East Cove days ago to go to Talo.'

'Oh!' Havvity's hand went to her mouth in horror. 'Then you know about the killings?'

Kal nodded. 'I was there, Havvity. I saw it happen. Two assassins, not Herring folk. Professional killers. But here's the thing. They had two Herring bodies. They put weapons in their hands and…'

Kal's voice faltered at the remembered horror, but Havvity didn't need to hear the rest

'They wanted to make it look like Herrings did the killing!' she said.

Kal nodded again. 'Whoever's behind all this wants me dead,' Kal said. 'Because of what I saw.'

There was a sudden ring of military boots on the cobbles right outside the door. Kal laid a hand on Havvity's arm, and the two friends froze in alarm. Voices came from the doorway, just audible over the rain that fell on the roof above. Their low whispering told Kal that these speakers didn't want to be heard. Kal peered through a knothole to see to whom the voices belonged.

Two black-uniformed officers had taken shelter underneath the arch. One was older, with close-cropped, steel-grey hair, the other younger, with a sandy moustache like a pale pencil line above his thin lips. The older had an air of authority.

'Wretched weather!' he snarled. 'Why didn't you bring an umbrella, Reeven Dopp?'

He spoke in Nordsky, the second language for everyone in Erem. But his companion answered in Rumyc that few outside the port towns understood.

'Apologies, Commander Lazit.' The mustachioed man, Reeven Dopp, was all but cringing.

The older man, Lazit, was instantly angry.

'Speak Nordsky, you fool. We don't want Rumyc involvement here to be obvious.'

The reply came at once, in Nordsky.

'Forgive me, Commander.'

'Just give your report then, while we are stranded here!' the Commander snapped. Reeven Dopp seemed reluctant to reply. He cleared his throat. Lazit rolled his eyes. 'Oh, get on with it!'

'Well, Commander,' the man began. 'Our special operatives completed the two missions.'

'And were the necessary terminations achieved?'

'The what?' Reeven Dopp stuttered.

'Oh, for goodness' sake, man!' Lazit growled. 'Did they kill everyone at Talo Numikalo and East Cove?'

'Oh, yes.' Reeven Dopp nodded eagerly. 'But there was a small problem ... a witness at Talo.'

Lazit let out his breath in a hiss.

'Tell me they didn't allow this witness to escape?' Lazit snarled. Reeven Dopp hung his head. 'I'm afraid so, sir.'

Lazit spoke through clenched teeth. 'And where are our special operatives now?'

'On the way to their next assignment, sir.'

26

Lazit passed a hand over his eyes. 'You do understand that this civil war is vital to our plans, Reeven Dopp?'

'Oh yes, of course, Sir.'

'Then *deal with this witness.*' The venom in Lazit's low whisper almost made Kal gasp. 'They must be *silenced, destroyed, discredited*. I don't care how you do it. The witness must not be allowed to tell what they know.'

Reeven Dopp nodded so hard his head might have come off.

'I have taken immediate steps. Issued a description of the person and named them as a murderer. I have…'

'I don't care. All I want to hear is that the *witness is dealt with.*'

'Of course, Commander. Yes, I will do all the…'

Lazit waved a hand in irritation. 'Just get on with it, you idiot. Now, seeing as the rain has stopped, I will continue to the town hall to address our forces. I have a war to start and a gold mine to dig.'

A moment later both the men had vanished, and their footsteps had receded up the street.

'A gold mine to dig?' whispered Havvity.

'They want the gold that's under Tamen Haja,' Kal said. 'That's why they want to start a war. So everyone will be too busy fighting to stop them.'

Havvity was pale with shock. 'It's going to be terrible. Like that mob and the old man!' She grabbed at Kal's sleeve with desperate fingers. 'You could stop it, Kal. If people know the truth, they'll stop fighting.'

Kal stared at Havvity.

'Who's going to listen to me?' Kal said. 'I've been a misfit all my life. You heard what that man said. They'll call me a murderer and they'll kill me. Who will that save? There's nothing I can do.'

Havvity's eyes filled with tears.

'Couldn't you try, Kal?' she said.

'It's no use, Havvity,' Kal said softly. 'You know it's not.'

Yes, she did know, of course. Kal was 'the witch's child' to the Herrings, 'the feckless drunk's spawn' to the Horses. Nothing about Kal fitted anywhere and never had. As Kal saw Havvity's slow sad nod a new fear sprang up.

'I shouldn't have come here. Now you and Roko are in danger too!'

Havvity looked so small with Roko now fast asleep inside her coat. Kal wanted so much to protect the two of them, but the best thing to do now was to push them away.

'Go!' Kal cried. 'Go now!'

Havvity's eyes grew wide. 'But where will *you* go, Kal?'

'Somewhere! I don't know,' Kal replied. 'It doesn't matter. What matters is that you stay safe. It's better you don't know where I am. Kal creaked open the door and began to push Havvity and Roko through it.

'Wait!' said Havvity. 'Wait.' She rummaged in a pocket, pulled out a crumpled piece of paper and thrust it into Kal's hands.

'I kept this for you,' she said. 'I thought it was a chance for you go somewhere you wouldn't be a misfit!' Havvity smiled, then she turned and clattered down the street towards the café.

Kal looked at Havvity's piece of paper.

Majak's Marvellous Circus!
Nordsky's Finest Circus needs new talent
visit our ship at Central Quay
show Itmis Majak what you can do.

Kal's forehead rested against Luja's. The noble, quiet mind that loved the grass and the wind thrummed just beyond the boundary of bone and blood. Kal longed to see his thoughts!

'What should we do, Luja? What should we do?'

Luja didn't answer, but the rain fell again, heavy as glass beads. In minutes Luja's disguise would wash off and he would match the description on the wanted posters. They'd be found and *'dealt with'*.

Down at the quay, Kal spotted the ship at once, the vessel closest to the end which carried a banner down its side.

MAJAK'S MARVELLOUS CIRCUS

The crew were making her ready to leave. They would have to hurry. The sloping cobbles, wet with rain, were too treacherous for more than a walk, but a narrow strip of muddy grass ran the length of the quayside beside the granite blocks that held the sea at bay. It was just wide enough for Luja to find the easy canter that he loved. In a moment they were alongside the vessel.

The cargo was being stowed and everyone was clearly in a rush to escape the conflict that had suddenly erupted in Erem. In the middle of the foredeck, surrounded by boxes, enormous tent poles and a huge roll of striped canvas, stood a man in a

29

red frock coat and a blue top hat. He was tall and elegant, and even from a distance Kal could see that his face was striking. He seemed young to be the proprietor of a circus. Kal called out in Nordsky.

'Mr Majak, we wish to try for your circus.'

As the man looked up, the last mooring lines were cast off and the ship began to glide forward, slowly, almost imperceptibly, pulling away from the quay toward the grey waters of the Strait of Swans.

Mr Majak raised his hat in greeting in spite of the rain. 'You are a little late!'

The ship began to move more quickly and the distance between it and the quay widened. Kal and Luja kept pace with it. The crew laughed and pointed at the rain-soaked horse and rider. Kal and Luja were one creature now, rolling with water that ran like a river over them out of the sky.

'You do not seem to be giving up,' the man cried.

'No,' Kal replied.

'What can you do? Cantering is all very well, but really more is required of a circus performer.' The man shrugged his elegant shoulders.

'Give us space,' Kal shouted, 'and we will show you!'

Just in time, the ship's crew read the body language of this crazy person and the horse. With cries of alarm, boxes, crates and cages were hastily shoved aside to clear the deck and all stood out of the way.

'We're going to jump, Luja,' Kal whispered, 'jump for our lives!'

Kal felt the horse's spirit rise, courageous and desperate in equal measure, wild, joyous and completely at one with Kal's own. Like a great 'yes!' cried out through his whole body, Luja bunched his back legs under him and sprang. The hooves of his front feet rang on the very edge of the quay, striking a shower of sparks from the granite, pushing the ground away as if it meant nothing to him. Below them, in the green waters of the harbour, astonished crabs looked up at the biggest flying creature they had ever seen; above was the swirling cloud.

For a moment they soared, then landed, skidding at speed and threatening to slide clear off the deck and into the harbour. But the sturdy deck hands rushed forward and pushed against the horse's considerable momentum to bring the fatal slide to a halt. The crew cheered and Mr Majak stepped forward, beaming.

'Bravo! Bravo, everyone!'

Kal slid from Luja's back. Stand straight, think bold, a voice inside seemed to say. Kal looked the man in the eye and stood tall.

'Do we get a job?'

Mr Majak smiled.

'Yes! Yes indeed, Madam, you do!' He put out his hand to be shaken.

Madam? Kal hesitated, hand hovering.

'Madam Numiko at your service, Mr Majak,' Kal said, bowing slightly from the waist.

'I am delighted to make your acquaintance. Please call me Itmis! Mr Majak sounds like my father.' Kal noted that the man's smile did not light up his eyes. He continued, 'Do let me introduce our other newest performers: the Acrobat Twins, Spion and Listig. They have just joined our company!'

Two women dressed in identical red jumpsuits, with identical yellow curls popped up from between the piles of boxes. Their faces were like dolls, their eyes were as pale as glass, they smiled and yet looked like something that would bite.

'We look forward to working with you!' said the one called Spion, whose face was the sharper of the two.

'Yes,' said the other, more round-faced one. 'We *love* horses.'

Just then, the rain became fierce and slapped the deck, so Kal didn't notice the little sidestep Luja took to avoid Listig's reaching hand.

'We are getting soaked,' Itmis exclaimed. 'We should get under cover. I have just one question, Madam Numiko: why is your horse changing colour?

As Luja shook the water from his coat and, with it, the last of the berry dye, the twin acrobats exclaimed in delight.

'He really is very striking!' said Spion.

'Milk white with dark stars!' said Listig.

'*Very* distinctive indeed,' Itmis added. A look passed between him and the two acrobats that, although unreadable, sent a shiver up Kal's spine.

3
Skrimsli

The Elephant's Eye

 The cub's eyes opened on a blurry world. Things loomed out of it. A snout and a warm tongue, cleaning his face. He gave a short 'mew' of protest, but the warm tongue took no notice. A firm paw held him still until he was clean all over.

He slept, and drifted about in warm, milky dreams. When his eyes opened again, another face loomed: pale and round, with dark eyes, furless. It showed its teeth but was friendly. Its paws smoothed the cub's fur and scratched his ears, so he wriggled with pleasure and purred. A sound came from the face, a 'huh huh huh' sound that attached at once to the feelings of warmth and pleasure. When he slipped back to sleep this time, the being behind that face slipped with him. Together, they entered dreams of green where they walked between tall trees beside flowing water.

Long Snout and Round Face were his safety, always there to care for him. Their faces, sounds and smells imprinted on the cub's mind and made a mould to help shape the sort of creature that he would grow into.

The cub found his paws. When he thought 'move', they moved! At first his tail was chasing him, but he found it was

33

himself too. There were smells and noises all around. Curious, he crawled towards them. He grew cold and very tired. A huge rubbery tube came for him. It huffed and snuffed, hot wet breath, then curled around his middle and lifted him off the ground. He mewed with terror, certain he would be eaten by the tube creature.

But he was not eaten, or even harmed, instead he was held level with an eye, nested in wrinkled skin. The cub looked into it and saw a world so much bigger than the one he knew. He stopped his mewing and stared into the eye in wonder.

Long Snout and Round Face came running to his rescue. He was lowered into Round Face's paws, into warmth and safety. They would protect him always. But he remembered the big world inside the elephant's eye, and it sang to him in his sleep.

Day by day the cub grew stronger, saw further. He found three faces in a puddle. Long Snout, Round Face and another. The Another poked the puddle with its paw just as he did the same. It broke the faces into lines of light. When they reappeared, something spoke inside him, and he recognised Another as himself. Why was he so different from Long Snout and Round Face? What sort of creature was he?

He explored his little world, the floor of mud and straw, the cages and food hoppers, the rats that scuttled in the night. He met the other beings who lived there, the big tube noses, the humpy backs, the claw paws. Every day they greeted him with deep rumbling sounds he felt through his feet that spoke of alarm and comfort, anger and love. Soon they knew each other well. But none of them were like him or either of his parents. Where did he fit? He did not know.

He explored the place inside his own head too. There he found Round Face as if they sometimes shared the same head. It did not seem strange to Skrimsli since he'd never known another way to be, but Round Face's thoughts were so different from his own. They contained the thought shapes that Round Face used to label things in the world. These were called *words* and finding them so often in the shared part of their two minds, Skrimsli could not help but learn them. He grew to understand words, whether they were just the thought shapes inside Round Face's head or the sounds that Round Face made through his mouth and put in the air. The cub heard the inside and the outside words and understood.

The word 'Owl', he learned meant Round Face. 'Taze' was Long Snout. 'Skrimsli' was himself. Other beings like Owl were 'human'. Galu Mak was human but her companions, like Taze, were 'dogs' – although they looked quite like the 'rats' that scuttled round the tent at night, their smell told him that they were indeed kin to Taze. He learned the labels for the tube noses, 'elephant'; the humpy backs, 'camel'; the long claws, 'bear'. He learned another category: 'friends'. These shared no physical features, only their behaviour, which Owl said was called 'kind'. 'Kind' meant giving food, or help, or comfort. 'Kind' was what held Owl and Taze and Skrimsli together. The cub saw that 'kind' made them stronger than they would be alone.

Dogs, humans, camels, elephants, bears, but there were no Skrimslies. What *was* he?

At last Owl told him. 'Tiger', Owl said. Tiger was the label for the kind of being that he was. His own body gave him clues about what 'tiger' meant. His eyes were drawn to

35

movement as a magnet is to iron, his ears alerted him to the smallest sounds. He noticed, he remembered, and he thought. He soon knew the meaning of every sound he heard. The creak of the hinge at dawn that meant Galu Mak had cracked open the window to let out the steam from the first boiled kettle of the day; the twin sighs that came from the sloth bears as they settled into their straw bed; the muffled angry voices that said the jantevas were fighting over cards again.

In play fighting with Taze, the cub found strength; when he grew stronger than her, he found control.

His body told him that tigers were built for killing, and that his claws and teeth were tools for delivering death. When a thing was made dead, he could eat it and then its body became part of his. This was a solemn thing, which he carried like a weight for days until his hunger made the heaviness light. Owl took him to the snowy forest at night. Everything was new and unfamiliar and, at first, he didn't know what he should do. But his instincts spoke to him, and he found they told the truth. If he acted on them, he would not fail. He sensed the hiding places of rabbits, killed, ate, and felt invincible.

He was a tiger born to the legacy of his kind: great strength, sharp senses, deep intelligence. Born to be wild. When the sounds of the mountain nights came to him – the sighing wind, the calls of wolves, the snap of frost – they spoke of the world beyond the circus. It was the world he had glimpsed in the elephant's eye and visited in Owl's green dreams. It called to him and his heart sang back in longing.

But he was not just tiger. Those sound shapes that he

learned, those words, were changing him. When he was alone, he tried to make them for himself. Although all that came out of his mouth were yowls and growls, inside his head, he could speak a little, almost like a human.

4
Owl

The Iron Collar

Taze and Skrimsli were having their morning play fight, chasing each other around the menagerie, startling the elephants and the camels, and rolling over and over in front of the sloth-bear enclosure. Owl could hardly believe how much the cub had grown in six months. That autumn day when he had been pulled from the lake he had been small enough to fit inside one of Galu Mak's jewelled handbags, the way her little show dogs did. Now he was bigger than his foster mother Taze, with huge paws and shoulders rippling with muscle.

Owl was proud of the job that he and Taze had done raising the cub. He could not remember his first family from the house in the tree, but he knew that he, Taze and Skrimsli worked like one. Like all families, they'd had to struggle sometimes, especially when Taze's milk was no longer enough and Owl had had to find meat to feed Skrimsli. It had meant doing the thing Owl hated most: talking to people. People could be cruel, they called him freak, laughed when they heard his cracked, squeaky voice. So Owl had learned to keep silent, safe and separate. Stepping from the invisibility he had made for himself had been hard. But to Owl's astonishment he had found some friends: Gruff old Anasta, the provisioner whose job it was to keep the whole circus fed, both animals and people, had simply added Skrimsli's food to his list.

'As far as the boss is concerned,' Anasta had told Owl with a wink, 'the bears are eating more because of the winter weather.'

Galu Mak had been helpful too, popping by with treats for Taze.

'She's mummy to a super big pup. She needs extra!!'

And Mappa Po, the biggest, fiercest of the cooks, had started smiling at Owl and giving him extra portions when he turned up at the mess tent.

But the best thing about raising the cub was something invisible. Almost from the first day that Skrimsli had been in his care, Owl had felt the cub inside his mind. Owl had never had the gift of Listening, the ability to slip inside an animal's mind and hear their thoughts or even speak to them. So, at first Owl had thought he was imagining things. He asked Galu Mak how she read the thoughts of her dogs and used that ability to train them, but the old lady just told him to 'shush'.

'It's not safe to talk about these things now!' she had scolded. 'Anyway,' she added in a whisper, 'not a thing you learn, boy. A thing you *know*, or don't.'

He asked Akit, who had once told Owl that in his land, in the White Sea, all people spoke to animals; but Akit was just as unhelpful.

'My mind is like ice. It melts to open.'

Owl didn't feel he 'knew' anything and staring at the cub, imagining a wall of ice melting and himself stepping through, didn't help at all.

But as the cub got bigger and more independent Owl grew more certain that something in their two minds was joining up. When Skrimsli was close, it was as if he could see through the cub's eyes. He could feel the cub exploring inside his head, gently padding about and sniffing at things.

One day, when they were spreading clean straw in the elephants' enclosure, Owl decided to try out this connection. Skrimsli was pouncing on the strands that had caught the breeze from the open tent flap. Owl could see that the old elephant, Mallamalla, was getting cross. She'd been fond of Skrimsli ever since she'd almost stepped on him when he was tiny, but like many old ladies, she sometimes found the playing of children a bit too boisterous. Any moment now, she would lose her temper and send the cub flying with a whack of her trunk.

Skrimsli! Stoppit. Owl told the cub inside his head.

Skrimsli froze, mid pounce and turned his bright face towards Owl, ears forward, whiskers twitching.

'Stoppit!' Owl repeated, with his voice. 'Mallamalla will hit you.'

Skrimsli looked over his shoulder at the elephant who was flapping her ears in irritation and swinging her trunk. He flattened his ears to his head and slunk away, giving Owl a head bump of thanks as he passed. Owl's heart sang. From then on, he spoke to the cub all the time, outside and inside his head. The cub didn't always hear or understand, but Owl kept doing it anyway.

The thing Owl most wanted to tell the cub was to keep out of Kobret's way. As long as Kobret didn't notice him, he was safe from his cruelty. But it was tricky. Kobret and Karu came to the menage almost every day to put the animals 'through their paces'. Which meant reminding them all how much fear and pain he could inflict if they didn't do exactly what they were told, the moment they were told to do it. The stable hands helped to keep the cub out of Kobret's way by giving a special, high-pitched whistle when the ringmaster was heading towards the menagerie. Luckily, growing tigers need lots of sleep, so Skrimsli spent much of every day out of sight, curled up under the stack of audience seating.

Deep into the night, when Kobret and the rest of the circus were asleep, Owl took Skrimsli and Taze out into the snowy woods. They caught rabbits together, Skrimsli pouncing on the ones he found crouching in clumps of frosted grass; Taze chasing after those that broke cover and made a run for it under the starlight. They both crunched them up with great relish. Sometimes Owl thought they should just keep on walking away from the circus. But he wasn't sure they could survive in the mountains and knew they would be easy to track through the snow. He feared how Kobret would punish them for trying to get away.

As Skrimsli grew, it became harder and harder to hide such a big, orange secret. It was just a matter of time before someone whispered in the ringmaster's ear and Kobret came looking. And when Owl heard the circus was to move from the mountains and cross the country by train to reach the Sand City he knew it would be impossible to keep a half-grown tiger out of sight. Yet every day Owl said to himself *not today, not yet.* Not until he had come up with some plan of escape for them both or some way to keep Skrimsli safe from the harm that Kobret could do.

Owl was saying 'not today, not yet' to himself again, as he pulled two ox bones from the snow drift that served as their larder. There was a crunch of footsteps in the frost behind him and the low rumble of the bear Karu's voice. Then, Kobret's huge hand grasped his shoulder.

'Well, my little freak,' said the man, giving Owl a shake. 'I'm sure *you* aren't going to eat *those*. Shall we see whose breakfast you *are* preparing?'

He dragged Owl, still holding the bones, inside the marquee, with Karu lumbering along behind. Skrimsli had allowed Taze to pin him to the ground and was affectionately gnawing on one of her ears. As soon as Taze saw Kobret she sprang away, her tail between her legs, already whining. Skrimsli simply stood up and shook himself, and stood very still, his nose twitching towards the delicious scent of bone.

Kobret stared at the cub.

'Well, well, well,' he breathed. 'So *you* are the secret our little freak has been keeping all this time.' He caught Owl's face in his hand and twisted it to look into his own. 'You cannot have secrets from me, Freak,' he whispered. 'You belong to me and so does everything you think and do.'

Karu made a moaning sound that didn't sound much like support to Owl, and Kobret snarled at him.

'Shut up, Karu.'

The bear sat back on his haunches and hung his head.

Kobret turned his attention back to the cub, his eyes glittering. Skrimsli had grown used to all the different people who came and tended to the circus animals but he was still young and wary of anyone new. Usually he backed away from strangers, sometimes snarling and spitting, as he had done as a very small cub. This time, he didn't move at all. He simply stared back, holding the ringmaster's gaze, and staring at the dejected bear. Skrimsli was so still that Owl wondered in alarm if Kobret was already slipping inside the cub's mind. Would Owl sense it if that happened? He didn't know.

Kobret walked around Skrimsli, taking in every feature, like a shopkeeper totting up his stock: the deep, fire-coloured coat, the sharp black markings, the massive paws that showed how very, very much bigger the tiger would grow.

'You are going to make me a *great deal* of money!' he crooned. 'You will be more than enough to impress the Palatine of the Sand Sea!'

Slowly Kobret ran his hand over the cub's dense coat, from shoulder to tail and Owl felt the whole menagerie holding its breath. Skrimsli froze as Kobret's touch grew heavier and his hand shifted to wrap the pale fur of the cub's throat.

'You will be the star of our new show! I will train you myself as soon as we reach Shamanow.' Kobret began to tighten his grasp, closing his fat fingers on the pale fur. Owl shuddered. It looked as if the cub would allow the ringmaster to do anything. Then Skrimsli began to growl, not the rasp of a cub, but the deep, bone-shaking rumble of an adult tiger. He seemed to grow larger and brighter; his eyes flashed, and his bared teeth glinted. Kobret snatched his hand away and the dark hairs that covered it stood on end.

'Oh, a feisty one you are!' the ringmaster snarled. 'But I will *break* you all the same, my stripy friend!'

43

The man stalked out of the menagerie with Karu in his wake, leaving Owl shuddering with dread. Skrimsli stood on his hind legs and wrapped his front paws around the boy, purring, and pushing his whiskered nose into Owl's hair again and again.

The rumours were true. The circus was heading east to the Sand City, Shamanow, in Yuderan, the vast country of sand and mountains ruled by a person called the Palatine. Everyone was excited. All the trials of the last months, the snow and ice, even Kobret's tyrannical rule, were temporarily forgotten; they would be performing in front of all manner of Nordsky dignitaries and the Queen of the Desert herself.

'The Palatine of Yuderan!' Mappa Po said in wonder as she handed out hunks of bread to circus folk too busy to stop and eat a proper meal.

'I heard them Yuderans need cheering up,' one of the jantevas said through a full mouth. 'They've had a drought, all their crops failed. Haven't had more to eat than grass in a year.'

'You'd better watch out then, mate,' another quipped. 'Your fat backside would feed a family!'

The very next day the menagerie tent was taken down and packed away. A long train arrived from Pokov, mending the fractured railway lines as it came. Gear, animals, people, caravans were loaded onto its one hundred and twelve carriages and box cars for the journey to Shamanow. The whole circus buzzed with excitement; their mountain exile was over at last. Majak's Marvellous Circus would be part of a diplomatic mission sent specially by the Nordsky Government to the people of Yuderan.

Owl couldn't share the excitement. The journey would take ten or eleven days, first to Pokov, where they would pick up the new performers that Kobret's son had engaged, then along the northern edge of the Sand Sea. Owl resolved that in the time it took them to make the journey, he would find a way to protect Skrimsli from Kobret, or escape. But it was obvious at once that Kobret was not going to let a precious asset like a tiger slip through his fingers. The jantevas hustled Owl, Taze and Skrimsli into carriage number fifty-one: a locked box-car cage, that would only be unlocked once a day. Escape would be impossible.

As the long train pulled away from the mountains the musicians played a jolly marching song and the entire company cheered. Except for Owl. The countdown had begun; he had ten days to find a way to keep Skrimsli safe.

The train rumbled on day and night. Taze and the cub slept, played, slept again. Owl worried and worried. He warned the cub over and over.

Kobret will try to hurt you. Do not let him in your head.

In the shared space inside their heads in a voice that was part growl, part purr, part breath, Skrimsli responded bravely.

Bite Kobret! he said. *Bite Kobret.*

But Owl knew that Narastikeri's strength and cunning had been no defence against Kobret's cruelty, and Skrimsli was just a cub.

Owl stared through the bars at the land slipping by: farmers' fields and towns. Where, he wondered, was his old forest home? How would a freak boy, a hound and a tiger find their way to a place no one had heard of? Bayuk Lazil? No one knew where that was.

They reached Pokov and were joined by Kobret's son Itmis, 'the Little Boss' as he was known, and his new performers. Owl took no notice. It only meant that the time before they reached Shamanow was getting shorter and shorter.

But Galu Mak walked half the length of the train from her carriage (number ninety-six) to tell Owl about one of them.

'She's a trick rider,' Galu Mak told him. 'Called Numiko or some such name. The horse is very smart. They share a carriage, like you and the cub. You watch out for them!'

So, when the train stopped towards the end of the first day out of the capital, Owl did watch out. Numiko and the horse had the carriage two down from Owl's. As soon as its door was opened, the horse leapt out with the rider on his back. They galloped at full speed until they were a tiny speck in the distance. There was no saddle or bridle; the rider didn't even hold the horse's mane. They simply operated like one animal. The wild freedom of that gallop made Owl's heart lift.

Skrimsli too was fascinated. He gave up tussling with Taze and sat beside Owl at the open door of their carriage. When the rider and horse returned from their gallop, they came close to look at the boy and the cub.

'I have never seen a tiger!' The rider's accent was strange, the voice light but with a deep resonance. 'I am Kal,' the rider said, 'and this is Luja.'

Owl nodded and smiled, as usual a little afraid to let anyone hear his squeak of a voice, but the rider was waiting for him to introduce himself and the cub; speaking could not be avoided.

'I'm Owl,' Owl squeaked, 'and this is Skrimsli and Taze.' Kal didn't seem to mind the sound of Owl's voice at all, and the horse reached his soft muzzle to go nose to nose with the cub. He breathed deeply, sucking in the cub's scent with obvious pleasure, and the cub's pink nose sniffed back, his whiskers trembling. Then the cub got up and rubbed his head against Luja's face and purred.

'They like each other!' Kal smiled. It was an unexpected sort of smile, Owl thought, as if it didn't get much use; it was gone in an instant, leaving the face looking uncertain, as if it might change into something else entirely, the face of a different person, or even a different creature. It was the face, Owl thought, of someone who didn't want to be seen. He smiled back as warmly as he could. He knew about not wanting to be seen.

'I loved watching you ride,' Owl said.

'Oh.' Kal looked down and away. 'I don't really ride. He just lets me sit on him while he does what he loves best, which is running!'

Taze came from the back of the carriage where she had been sleeping. Kal leaned in to fuss her and Taze, who was normally wary of strangers, let her ears be scratched and wagged her tail.

'She is lovely!' Kal exclaimed. 'The tiger also!'

'Luja is beautiful!' Owl said and wanted to add, *and you are beautiful too*, but he didn't. Instead he just smiled, and felt a strange glow as if the five of them were in a little bubble, quite away from the rest of the world.

'Back to your carriages!' the jantevas barked at them. 'Quick about it.'

And, just like that, the bubble burst.

On the days that followed the jantevas tried to stop Kal and Luja coming to call, but once in a while they were busy or distracted and Kal and Luja would snatch a few minutes to stand at the door of the carriage. Little was said, but each time there was that feeling of being together in a sunny bubble, safe and warm, even happy.

The landscape grew barer. Farms vanished and plants diminished to a low blue-grey fuzz, with occasional cacti like huge statues. The nights were clear and very cold and the days blazing. The train began to stop just before sundown to give the circus people and animals time outside in the air and to allow the carriages to cool as the sun lost its greatest power.

They could not be far from Shamanow now, but Owl had not seen Kobret for days. He allowed himself to believe that perhaps, with the arrival of the new performers, with Kal and Luja and the two acrobats he had heard so much about from Galu Mak, Kobret had thought better of training the cub. But one afternoon before the jantevas had opened the bars of their box car to allow Owl, Taze and the cub to stretch their legs, the ringmaster and his son came to visit. They brought with them the bear and two of the meanest jantevas.

They peered in through the metal bars. Kobret looked at the cub as if he could carve him up and eat him bite by bite.

'Ooh yes, you will certainly be a star!' he exclaimed. 'I'm going to begin your training at once.'

He turned to the son, Itmis, a thinner version of himself.

'Show them the collar!' Kobret ordered. Itmis held a heavy metal collar and a chain up to the bars, reluctant at first and then with the same hard gleam of cruelty that Owl had seen in Kobret's eyes.

'Jantevas!' the younger man ordered. 'Unlock this car.'

The sight of the metal collar made Owl feel sick. It was clear that the cub understood what it was and who it was meant for. His fur stood on end, he growled, and his mind filled with thoughts of attack that rang in Owl's brain.

Bite! Bite! Bite! The cub was almost chanting.

Taze retreated to their sleeping corner. She was terrified of Kobret. She whined and shivered and tried to burrow her way into the straw. But the cub stood his ground as the jantevas unlocked the barred door and Kobret walked up and into the car. The ringmaster looked even bigger than normal, with the two burly jantevas on either side of him, heavy clubs in their hands, Karu and Itmis at their back. Together they made one, big, dark shape, coming closer and closer.

Owl had never wished more fiercely that he was huge and strong. He wanted to push Kobret to the ground and put that cruel metal collar around *his* neck.

Kobret drew closer to the cub.

'So, my feisty little star,' he said. 'I'm going to show you who's boss. By the time I'm done with you, you won't dare growl at me anymore. You'll do exactly what I want.'

Kobret gave a low laugh like the sound of something slithering over a floor and the white of his smile glowed in the gloom.

Owl knew he was weak and tiny, but he stood up and made himself as straight and tall as he could.

'You won't hurt him!' he cried. 'I won't let you!'

Itmis stepped back but the jantevas only laughed.

'Did I hear a mouse squeak then?' one said to the other.

'No,' replied the other, 'that's a hinge that needs oiling.'

With one flick of his big boot Owl was kicked to one side. He hit a wall and slid to the floor.

Taze too had overcome her fear and had stopped whining. She turned to face Kobret growling and snarling, snapping her jaws as if she simply couldn't wait to sink her teeth into his flesh. Kobret reached a hand towards her, and Owl guessed he was inflicting pain inside her mind; but this time it made no difference. Although she yelped, her eyes white-rimmed with the terror he was busy planting in her head, she bared her teeth. Skrimsli was her child, and she would save him from Kobret if she could. She sprang, aiming her teeth straight for the ringmaster's fat neck.

The jantevas were ready. They brought their clubs down with all the force their angry hearts could muster and struck Taze down. She hit the floor and lay quite still. She was not breathing anymore.

There was a high-pitched scream. Owl realised that it was coming from his mouth. He threw himself at the jantevas, but another kick left him dazed and helpless, unable to do more than look up from the floor.

Every hair of Skrimsli's coat was on end, every tooth bared, his eyes green flames, his claws out, his muscles tensed and ready to spring. But it did no good. He could not shut out the dagger of Kobret's power and it plunged into his mind. Kobret could see just what the cub would do before he did it. Before Skrimsli could strike, Kobret yelled, 'Now!'

The men fell on the cub and Itmis stepped forward with the collar and chain.

'Put it on!' Kobret ordered and, in a moment, the cub was

collared and yowled as Itmis pulled on the chain. The other end was clipped to Karu's collar. Under Kobret's command, Karu and Itmis began to drag the protesting cub from the car. The door clanged shut behind them.

Owl looked over Taze's broken body into the brightness of the day. Outlined against the blue sky were the rider, Kal, and her horse.

'Get back to your own car!' the jantevas snarled. 'Go away! Be off!'

As the horse turned, Kal looked at Owl and met his eyes.

'I saw,' the eyes said, 'and I won't forget.'

Owl managed to nod once in response before blackness swallowed him.

It was night by the time Owl came round. There was a familiar smell of wood polish, the smell of the benches that he had spent all winter sleeping under. Now that there was no valuable tiger to keep in box fifty-one, it had been filled with other things. The barred iron doors had been removed so that long sections of bench could stick out through the car openings on either side. In the half light, Owl could make out coils of rope, canvas bags of safety nets, bunting, lights, costumes.

Painfully he pulled himself into a sitting position and looked around. He couldn't see a thing. With his heart in his throat, he called out, 'Taze! Taze!'

There was no reply. He crawled towards the back of the car, where he had last seen her lying and felt about in the darkness. His hand touched something sticky: blood, and then a paw. But it was quite cold, a thing now, not part of a living body. Very gently he felt his way up her leg to her chest and laid his hand on her wiry fur. He stroked her head and whispered her name. 'Taze, Taze.'

A loud thump on the roof of the car startled him. Owl's head throbbed where the janteva's boot had struck it. In his pain and confusion, it was easy to imagine that the thudding on the roof meant all kinds of horrors. There was a sudden clattering, and something swung in through the space above the protruding benches and landed with a crash beside him. A switch flicked and a pool of yellow light materialised. Inside it were himself, Taze, and Kal.

The rider put out a slender hand, and smiled that lopsided, wary smile.

'I saw what … that man did, and so I came to see you.'

There was a satchel slung around Kal's shoulders. Kal pulled it off and rummaged inside.

'I have water. Some food. And some medicine. I'm not skilled with healing but I can clean the wounds.'

Owl nodded and Kal's long fingers were soon patrolling every inch of his scalp, checking all the cuts and bumps.

'You will live, perhaps!' Owl felt a pulse of anxiety. Only perhaps? Was he so badly injured?

'I'm joking,' Kal told him gently. 'It's just a bump, a headache. In two days, you will be fine. Here, drink this.'

Obediently, Owl took the bottle he was offered. The water tasted good, sweet, with a tinge of an unfamiliar fruit.

'Please,' Owl said. 'Please … Taze!'

Owl thought desperately that this Kal might find life in Taze that he had failed to detect.

Owl watched as Kal checked Taze over. Felt her chest, carefully spread fingers over the dog's head, opened her eyes, looked in her mouth. Then Kal sat with one hand resting on the dog's chest. At last, Kal looked up. Owl didn't want to meet the rider's eyes.

'She is gone,' Kal said. 'I don't believe she suffered. They cracked her skull with the first blow.'

Kal helped Owl sit up so he could hold Taze in his arms. He pressed his nose into the dark crinkled fur, breathed in her dear smell and said her name. She would never wag her tail at that sound ever again, never lean against him with a sigh, never tussle with the cub.

All the while, as Owl sobbed, Kal sat close, quiet and kind. At last, Kal said, 'Let me take her for you.'

Kal took Taze from his arms and gently wrapped the dog's body in some sacking.

'Now, you must rest.'

Kal began to pack up the satchel, then stopped and looked at Owl.

'Why did Kobret beat you? Why did he take your tiger?'

There was so much that Owl wanted to say in answer: about Kobret's cruelty, about the evil way he used his power; about how all the animals in the circus feared him. But his heart hurt, his head throbbed, and it was hard to organise thoughts and pull them from his creaky little voice box.

'Wants to train him for the circus,' was all he could manage.

Kal's face looked grim.

'With a *beating*? And an *iron* collar?'

'Worse!' Owl tapped his head. 'He is a Listener, though he says he's not. But a horrible kind. He goes into animals' heads and makes fear inside. I tried to stop him hurting the cub but...'

Owl felt his throat close with tears. He was suddenly overwhelmed with grief and with the feeling that he had failed Skrimsli completely; he hadn't protected him, or Taze, and now Kobret was 'breaking him' just as he'd promised. Owl was a hopeless little freak, just as he'd always been told.

There was a silence. Kal sighed.

'Listen, Owl. I saw what you both did. Your dog was so brave. You were so brave. You stood up in front of those big men, though you could never win. Your tiger knows that.'

Owl raised his head. No one had ever called him brave. Kal nodded at him.

'Yes, *brave* is what you are. Braver than I could ever, ever be.' Kal repacked the satchel.

'I will leave the lantern and water,' Kal said. Owl nodded.

He wondered how Taze had grown so small in death, that Kal carried her wrapped-up body so easily.

'I will try to find out something about your Skrimsli. Try not to worry. He is clever and young and very strong.'

Owl nodded. 'Tomorrow,' Kal said, then swung up onto the roof of the car, leaving Owl more alone than he had ever felt in his life.

5
The Palatine

Eagle Eyes

The Palatine slipped between the tent flaps and out into the night. The sand was smooth and cold as water; the sky was deeply black and singing with stars. She felt the need for escape so keenly that she could have cried out and simply raced off into the night. But that would wake the encampment and her chance would be wasted. It wasn't simply solitude she sought, after all.

She held herself quite still, breathing with care. The hunting birds were on their perches just a few feet ahead, beyond the last tent, where one of her entourage snored like an ox. Even though they were hooded, the birds would startle at her approach; very gently she entered into their minds, one by one confirming their decision to stay asleep. How strange it was that a sleeping bird of prey could be so peaceful when their waking minds raged and rang with the vivid, fierce experience delivered to them by their sharp eyes and beating wings.

Last of all, she entered the mind of Sayka, her own bird. He'd been hers from the moment his small, pink head with its too-big beak poked from the broken shell of his egg. He was a *tayir alraed*, a thunder bird: a variety of eagle bred for generations for great size, strength and vision. Once they had been used in war as deadly weapons that snatched riders from the saddle. The Palatine could never imagine Sayka being used for such a purpose. He was as gentle as a lapdog and what he lacked in intelligence he made up for with his miraculous vision and steadfast loyalty.

He was already awake: his mind, as always, open as a blank page. She showed him the thought of herself, about to round the tent and pass between the sleeping falcons. It was a thought that said *I'm coming. Be ready!* The Palatine felt Sayka's answer: a deep *yes*, that was part acceptance, part welcome.

She pulled the leather gauntlet onto her hand, undid the jesses that tied him to the perch and took his weight onto her arm. His huge, taloned feet enclosed her forearm. If he gripped hard, he could crush her bone to dust. She felt his calm, his trust as she walked with him. Even though he was hooded and couldn't see, he knew her muscles were strong enough, trained through the years, to hold his weight. She wouldn't let him fall.

Together they walked into the desert. A low scribble of dead plants was etched against the pale sand. The long drought had killed even the small spiky silver-leaved things that normally flourished in this harsh environment. Only the tall cacti remained, and even they had begun to stoop and curl as the dry air sucked the last water from their stores. The failure of the rains was bringing Yuderan to its knees. Crops had failed, and even the rats in the grain stores were going hungry. The Palatine shuddered. She feared for her country and its people.

A mile from camp the moon rose: a great, gold fruit floating in the garden of the sky. She removed the eagle's hood.

'Fly, old friend,' she told him. 'Show me what you see.'

No wild bird would fly over cold sand without warm, rising thermals to carry him up. No wild bird would fly by moonlight. But Sayka and his kind had never been wild. He was fed on goat meat and so used to doing the Palatine's bidding that he could not separate her wishes from his own. He climbed laboriously into the night, higher and higher over the blue and silver desert. High enough to see the path the Palatine had taken from her home in the Yuderan capital, Bisque City, to the south; high enough to see the long, winding trail that she was to follow through every desert town before finally arriving at Sand City on the border with Nordsky. It would keep the Palatine from her palace for a month or more.

Sayka's keen eyes, that even in moonlight could spot a desert hare from more than a mile away, saw every detail laid out below him. The eagle saw the lanterns lighting the way for the trains of camels, heading through the night in the direction of the capital city. He saw the figures marching alongside them. He caught the flash of their foreign weapons – strange, long rifles – and of their dark uniforms, peeping from the slits in their pale Yuderan tunics.

Far to the north he saw the smoke of many fires. There was a great encampment gathered round the place where the railway line from Nordsky snaked along the Yuderan border at the edge of the Sand Sea. He saw the herds of vast machines that laid the railway. He saw the mountainous stacks of wooden sleepers, ready for the iron of the rails, a whole forest felled and brought to the edge of the desert.

It was not within Sayka's ability to understand the things he saw. His mistress would do that. It was just his job to see, to be her eyes. He descended and took his reward of sweet goat meat. While he tore it with his beak, he left his mind wide open, so the Palatine could look inside more easily.

The Palatine hooded her eagle. She filled him with thoughts of blue sky and rising air and sent him, full bellied, into sleep. Then she lit a fire and sat staring into the flames, singing softly to herself. What the eagle saw was only what she had feared, but to see it all confirmed was still a body blow. An army was heading to overthrow her government, masquerading as a Yuderan rebel force. She recognised the dark uniforms Sayka had glimpsed: soldiers brought all the way from Rumyc, paid for with Nordsky money. She'd heard whispers of these forces; Automators, they were called. They gathered power and wealth like army ants, to carry it back to their own nest.

This time it was all about the railway. The Nordskys were determined to build it across Yuderan. They were so sure of themselves that they were waiting at her borders to begin its construction. They would tell her countrywomen and men that it was for their good; that it would relieve the suffering that the long drought had brought; that it would flood their country with wonderful things. But the Palatine knew that was not the truth. The railway was like the stylet of the mosquito, it was a parasite's device for sucking out the blood of her land and her people. They would dig up the desert, take over the towns and cities, put the people to work. Yuderan would be robbed, ravaged and enslaved. All her plans to turn their land green with irrigation and save her people from another drought would be thrown aside.

Someone close to her was behind this betrayal. Her mind said the name even as her heart refused to hear it: Yalen, her own brother. The Palatine had always known his nature and his ambitions. Like many things, she'd kept them hidden from herself. It had been his idea for her to go on this long route to Shamanow to meet the Nordsky ambassadors.

'Go,' Yalen had told her. 'I will mind your throne for you.'

Indeed he would! Mind it and then keep it for himself.

She saw now what would happen. In Shamanow, they would ask for her signature, her blessing, on the railway. When she didn't give it, her brother would be ready, already sitting on her throne. He would support the railway because he had been bought. He was nothing if not practical, her brother.

Then he would offer her a share in her own throne, in return for her silence. She would be his mute puppet, forced to watch as he ruled over the destruction of their country.

Her handsome brother, with his dazzling smile. How much the people of Yuderan would prefer him, she thought, to herself. Right from the start they had questioned her mother's choice of successor. She was too young, they said; she was too serious; they even said she was too big, too strong – whoever saw a woman that tall? They would be smiling at handsome, charming Yalen, even as he knifed them in the back!

The Palatine could see it now: the entourage she travelled with could not be trusted; the meeting with the Nordskys was a sham. Betrayal lay on every side. Sayka was now one of only two living beings she could still trust.

But some things were not clear. This 'circus' that the Nordsky ambassador had made so very much of, and Yalen had been so very interested in, was that some part of their plotting? In that uncertainty there was perhaps a chance to regain some small advantage.

The Palatine doused her fire with sand and walked towards the camp with the sleeping eagle weighing on her arm. She thought about her mother's ancestors, nomadic beekeepers who followed the clouds to find the flowers that bloomed after scattered rainstorms. Without a place to call their own, they had lived lives of great hardship and great beauty. She remembered her grandmother's voice calling the name that had once been hers.

'Najma! Najma!'

She felt again the rough skin of the old woman's hand, tender on her brow, smoothing away all tears.

'Happiness is as fleeting as the rain. But purpose, Najma, that is what endures. *Purpose!*'

It was a long time since anyone had called her Najma. She had become the Palatine; she had *become* a purpose and indeed happiness *had* proved fleeting. She breathed the dry desert air, cool and sweet, then sighed it out. Yes, purpose was the key. Her enemies might take her title, take her palace, but they could not take her *purpose*. Somehow she would stop her brother and his railway-parasite from sucking out the life of Yuderan.

The Palatine placed the sleeping Sayka back on his perch and slipped back into her tent. Tiff, her bodyguard, was waiting of course. In her close-fitting armoured clothes, her head enclosed in a leather helmet, a stranger might miss her resemblance to her mistress. But dressed alike, they could be twins. It was an attribute that the Palatine had found very useful.

Tiff waited, poised for any instruction, one hand on her sword.

'It's worse than I feared,' the Palatine breathed.

'Do we leave, my star?' Tiff whispered in reply.

The Palatine shook her head. Tiff's shoulders drooped very slightly. She had hoped for a different answer that would have meant a stealthy escape across the midnight desert. Immediate danger and physical challenge was what Tiff relished most of all.

'We stay on this road. We do just as they expect.'

Tiff frowned. She began to speak but the Palatine held a finger to her lips.

'We do as they expect, Tiff. And in so doing, we do the unexpected. It is the only weapon we have left. Now, take my clothes; you are going to be me for a while.'

'And you, my star?' Tiff asked.

'I...' the Palatine replied, 'I am going to join the circus!'

6
Kal

Night Visitors

Kal carried Taze the length of the train, to the engine. The stokers were kind enough and gave the dog's body to the flames.

Dark thoughts crowded round as Kal climbed back along the snaking train. The true nature of this circus was not Itmis and his enthusiasm; it was his father's brutality. Itmis was too weak and vain to stand up to it but Owl, the little odd-shaped child, had! What an extraordinary being he was! So young and yet so old, radiating peace and courage. If Owl had witnessed what Kal had seen, *he* would have done *the right thing*, as Havvity had wanted. Owl's bravery made Kal feel ashamed all over again.

The newspapers in Pokov had been full of the lies from Erem: how civil war had broken out between the 'ancient enemies' the Horses and the Herrings and how Automator Forces under Nordsky command were fighting to 'restore peace'. Nothing about how Horses and Herrings had always got along and worked together; nothing about the sinister murders or their plans to steal the gold from underneath the Erem mountains.

Kal pushed these thoughts aside.

'I don't owe Erem anything! They branded me a misfit from the start,' Kal whispered into the dark. 'Freedom is what matters!' But the circus was not freedom. Kal knew it, and knew too that what was owed or not to Erem was unimportant; what mattered was Havvity and Roko and the growing feeling that Kal had abandoned them to whatever evil war would deliver.

Escape began to occupy Kal's thoughts. Once they reached Shamanow one horse and one rider could gallop away quite easily, Kal was sure of it. But what of Owl and his beloved tiger? The sight of the boy, his small fists raised against those big, violent men, was one that would not leave Kal's mind. Owl could not be abandoned. Kal cursed fiercely into the night air, damning Kobret Majak to flames and destruction, damning Owl for slipping into the closed places of Kal's heart so easily.

Escape for a rider, a horse, a boy and a tiger? Not so easy!

Oh, Luja, why can't it be just you and me? Kal thought.

As if in answer, a faint whicker cut through the clatter and clank of the lumbering train. Luja's voice coming from their shared truck. It conveyed a warning: *I know you are close; be wary, someone's in here.*

Who would have climbed along the train in the middle of the night to pay them a visit? Kal could think of no good answers. Kal scrambled as quietly as possible along the sides of the last two trucks and into the space at the end of their own. Ear to the wall, Kal stopped and listened: silence. No sound at all. It set every hair on end, every nerve tingling. As stealthily as possible, Kal climbed onto the roof of their truck, listened again then swung down into the darkness, and landed lightly on the straw-strewn floor.

As if materialising out of the air, a blade was drawn across Kal's throat, only just lightly enough not to draw blood. A whispered voice, so soft and rasping as to be barely human, spoke in Erem.

'Keep still,' it breathed.

Two pairs of deft and expert hands had Kal bound, gagged and blindfolded in a few more seconds.

'Sit here,' another slightly different voice said in the same, barely audible whisper. Kal was pushed to the floor next to the curve of Luja's withers. His breathing was deep, too deep for ordinary sleep. Kal realised, with a wave of nausea, that whoever these people were, they had drugged him.

There was a long silence in which Kal's fear grew big enough to fill the whole carriage. Any second Kal expected death to be delivered with that cold blade. But the silence just continued, so profound that Kal wondered if the two attackers had left. Then, the ghost voices spoke again, even more quietly, so that Kal had to strain to hear over Luja's breaths and the train's rattle.

'We know who you are, exactly.'

'And we know what you saw at Talo Numikalo.'

'We could kill you, just for that.'

'There are many who want you dead.'

'But we think you could be useful.'

The voices alternated, Kal thought, but it was hard to tell where one voice ended and the other began. Both were so close to not being any voice at all, so quiet, so flat. The voices of things, not people, one, then the other. Who were they? There was no one in the circus who spoke Erem?

'This is what we require.'

'First, that you make no attempt to escape.'

'Next, that you perfect your performance for Kobret Majak *exactly* as he instructs you.'

'During the performance for the Palatine the tiger will appear to attack. You will attempt to shoot the beast, but instead you will shoot the Palatine. A head shot will be necessary.'

'We will furnish you with the weapon.'

Was this a dream? A nightmare? Kal tried to yell, to struggle, to protest. But as the words clouded in Kal's mind the realisation came that Luja was not the only one who had been drugged: speech and movement were now impossible. Kal could only listen to these ghost voices that demanded blood and murder.

'You *will* comply.'

'Your life is in our hands.'

'And the lives of those you love.'

'We know who you know.'

'Havvity.'

'Dear *dear* little Roko.'

'Luja, too, and your new friend, the little freak boy.'

'If you do not do as we tell you, they will *all* die.'

'We are ghosts in the night, with long, long fingers.'

'We cannot be opposed.'

'You cannot escape us.'

'You are powerless.'

'Do as you are told.'

'We always know everything.'

'We always see everything.'

'This will help you to remember.'

A sting, sharp as a sudden burn, seared Kal's neck, and then nothing but blackness and a long fall.

Kal's eyes flickered open. This wasn't the railway truck. It was a tent, a very nice one. And a bed! A *proper* bed. Soft air billowed through the open tent flap, carrying sounds of voices, carts, animals.

Kal sat up. There was a table and a jug of water, with a cup. Kal was overtaken by thirst. For a few moments, until the contents of the jug were gone, there was nothing else in the world. And then, where was Luja? How long had this sleep, or whatever it was, lasted? Kal's hand found the stinging line of a knife wound, running from left ear to left collar bone. It was a scratch that hardly broke the skin and was already scabbed and healing, but it was a reminder:

You did not dream us.

Do not forget.

We know who you know.

All will die.

Who were those ghost people? How did they know what Kal had seen at Talo and why did they want to kill the Palatine? Where were they now? Kal glanced around the tent; were they here, somehow hidden in the billowing folds of fabric? Floating in the shifting shadows? Kal shuddered. Whatever they were, they were somewhere close, hiding in plain sight. No one and nothing could be trusted.

'Madam Numiko? May I come in?'

It was Itmis Majak. Kal pulled the bedsheet up to cover trembling hands. Itmis did not wait for a response and breezed in, still trying to be the prince charming of the circus. But Kal knew better now. Itmis might not have his father's ability to manipulate animal minds, but Kal had seen his cruelty. He was his father's son.

'I'm so happy to see you looking, well *looking*...' Itmis was clearly relieved, but there was something shifty about him. What did he know?

'How long was I...?' Kal began to ask.

'Unconscious, dear lady. *Unconscious.* Yes. A fall, in the railway carriage.' Itmis was so quick to offer this explanation! Too quick. His nervous laugh betrayed him. He knew something, Kal was certain.

'You have been quite insensible for almost three days,' he added.

Three days? Kal remembered the promise to Owl. *Tomorrow.* But there was a more pressing worry.

'Where is Luja?' Kal asked.

'Ah, Luja. Well, that is *precisely* the reason for my visit. We have, as you may have guessed, arrived in Shamanow. As I speak, we are setting up accommodation, mess tents, rehearsal space and so on. It is all most exciting! But Luja is not *cooperating.* At this moment my father is...'

The words were out of Kal's mouth before there was time to think.

'Your *father*? Your father will not *touch* my horse!'

Itmis swallowed and looked at his feet.

'Ah. Quite so,' he mumbled.

'Itmis,' Kal snapped. 'Outside! I must dress.'

Kal and Itmis walked into a scene resembling an ants' nest: people, carts, animals rushing around carrying, pulling, unloading, putting up, taking down, shouting instructions in a number of different languages. But, like an ants' nest, what appeared to be random activity, achieved a great deal. The Big Top itself was laid out like a giant, deflated balloon and jantevas swarmed around it with ropes and pulleys.

The Menagerie Marquee was already erected and, outside it, pens and cages were assembled under a sea of awnings, with camels, elephants, horses and sloth bears already wandering about, looking a little dazed to be out in the open air after so long in the stuffy confinement of their trucks and carriages.

The circus occupied a wide, flat island on the bed of the Shamanow river. The Shamanow carried rainwater from the great forests that cloaked the distant mountains to the north in a blue-green haze. Every year the dry season reduced it to a narrow strip of deep water that cut under the cliff beneath the city, then fanned out into a delta to lose itself in the ocean. The long drought had reduced it still further, to a muddy trickle. The ground under Kal's feet was a mosaic of cracked mud, hard as a tiled floor. Only the deeply eroded banks to either side showed that, when the time came, the river flowed deep and wide.

Beyond the southern bank stood the train, lost in a line of trees, like a giant snake. There was no station of any kind, just the place where the line finally ran out. Beyond that was the city of Shamanow, on a rocky outcrop high above the dry riverbed. Its towers and minarets were enclosed in high walls of yellow stone. To the east, where the light bleached both land and sky to whiteness, lay the river delta and the ocean.

The desert light was blindingly bright, but the morning air was still cool from the cold, clear night. In a fenced enclosure, Kobret stood with a horse on a long lead rein. Kal lifted a hand to cut the dazzle that had brought back a throbbing head and saw that the horse wore an iron head collar, like a vice around its face. It was sweating, its eyes wide and cloudy with horror. With a shock that felt as violent as a blow, Kal saw that the suffering, terrified horse was Luja!

Kal ran, anger burning as hot as the sun-baked mud: over the fence in one clean vault; three long strides to reach Luja's side and one leap onto his back. One vicious tug pulled the lead rein from Kobret's hand. In one more movement the head collar was undone and thrown down. In another, the two of them had cleared the fence and were galloping up the dry riverbed and away, away, away.

Kal's body moulded to Luja's movement and the rhythm of Kal's heart beat with Luja's flying hooves. Running was the answer to all questions, the healing for all hurts. Kal's anger was like an explosion. In its white heat nothing existed but the exhilaration of this escape, the desire to keep running until the two of them evaporated into the air and vanished forever.

Luja hit a stride that he could maintain for miles. On and on they ran, around a long bend in the dry riverbed, where the banks grew closer together and tall trees topped them, cooling the dried mud with shade. The circus was far away, out of sight, far behind them. They would never go back. Kal would not have to agree to be an assassin.

Then that rasping ghost voice wriggled into Kal's ears:

Do not forget.
We know who you know.
All of them will die.
All of them will die.
Do as you are told.
Tell no one.

Kal had no doubt the ghosts would keep their promises. The heat of anger cooled. Running away was not an answer to anything.

'Stop!' Kal cried. But the fear that Kobret had planted in Luja's mind still drove him. It had triggered the response to flee, woven deep in his every cell. Kal realised he would run now until he was exhausted.

Or until something stopped him.

Basking on the hot mud, her belly full of eggs she needed to incubate, was a snake. When Luja's hoof struck the ground beside her, she too had just one response. Her fangs had delivered their venom before Luja's other forefoot had hit the ground. In two more paces he was felled, mid-gallop, throwing Kal over his head as he hit the ground.

Kal stared up, dazed, into the pale sky, head spinning. A huge bird wheeled overhead and let out a high, thin cry. Moments or hours later, Kal could not be sure, a figure stood over them, dressed for hard travel, masked against the cutting cold and fierce sun of the desert, a sword and a dagger in a sturdy belt.

'You are unhurt?' The question was in Nordsky but with a strong Yuderan accent.

Kal nodded.

'Then I attend the horse.'

The figure vanished. Painfully Kal got up. Luja was on his side, white eyed, and rigid. Cradling his right foreleg and pulling things from a backpack was the armed figure: a young woman, Kal now saw, very tall, strong, with dark eyes showing above the line of her mask.

'Hold your horse's head,' she ordered in a voice that was clearly used to being instantly obeyed. Kal didn't argue. Luja's eyes were wild and his presence far away and drifting further. But he didn't struggle as Kal's arms wrapped his head and cradled him.

'Be calm, old friend. It will be right. Just be calm,' Kal told him in Erem.

The woman looked up from her work binding his foreleg, just above the fetlock.

'That is a tongue I do not know,' said the woman.

'Erem,' Kal replied in Nordsky. 'That's where we're from. What's the matter with him? Will he die?'

'Snake bite, here.' The woman indicated a point just above the hoof on the inside of the pastern. 'Not bad. He is shocked. The bite gave little poison. I have…' She searched for a word then shrugged and held up a small glass vial from her bag and filled a syringe with its pale liquid.

'Hold him well,' the woman said, and before Kal could protest or ask for any explanation, she had plunged the needle into Luja's neck and injected the contents of the syringe.

'What is that?' Kal asked in alarm.

The woman shook her head.

'I do not know the word in Nordsky. It is against poison. A cure. You do not need to fear. He will live.'

She got up. 'Now. He must be up, and we must find shade, water.' She placed hand on Luja's face. '*Bidaar shoran,*' she whispered. It could have been a spell, so instant was the effect. Luja's eyes opened, he got up and stood unsteadily, leaning not on Kal, but the woman.

'You speak in his mind?' Kal knew it sounded like a kind of accusation, but the tone was ignored.

'Don't you?' she replied and lead Luja away so all Kal could do was follow.

They walked to a nearby grove of thorny trees where a camel was lazily browsing leaves and a dark-coated horse cropped what remained of the grass. The woman introduced the camel as Harib, and the horse as Zait. Luja and Zait whickered a low greeting. Harib took no notice of either of them, but Zait was friendly enough.

'And this,' she added, 'is Sayka.'

An enormous bird of prey perched quietly on a rock, looking about with intent yellow eyes.

'He is an eagle,' the woman explained, 'of a kind bred for war. But my Sayka is no fighter.'

She scratched the space on the bird's neck, and it gave a very un-eagle-like chirrup of pleasure. Kal couldn't help but smile.

'He is my eyes,' the woman explained. 'He saw you fall and so I also saw and came here.' She slipped a hood over the bird's head, and it submitted to this imposed darkness without complaint.

The woman gave Luja water in a leather bowl and offered Kal water from her own water-skin. She removed her mask to drink herself. Kal saw that in spite of her stature and commanding presence she was young, only a few years older than Kal. They rested silently together in the shade. From time to time the woman checked on Luja's recovery and it seemed her horse Zait did the same, standing companionably beside Luja and gently touching his neck with a soft grey nose.

Luja snuffled Kal's hair – a small signal of reassurance. Kal felt a rush of love for this oldest, dearest friend and another rush of gratitude to this unusual woman who had saved him.

'Thank you,' Kal said, 'for saving Luja.'

'It is nothing,' she replied. 'I'm glad to see my snake remedy useful.'

'You made that medicine in the bottle?' Kal asked. The woman nodded.

'From horse blood,' she said. 'If you can believe such a thing. Many of my countrymen do not.'

The words were raw, and the woman was instantly embarrassed by them, as if she had given away too much.

'I am Kal,' Kal said. 'May I know your name?'

'I am Najma,' she replied, but she spoke as if the name was unfamiliar to her. Was Najma this woman's real name? What did it matter? There was no avoiding the fact that Kal must go back to the circus with all that meant.

'We must be on our way,' Kal said, 'back to the circus.'

'The circus?' Najma stopped packing her saddlebags and looked up, her eyes needle sharp. 'That is where I am going, to offer my services as an animal healer and horse trainer, if they need such things.'

Kal stared at her. This was too much of a coincidence,

73

wasn't it? Or were the ghosts just making Kal fear every shadow.

'It's close,' Kal said. 'Closer than the city. Round the bend in this dry river.'

'Then we will go in company,' Najma replied. 'Perhaps you can tell me about this "circus".'

They walked beside their animals, as Luja was still too weak to bear Kal's weight. It was soon clear that Najma didn't really understand what the word 'circus' even meant! Kal explained about the Big Top and the performances, the acrobats and trapeze artists, the animals and all the tricks they were trained to do.

'And you perform, with your horse?' Najma asked.

Kal had not really thought of performance. Only of escape and now of the rasping voices of the ghosts in the night. If it had not been for their vile demands, Kal might indeed be looking forward to 'performing', showing off horse-skills a lifetime in the making. Now the thought of it was tinged with dread. It was good that Najma was too interested in her own next question to notice that Kal didn't answer.

'How are they trained to do the tricks you describe?' Najma asked. 'Are the circus people Listeners?'

Kal gave an evasive answer without even thinking.

'Oh, lots of different ways. All the trainers have their own methods.'

Why did I say that? Kal wondered. *Doesn't she need to know lies and cruelty that are at the heart of Kobret's circus?* Kal did not reflect on the answer that came to mind at once.

Because if I tell her, she might not come.

74

They made slow progress, as Luja needed frequent rests. By the time they rounded the long bend in the riverbed and saw the circus laid out on the delta, the sun was sliding down the sky. Kal estimated that they had been gone for four hours at least. Was that long enough for the ghosts to send a message back to Erem? Kal imagined some hooded assassin slipping into the Black Fish Café at dead of night, climbing the stairs, opening the door to Roko's room without a sound. The ghost voices went round in Kal's head like a whispering tide.

Najma noticed something was wrong and turned her dark enquiring eyes on Kal's face.

'You are anxious, I think?'

Kal felt the keen edge of Najma's question. The woman missed nothing. She knew Kal had not given straight answers. She had seen the dread as they had turned back towards the circus. Kal felt exposed. But the truth, all the truth, was too much of a risk. A half-truth would have to do.

'He was punished,' Kal said. 'Not by me. It made him afraid. I worry that he will not perform, no matter what is done to him by our ringmaster. And if he does not perform, we are in danger.'

Kal looked at the ground. That last part had slipped out by mistake. Kal's skin crawled. How was it possible to return to this and become a murderer?

Najma rested a strong, broad hand on Kal's arm.

'Let me help.'

'How?' Kal eyes met Najma's. Never had Kal felt so seen. It was terrifying. It was irresistible. For a long moment Najma held Kal in the spotlight of her gaze. When at last she spoke

Kal knew that this voice came from her true self, whoever that was, whatever her name.

'We have secrets, you, me,' Najma said. 'I cannot tell you mine, and I can see you cannot tell me yours. But knowing we each have secrets, makes us kin. I can train any horse. I see into their minds. I use that understanding, not for harm. In my culture that is not something shameful or old fashioned. You and I will train Luja together, to do whatever is required of him, without hurt. Bring me to your ringmaster.'

'What do *you* gain from this?' Kal asked.

'A job and the chance to see the circus from the inside.'

That was just a part-truth, Kal could see, but it was enough for now.

'Alright,' said Kal. 'Alright.'

'First, I must send my eagle home.'

Najma took off the bird's hood and whispered some words into the feathers of his neck. Then his wings spread, and he pulled himself higher and higher into the blue sky. Kal didn't ask where he was going.

7

Skrimsli

You Are Not Prey

Skrimsli lay in the dark, cramped space of a box too small for his body. His heart raced and his breath came in shallow gasps. His mind was a tangle of confusion. He had felt so strong, so sure of the power of his muscles, his teeth and claws. But he was weak and helpless and utterly alone.

When he saw Owl and Taze struck down and felt Taze's life go from her like a light snuffed out, he was engulfed in darkness. Through that blackness Kobret had shot pain into his mind. It was so great that Skrimsli had thought that he too must die, that he would be killed and eaten, like a rabbit. But when he found he was not dead, it made no sense. What purpose did the pain serve?

He soon found out. After a time he could not measure, the box was opened and he was pulled out into the space of an empty railway car, rattling over the rails. Sunlight streaked through the slats of its wood and showed Kobret, the bear, and the two jantevas who had hurt Owl and killed Taze. Itmis the cub stood by in the shadows, watching. Hatred raged in Skrimsli's mind and body. He snarled and spat and tried to attack. But Kobret was inside his head and heard the intention in his thoughts; the ringmaster struck first, pinning the cub to the floor with agony.

Kobret spoke in his mind:

Do as I tell you. Or there will be more pain.

Do as I tell you or there will be death.

He fired pain directly into Skrimsli's brain, so that every part of his body screamed with it. And then he showed how death would come: with Karu's claws, or with the gun. That was the long metal object that one of the jantevas carried. It cracked then spat a tooth that flew too fast to see and was strong enough to bite a hole in wood. It could bite a hole straight through Skrimsli's heart.

Kobret barked orders, single words, and when Skrimsli did nothing, he filled each word with shots of pain. Pain and pain and more pain, until Skrimsli did whatever the words said. There were brief moments when the pain stopped. Oh, the sweetness of those short seconds! To get to them, Skrimsli did what Kobret told him more and more quickly: *sit, lie, roll, jump, growl, roar, snarl.*

Always somewhere close were the son and the bear. Itmis, looking on with a kind of envy, as if he longed to be able to exert the power that his father did; Karu carrying a silent promise of further violence and a terrible model of what he, Skrimsli, might become. The cub looked at Karu with dread. Was that his fate too, to become a puppet monster for this monster of a man?

Soon something worse than pain controlled what Skrimsli did: that was *fear of the pain.* The fear ate him from the inside, like a worm; it made him cringe and writhe. It made him weak.

Every day that followed was the same. Hours of learning orders, sequences of movements to be performed perfectly. Any mistake, no matter how slight, earned instant agony. Fear of that torture hung round the cub like a cloud heavier than the awful iron collar that tugged and rubbed at his neck.

At the end of each day, he was given a hunk of stinking meat, then pushed back into the box by the irresistible pressure of Karu's massive paws. He lay curled, too cramped to sleep properly, his heart still racing with anxiety, his body aching. Some days, Kobret did not want to work with him. Then they fed him something bitter hidden in the meat. It made him sleep, but a horrible sleep, from which he woke with no sense of time or place, his bones leaden, his muscles cold as stone.

By the time they arrived in Shamanow, Skrimsli's life with Owl and Taze was a bright dream, floating somewhere in the past, unreachable.

Kobret took him into the ring every afternoon to 'rehearse', which meant to do something over and over again. The cub was required to jump between tall pillars, controlling his landing and balancing four paws on the top of each one. It was hard, as the time in the box made him stiff and tired. It made no sense at all to Skrimsli. Kobret used a word for it, 'finale', which he did not understand.

Each day, more was added to the sequence of actions he was required to perform: another pillar; another leap; a greater distance between them; hoops that he must jump through. The ringmaster was meticulous. Only when the cub had mastered every jump, every pillar and hoop, was another trial added. Skrimsli knew his routine of tricks with every muscle, every bone. They entered into his shadowed dreams.

Kobret's pleasure lay in cruelty and Skrimsli never knew when a bolt of pain would be delivered. He felt more like a thing than a living being.

After a time, horses were added to the routine of tricks that was the 'rehearse', the 'finale'. They ran around at the bottom of the pillars under the command of Owl's friend, Kal. The horse, Luja, was there too. Skrimsli hardly noticed. The peaceful bubble that he, Owl and Taze had once shared with them, and the calm that Luja's mind had radiated, were as distant as the stars. Two more humans became a part of it: strange and skinny, slithering down from high in the Big Top to dance and prance across the backs of the moving horses. At first their smell made Skrimsli's fur prickle with unease and dislike, but after a few days, they too faded into the background.

Time blurred into a fog of misery and pain, and then one day when Skrimsli was brought to the ring something was different. The stink of burning smeared the air and, with a shiver of horror, Skrimsli saw that the hoops through which he had got so used to jumping had been set alight! Skrimsli's body tingled with the ancestral fear of fire. When Kobret spoke the words that meant he must begin his tricks, the cub did not move. He was frozen.

Kobret reached into his mind with the usual dagger of fear and pain.

Jump through the fire or die, it said.

Jump through the fire or you will be killed.

Two fears, the fear of fire and the fear of Kobret, closed on Skrimsli's mind, like a vice crushing him with terror, paralysing him. Kobret grew more and more angry as Skrimsli remained motionless on the top of his first pillar. The ringmaster came from where he stood at the side of the ring, getting closer so as to be able to get into Skrimsli's mind more easily. Skrimsli watched him approach, knowing that he would inflict more and more pain, but he felt powerless to do anything about it. The cub looked about in panic and saw no escape, but something caught his eye. To his right, to the side of the ring something was wriggling under the edge of the canvas, squeezing through a small gap. The something ran towards him across the ring, its little tail erect, its ears pricked. Skrimsli knew it! It was one of Galu Mak's little dog-creatures. They were kin to Taze. He'd played with them many times: long, long ago it seemed now. A tiny gleam of remembered pleasure flashed in the dark of Skrimsli's mind.

This dog was one of the smallest. Her carefully groomed black coat shone and her red ruff stood out from her delicate neck. She stopped in Kobret's path and bared her teeth at him. He laughed, then cursed and drew back his foot to deliver a kick that would break the dog's fragile body into pieces. Even as his foot was about to make contact with her body, she stood firm and snarled louder. Her ferocity took Kobret by surprise; he put his foot back on the ground and backed away from her!

She looked from Kobret straight up to where Skrimsli cowered on his pillar. She met his eye and, at once, her being slipped into his mind. She appeared there not as a tiny creature with a ruff around her neck but as she was inside her own heart: a great, black she-wolf! Her voice was like boulders rumbling along a mountain riverbed.

I am Blit the Wolf, she declared, *and I am not prey!*

He stared at her and felt her fierce, proud energy flood into him.

You are Skrimsli the tiger, she told him. *You are not prey! Fear does not know everything.*

Then she snarled once more at Kobret and raced back across the ring, to squirm under the edge of the tent and away.

Blit the Wolf was right! He was *not* prey, made to run and be ruled by fear. Fear *didn't* know all there was to know. A new calm space opened inside his mind. Into it he could move thoughts and observations like pebbles being patted by his paws.

Skrimsli looked again at the hoop of fire. Yes, there were flames, but there was space for him to pass through unharmed, if he kept exactly to the centre. His fear had not seen that. He looked around at the pillars and the rings. All of it was about *him*, Skrimsli the tiger. Kobret was not going to kill him. Not right now. Fear didn't know much at all it seemed!

Skrimsli leapt through the fire. He realised that the weeks of training, jumping, balancing, jumping again, had made him strong and skilled. He felt the agility of his tiger ancestors flowing in his body, as he leapt through one flaming ring after another. Effortless and powerful once more.

He was almost at the end, one more hoop, and one more pillar. But now the fog of fear had lifted, Skrimsli's sharp awareness shone bright. He paused and looked around. There was an electric buzz of tension that he had never sensed before. Many dark uniformed guards with weapons stood around the perimeter of the ring. Kobret had moved back to the side of the ring and stood with his cub, Itmis, and three other males. Their heads were bent together, their eyes flicked to and fro looking at him, looking at the last pillar where he was supposed to land next, and talking, talking. Skrimsli did not understand their fast words, but his ears picked up a sharp intensity. Currents of human thoughts snaked and tangled all around, turning the air sour and bad.

The horses wheeled around and lined up on either side of the last pillar. They were different too. Luja, normally an oasis of peace even when he was galloping, was jittery and Kal his rider gave out a jagged, miserable anxiety. Skrimsli had been insensible to such things for so long but now he noticed every detail. He breathed deep, listened hard, looked carefully, and drew in all the other currents that his mind picked up. Time seemed to slow, the way it had in the last moments of those nighttime rabbit hunts. Something was hidden under the surface of things here. Something bad. He knew it. There was a stink of death. Not clean death, the death of prey that would be eaten, but a kind of death whose smell made him recoil. Kobret wanted it and the three men who stood with him wanted it. Even Kal somehow wanted it.

These hoops of fire, these pillars, and all the tricks that he'd been made to do were part of this badness. It made his paws feel dirty. He'd be part of such filth no more! He jumped to the ground.

Immediately fear sparked in all the humans. Skrimsli sensed it so clearly, it surprised him.

'Get back up there!' Kobret shouted and sent pain towards the cub's mind. Skrimsli watched it coming, and for the first time saw it clearly. Why had he not seen before that the fear Kobret used was his *own* fear? Cruelty, control and power

83

were merely ways to deflect the nightmare of terror in his head. Skrimsli simply pushed the fear away and forced it back into the ringmaster's own ravaged mind.

Kobret staggered and fell to his knees. Itmis rushed to his side and helped him to the side of the ring. Karu raised his paws to either side of his head and gave a long moan of pain. The horses stamped and whinnied and were hurried from the Big Top. The men, who had been so deep in conversation with the ringmaster, trembled. They were afraid of Skrimsli's teeth and claws. Good! Itmis shouted orders and the dark-clad guards raised their guns and made a ring around the cub.

Skrimsli was no longer afraid. He was back in command of his body and of his life, whatever remained of it. He knew that before he was killed, he would deliver death to many of the humans in this place. The ring of guards closed in, their eyes glittering as they stared down the barrels of their guns, aiming for his head, his heart. He snarled and gathered himself to pounce. He would take the big one first, the one to his left who looked and smelled most afraid. Then the way would be clear to get to Kobret. He could sink his teeth into the man's neck before their flying teeth bit him and brought him down.

He was *not* prey! He was a *tiger*! Built to deliver death when he chose to do so. He would not be a puppet to be used for whatever filthy business the humans hatched here. He snarled again and felt the fear ripple through the humans all around.

Kobret got to his feet at last. His voice had a satisfying quiver in it but it was still loud enough.

'Bring me the freak boy!' he shouted. 'Now!'

8
Owl

Bargains

Kobret was always keen to make as much money as possible, so in the run-up to the gala performance for the Nordsky toffs and the Palatine, he had opened the menagerie to the public every afternoon. The circus with its tents and Big Top was now the centre of a small town of shacks, shelters and stalls so there was always a fresh supply of visitors, willing to pay to see the 'Circus Animals and Attractions'. Owl was not sure if he was an animal or an attraction. Maybe, with the 'Face of an Owl, the Body of a Boy', as the sign over the booth said, he was both.

He looked out from his booth at the faces of people from the Sand City. They didn't laugh and point at him the way the Nordskys did. They just stared and whispered to each other. Some even came back for another look after they'd wandered down the line of animal enclosures.

At least it was a rest from his new job, which was cleaning the latrines. With the circus people and the stream of visitors from the city, it took up every other hour when he wasn't required to sit in the booth. The jantevas inspected his work. If the latrines were less than spotless, he was beaten. He was once again the Freak, taunted, or ignored.

When Owl wasn't cleaning latrines or being an exhibit, he helped Akit to care for the animals. Akit didn't talk much, but he was kind, and being close to the animals made Owl miss Skrimsli a little bit less. The elephants, Mallamalla and Tooti, were especially friendly. It comforted him to be near them. They seemed to understand that Taze was gone and how Owl grieved for her.

Owl had tried to see Skrimsli, but the cub was Kobret's creature now. He was to be a star of the finale of the grand gala performance. Usually, it was possible to slip into the audience seating and watch rehearsals for circus performances. Owl had often sat in the shadows, his heart thumping, his spirit soaring with the trapeze artists and acrobats, but Skrimsli's rehearsals were held in secret. New guards, with black uniforms and big guns guarded all the entrances to the Big Top. Only the performers were allowed to watch, and when rehearsals were over, the cub was marched to the ringmaster's compound, and that was guarded too. Owl had caught a glimpse of Skrimsli just once in weeks, enough to see that the cub was thin and sad and that his coat no longer shone.

Visiting Kal or Galu Mak to try to get news was impossible too because metal fences surrounded all the living quarters now, and guards and jantevas stood at the gates between them night and day. The whole circus had become like a prison.

But there was an advantage to being small and ignored and doing a job no one wanted to think about: Owl overheard things. He only had to keep his eyes and ears open and little scraps of information fell into them.

He heard the jantevas talking about the guards and their

dark uniforms, masks and sober eyes. The story the jantevas told was that they were mercenaries, professional soldiers called Automators, from Rumyc. They were here to protect the Yuderan queen, the Palatine, paid for by the Nordsky government.

But what Yuderan stall-holders said was quite different. They said the soldiers were in cahoots with the Palatine's brother. Some thought that this might be a good thing because the prince – Yalen was his name – was handsome and dashing and the Palatine was *too clever for her own good*. But other stall holders didn't trust that 'flashy Prince', and thought the Palatine was more loyal to her people.

Owl didn't care what the soldiers were really up to, and he didn't much care whether the prince was flashy or the Palatine clever. The information that interested him most was about Kobret and his mysterious finale. Circus people gossiped about how Kobret, the Nordsky ambassador, the boss of the soldiers in Sand City, and a mysterious Yuderan businessman were often seen together. They were, people said, up to something, but no one could say what, only that the gala performance was very, very important; some said important in a bad way, and some said important in a good way. There were really only two things that the whole circus could agree on: that the tiger cub was the star of the show and that Kobret was even more angry and cruel than ever.

Thinking about all he overheard made Owl tired and anxious. He shut his eyes now against the late-afternoon sun and tried to think for the thousandth time of how he might free the cub from Kobret's clutches. But once again, his brain failed to come up with any sensible ideas.

Owl looked out of the booth and noticed nothing at first except that the visitors had drifted off, and the janteva on the ticket booth had gone to deposit his takings with the purser. But there *was* something else: the black uniformed guards had vanished! The gate that led from the menagerie compound to the rest of the circus was unattended. This was Owl's chance to see for himself what Kobret was doing with Skrimsli. He pushed open the door at the back of his booth and ran.

Owl had grown so used to the circus feeling like a prison that it was odd to find that every gateway had been left unguarded. Owl wound his way past open gates and though gaps in fences. He never even saw a janteva or a guard. It was odd.

He slipped through one last gap between two bits of fencing and into the space in front of the entrance to the Big Top. The whole space was filled with a colourful mosaic of human performers. Those not involved in the finale were taking every possible moment to perfect their acts. The tumblers did triple back flips; the clowns were falling over; the jugglers juggling with their brightly coloured clubs; the trapeze artists were doing all sorts of stretching exercises to ready their muscles; and the costume makers were darting around with pins in their mouths and half-made costumes, taking measurements and attempting to get performers to stand still long enough for final fittings.

But it was clear now why the guards had vanished: they were all *here*, making a wall of bodies and weapons around the entrance to the ring.

How ever was Owl going to get a look inside?

'Yip yip yip.'

It was the unmistakable sound of small dogs – Galu Mak and her pack of miniature performers were coming towards them.

'Well! I'm super pleased to see you!' She crouched down to be at eye level with him and put a bony hand on his shoulder.

'I sorry about Tiger Mummy. And I'm sorry I didn't come see you before,' she said softly. 'Too many guards. This place is one big jail! You want to see your cub, eh? He's in the Big Top now with Kobret, and that boy Itmis and those weird acrobat people.' Galu Mak spat on the ground to show what she thought about them. 'Numiko and the horses also. Funny business. All secret.'

'I want to get in there, to see what's going on,' Owl said.

Galu Mak shook her head. 'Many guards. Very hard.'

'I have to see the cub, Galu Mak.'

The old lady pursed her lips, and straightened up for a moment, rubbing her back. She looked over her shoulder as if afraid she might be watched, then leaned down again to whisper in his ear.

'That Kobret, he's in cahoots with these soldier boys and I dunno what else.' She shook her head. 'Bad, *bad* stuff is going down, I just *know* it. My doggies know too. After this, I quit this damn circus.'

'Will you help me get in the Big Top, Galu Mak?' Owl asked her.

Galu Mak gave him a long look.

'You're one brave kid, you know? OK. The only way is up the ladder at the back, in through the top. You good with heights?'

Owl wasn't sure if he was or wasn't, but he nodded all the same and she winked back.

'Me and the doggies will keep those guards busy, eh?' She stood up straight, with a gap-toothed grin, and looked at the pack of mini dogs around her legs.

'You ready, doggies?' The dogs looked back at her and wagged their tails.

Owl wished he could stay to watch this performance: Galu Mak pretending to call her dogs back as they galloped towards the guards barking in piercing little yips, like needles on the ears. The dogs swarmed round the guards' legs. They moved like lightning, rushing in to nip, then retreating. Every time a guard moved in one direction, the dogs attacked from another; every time a guard threatened a dog, Galu Mak screamed loud and high enough to break glass and all the other performers turned and stared and started yelling too. It was wonderful and the perfect diversion. Owl darted to the side of the tent and round the back. The few guards on patrol at the rear were running towards the sound of the commotion at the front. They would return, Owl knew; he must be quick.

The tent edge was so stiff, so tightly pegged and guyed that only something the size of a tiny dog could get under it. Galu Mak was right, the ladder to the top was the only way. Owl had watched the jantevas raise the Big Top enough times to know just where to go. It wasn't really a ladder, just a criss-cross of metal supports on the outside of the massive tent. It ran from huge poles driven into the ground, over the roof, and down the other side. At the very top was a covered vent, like a little hat on the apex of the Big Top. That was Owl's way in. But first he had to reach the lowest of the cross struts that ran between the metal supports like slanting ladder rungs. Low enough for an adult human, but not so easy for a child with owl-sized legs to reach. It took three running leaps and then a lot of swinging and straining to get onto it. He would never make a trapeze artist.

Owl climbed as fast as he could. He knew he stood out against the bright white and red of the huge tent and that as soon as the guards returned to this side, he would be spotted. Up he went as fast as he could, trying to look only at his hands and feet. He reached the place where the 'ladder' curved over the top of the roof; up ahead was the little vent and he could see the hole that led inside the roof. Owl would have to climb in through that, but he couldn't remember what was underneath. Was it the metal frame of the Big Top? A platform? Or nothing at all but a long drop to the floor of the ring below?

He paused to get his breath and, because he didn't want to think of looking down, looked up. Clouds were rising, billowing higher and higher and starting to cover the clear blue of the desert sky. Was it really true that it never rained at this time of year? For the first time since they had arrived in Shamanow, a breeze was blowing. More than a breeze, a wind. A wind from the north, carrying an unmistakable scent. Even in his hurry, Owl could not ignore that scent. It was scent of green: deep green. The scent of home! His heart turned over in his chest. He looked to the north, to the ranks of hills covered with a fuzz of blue-green and fading to blue distance. Trees! That was where his forest lay.

But it was not the time to stand and stare. He could see the other side of the tent now: the performers, the guards, the tiny darting dogs. Just one face was lifted towards him: Galu Mak.

He could guess what she would be saying so well he almost heard her voice scolding him.

'Are you a fool or what? Get inside. Now! You want to be seen?'

Fearfully, Owl crawled towards the vent and crept inside. It wasn't a clear drop to the ring floor. Immediately below the vent was a ledge made of wooden planks, suspended by more metal struts; he slid down one and landed on the platform.

Far below him he could see the ring. The flaming hoops and gold pillars looked like toys, the horses and people smaller than mice. But the sounds travelled up, easily loud enough to hear that things were not going smoothly.

Something bad had happened. The horses were all rearing and bucking, milling around and whinnying in alarm as Kal tried to get them under control. The two acrobats, those weird twins, Listig and Spion, were there. Three other men were all cowering in fear. Far from commanding everything with his usual bullying and cruelty, Kobret was crumpled in his son's arms on the side of the ring!

Most alarming of all was Skrimsli. The cub stood growling in the centre of a circle of guards, their rifles cocked and pointing right at him. Even from this far away, Owl could feel the cub's aggressive intent; any second now, Skrimsli was going to attack that ring of armed men! Didn't he understand that he would be shot and killed at once?

Owl had to stop him. There were just seconds to prevent the cub being riddled with bullets. There was a narrow ladder leading down the ring but that would take too long. Two skeins of red fabric hung coiled on the platform, each with an end tied to its metal frame. Owl had seen acrobats use these to slide from the big top to the ring. He grabbed one now, wrapped it round his body, and jumped.

He had just enough time to think that he was about to die but at least that might distract the cub and the guards from imminent conflict. The unfurling silk rolled him round and round and then dropped him in a heap, dazed but unhurt, onto the sand and sawdust of the floor of the ring.

Kobret stood up. He was shouting something, but Owl's head was spinning too much to make out what he said. Probably, Owl thought, commanding the guards to shoot. He was just in time! Owl ran in between the legs of the soldiers and stood in front of the cub.

'Stop!' he cried. 'Don't shoot!'

Owl wrapped his arms as far around Skrimsli's body as they would go, which wasn't very far any more. He expected that they would both be shot to pieces. He almost didn't care. Owl had missed his cub so much; he buried his face in Skrimsli's fur and felt the tiger's deep purr ripple into his body.

Friend, friend, friend, the cub said over and over inside Owl's head.

The bullets did not come. When Owl opened his eyes again, the guards stood astounded, their arms limp at their sides, their guns dropped. The snarling monster that had been before them a second ago was now nothing more than a giant kitten in the arms of a small, strange-looking child.

Kobret stared at Owl and Skrimsli. His expression was hard to read. Astonishment? Anger? Yes, they were part of it, but Owl saw something else; Kobret looked bewildered. As if the sight of mutual affection and respect between a human and animal was beyond his understanding. For a long moment he stood, dumbstruck. Then, his expression changed. Cold calculation stole into his face, as he realised, as always, how to turn what he saw into something useful, *profitable*. Everything, in Kobret's mind, had a price tag.

His look of bewilderment vanished, and he addressed the three men standing uncertainly to one side of the ring.

'Colleagues! Have no fear. The situation is very much resolved. All will go as we planned.'

Then he walked towards Owl and the cub.

'Well, well, well, little Freak,' he said. 'You are full of surprises. I call for you and you simply fall from the sky.'

Skrimsli drew back his lips and flattened his ears as Kobret's huge hand fell on to Owl's shoulder and he leaned down to speak quietly.

'Yes, yes, my little stripy one, you are very cross.' Kobret's voice was a low croon now, like a quiet knife slipping under a rib.

'But now I know something about you, don't I? How much you care for this little freak. Let me escort you both to my quarters.'

He stood up and called to Itmis.

'Itmis, I leave the care of our esteemed guests and remaining rehearsal to you, I have a proposition to discuss with the boy and the tiger.'

Owl and Skrimsli walked with an armed escort out of the doors of the Big Top and through the throng of staring circus performers to Kobret's private compound. Owl kept one hand on the cub's shoulder as they walked, to keep from trembling.

He knew Kobret would neither discuss nor propose. He would dictate because it was all he was capable of.

Kobret kept up the pretence of the kind and jolly ringmaster until they were safely out of sight behind the fence of his compound, when the guards were ordered once again to point their guns at the tiger. They dropped a net over the cub and soon he was snarling and struggling helplessly inside it.

Kobret laughed. He grabbed Owl by the scruff of the neck and lifted him off the floor, to shake him like a rabbit in front of Skrimsli's face.

'This is your little friend. And your little friend will die before your eyes if you do not do exactly as I say in the ring tonight!'

The look of pure hate that Skrimsli shot at the man was answer enough. Kobret laughed again.

'Yes, I see you understand. You know I am a man of my word.'

He dropped Owl to the ground and Karu held him there with one huge paw. Now he looked down at Owl and spoke to him.

'Karu is very strong and very practised. If your cub disobeys, he will have your guts out of your belly with the flick of a claw. If you attempt to escape, the cub will meet the same fate. Understand?'

Owl gave the smallest nod.

'Good. Now time for you to rest!' he said. 'Guards, please accommodate our guests.'

They shoved Skrimsli into a wooden box with holes. With a shudder Owl realised that was where Skrimsli had been kept for weeks now, whenever he was not in the ring. Owl was tied up and dragged into Kobret's caravan. He hoped Skrimsli had never been in here because his mother's skin had been used to decorate the wall. Owl was shoved into a cupboard and the key was turned.

Hours passed. Owl tried to reach out to Skrimsli's mind, but the cub's box was too far off. Perhaps he'd been taken back to the ring. Perhaps the performance had already taken place. Owl's mind swirled with misery and confusion. He simply couldn't think at all.

After a time that could have been minutes or weeks, Owl woke. There were voices on the other side of the door and the clink of glasses. Owl pressed his eye to the tiny line of light at the door's edge and peered through.

He saw a table set with glasses and dishes of food. Several people were standing around it, moving a little to refill glasses or take snacks from the plates. Owl could see them as they moved about. Kobret was there, and the three men from the ring, the three who were 'up to something': the Nordsky ambassador, the Automator commander and that 'mysterious Yuderan businessman' dressed in a long, flowing coat. There was a flash of red costume too: it was the acrobat Spion, the skinnier of the twins. What was she doing here? Owl pressed his ear to the crack and listened harder.

'We are grateful to you, Mr Majak, for your cooperation.'

This was the black-uniformed man, the boss of the Automators. He spoke in Nordsky, a voice flat and grey as an icy lake.

'Your help will not be forgotten by my colleagues,' he went on. 'The Automators will always remember you!'

'Well said, Commander Lazit,' the 'businessman' replied. 'Nor will the new Palatine leader of Yuderan forget!'

'I am honoured to serve you, Prince,' said Kobret, adding in a low voice. 'I don't believe I have ever hosted a Palatine prince before!'

Their glasses chinked in a toast. Then Spion spoke. Owl had seen her and her twin from a distance but never heard them speak. Her voice was sharp as broken glass.

'Commander,' she said. 'I must take my leave, sir; it is time for me to go and prepare.'

'I trust there will be no mistakes this time, Spion,' the Commander said. 'I return to Erem tonight and I want nothing to stand in the way of the continuation of the civil war...'

'Nor,' the man they called Prince added, 'to my accession to the Yuderan throne. Failure on your part is not acceptable.'

'I assure you both, Commander, Prince, there will be no errors,' Spion answered. 'The tiger will create chaos, the assassination will be completed, the Erem witness will be held responsible...'

'And terminated!' the Commander added.

'Of course, Commander,' Spion replied. 'Terminated.'

A new voice boomed in, as deep and fat as the commander's voice was cold.

'Excellent! Excellent,' the voice rolled, and a large arm with a ringed hand waved over the table. The voice continued. 'There will be no opposition to the railway and no obstacle to the flow of gold to pay for it! We will all prosper.'

'Quite so, Ambassador!' said the prince. 'And I will personally compensate Mr Majak for the loss of the tiger.'

'Deepest thanks, Sir,' said Kobret. 'It is a valuable animal, although I will keep the skin, if I may?'

'You may dispose of the body as you see fit.' The prince laughed. 'I have no use for dead cats!'

There was more laughter and another chink of glasses.

'To success then!' Kobret cried. 'But now is the time for us all to be about our business.'

Kobret's guests left and the door to the room was pushed shut so Owl could hear and see no more.

Assassinations and witnesses? Owl didn't understand half of what he'd heard, but he knew now that whatever Skrimsli did or didn't do in the ring in the finale, he would end up dead, another skin pinned to Kobret's wall. Desperately Owl reached out again to touch the cub's mind and warn him, but there was nothing but darkness.

Muffled sounds of the crowd came through the walls to where Owl crouched, telling him that the Big Top was filling with an excited audience. The performance was about to begin. A janteva hauled him from the cupboard and marched him towards the Big Top.

'You'll sit with Karu, Freak,' the man told him. 'So your little stripy mate won't forget what'll happen if he kicks off.'

Owl looked up at the sky. Dark clouds rolled and thunder rumbled as a storm gathered itself. There was nothing now that Owl could do to help the cub except hope that Skrimsli was clever and strong enough to find a way to survive.

9
The Palatine

A Prince and his Plot

 Even Luja was a little spooked by the tiger's rebellion. He was upset, the Palatine suspected, because of his fondness for the creature. But the other horses were almost ready to bolt when Kal brought them from the ring. It took all the Palatine's Listener skill to enter their minds and calm them with thoughts of green grass and soft rain.

Her own heart was racing too because Yalen was here! She had seen him, standing with Kobret, the Nordsky ambassador and the captain of the Automators. His disguise was good. He looked every inch the rich merchant, soft and fat, dripping with gold chains. She had almost been fooled. But those sly eyes? She'd know them anywhere!

Why was he here? Why wasn't he back in Bisque City commanding all those fighters that Sayka's eyes had spotted creeping across the Sand Sea? What was he up to?

Kal stood close by, calming Luja, standing as they often did forehead to forehead.

'Is all well with Luja?' the Palatine asked quietly.

'Oh yes, he's calm again now, thank you!' But Kal's words did not match the clouds that the Palatine saw in her friend's eyes.

'And you, Kal. How are you?' The Palatine laid a hand on Kal's arm. Kal flinched; neither touch nor question were welcome.

'I'm fine. Fine,' Kal answered. 'Just anxious about the performance.' Kal stalked away with the horse to find food and water. The Palatine watched them go. She knew quite well that Kal was hiding something. Of course, they were both pretending to be something that they weren't. But that pretence had been acknowledged and laid aside, and still they had grown close, then closer. Lying under the desert stars one night, Kal had said, 'Perhaps one day we'll tell all our secrets.'

The Palatine had been sure that one day they would, and that at some deep level they understood each other.

Yet as the gala had got closer, Kal had drawn away, become once more a wary stranger. The Palatine had tried to examine this behaviour, to dissect it with her mind, without feeling. But she could not bear to cut open *that* sore place to see what lay inside. It would mean admitting how much she cherished her time in the circus. In spite of the bullying monster Kobret, she and Kal had created a beautiful performance together.

What was she thinking! She was *the Palatine*. Her duty was to her people, *not* to her own heart. She *wasn't* an animal healer; she *wasn't* a part of the circus; she was a servant of Yuderan and now it was time to remember that. There was a reason that her brother was here in disguise, and it could not be a good one. She must get to the bottom of it at once. Besides, she could not leave Tiff to handle the Nordsky ambassador. It was time to leave this role, and Kal, behind.

The Palatine walked the black horses to their stalls, rubbed them down, watered and fed them. Then, she ran through their minds all they had to do in the performance. She reinforced all the commands and signals they would expect from Kal. Her job was done. The performance would go smoothly without her.

The Palatine fetched Zait and Harib from their stalls and led them past her tent to pick up her few belongings. She was glad to find no sign of Kal or of Luja. There would be no awkward goodbyes, no need for more layers of lies for either of them. She left her last phial of snake medicine in a leather pouch hanging at Kal's door, so that Kal would know she was gone, and not to come looking.

The Palatine knew how to divert attention from herself and remain all but invisible. She passed from the circus compound out into the crowds unnoticed, even while leading a camel and a horse. In the shadows behind a stall selling trinkets she shed Najma's clothes for Tiff's uniform. After that, just a change of posture and expression were enough to let her pass unchallenged, as the Palatine's bodyguard, into the Yuderan Royal Compound beneath the walls of the Sand City. A groom took Zait and Harib.

At the Palatine's tent, Alhamis, head of the Palatine's personal guard, greeted her.

'Ah, Tiff. The Palatine will be glad you have returned safely. I trust your mission was successful.'

'Very successful. Thank you, Captain. Is the lady within?'

'She is. The Nordsky delegation is expected within the hour. And then the gala.'

101

The Palatine bowed respectfully and entered.

Tiff, dressed perfectly as the Palatine, sat stiffly in a chair pouring mint tea from a silver pot. Of course, it wasn't safe to talk here but Tiff understood that.

'How pleased I am to see you!' Tiff-the-Palatine said, graciously offering her hand for the Palatine-Tiff to kiss.

'I have very little to report, Madam. My mission has been most uneventful.'

Tiff allowed herself the smallest smile and gave a theatrical sigh.

'With so little to report then,' she replied, 'you may easily tell all quickly. Come, I must bathe before the Nordsky delegation arrive. You will attend me.'

The filled bath stood in the adjacent tent, just far enough for whispered conversations not to be overheard.

'I think you need this bath more than I do,' Tiff breathed. 'You stink of horse, my star!'

The Palatine smiled. 'I see you have lost none of your customary respectful behaviour in my absence!'

The two of them stifled their laughter

'But you are right. I do stink.'

The Palatine stripped and climbed into the scented water. It felt *so* good but there wasn't time to savour it. She splashed a bit to give their conversation an extra layer of cover.

'My brother is here,' she whispered. 'I saw him with the chief of the Rumyc mercenaries, the Nordsky ambassador and the circus boss. He was in disguise.'

Tiff raised her eyebrows. 'He's supposed to be in Bisque City, keeping your throne warm.'

'Taking over, in other words,' the Palatine replied.

Tiff frowned. 'Perhaps he wants more than a takeover. Perhaps he wants *real* succession? An assassination far away from home would work very well and he has the resources to pay for it.'

'You think he would do that?' she breathed. Tiff looked sadly into the Palatine's face and nodded.

It was a hard conclusion to draw that her own brother would sink so low, but it was obvious, now.

'You can't go to the gala,' Tiff told her. 'It's too dangerous. I can't protect you, surrounded by a crowd of thousands. I have to keep being you.'

'No, Tiff,' the Palatine replied. 'I won't allow you to take that risk. Besides, an assassination in front of witnesses is not Yalen's style. He is more likely to try a knife in the dark. After the gala, that will be the dangerous time. I will see the delegation about the railway, go to this "gala" and then, well, we'll see.'

Tiff opened her mouth to argue.

'No arguments, Tiff. Get dressed in your uniform, then get out there and tell Alhamis that I'll be ready to receive the delegation as soon as they arrive.'

The delegation was full of sweetened nonsense about the great benefits that the railway would bring her people. The Palatine listened patiently to the Nordsky ambassador's words but noted the look in the eyes of his friends from Rumyc, the sinister members of the Automators. The message *there* was clear: 'cross us and you die'.

So she had smiled and dipped her head and said that she would give her answer after the gala performance and before their departure for Bisque City. She let the Nordsky believe that her approval was possible and hoped that would buy her some time. Perhaps her brother's ambitions could be controlled without anyone having to die for them.

It was getting dark. Almost time for the gala, for more empty smiles and more Nordsky lies and Automator dark looks. By now Kal would have discovered the phial and understood its message. The Palatine sighed. There was no way back. Surely she was used to putting the desires of her own heart to one side?

The Palatine ducked beneath the awning that shaded the birds from the sun. Sayka had done as she had bid him and made his own way to his accustomed place in the royal mews. She quieted the bird's mind before taking him from his perch and walking into the open with him. The sky was black with clouds, and thunder rumbled. Rain at this season was unknown in the Sand City but the sky told a different story. Would an unseasonable storm be the end to the long drought? What would the night bring? There was no way to tell. She slipped the hood from the eagle's head and then removed his jesses. If she was no longer in the world to be his mistress, she wanted him to be entirely free. She raised her arm and threw him into the air.

'Wind to your wings, dear friend. Go now, my eyes!'

10
Kal

The Breaking Storm

 Kal took the phial from its leather pouch. So, Najma had gone, vanished as inexplicably as she had appeared. Well, that was good, wasn't it? Najma wouldn't have to witness the evil that Kal would be forced to do by the ghosts and their threats.

For days after Najma had joined the circus, the ghosts had not appeared. It was possible to forget, even to *believe*, that the awful deed they'd asked for would not be necessary, that all that was required was the performance with the horses. Najma's skill was breathtaking and what she could achieve by tuning in directly to the horses' minds was extraordinary. Kal stopped feeling resentful and simply wondered at it.

Kobret kept out of their way and even Itmis was too occupied to interfere. They were left in peace. Although Najma would not be in the ring performing, she and Kal created the performance together. Kal escaped into it and sensed that Najma was doing the same. They were both hiding from something, and this was their refuge. They collaborated on every move and spent long hours talking about the music and explaining what they wanted to the musicians. The day they ran through the whole first part, where Kal and Luja were alone in the spotlight, Najma had taken Kal's hand and said: 'We have made something beautiful!'

Luja was happy too. He basked in Najma's presence and worked well with the black horses she had found for the performance, although it was clear they were nothing like as clever as he was.

Their little bubble was invaded first by the acrobats, Listig and Spion. Itmis said that they had to be involved in the finale. They were such a strange pair. On the surface they behaved like sweet-natured girls, with their odd, poorly spoken Nordsky. It was true their ability was incredible, and the perfection of their physical abilities sometimes made the hairs on Kal's neck stand on end. Yet there was something weird about them; something not quite alive. They certainly gave Luja the shivers. At their touch, his skin twitched as if bitten by a horsefly. Only the black horses, who were beautiful and fast, but not bright, could endure them.

Then came the business with the tiger, Skrimsli, jumping from pillar to pillar while the horses ran through their routine below. He looked magnificent, of course, but it was obvious the brave and noble creature was trying to resist Kobret's cruelty. Kal sometimes had to turn away from the pain and intelligence in Skrimsli's deep-green eyes. It must break poor Owl's heart to see his friend so mis-used, but Kal had hardly seen the boy since their arrival in Shamanow. Fences and guards divided the circus now and kept friends and colleagues apart.

Slowly but surely, the horrible reality of what the circus *really* was pressed itself into Kal's mind, souring the pleasure of the time spent working with Najma.

106

Finally, the ghosts had come again. This time Kal didn't hear or see them, only found what they left behind. A pair of tiny blue riding boots that had been Kal's gift to Roko on his last birthday and a scribbled note, smudged and bloodstained but the hand still, unmistakably, Havvity's.

They've got us, Kal. Many others too. They came in the night. Dragged us from the house. Took Roko from me. I heard him screaming. Please do whatever they want. Please.

Kal felt sick.

'Can't you try?'

That's what Havvity had said wasn't it? So why hadn't Kal tried? There was only one answer in Kal's mind: cowardice. If Kal had been courageous Havvity and Roko, perhaps all of Erem, might be safe.

Well, the blue boots made it easier. Kal could take any life, from anyone, if it would save his family, as he thought of them. What tortured him was the doubt – could the ghosts be trusted? Perhaps Havvity and Roko were already dead.

The ghosts had left something else too. A gun and bullets to go with it. Attached to it was a brown luggage label with a single word printed on it: *'PRACTISE'.*

Kal's skin pricked with revulsion at the feel of the gun: its cool grey metal. But every morning, as soon as there was enough light, Kal had ridden round the bend in the dry riverbed and obeyed that single-word command. Luja had taken the loud bangs of the gun quite calmly, but Kal sensed his quiet questioning on each occasion and turned from it. It was unbearable that Luja's noble mind should be touched by such wickedness. After every practice Kal's aim improved, but the sense of shame and contamination only grew.

'I'm doing what they want, Havvity,' Kal thought.

And yet, right up until today, the day of the gala, Kal had hoped that the new-found, unwanted skill of shooting straight would not be needed. When the tiger cub had rebelled against Kobret's awful control, Kal's heart had cheered. Kal could see why Owl loved the cub so much and now, thanks to Skrimsli's bravery, the ghosts would have to change their plans. But that hope had been short lived.

Itmis called by to explain that the *'problem with the tiger'* had been solved. There was no escape now. Grimly, Kal fitted the weapon inside the waistcoat of the blue and gold costume.

Roko and Havvity.

That was the trick to it, to think of *them* all the time. And what came after? How would living feel when you had taken a life? *Perhaps,* Kal thought, *I won't need to find out.*

Like a thing already dead, Kal fetched the horses from the stable. Luja snuffled at Kal's neck, breathing in the scent of unease and trying to make sense of it. Kal pushed him away.

'We've work to do!' Kal told him.

The little boots.

The bloodstains on the letter.

Do whatever they want.

Please.

Think of this, just of this and then it will be easy.

But it didn't feel easy. Not easy to stand smiling as other performers milled around, exiting or entering the ring. Not easy to remind the stable hand politely when to put the black horses in the ring. Not easy to get on Luja's back and feel his concern. Not easy to watch the jantevas run in to set the golden pillars in their place and be ready to light the swinging hoops. Not easy to...

'Madam Numiko, for me, moment?'

It was Spion, one of the twin acrobats. They spoke Nordsky badly with heavy Danet accents. Spion was dressed from head to foot in gleaming scarlet, spangled with gold sequins so that her hard, slender body looked like a lick of flame. Spion and her twin both had a way of smiling that suggested they had taught themselves to do it by staring into a badly damaged mirror. But of the two, Spion was definitely the weirdest. Kal's teeth clenched.

'Yes, of course.'

Spion stood at Luja's head and tried to put her hand on his nose. As always, he jinked away.

'Ah, he nervous for the big performance, yes?' she placed a hand on her own chest. 'I also. Also, my twin. We wish our mamma back in Danet could see.'

Kal's patience was wearing thin with this chit-chat.

'What is it you wanted to say?' Kal asked and, without hesitation, Spion leapt onto Luja's back. The horse gave a low whicker and a wave of loathing flowed from his body. Kal was about to ask the woman to get down as she was spooking the horse right before the performance but then Spion leaned close and spoke into Kal's left ear. As she did so the sharp point of a knife pushed against Kal's spine. No more Danet-accented Nordsky; she spoke, or rather breathed, in Erem.

'Do not speak or move.'

It was unmistakable. The voice of a ghost!

'You!' Kal managed to breathe. 'You!'

The ghost gave the breath of a laugh.

109

'You want little Roko to live, don't you?'

The blade in the back bit a little harder. Kal nodded.

'Here is what will happen. The last gold pillar will collapse as the tiger lands, pitching the beast towards the Palatine as if in attack. You will be perfectly placed to take the shot to the Palatine's head. Afterwards you can claim you were aiming at the tiger. A head shot, remember. It's essential for Roko that she dies.'

She slipped to the floor and pressed something into Kal's hand. Then she ran off to take up her position.

'Good luck, Madam Numiko,' she called gaily, in her usual Danet accent. 'You will be big hit. Sure.'

She waved, a casual gesture, but something about the way the wrist flexed made it completely unique. Recognisable at once as a gesture Kal had seen before. It was the wave that had passed between the two identical killers at Talo, with the slender bodies and their machine-like determination. The acrobats were ghosts, and they were assassins too. They had killed friends and relatives and made the lie that began a war.

Kal looked down at what Spion had left: it was a small curling lock of Roko's hair! Luja tossed his head and whinnied as Kal's shock and distress leaked into him.

'Calm, my friend. Calm,' Kal told him.

Yes, calm. Calm was what Kal must try to feel or if not calm at least numb. Numb enough to do, now, what needed to be done.

'Madam Numiko, two minutes!' Masto the stage manager announced. He stepped close to Luja and smiled up at Kal.

'It has gone very well,' he said. 'Very well indeed! Even Mr Majak seems pleased. The Palatine is *most* attentive as far as

110

one can tell through those veils. Truly the woman is wrapped up like a parcel! The crowd adored Saldo and Zuta – flawless performance tonight. They will love you, Madam, I *know* it!'

Kal's face managed something that hopefully resembled a smile and then the music began.

On the other side of the curtain Itmis Majak's voice boomed out.

'Our gala is drawing to its close, but we have one last set of wonders to present to you. In our grand finale, humans and beasts will once more work in total harmony. But I assure you, there is no hocus-pocus here. Our beasts are trained by science, through reward and kindness, not through the primitive art of Listening. Majak's circus is a circus of the future, not of the past.'

Stupid lies, of course, turned out to please the Nordsky high-ups and their mercenary friends from Rumyc, those slit-eyed Automators in their suits as black as death itself. Itmis droned on.

'Most honourable Palatine of all Yuderan, esteemed guests, ladies and gentlemen, I present to you our finale! Mistress Numiko, her extraordinary horse companions and the Cat of Fire from the great green forests of the north!'

At last, the waiting was over. Two lives depended on what Kal did in the next few minutes. All must go smoothly. Nothing must be suspected. Kal breathed deep, calmed the skipping heartbeat, focused all thought on the sequence of actions that must follow. Kal lay down along Luja's back, so they were spine to spine.

'Begin!' Kal told him. 'Begin!'

Slowly, delicately, the great, pale horse moved into the darkened ring. He stepped into the silver circle of the spotlight that made horse and rider into the only creatures in the whole wide world.

What the audience saw was something extraordinary: a milk white horse, darkly spangled with black stars, which side stepped, turned, bowed and stretched. The Yuderans, great horse trainers though they were, had never seen anything like it. The horse's movements were so perfectly tuned to the deep, sad melody the orchestra played that he must surely understand the music! More extraordinary still was the slender figure on his back, with dark hair falling in a cascade, almost to the floor. This figure too began to dance on the horse's back as if it was solid ground, not the moving back of living animal!

Together, the tempo of their dance responded to the quickening themes of the music, until they moved around the ring, entirely possessing it, the spotlight only just managing to keep track of their quicksilver progress.

Just when every heart was caught in every throat, two more spotlights flashed to life, illuminating two beautiful black horses, as sleek and gleaming as polished jet. They joined the dance: whirling, turning, leaping with unthinkable speed and precision, all three horses now moving as if driven by a single mind.

Then the acrobats! Suddenly two swathes of shimmering blood-red silk unfurled from high in the Big Top. From them dropped two acrobats, as taut and supple as willow wands, encased in scarlet like living flames. Each landed on the back of one of the galloping black horses. They moved over the horses' backs, sometimes with one foot on each of two backs, sometimes almost seeming to float above them. They flipped, somersaulted and balanced in ways that seemed impossible, otherworldly, in ways that made the audience almost forget to breathe.

Finally, when the audience was excited almost beyond endurance, the tiger appeared, picked out in light, perched on top of a golden pillar, surrounded by hoops that burst into flame. The big cat glowed, beautiful but terrible, bringing to the ring a gorgeous, awe-inspiring wildness. With every leap the gasps and shrieks from the audience grew louder. The thunder that now shook the roof and the trembling of the ground beneath seemed just a part of this extraordinary performance.

The music swelled to a crescendo. Kal glanced towards the velvet-covered box where the Palatine and the other dignitaries sat. Just above the box, screened from the audience by the two high-sided staircases that led up to it, Kal could make out Kobret Majak and his bear, standing on its hind legs. One of its forepaws rested on the head of the boy, Owl. Kal's heart went out to the child. He was innocent, like Roko. The threat was clear: if the tiger, Skrimsli, didn't do exactly what Kobret told him, the boy would die. The tiger had defeated Kobret's hideous control of his mind, but he could not defeat his own love for the boy. Shame washed through Kal like a fever; it was terrible that such fine beings as Skrimsli, Owl and dear Luja were now ensnared in this filthy business. It was a bitter thing to know that Kal, Owl and Skrimsli were all being controlled by love! A pulse of white-hot anger shot through Kal's body. It would be easy to draw the gun and shoot the monster Kobret right now.

Roko, Havvity.

Kal repeated it like a spell. There was only one way to make

113

anything good come of all this. Focus. Concentrate. Do this job. Then whatever came afterwards would come.

Kal wheeled Luja and the other horses in a final, elegant arc that brought them into a line, close to the box. It was raised only a little above the level of the ring so the tiger on his pedestal was just above it. On horseback, Kal was on eye-level with those who sat there. Kal didn't want to look at any of the faces. When the horses bowed their heads as they had been trained to do, Kal did the same.

Now was the moment for the tiger's last leap. To the audience it would appear as if his whole body had become fire itself. Everyone would be looking at him; they would see nothing else.

Now, Kal's mind said. The moment had come, dread, dark and evil. Every detail of it at once unnaturally clear and strangely distant. The tiger's muscled body passed within a hand's breadth of Kal's left side, where the gun lay waiting.

Roko, Kal thought, *crying in some dark cell; Havvity, beaten and afraid.*

The big cat's soft forepaws made contact with the pillar, but it didn't give way at once. Whoever had made the weakness in it had judged it perfectly. Only when the tiger tucked his back paws neatly beside the front ones, his full weight resting on the pillar's top, did it crumble, pitching him toward the Palatine who sat in the middle of the box.

Kal pulled out the gun and pointed it. Sound and vision narrowed to a cylinder of existence extending forwards from the black barrel. At one end was Kal's own breath and heartbeat, horribly loud, grotesquely slow. At the other was the Palatine, a figure wound in layers of cream silk, more

114

parcel than human, an aristocrat removed from the ordinary lives of her people. What was the life of such a person against the lives of Roko and Havvity?

Kal's practised finger pulled the trigger, a movement that seemed to stretch out for minutes. In that small eternity, the Palatine looked up. The eyes were unmistakable. With a lurch of the heart, Kal knew that this was no stranger, no distant aristocrat. However impossible, however strange, *this was Najma*. About to be killed by the bullet which Kal had set in motion, spinning now from the end of the grey barrel.

How cruel that only now was understanding delivered of the place that Najma held in Kal's heart. At the very moment of this sweet realisation its light would be extinguished.

But the bullet did not reach its mark. A blur of dark clothing came between it and the cream silk! Relief and horror jolted Kal back to the world. The ordered rows of seating unraveled into a chaos of pushing, running, clambering panic. But it was not the gunshot that had terrified everyone. A deep roaring noise built all around and then the night sky broke through the ripping canopy of the Big Top as the tent poles the size of tree trunks snapped like matchsticks.

A wall of water burst in a torrent, a barrage, through the ring. Luja's terror and utter incomprehension rushed up to meet Kal's own. Then two more gunshots exploded, one from the left and one from the right. Kal stared, stupid with shock, at the Palatine – at Najma – as red blossomed on the cream silk of her clothes.

Then the lights went out and the flood engulfed everything.

11
Skrimsli

A Reckoning

 Kobret, his bear and twelve of the armed men had come to bring Skrimsli to the ring, ready for the start of the jumping and fire nonsense. As they walked, Kobret did that smiling thing that humans did. He believed he was back in control, but Skrimsli knew better. Kobret had been defeated; without these men, these guns, Kobret and his sad old bear would be dead meat.

The tiger reached out, trying to find Owl's mind, to reassure him that all would be well, but he was hidden somewhere, too far away to reach.

They stopped at the special entrance, no more than a loose flap of tent that led, via a narrow gap in the audience seating, to Skrimsli's first position. The Big Top was already full of people, buzzing like a hive of bees, waiting for this 'gala' to begin.

Kobret paced about, talking to himself, fear and anger rippling from him with growing intensity. Skrimsli was calm. He was waiting for the greatest hunt of his short life to begin. When Kobret, with two armed men on either side of him, strode up and seized the chain on Skrimsli's collar, he met the man's eyes.

'You will see the freak boy,' Kobret told him. 'He will be with Karu. Do what I trained you to do or the freak dies!' Kobret tried to sound strong, but Skrimsli saw his lip tremble and noted, with satisfaction, that the man did not attempt to enter his mind.

'One mistake in there, Stripy,' Kobret snarled, 'and Karu will take the freak's guts out. Understand.'

Skrimsli stared at him and watched his eyes slide away.

All you have now is words, Kobret, Skrimsli thought. *And words will not be enough.*

Skrimsli wanted very much to kill Kobret now. For Taze, for Owl and for all the other beings Kobret had broken and terrorised. But it was best to wait.

There was something big going on which the humans didn't seem to notice. Skrimsli sensed it in the crackle in the clouds, the thrumming of the ground. It drew closer every second. An opportunity was on its way and, when it came, the score with Kobret would be settled.

Kobret left to take up his position at the side of the ring. He had many other animals to rule and terrorise tonight, to make them do their tricks, while Itmis, his cub, pranced and shouted in the spotlight.

There would be a time of waiting now, he knew. Skrimsli sensed the fear of the guards around him. They gripped their guns too tightly. Fear might make them dangerous to him. It was better if they relaxed. So he lay down and rested, closed his eyes and felt their fearfulness recede.

It was good to rest while there was nothing else to be done, but he kept his eyes a little open and all other senses on alert. Thoughts came into the new space that had opened in his

117

mind. He pushed them into order as if arranging stones with a paw.

Inside the tent many humans were watching other humans and creatures do tricks. Would a crowd of tigers watch other tigers like this? He didn't know. He didn't think they would. Were there even that many tigers in the world? Many tigers! *That* thought was a good one. He liked it and thought it again.

The emotion from the crowd of humans was like a wind. So many humans, all feeling the same thing all at once! It was strange and fascinating to him. The feelings ebbed and flowed in time with the noises from the group of people who made squeaks and bangs with the objects they held in their hands. Owl had a word for these sounds: '*mew-sick*'. that was it! The humans who made it were '*orkestra*'. *Mew-sick* usually caused Skrimsli's ears to complain, although he had got a little more used to it in recent days. Now he heard that the waves of fear or excitement were connected to the *mew-sick* and to whatever it was that was happening inside the tent.

Underneath the hum of noise and feelings from the Big Top, Skrimsli felt the ground shake. All sorts of smells rose from the cracks in the mud, smells long held underground awakened now by moisture. His deep, tiger self knew the meaning of these smells. Somewhere, a lot of rain had fallen in a very short time. The long fingers of the river were gathering it up faster and faster, more and more. Soon they would bring it here. Skrimsli took a long breath. Yes! Very soon. Just in time!

One of the guards pulled on the chain and jerked the metal collar that was around his neck. The waiting was over.

'Inside, onto the pillar!' one of them growled. A flap of canvas was pulled aside and in Skrimsli went.

The guard was afraid when he unclipped Skrimsli's chain. Just for the amusement of seeing the man cringe, Skrimsli snarled.

Then, he jumped to the top of the first pillar.

Kobret's cub was shouting something on the other side of the ring. Skrimsli scanned the sea of faces in the dim light and picked out Kobret, the bear and Owl too, his head just visible under one of Karu's huge paws. He reached out to Owl's mind one last time before the hunt began and all his concentration would be on it. For a fleeting second, he flickered in the boy's brain. He wanted Owl to know that even though this was bad human business, he would make it right. Fear was pushed down underneath his paw now. He was strong and knew more than humans did. Skrimsli would free them both, he *knew* it. But he lacked the words and the time to say all that, so he said what he could.

I am Skrimsli. Do not fear. And hoped that Owl heard.

Itmis finished shouting and the mew-sick began again, the slow kind that played for the horse, Luja, and his companion, Kal. A beam of white light followed Kal and the horse around the ring. Sadness came from the audience. It was as if the mew-sick, the horse and rider hurt them. Why did they stay and watch if it hurt?

Skrimsli gave his head a shake. Those thoughts needed to be quiet now.

He was hunting.

The horses did their running about. The humans did their leaping on the horses' backs. The two acrobats, the skinny female ones, slid down from high up and the audience made a great deal of noise. They liked these acrobats. They could not smell what Skrimsli smelled which was that they were bad, wrong in every way, and always tangled in some knot of human business.

Skrimsli took little notice of any of it. His attention was on Kobret; on the water that was coming closer every second; on the wind that was already tearing at the canvas overhead.

Skrimsli jumped through hoops and between pillars. He was approaching the last jump and the last pillar where Kal and Luja would be very close. Skrimsli remembered the peaceful moments on the train, spent with Taze and Owl, Luja and Kal. The Kal in the ring now was not the same as *that* Kal. This Kal was hiding something; was tangled in the same bad human business as Kobret and the skinny acrobats. Skrimsli could smell it in the trails of wants and emotions that looped around them all.

But none of that mattered.

He judged that the river and the wind would create a distraction just at the moment that he needed it. It wouldn't take long to dispose of Kobret. Released from the ringmaster's cruel control, Skrimsli guessed the bear would crumble. Then Skrimsli could grab Owl and they would get away. He could see it in his mind. It would be easy.

But as he leapt through the last fire and reached for the pillar that provided excellent access to Kobret's throat, several things happened that he had not expected.

The pillar broke, cutting his leap to the box short. Kal pulled out a small gun and with a bang, a flying tooth came from it. That was what Kal had been hiding! A figure he had failed to notice, covered in a dark cloth-skin, threw itself in front of him. To his left, another gun fired and fired again. One of the acrobats had a gun too!

At the same time, the water and the wind arrived, and they were much, much more than the 'distraction' Skrimsli had anticipated. The whole world was about to wash away!

A cold shoot of doubt sprang up inside him. He pushed it down. He wasn't a fearful cub now. He just needed a change of plan.

His front paws landed on the body of the dark-clad figure as it fell. Dead already, Skrimsli noted. One of the guns had done that. His back paws grasped the edge of the box. He curled his hind legs like a spring and released their energy to leap up. He rose over the people in the front of the box and straight to Kobret.

The tearing Big Top, the water rushing into the ring, had indeed distracted Kobret and his bear. Skrimsli leapt so quickly that neither of them had time to react. He swiped at the bear with his right paw, his claws leaving deep cuts along its snout. Karu was not at all used to creatures fighting back. He released his grip on Owl and fell back, yowling.

Then his left paw made contact with Kobret's chest and pushed the man backwards and down.

The water was rising very fast. There wasn't much time. Skrimsli stood over the ringmaster. He tensed his muscles and the iron collar burst and fell away. He drank in Kobret's fear. It was paralysing. Overwhelming. He let the man feel that fear, the fear he had used on so many others for so long, before delivering death in a single bite. Nearby he heard Karu the bear let out an ear-splitting scream and saw him tumble over the wall of the box into the dark well of the staircase.

The lights had gone out and humans, whose eyes did not work unless the daylight was bright, were screaming in blind confusion. Skrimsli's eyes worked well enough in normal nighttime but under the remaining canopy of the tent it was darker than night; the tiger had to peer around to find Owl, ready to grab him and make their escape. But Owl was no longer in the box. Skrimsli scanned the crowds of people running from the collapsing tent, bumping into things and falling. Owl wasn't among them. Where *was* he? Skrimsli turned to look in the opposite direction and saw the wall of water coming towards them. It hit the box, tipping it like a straw, plunging Skrimsli into the dark swirling waters.

12
Owl

Ancient Fishes

 The fish were old, gnarled and armoured. They had smelled the rain coming for days. The news of it had filtered down to the green depths of the sea where they swam, feeling for the shiver of prey in dimness. They had breathed it through their gills, felt it tingle on their skins. The river would flood into the rising tide of the full moon; the gate to their other life upstream would open at last.

The breaking of the drought by an out-of-season storm that was far beyond any human memory, made hardly a ripple in the rhythm of creatures with the lineage of a sturgeon. When their kind first made these journeys from salt to fresh, the stars had formed other constellations. Their knowledge was ancient, built over uncounted eons. They moved inexorably into the mouth of the river, into the champing teeth of the greatest flood in a hundred human generations.

Their journey was not without danger. The unusual storm, created by a broken weather pattern, had brought torrents of rain to mountains stripped of their forest cover. So the flood had a swiftness and a violence that had carried with it almost all it encountered on its way: logs, rocks, branches, bodies. To

123

this, all the debris of the circus was now added: broken wooden seats, with humans and animals clinging to them; hats and shoes and bags; diabolos and lanterns; plates and cups; blankets; a cake inside its tin; huge tent poles and a tent canvas; animals swimming for their lives; Mallamalla, her trunk like a snorkel above the surface; bodies drowned in a tangle of rope and canvas. The circus-owner's caravan had broken open, its contents floating free: top hats and gilded jackets; banknotes; Narastikeri's skin. All reunited with the man himself, Kobret Majak, floating blindly in the water, as it turned him over and over on its journey to the ocean.

High above, the storm clouds grew thin and ragged and allowed a little watery moonlight to filter through. Owl could see the surface at last! He kicked off the boots that were dragging him down and pushed for the light. His head broke into the air for just long enough to take a breath, then something tumbled him over and down again. At first he thought it was a huge log, but it was moving against the push of the flood. It flexed its huge, gnarled body. It was a fish! A giant fish! He bumped along its side as it beat its tail, swimming upstream. It was ten, no twenty times his size: its rough scales as big as roof tiles.

Another came. Its huge snout brushed his face with fleshy whiskers.

Owl was not afraid. He knew this creature; he had carried a tiny wooden replica of it on a string around his neck all his life. He found he remembered the touch of its skin; its vast presence was familiar to him. It was a sturgeon. A keeper of the forest: *his* forest. A keeper of the forest just like him!

An image flashed into his mind, bright and clear. Sunshine on a riverbank. All around people were singing:

Great fish, great fish, welcome,
You bring the green.

He had been very small, and he had been carried into the water where the huge fish crowded. The person in whose arms he was held lowered him into the river to touch their reaching snouts, one after another, while the people sang:

Welcome, great fish, welcome,
The owl child bids you come.

The words were not in the Nordsky that Owl used every day in the circus. They came from another language, another place and time; the one from which the cub's name had come. This was a memory of a *real* day in his own life! The proof of that was here in the giant fish that thronged the flood and pushed him to the surface like a cork from a bottle.

Huge bodies were all around and Owl feared he would be crushed. He grappled himself between two of them, pushing with his legs against the side of one, to struggle onto the back of the next. Breathless and shivering he sat upright and looked at the strange scene that surrounded him.

The backs of a thousand great fish broke the surface of the flooded river; their knobbled scales caught the moonlight like a range of mountains. They were swimming upstream, pushing against the debris that the flood had caught. And he was being carried with them. They would swim all the way to where the fingers of the river stretched into the forest. The green place. For a moment Owl believed that he could ride like this all the way.

But the logjam of debris in the river was clearing, unlocked and untangled by the determination of the water. As it swept away towards the sea, the river was no longer clogged with obstacles and the fish were not forced to swim so close to the surface. One by one, the sturgeon began to dive, to swim into the current in the dark depths, where they felt most at home. Owl tried to hang on, but he was Owl and not a fish. Coughing and spluttering he fought back to the surface. The fish had vanished and the idea of riding on a moonlit back all the way upstream faded like a dream.

Clinging to a floating ball that one of Galu Mak's dogs had once balanced on, Owl kicked for the shore and crawled out on to the bank. There, shivering among the washed-up flotsam, was Blit. Not so long ago Owl had shared his sweetened tea with her in Galu Mak's caravan. Already, it seemed like another life. The little dog leapt into his arms and for a while they sat wrapped up together, adjusting to the new world in which they found themselves.

At length, Owl looked up.

'I have to look for Skrimsli,' Owl told Blit, and she seemed to understand.

They had walked some way downstream before finding any remains of the circus, showing Owl just how far the fish had carried him and, he guessed, Blit too. Objects and bodies lay tangled together, mired in mud. Everything looked long dead, as if from some ancient catastrophe. Owl didn't want to look closely at the horrors that the flood had washed up but sometimes Blit barked so loudly he knew she wanted him to inspect what she'd found. Once it was a dog, one of Blit's companions. She sniffed at it and whined. Another time it was a cake tin with the cake inside, quite safe, if a little battered. They shared it sitting on a half-rotten log. Another day, Owl would have found it delicious but now he ate it only to have the energy to go on searching.

Over and over Owl reproached himself for having run from the box the moment that Skrimsli had attacked Kobret and so become separated from the cub. He had wanted so badly to escape from the bear and the threat of those long claws that, the moment its paw lifted, he'd darted away. He had been sure that Skrimsli was just a step behind him. But when he'd looked around, there had been a wall of water. If only he'd stayed close, they would be together now. Without the cub, Owl felt bereft.

Thinking these gloomy thoughts, Owl lost track of how far they'd walked until his feet began to hurt and reminded him of the boots he had kicked off as he struggled to the surface. The debris was thinning out; whatever else the flood had taken was now out at sea. Perhaps they had somehow missed the cub in the darkness, and he was looking out for them back the way they'd come.

'C'mon Blit,' Owl said. 'We turn around and go back.' But Blit had found something. She stood back from it, her fur on end, whining now between barks.

Owl came closer. He didn't want it to be true. Half buried in the mud, held beneath a huge log and only just visible in the thin grey light, was the unmistakable pattern of a tiger's coat. It didn't move. It could only be Skrimsli's drowned body;

Owl couldn't bear to touch it or try to pull it clear. What was the point? What was the point of anything now?

He stared at the dark river where he had sat on the back of the sturgeon and thought again of being carried upstream to the green forest. Words from that lost place and time spoke inside him again.

'The tiger and the sturgeon and the owl are the keepers of the forest. Each must speak to each to keep the forest whole. But the owl, who speaks both to the river and the trees, is the greatest keeper of them all.'

They seemed hollow now, like a kind of taunt. A mockery. What did those words matter?

Skrimsli is dead.
Skrimsli is dead.
Skrimsli is...

A deep growl interrupted Owl's thoughts.

Before him, in the real world, Blit stood with her teeth bared while in his mind a great she-wolf snarled, then spoke.

Wolves are forest keepers too, you know. We could find the forest together.

Owl looked at the tiny dog that was a wolf inside. Perhaps she was right. In any case, what else was there to do?

We will find the forest, Owl told her. *We will follow the sturgeon up the river.*

Owl dried his eyes, straightened his back, and began to walk upstream, with the littlest wolf in the world at his heels.

13

Skrimsli

The Unexpected Friend

 Skrimsli did not expect to be afraid of water. Yet the moment the flood closed over his head, he was. How had fear slipped out from under his paw again? He felt just like a tiny cub, cold and powerless inside a sack of terror. He sank, bombarded by all manner of alarming objects; mud filled his eyes and ears.

Something grasped the back of his neck. Not a bite, although Skrimsli could feel teeth; no, this was the way mothers picked up cubs. Taze had picked him up like this when he wandered too far away inside the menage tent. It made him a little calmer.

The something that had hold of him was very big and very strong. It dragged him to the surface where he took a ragged gasping breath. Then another. He pushed the fear down, out of the way again. He found his paws were moving: one, then the other, one, then the other, back and front. His body knew how to swim! He lifted his whole head above the surface and shook out the mud from his ears and eyes, rather ashamed of how foolish he had been.

There, in the water beside him, was a huge head. It turned towards him, a wide furry horizon of forehead with two small ears and a pair of eyes. It had a long snout with the bloody marks of Skrimsli's claws still oozing blood. Even in this poor light there was no mistaking the bear, Karu, Kobret's dark shadow!

There was no mistaking it and yet the transformation was astonishing. The eyes that had been dead holes gleamed with life; the great paws had been drained of their violence and now reached to help Skrimsli scrabble up a steep bank, through a scrub of spiky plants, to dry land.

Tiger cub and bear each did the spiral shake from nose to tail that spun the water from their pelts. Then, they stood looking at each other. What was the bear thinking? Skrimsli could tell what was going on inside Owl so easily, but Karu was unreadable. Even his smell gave nothing away for now, clouded as it was with all that his fur had absorbed from the flood water.

The bear sniffed at him, running the end of its snout over his face. Skrimsli stood very still, not sure yet if Karu could be trusted. But the bear just huffed through his long nose and sat down, with his front paws in his big lap, like a human. His head hung; he seemed once again as dead as he had been under Kobret's command.

Skrimsli turned and began to walk away. But he could not help considering this bear. It had, a very short time ago, been an enemy that Skrimsli would have been happy to kill. But the bear had saved him from drowning. That was what Owl called 'kind'. Kind required repayment. Skrimsli recognised this as a human thought that he didn't want to have. Yet here it was in his mind. Unavoidable.

He turned back and sat down beside the bear. Very gently Skrimsli put his mind into the space where, usually, he met with Owl's mind. Perhaps it was a way into Karu's mind too. He didn't know what else to try, as Karu sat there staring at his own paws, not moving.

Skrimsli felt himself fall into Karu's head as if into a deep hole. Immediately Karu snarled and pushed him out. Skrimsli felt as if he'd been thwacked with a big paw. Good. If the bear was no longer kind that made it easier. He got up and set off downriver. He had to look for Owl. That was the hunt now. Owl was small and weak; the current would have carried him a long way downstream.

Skrimsli picked up his pace and began to trot. The bear gave a kind of yowl and began to lumber after him. Skrimsli turned and the bear stopped. Skrimsli set off again and the bear followed. Skrimsli stopped again and then, to Skrimsli's surprise, the bear spoke in his mind, not quite in words, not quite in pictures. Rather, the bear's thoughts appeared like faint gleams of light that Skrimsli recognised, the way you would see a tree reflected in a rippling pond.

You kill Kobret! Karu the bear conveyed.

Kobret bad, Skrimsli replied in the same tree-reflection way. *Cruel.*

Kobret dead, Karu replied. *Still in my head.*

Karu began to shake his head.

Get out! he growled. *You dead. Get out!*

Now, Skrimsli understood. The memory of Kobret's cruelty still lay like a shadow over his own mind. How much worse would it be for poor Karu who had suffered under the man's control for so long?

The bear flopped down again, his back legs out in front of

him, his forepaws in his ample lap and sighed. *What do now?* he asked.

It must have been a long, long time since Karu had been able to decide what to do for himself. What *would* they do now? Kobret and his circus had been horrible, but that was all that Skrimsli had ever known, perhaps Karu too. The question was a little frightening. But for now he had an answer that he knew was good.

Find Owl! he told the bear. *You search that way. I go this.*

Karu sighed, huffed, shook his head a bit then got up and began to lumber away upstream, sniffing the air and turning over objects with a deft paw. Skrimsli set off in the other direction. What would happen if they didn't find Owl? No. He would not ask that yet. Now, he would hunt.

The river had washed all smells into one smell. Skrimsli had to paw at the piles of flotsam, and sniff at them close up to check that Owl wasn't in among them. But of course, Skrimsli realised, if he was *that* tangled and *that* still, he would be dead. Skrimsli pushed the thought away and hurried on. There seemed to be nothing alive on this side of the river whereas, on the other, figures moved about and lamps burned. Perhaps he should swim there and look? He sniffed the breeze. There were many humans on that side, perhaps they would want to put him back in another box. No, he reasoned, if he and Karu had washed up on this bank then Owl would have done so too.

Skrimsli found nothing. After a while he turned round and went upstream to find Karu. At first Skrimsli thought the bear was once more staring into space, but he wasn't. He was staring at a pair of boots, half buried in the mud. They were very small boots. Skrimsli hooked them with his claws and sunk his nose into them. Owl. *Owl.* He waded into the water to see if the boy was swimming nearby or clinging to some floating object. He dove and dove, but all was darkness down there.

Gone, the bear said in Skrimsli's head. *Gone.*

With a snarl of sudden fury, Skrimsli knocked the bear over and grabbed his throat. *You kill boy?*

No!

Skrimsli could feel the truth of this. He let go of Karu and stood staring at him.

Boy gone, Karu's thought said and he waved his snout out towards the river and *upstream.*

Gone. There. Water.

Skrimsli ejected Karu from his mind as sharply as the bear had at first pushed him away. He was tired, he was hungry, he was cold. He would not think these thoughts. He walked from the river and found a patch of scrubby trees where he curled up and burrowed himself into sleep.

Sunshine, warm on his fur, woke him. He opened his eyes. Karu was sitting close by, in that same oddly human way, back legs stretched out, front paws idle in his lap, big head lolling down. He didn't look up as Skrimsli stretched, but he followed when the cub walked down to the edge of the water to drink. In broad daylight the edge of the water felt exposed and unsafe. They both slunk back into the shelter of trees and shadows as soon as they had drunk.

Skrimsli didn't have to look to know that Owl was not anywhere here. His heart told him. The bear was right.

Gone, but what sort of *gone*? Gone dead, or just gone? Gone now? Or gone tomorrow too?

Gone now, that was enough. Skrimsli was alone. The circus was over. Kobret was dead, there was no one to fight, and no one to tell him what to do. Perhaps Owl would not stay gone, but right now Skrimsli had to decide for himself what to do, where to go. He felt as if a huge hole had opened up beneath his feet.

Karu came and stood close beside him. *Long, long time Kobret keep me*, Karu said. *Like dead bear.*

Skrimsli shuddered to think it was the fate he himself had only just escaped.

Now, the bear went on, *I am alive.*

Skrimsli felt warmth seep into his mind from the bear's presence.

We are alive.

Karu lifted his nose into the breeze that still blew from the north and took a huge breath. *Smell!* Karu said. *Smell!*

Skrimsli did as the bear asked. He closed his eyes and pulled the air in through his nose. It contained many strands of information, scents of wet earth and vegetation, the traces of many, many kinds of living thing. The air was alive with details, none of which Skrimsli could identify; all of which he instantly wanted to know more about. He had jumped through the elephant's eye and this was the first part of the big world that he had seen there.

Green, the bear said happily. *Smell is green.*

Green! Green was the place Skrimsli had shared with Owl. The green forest that filled his dreams. Owl's voice came to Skrimsli.

'The tiger and the sturgeon and the owl are the keepers of the forest. Each must speak to each to keep the forest whole.

'That's where we belong, Skrimsli, in that great, green forest in the north!'

If Owl was still alive that was where he would go.

Green smell from the north, said Karu.

Yes! We head north? Skrimsli asked.

We head north, Karu agreed.

Just like that, the decision was made. Together the bear and the tiger turned from the westward bend of the Shamanow river, heading north into the wind, towards the smell of the forest.

14
Kal and the Palatine

Silken Layers

 The Palatine clung to Tiff's body. She would not let the river have her. She wound the unravelling strands of her own clothing around the dead bodyguard to bind it to her. It was impossible to swim against the flood, so they floated together downstream. She grabbed at a floating door and managed with a huge effort to pull them both on top of it. It wasn't exactly a raft, but it would at least hold them up in the water. She lay on her back and held onto Tiff with her right arm. Her left no longer seemed to be aware of what her brain was telling it.

Every now and then she caught a glimpse over the surface of the swirling water. Their door had been washed to the north side of the river but along the other shore she could see the yellow dots of lanterns and the silhouettes of people and animals. Rescuers had come from the Sand City to pull out survivors. Many of the audience had got out of the Big Top before it collapsed and had made it to the south bank. Perhaps the death toll of Yuderani wouldn't be so bad.

She was very tired. Tiff had taken the first bullet but not the second. That one had pierced her own shoulder just below her left collar bone. Blood loss was making her confused.

Where had that bullet come from? Oh, yes. She remembered. Kal! It was Kal! Why had Kal shot her? Something to do with her brother? Her mind drifted and wandered. She forgot for a moment why Tiff wasn't moving and shook her, before remembering. They would both be dead soon. Two bodies drifting out into the ocean. Yalen would have his railway now. It would march across their land like a foul scar. She looked up into the night sky, where the remnants of the storm clouds trailed like torn scarves. High, high up a bird was wheeling against the background of the stars. Sayka! Sayka! Goodbye, dear friend, she told him; carry my heart from this broken world.

**

Despair would have washed Kal clean away even without the force of the flood. But Luja was a strong swimmer and very determined that they should both survive. As the water swept them off their feet, he had stepped from the shadows at the edge of Kal's thoughts and said, *Stay on my back. I will not allow you to drown.*

He answered Kal's surprise calmly. *I have always been here with you and you with me, in our shared mind. Now, hold on to my neck!*

The water was deep, cold, muddy and the darkness absolute but through it Kal felt the horse's resolve and his love. It was not possible to decide to die in the face of such devotion. No matter how bad Kal felt, giving up was not an option.

The metal structure of the Big Top broke apart and shot down into the water around them. Under the water, stray ropes and swathes of canvas grabbed at their feet and tried to pull them under. All around in the darkness were sounds of tearing and breaking and the screams of humans and animals. Luja's legs worked steadily. *Hold on*, he kept repeating. *Hold on.*

There had been another shot after Kal's gun had fired. And then another. Perhaps more. Somewhere in their skintight costumes the twins had concealed their own guns. They'd fired to kill Kal but the shot had missed. Kal saw now what their plan was: Kal would kill the Palatine and then one of the ghosts would kill Kal. How neatly that would tie things off. 'EREM TERRORIST SHOT WHILE ASSASSINATING PALATINE.' The Nordskys and the Rumyc mercenaries could paint themselves as defenders of Yuderan as well as of Erem.

Luja's pumping hooves had found solid ground at last. They could scrabble out and onto dry land. Kal let go of Luja's neck and slithered to the ground.

Thank you, Kal told him.

He didn't reply. Now the immediate threat of death had passed, he had melted back into the background noise of Kal's thoughts.

Kal looked around. They were on the north bank of the river, quite a long way down from where the circus had stood. The lights of the city were in the distance to the right. Further upstream the yellow of lanterns dotted the shore where people were already searching for survivors. Kal sank down on the mud. The image of the blood spreading on the Palatine's pale costume was printed on the darkness all around. The Palatine was Najma; Najma was the Palatine. How? *How?* Kal could not imagine.

Perhaps the ghosts had drowned. Kal hoped so. It would not bring Najma back, but it might mean that Roko and Havvity would be safe. There was no way to know. Luja's soft nose rubbed the place on Kal's head where the blood oozed. Kal raised a hand to the soft muzzle. He was exhausted from his swim. Kal owed him a little care: water, a fire for warmth at least.

Stay here, Luja, Kal told the horse. *I'm going to see if anything useful has washed up.*

Kal began to pick a path along the ragged strandline. Luja walked right behind.

Stubborn, Kal told him. Once again, the horse did not reply, just kept walking.

It was hard to see anything in the moonlight that flashed between the scudding clouds. Most of what had washed up was so mud-covered it was impossible to determine what it was. There were several bodies: a woman with a child in her arms, one of the jantevas. Kal checked each one for signs of life. There were none. Then they found Zait, the horse that Najma, the Palatine, had brought to the circus. He lay on his side, legs washing in the shallows, eyes closed. Luja sniffed at him, pushed at him with one hoof, and Zait's eyes popped open. He struggled to his feet in a flurry of panic. For a moment Kal thought he would run off. But Luja seemed to calm him down, and the three of them continued on their way.

They found nothing useful and Kal decided it was best to head away from the river and find dry wood to make a fire. But as they turned their backs on the water, a thin, piercing cry came out of the sky. It made Kal's hair stand on end. Whoever

139

heard of an eagle flying in the night? It could only be Sayka! The huge bird dropped fast towards them, so fast that even Zait, who knew him well, whinnied in fear, and Luja did a little hoof-shifting dance of anxiety. The bird landed a short distance away and then walked towards them very purposefully. It looked ridiculous, lifting its feet over the muddy ground, its leg feathers like bedraggled skirts. It fixed Kal with a mad, yellow-eyed stare then flapped it wings in frustration. It walked away, walked back several times, until Kal realised it wanted them to follow! As soon as Kal began to walk after it, the bird took off, flapping as low and slow as possible and wheeling round to check that they were keeping up.

After a few minutes the bird gained height and vanished into the blue dark. Then it cried out again and flapped rapidly, out over the river, downstream, its silhouette just visible against the faint gleam of the surface. Eagles – especially giant ones – are not made for hovering but Sayka did his best. Kal peered at the water below where the eagle circled. Something pale was floating there. Could it be a long piece of fabric unravelling in the current? Cream silk even?

Kal leapt onto Luja's back.

It's Najma, Kal told him, *in the water.*

Luja didn't need to be asked twice, exhausted as he was. He must have told Zait because the two of them picked up their heels and ran like the wind along the edge of the flood.

As they drew closer, Kal could make out some kind of raft on which two bodies lay: one wrapped in pale material; the other a dark silhouette. *That* had not happened by chance. Hope sprang up in Kal – perhaps Najma was not dead.

The current here was picking up, pulling the raft ever faster.

In the distance. Kal could hear the roar of surf where the flood waters ran into the stormy sea. Luja understood what to do without being told. He plunged back into the river with Zait bravely beside them.

We need to get downstream of them, Kal cried.

The eagle too seemed to understand the plan. Flapping slowly, as close to the surface as he could, he tracked the progress of the raft.

Their progress was agonisingly slow; the current fought them every inch of the way, and the pale flash of the Palatine's clothing appeared and disappeared in the dark turbulence of the water. For a moment Kal was convinced that they had missed their chance and would have to battle to the bank, gallop further downstream and try again. Then, there it was, the raft with the two insensible figures on it. Somehow Kal and Luja had manoeuvred exactly into it's path.

The raft came closer, Kal reached out from Luja's back towards it, ready to grasp it in whatever way was possible. But two horse lengths away, the current jinked the raft sideways, and the two figures slid off into the water and disappeared.

Kal jumped from Luja's back. In seconds the Palatine would be washed downstream, lost in the dark of the river and then the infinite darkness of the sea. Desperately, Kal dived and dived, lungs bursting, heart breaking, trying to hold a place in the current. It was impossible to see anything under the water… Was that the flicker of something pale? Kal's hand grabbed and found wet fabric. Using every last ounce of strength, Kal wound in the silk. Then, with the two horses on either side, they towed their catch back to the shore and dragged the two bodies out of the water at last. Najma – the

Palatine – must have managed to wrap herself and the body of the guard in the silk of her clothing, a binding that had held them, for a time, on the raft.

There was light in the eastern sky now and it fell on the two faces, laid side by side. They were very alike, Kal noticed. Had the guard played the part of the Palatine while she had been Najma? There was a great difference between them now, however. The guard was dead; Kal saw that she must have taken the bullet that Kal had fired, through the heart. But her mistress was alive, and it was some comfort that the wound in her shoulder had not been caused by Kal's bullet. Kal had fired only once; the other shots had come from the assassins. The Palatine was breathing, and there was a pulse, but it was no more than the beating of a moth's wing.

Kal's misery lifted! Here was purpose and a chance to save the life that the ghosts had plotted to destroy. First, the bullet must be removed: that required fire, water, and a knife.

The guard's body furnished two knives and another search along the strandline revealed a metal pot. Dry kindling took longer to locate, but the spark struck with the knife from the river rock ate the grass hungrily and the warm flames grew.

The bullet wasn't deep. It came out cleanly. Najma cried out when Kal cauterised the wound. But then she lay quiet. Her pulse was stronger, and her breathing deeper. She would live. *She would live!*

The dawn light grew brighter. The far bank was still a grey blur dotted with the yellow spots of lanterns but in the stillness voices carried. Someone was barking orders. Luja's ears swivelled like a rabbit's to catch them.

142

Find the Palatine!

The cry grew louder and was repeated along the bank.

Find the Palatine!

Who was searching? If the ghosts and their masters had survived, they would make sure their job was done properly this time. It wasn't safe for the Palatine here. They would have to leave at once. Then came a thought: Kal's own or Luja's? Perhaps now it would always be impossible to tell. It didn't matter. It was a very good thought.

You cannot kill what is already dead.

Kal looked at the dead guard and Najma. Yes, they were alike. Very alike.

It was probably against all Yuderan law to undress an unconscious queen. But Kal did it. Unwinding the layers of silk was easy compared with removing the tight-fitting uniform of the guard. Then Kal rewound the silken layers around the dead guard. Kal silently apologised to the dead woman but somehow knew that she would be pleased that even in death she was protecting her mistress. It was too difficult to get the tight-fitting uniform on the insensible Najma. Instead, Kal put it on and dressed the Palatine in the blue-and-gold circus costume. Luckily it was loose, or it would never have fitted the larger, stronger Najma. The guard's boots were far too big for Kal, so they were tied to Kal's belt. One of the knives was tucked back into its place on the guard's uniform. Kal kept the other. It was a good knife.

At last, Kal lifted Najma to her feet and, somehow, got her onto Zait's back. She came round a little and stared in confusion into Kal's face. How much did she remember? Kal could only hope nothing at all, but the Palatine was conscious enough to hold the makeshift reins that Kal had fashioned from a length of rope.

Kal dragged the bodyguard in the Palatine's clothes to the edge of the water as if she had just washed up. A twiggy branch brushed away the traces of the fire and the marks of feet and hooves. As the mist over the river swirled and the sun came over the horizon in a pale haze, they turned from the flood and headed north.

Fate was offering a second chance, and Kal resolved to be worthy of it. To keep the Palatine safe; perhaps find the courage to go back to Erem, to find Havvity; perhaps, even, tell the truth and stop the war.

15
Owl

Learning the Story

For a dog small enough to fit in a top hat, Blit had very wolfish habits. The flood had taken many small animals by surprise and Blit was happy to make their drowned bodies her dinner. On the third day of their journey, when Owl had eaten nothing but the last crumbs of the cake they had found, he envied her. How hungry would he have to be for semi-decayed rat to seem appetising?

The river, having been in such a tearing hurry to get back to the sea after its long absence, had slowed. Mostly it now confined itself once again within its banks. It wound its way through the land, turning east, then west, then east again. Owl followed its course, knowing that this was the only route the great fish could have taken. Perhaps, he thought, they were going as slowly as he and Blit and were right there, in the green depths. He stared down and down through the water but could make out nothing but his own reflection, or that of the sky and clouds.

They had been covering great distances for two beings with quite small legs and at the end of each day had been so exhausted that they had slept pretty much where they fell. But yesterday, clouds had threatened more rain, so Owl had been glad to find a large, empty barrel, which the flood had carried onto the bank. He had rolled it a little further from the water, into the shelter of a tree, crawled inside and fallen asleep, with Blit curled on his chest.

The barrel had been used to store brandy so that Owl and Blit breathed the fumes all night and slept rather *too* soundly. Only when Owl felt something tickling his feet did he wake. He sat up suddenly, banged his head and lay down again. Blit woke up too and, rather embarrassed that her 'wolf senses' hadn't alerted her to danger, she began to bark very loudly.

The someone who had tickled his feet could be heard giggling outside. Owl pushed the furious Blit out of the barrel and wriggled after her. There, standing with hands on skinny hips and dressed in a pair of shorts and vest that might once have been red, was a small, very dirty child.

Blit stopped barking and sniffed suspiciously at the child's dusty feet, while she stared at Owl with solemn wide eyes. Owl had seen children many times, during his years in the circus. They often pointed at him, laughed or jeered. But sometimes, not very often, one of them smiled. And that's what this child did now. She smiled and her eyes danced, and her finger beckoned. Then, with another giggle, she turned and ran.

Owl's heart sank. She had smiled but she was just running away from him. He had seen fear before in children's faces when they saw him. He sighed and began to turn back to the barrel, but Blit was barking at him. She barged into his head, her she-wolf fur bristling, her tail wagging.

Follow! Follow! Blit announced. *Play! Come on!*

The child, although small, had ordinary child-length legs

146

and could run faster than Owl could ever hope to do. But Blit was speedy and could keep up. Within moments, both dog and child had vanished ahead into dappled green shadows.

The bank of the river was clothed in trees here but there was a well-worn path that wound between them. Owl hoped there was not more than one path. He was feeling a bit faint with hunger and didn't want to have to walk up and down several different paths to find Blit and the child again. He remembered something else he knew about children: they usually had parents with them. And parents often had food. The thought of a meal that wasn't dead rat made him move a little faster.

The path wound like the river, left, right, left again, but suddenly the trees ended and Owl found he had walked out into a sunlit yard of beaten earth. Before him was a long low building with mud walls and a roof made of thatch and solars. A woman sat on the roof fixing a solar that had come loose, helped by a bigger child. A small flock of birds, with bright-blue wings and yellow beaks, sat along the ridge of the roof as if in conversation with the larger child. They flew off when they saw Owl.

The three humans were all very alike: skinny, dirty, with long hair and dressed in shorts and vests. Smoke snaked from a chimney into the sky and the most delicious smell came out through the doorway of the building. Blit and the smallest child seemed to have got over the difficult start to their relationship as Blit had rolled over in the dust to have her tummy rubbed.

Some wolf! Owl thought.

But the woman on the roof seemed convinced.

'Your wolf?' she asked in Nordsky as she slithered down the roof to land as nimbly as an acrobat on the ground. Owl shook his head, then found his voice.

'She is her own self. Not a belonging,' he replied.

No one seemed to mind that his voice was just a squeak.

The larger child dropped to the ground too, smiling.

'That's what *she* told us,' he said, nodding towards Blit.

The woman smiled again.

'You look hungry,' she said, 'and we are about to have our breakfast. Want some?'

A voice from inside the hut called out, 'Fooood.'

And a fourth human, a large man, also in a pair of almost worn-out shorts, emerged from the door, with a steaming pot and four bowls on a tray. He smiled too and spoke to the smallest.

'Get another bowl, will you, there's good girl!'

The tray was placed on the floor and the family sat around it, including Owl and Blit in their circle. Carefully, the man ladled the food out of the pot, dividing it meticulously between the five bowls. The rest of the family watched him with such silent concentration that Owl guessed they must be almost as hungry as he was. Was it right to take some of their food? He wasn't sure.

'You look worried, little friend,' the woman said. 'What is it?'

Owl's mouth opened and for a few moments nothing came out, but no one seemed to mind that either.

'I am taking your breakfast,' he squeaked.

To Owl's enormous confusion the littlest child put her arms around him and gave him a hug.

'Don't worry!' the man told him. 'We like sharing.' With that, he placed the pot on its side so that Blit could lick every morsel that remained stuck to the bottom.

'Eat up, little wolf,' he said.

After breakfast the family told him their names. Map was the father, Ead the mother. The children, both girls, were Moss – the larger – and Nettle – the smaller. Nettle brought Owl a bit of the plant for which she was named. She grasped its toothed leaves without flinching even though, as she told him, it was 'a stinger'.

'It's home for lots of wigglies,' she explained. 'They's buttlebyes presently.'

Owl had no idea what 'wigglies' or 'buttlebyes' were, but Nettle seemed very proud of them, so he smiled and nodded. No one asked him anything about himself. This was good because he felt like an escaped prisoner and feared that someone might be on his trail. He certainly didn't want to talk about the cub. Or even think about him.

The family accepted Owl as they accepted the sunlight and the rain. They simply folded him into their life without comment. They gave Owl a place to sleep in the bit of loft above one end of the kitchen where they stored dried vegetables, strung from the beams like necklaces. They fed him, chatted to him, and set him to work alongside them. It was so easy that within a day Owl could almost forget that he had ever had another life.

Blit too fitted into the family as easily as the silliest pup. She trotted round in the children's footsteps wagging her tail and hardly ever came to Owl's head as a wolf. She soon earned the family's approval by chasing any rats that found their way uninvited into the food stores and was allowed to eat scraps and curl up by the stove at night.

Owl found it was true that the family liked sharing. They shared their house with many creatures who came to visit. Birds dropped out of the sky to settle on a shoulder, exchange a greeting, accept a gift of bread. Squirrels, martens and little grey forest foxes came too, usually at dusk or dawn. It was never spoken of. It was just a part of life for this family, who all had the gift of Listening. Unlike Owl, who could only hear animals who *decided* to talk to him, all members of the family could hear the thoughts of their animal visitors. Through that, they worked out what each one needed – food, shelter, healing, rest. With some visitors, Owl could see that the communication went further and ran both ways as it had done with himself and the cub and did, at least a little, with Blit.

Sometimes, watching Ead or Map with a squirrel or a finch, Owl was overwhelmed by missing Skrimsli. Then he would take himself off and walk down the winding path to the riverbank and stare at the dark water. Often he saw floating rafts of tree trunks, being guided downstream by black boats which all carried the same red symbol that he had seen on the uniforms of the guards in the circus: the Earth with a human hand closing around it, the insignia of the Automators. How were they here too? He tried to count the logs in each huge raft but there were far, far too many. Could any forest be left if so many trees had been cut? That was another thing he didn't want to think of. On days when the dead trees were passing, he didn't stay by the river but walked back and started to do whatever task he had abandoned.

Once, he asked Ead about the tree trunks. She shook her head sadly.

'They started passing two, maybe three years ago. The river was clogged with them. Huge mother trees that must have been growing for a thousand years.' She spoke as if the trees were her kin and Owl feared he had asked something too upsetting.

'When the river dried, we thought that would put a stop to it. How else could you move such giants but by water?' Ead went on. 'But it seems they are cutting down the forest once again.'

'Why?' Owl asked.

Ead shook her head.

'They want a railway right across the Sand Sea to the south. The trees are for the iron rails to rest on. They burn more trees to make the iron too. Don't ask me why. It's wickedness in my eyes. But what can we do about it?'

They didn't talk about the floating trees again. It was sad, but where was the help for it? And there was so much work to do that no one had time for anything else. The long drought, when the river had almost vanished, meant that, now it was back, they must grow as much food as possible, in case the drought came again.

Owl knew nothing about seeds and soil and gardens. He was astonished when Moss gave him a handful of little dried things that looked like nail clippings and told him they would grow into food.

'But how?' Owl asked, staring at the wizened brown grains in his palm.

151

'Water and sunlight,' Moss laughed, 'that's all it takes, and digging of course. Lots of digging!'

Digging was hard. Owl couldn't manage a big spade, but the little one that Map gave him worked fine. Every bit of Owl's body hurt after his first day at it. But he got stronger very fast and began to enjoy the rhythm of turning over the sods and mixing in the smelly brown stuff that Nettle brought in her little barrow.

'It was poo!' Nettle explained. 'Now it's compit.' Owl decided it was best not to know any more than that.

After a week or so of digging, mixing in 'compit' and poking the weird little seed things into holes and grooves in the earth, Ead announced that the garden was ready. When rain began to fall at the end of the last day of planting, the whole family shrieked in delight. Nettle grabbed Owl's hand and led him and the rest of the family in a wild dance around the garden. They twirled and laughed until they were all soaked to the skin and had squidgy mud squeezing between their toes. Blit barked excitedly and her wolf-self appeared in Owl's mind.

You humans are crazy! she said, then wagged her tail. *But good.*

Afterwards, they sat wrapped in blankets round the stove while their clothes steamed on the washing line strung from the eaves. Nettle climbed into her mother's lap.

'Story!' she said. '*STORY!*'

Ead smiled. '*One* story, then bedtime!'

Nettle nodded solemnly and Moss snuggled close to Map. Everyone smiled and sat quiet. Whatever 'story' was, it was something good. Blit jumped into Owl's lap and curled up too.

Ead began.

'This is a story my granny told me, and her granny told her. It comes from the big green forest where she was born, where the river starts its journey to our land.'

Ead's eyes caught the firelight and her voice had wrapped around them all, drawing a veil between them and the dark and rain. Now all there was in the world were the flickering flames, Ead's voice and their eager faces. Owl felt a tingle go right up his back and down again.

'Once,' Ead said, 'there was a man who lived in a forest by a river. One day he looked at his own reflection in its water.

I am beautiful, he said to himself, *but I could be more beautiful. Then someone would surely love me.*'

Owl could not imagine looking at his own reflection and thinking that it was beautiful. But he felt sorry for the man, who wanted to be loved; Owl knew about that alright!

Ead continued. 'So the man took the wings of the bees and he twined them into his hair…'

Owl imagined the glistening wings, tangled in the man's hair. That *would* look beautiful, but what about the poor bees? Owl didn't like this man very much.

'Then he looked once more at his reflection.

'Goodness! he said, *I am very beautiful, but…*'

Ead paused here and the children joined in.

'I could be more beautiful. Then someone would surely love me.' Moss and Nettle chorused.

For a moment Owl was puzzled. How did the girls know what to say? Then he realised that this story was something that the children had heard time after time. It was like the words in Owl's own heart about the keepers of the forest.

'So, the man took the claws of the bear,' Ead said, 'and made a necklace for himself and looked at his reflection once again.'

Here Map spoke the man's words.

'*I am very, very beautiful, but I could be more beautiful still. Then someone would surely love me.*'

The words filled Owl's mind with pictures, feelings, questions. How would anyone take a bear's claws? What terrible longing would drive a person to do something so dangerous and so cruel? He stared at Ead, his eyes wide.

'Shall I go on?' Ead asked.

'Yes! Yes, please!' Owl cried, rather louder than he had planned.

'Have you heard this story before, Owl?' Moss asked.

'Never!' Owl said. 'Never!'

'Oh, Owl,' Ead exclaimed. 'I am honoured to be the first to tell it to you.'

Nettle was impatient. 'Come *on!*' she said. 'More story!'

'So, where was I?'

Nettle took her thumb from her mouth. 'He's got the bear claws in a necklace.'

'Oh, yes! *That's* where I was.'

Nettle removed her thumb again. 'And he's looked at his 'flection and says…'

'I am very…' Moss began.

'…*very* beautiful,' Map concluded.

Ead smiled and took up the story again.

'*But*, thought the man, *I could be more beautiful still, and then someone will surely love me.* So, he took the stripes of the tiger and spread them all over his skin.'

Owl's heart turned over in his chest. He thought of the

pattern of black and flame on the cub's head. How many times had he stroked it, since those very first days when Skrimsli was a helpless kitten, whose eyes were yet to open. Those stripes, so beautiful. If you took them, you'd be taking the very essence of the tiger! That was in a way what Kobret had tried to do, to take Skrimsli's stripes away. But he had not succeeded!

'Now, when the man tried to look at his reflection,' Ead said, 'the water in the river was gone. It had dried up to a trickle and the forest around him was dying. So, when the woman came along, the man said, *The river has dried up and I cannot see my reflection. Will* you *tell me how very, very, very, very beautiful I am.*

'But the woman told him no such thing.

'*I can tell you how very, very, very foolish you are,* she said. *What will we eat if the forest is dead? Where will we live? I must speak to Owl, to help me sort out all this mess you made.*

'When Owl heard of man's foolishness, she sighed. She went to the last pool in the river where water still remained, and she spoke to Sturgeon. Then Owl flapped her wings and Sturgeon thrashed her tail and together they made a storm and a flood that filled up the river. The water washed the bees' wings from man's hair, and the bear claws from his neck and the tiger stripes from his body and put them back where they belonged.

'So the bees could fly to the flowers to help make seeds…

'So the bears could dig in the soil to plant them…

'And the tigers could catch the deer, so the baby trees were not all eaten

And slowly, slowly, slowly the forest lived again.

'But now, said the man, *I am not as beautiful as I could be.*

155

'*You are beautiful enough*, said the woman. *Quite beautiful enough for me to love you.*

'And the woman kissed the man under the green trees of the forest. And that's the end!'

Ead sat back in her chair, rain pattered on the thatch again and the fire crackled.

Owl's heart beat hard in his chest. Although he was not the man, or the woman, or even the owl, Ead's story had told truths he felt in his heart. It had told the truth about the logs floating down the river; it had told the truth about Owl's own longing to be loved; it had told the truth about Kobret's greed and cruelty. Ead's words held thoughts and feelings that Owl could not have explained, even to himself.

'Owl's crying!' Nettle said.

'What is it, Owl?' Ead and Map asked together.

Owl knew he would need another whole story to explain what he felt and understood. But all that he could manage for now was to tell the family that it was time for him to go north and find his real home.

The next morning Map dragged a long, narrow boat down the bank of the river and set up a little solar to drive the paddle in its stern. Then everyone got in and they set off upstream. They were going to a town called Riverbend on the opposite bank of the Shamanow. Ead said Owl would find a boat there to carry him further.

'Right up to Otok,' Map said.

'The forest where my granny was raised is north of there. You can follow the river fingers to get to it.'

Owl didn't ask what river fingers were. He guessed he would find that out on the way.

No one said much on the journey; no one wanted Owl to go. Even Owl wished he could stay. He had loved being part of this family. But their story was not the same as his, this place was not his place. He must try to find the green forest he remembered, where the Owl is the forest keeper.

Blit stood in the prow, her small ears moved by the breeze, her tail erect. The boat sliced the water, still a little murky after the flood, and trees leaned out over the river. Some of them were only just clinging on where their roots had been almost washed away.

'There didn't use to be floods and droughts when I was a boy,' Map told Owl. 'The river was always full: a little low in summer perhaps. They've cut down so many trees up north, it's made our rains all cock-eyed. If you make it up there, maybe you can sort that out?'

'Maybe,' Owl replied. 'Maybe.'

All along the riverbanks were little settlements. Families were working in riverside gardens, digging and planting, making the most of the newly filled river in case of another drought. Many waved and smiled but many frowned and turned away.

'Some don't like us,' Map said sadly. 'Because we are Listeners. Listeners are not liked in the Pokov City anymore I've heard.'

Ead shook her head and whispered as if someone would overhear.

'Listeners are even being arrested, and now that nonsense is spreading here. We need to be careful, Map.'

As they got close to the town, the river became busy with long, skinny boats: boats carrying families, animals, bags of grain, plant pots. They had to weave their way between them and the rafts of logs pulled by the black boats with the red logo.

'More trees cut down for the damned railway,' Map grumbled. 'Will they take every tree in the forest?'

Ead shook her head. 'We won't stay in town, I think,' she said. 'I don't feel safe there anymore.'

They dropped Owl off at a jetty on the edge of town, without much time to say goodbye. Blit let Nettle cuddle her too tightly before she wriggled free and jumped down to stand beside Owl on the jetty.

You don't have to come with me, Owl told her. *This could be your pack.*

For the first time in days she came into his mind as her she-wolf self.

We are forest guardians, she growled at him. *Same pack.*

They stood together and watched as the sad faces of the family vanished into the distance downstream.

The family had given Owl a satchel made of sacking with a sturdy rope strap, packed with gifts. Ead had put in a small blanket; Map had given him a tinder box; Moss had added a knife. Nettle's gift was an egg in a small bag.

'It's a tree seed,' she'd whispered in his ear. 'I found it by the river. It's magic. You got to plant it when you get home. Promise.'

Owl had thanked her and made his promise.

He picked up the bag now and slung the strap across his shoulders. The family had given him so much more than its

158

contents. He walked towards the main wharf with new strength, his head held high and Blit at his heels. People stared at him, as they always had, whispering behind their hands, but Owl took no notice. They could call him a freak if they wanted; he knew who and what he was now, so their opinions didn't matter.

Owl walked along a line of boats and called out to the people on them.

'I'm looking for a ride upriver!'

They replied without taunts or mockery.

'Sorry, mate, fully loaded.' Or: 'No luck, son; we're heading downstream.'

And then at last, 'Try Madam Engedo. The ochre boat, five along from here!'

A woman with a yellow cloth wound around her hair was loading sacks into a boat with peeling paint the same colour as her headdress.

'Madam Engedo?' Owl asked.

She looked up and frowned. 'Yeah, who's asking?'

'I'm Owl, and this is Blit. We need a ride upriver to Otok.'

'Well, that's where I'm going,' the woman said, her eyes narrow, weighing them up. 'What is that, anyway?' she asked, looking at Blit. 'Some kind of rat?'

Blit snarled, showing her sharp white teeth. The woman frowned and Owl could see their only chance of transport disappearing fast.

Hush, he told Blit. *It's better she doesn't know you are a wolf.*

'She's no trouble really,' Owl said to Madam Engedo. 'She's very well trained.'

Blit stopped snarling, stood on her hind legs and did a little twirl. The woman laughed out loud.

'What about you then? Bit young to be travelling on your own.'

Owl stood tall and answered without hesitation. 'I'm older than I look.'

She smiled again. 'Good answer. But what can *you* offer me for your passage, apart from your little doggie dancer there?'

Owl thought. What did he have to offer? No strong arms or legs to make him really useful loading cargo. No funny tricks like Blit; no tumbles or somersaults like an acrobat. Then he remembered – *you are quite beautiful enough for me to love you...*

'A story,' Owl said. 'I think I have a story!'

Madam Engedo put out a hand to help him down. 'Better come aboard then!' she said.

16

Skrimsli

Skins on the Wall

 Karu had begun his life as a wild bear. He had been a small cub when his mother was killed and he was stolen and sold to the circus. But he remembered things and he knew that the forest where he'd come from lay to the north.

Long way! Karu said.

So together Skrimsli and Karu travelled north. North was something Karu knew as surely as thirst or hunger.

Feel it in the earth, the bear told Skrimsli. *In my body.*

Gradually, as they travelled, Skrimsli began to feel it too. When he lay with his belly to the ground, or his head resting on a rock, he sensed it. He felt the ridge of it as if he laid on a long grass stalk, but inside his skin not outside.

Karu kept as clear of humans as he could. It was hard at first, as there were many small farms close to the river, linked by tracks along which carts and herds of cows and sheep moved all day. The land was criss-crossed with the paths of humans and their creatures. But the further north they went, the more rugged the land grew, the fewer were the signs and scents of people.

They travelled only at night and found places to rest out of sight by day. Skrimsli was still cub enough to climb trees and rest on any branch that could take his weight. But Karu was too big for climbing, so had to find caves and tree hollows, or places where the shadows broke up his outline and he could see trouble coming before it got close. This allowed them to travel unnoticed, as most humans were not very observant and never paid attention to what their noses told them. Their dogs sometimes barked and growled when they caught the unfamiliar scent of bear and tiger, but humans didn't listen to their dogs either.

Everything was new to Skrimsli. He had been used to the protection of Owl and Taze, and to the warm presence of Owl in his mind. But he had also been used to terrible confinement and the tyranny of Kobret. Without either he found his mind in a tangle that alternately filled him with a fizz of energy or made him want lie down with his sore head between his paws.

At first, without the cover of a tent, he'd found wind and rain made sleep impossible. The constant walking wore at his pads and even made them bleed. But his feet grew tough, his coat grew dense and after two weeks of travel, his mind grew quieter. His tiger self was more awake with every day, and it told him things about this new life. He noticed how the moon waned and gave more darkness for their nighttime journey; he noticed the smell and signs and tracks of other animals, the wild ones for whom this land had always been home. He wondered what that would be like, to know each rock and tree, each stream and shadow as well as his own paws.

He guessed it would make finding food easier. In a place where you knew the way the light fell on every tree, how each stream smelled, when and where other creatures moved about, there would be some chance to catch a meal. But as the cub was only passing through, there wasn't time for any of that. His only hope of food was a stroke of very good luck.

Finding food seemed to give Karu no problem. The sort of meals he thrived on didn't run off; all he had to do was sniff things out along the way. When Skrimsli asked him how he knew what to look for he said, *I remember.*

Karu's wild-bear mother had taught him about ant nests, with seams of eggs like white beads hidden in the earth, wild beehives full of grubs and last year's honey, and birds' eggs. The bear even remembered what plants were good to eat. Finding food was healing Karu. Skrimsli could see it. Every day he grew less and less like the haunted shell he had been under Kobret's rule. Skrimsli was growing to like the self that Karu was becoming.

But Skrimsli was getting hungry! Pushing his nose into ant or bee nests just got him stung, birds' eggs were all shell, and as for plants! He wanted *meat* but he had no idea how to get it in the landscape of rocks and stooping trees through which they now passed. It was not in the least bit like the snowy pine forest where he had found rabbits so easily underneath the snow.

One afternoon as he slept, draped over a large branch, he heard bleating. Skrimsli was instantly awake and on his feet. Below him a little flock of flop-eared goats: three females and their half-grown kids browsed between the scattered boulders. Here was the luck he had wanted. Their smell was delicious. Even though he had never killed a goat, he had been given goat meat to eat and his body cried out *food.*

Without thinking any further, Skrimsli dropped out of the tree and sprang towards the nearest goat. Its terror rippled through his mind and distracted him for a moment, but he had felt the same from the rabbits he had killed. But the goat didn't cower in the grass the way a rabbit would. It leapt away and in less than a heartbeat the whole flock had scattered, leaving the cub standing in the sunlight, feeling angry, foolish and hungrier than ever.

You want eat?

In his hunger and haste Skrimsli had not sensed the presence of any other creature and yet here it was, uninvited and unannounced inside his head, a shape speaking from the shadows. He turned, and saw a large dog, a male, with a deeply scarred muzzle and only half a tail. It stood in the sunlight where a moment ago the goats had been feeding. The dog smelled bad, his fur was dirty, and his breath stank of illness and decay. Skrimsli backed away and snarled.

Friend, the dog signalled and wagged his tail. *You want eat? I show where!*

The dog pricked his ears just the way Taze used to. *Come! Follow.*

The smell and sound the dog communicated to Skrimsli's mind was that of many goats, all in one place and *very* easy to catch.

Skrimsli sent a thought to Karu's sleeping mind, but the bear was holed up deep in a rocky crevice some distance away. Too far to receive it.

Yes, Skrimsli told the dog. *I come.* And stopped snarling.

The dog set off down the rocky gully at quite a pace. It wagged its tail constantly and looked over its shoulder in a way that reminded the cub both of Taze and of humans. Dogs had lived with humans for generations and had forgotten their wild ancestors. Blit was the only dog Skrimsli had met who had remembered her wolf self. Many of them must be, like this one, more human than wolf, Skrimsli thought.

At the bottom of the gully the land softened into a green meadow. Skrimsli smelled water nearby. He smelled human, also very strong and very near. He stopped.

No, he told the dog.

Food, the dog said again, reinforcing the smell, sound and even the taste of goat in Skrimli's mind. *Food. Come. In there!*

The dog turned its nose towards a building, tall and windowless, which stood to the right of another smaller one with windows and a door. Skrimsli had seen many similar on their journey and before. *'House,' 'barn'*; the memory of Owl's voice speaking the words came back to the cub now. Those words spoken in Owl's high, rasping little voice had carried something warm and kind. House was good, barn was good; especially good if they smelled of delicious goat, the way these did. The dog trotted on and Skrimsli followed once more.

Down a path that reeked of human, dog and goat, and whose grass was worn away by their feet, to the big building, the *barn*. It had one large opening on the side.

Inside, the dog said. *Inside. Go inside. Get goat. I wait. Guard.*

It was true, the smell of goat wafted out of the door. There was no noise, but perhaps that meant the goats were sleeping. Then they would be easy to kill!

Hunger shouted very, very loud inside Skrimli's head and body, blotting out every other thought. He slunk through the barn door into the darkness.

Instantly, behind him was a huge noise, a scarping and a scrabbling of paws and claws on metal, then a heavy bang and clang. With sudden cold clarity Skrimsli identified all the sounds as those of a big door being pushed shut and of a bolt being slid home, by clever paws and pulling teeth. Too late, he rushed back and threw himself against the wood and metal that now blocked the opening to the barn. He was trapped.

Outside, the dog barked frantically, calling to its human owner. Skimsli heard shouting voices, running feet and through a tiny chink in the door he glimpsed an eye staring at him.

'You are one clever dog, Buster!' a man's voice cried. 'That must be the last damn cat round here!'

Skrimsli smelled the man's hate and fear, and the greedy excitement of the boy at his side.

'What'll we do with it, Pop?' the boy cried.

'Kill it and skin it,' the man snapped back. 'What other use is there for them creatures?'

'Aww! Can I show it to Cousin Mattie before it's dead?'

'Best we kill it soon, son. A live tiger is nothing but trouble.'

'Oh, Pop,' the child whined. 'She'll be here tomorrow early, Mammy says.'

'Oh, alright! But you don't go near this barn until then, nor your sister, you hear me?'

'No, Pop. We won't.'

The footsteps retreated, the child calling out excitedly about the tiger in the barn.

When they were gone, a deep growl came through the door and the dog pushed back into Skrimsli's mind.

Caught you, cat! Caught you! it said and was gone. In fury Skrimsli threw himself at the door, but it did not budge.

166

Skrimsli paced inside the barn, snarling to himself. There was no crack, no hole, no way out. The smell of goat in which the barn was steeped, together with his hunger, had made him foolish. Why had he trusted a dog that smelled so bad, that was so *human?* Because of Owl? Because of Taze? Foolish! Foolish! They were both *dead*. His mind was once again a tangle. He raised his head and yowled.

That was when he saw the skins stretched out on wooden frames and hung from the wall of the barn. They were the first of his own kind he had ever seen. Three of them; his nose told him they were a female and her cub, and an old male. They were long dead, and the smell of their lives was dusty and distant. Skrimsli leant his front paws against the wall below where they hung and stretched up towards them. In the faint light of the barn their patterns danced, still working to break up the outlines of their bodies even in death. Was this the only fate of his kind in a world of humans? He would never live to see another tiger like himself alive. Killing Kobret had done no good. He was not free. He would die here in the dark and be pinned to the wall just like the others. He lay down, weak with hunger, dejected, exhausted, and slept.

Something woke him. It was deep night. He could feel the dark and the silence even as he swam up from the depths of sleep. The something was close by. For a split second it looked like Owl, small and watchful. But it was not. It was another child, different from the one who had been outside the barn earlier. This one was female, small and very young. She smelled a little like the man, enough for Skrimsli to know she was his cub. She sat on the barn floor within easy reach of his paws and stared at him. Her presence slid into his mind.

I don't want you to be dead, the girl told him.

Skrimsli did not reply but cautiously got to his feet and checked the barn for signs of adults and guns. There were none.

I want you to live, the girl said. *You understand?*

Yes, Skrimsli replied, still wary.

I couldn't save the other ones, she went on, looking up at the skins on the wall, *but I can save you. This way!*

She got up and walked to a far corner of the barn where logs and broken cart wheels were stacked. The girl turned to look at him.

You're hungry, aren't you? Will you eat me?

Skrimsli had not considered this. But he did so now, pulling thoughts into the quiet space of his mind: the man had planned to kill him; to take the man's cub would be fair punishment; but then there would be no one left here to save other tigers who ended up inside this barn.

No, he answered. *No.*

She nodded, and he guessed that she would have nodded in the same way had he said yes. *There's a hole,* she said, *under here.*

The wood and cartwheels hid a gap beneath the barn wall. It wasn't much; another month of growth or even a meal or two of goat and Skrimsli would not have managed it. But now he stood under the thin slice of the new moon with the girl.

Go, she said. *Go north. Find the forest where you belong. They cut it down here long ago and now they only understand goats and corn.*

Skrimsli stepped away and turned towards the gully, which showed black against the hillside. He felt the girl's sadness follow him and turned to look at her. She too was the only one of her kind in an unfriendly place.

Come with me? he said.

She smiled and shook her head. *I have to stay. Help others.*

He walked back to her, bumped his head against her small body, then leapt away.

Halfway to the gully, he found the goats in a pen. How had he not seen before how to take one? It was clear now. He crept through the grass, low, and invisible and snatched the largest kid. Before it had time to be afraid, he'd broken its neck and carried it off up the hillside.

It was almost dawn by the time the cub tracked Karu to a tree stump where he was enjoying a breakfast of honeycomb and bee grubs. In spite of being very taken up by his meal, the bear gave out a welcome and showed how glad he was to see Skrimsli. He shook the last of the angry insects from his coat.

Good hunt? he asked.

Good hunt! Skrimsli replied. *Goat. Good.*

Long night? Karu asked.

Long night, Skrimsli replied. *Head north and north, now!*

Karu stretched his snout to read the story and the danger carried on Skrimsli's fur.

North and north, the bear agreed. They set off, even though it was daylight.

The country grew hillier and more forested. On the north-facing slopes pine and spruce began to replace the oaks and hemlocks. Karu breathed in the sharp, sweet smell of their needles.

More green! he said. *Keep north. Most green is north.*

Skrimsli looked at the bear. Was the *most green* place the same as Owl's green place? And when they reached it, how would they know?

What do you do in the most green? Skrimsli asked.

Be a bear! Karu replied. Skrimsli wondered if he would know how to be a tiger when no mother tiger had ever taught him? Even though he had never walked in the forest of his ancestors. Even though the only other tiger he had ever seen was a dead skin on a wall.

For now, there was no choice but to keep heading north. They heard the baying of hounds to the south. The farmer had raised the alarm after his goat had been killed.

They try to track us, Karu said.

They followed a stream bed, where their paws would leave no scent and no impression for the even the wiliest hound to find. Still, the thought that humans who wanted only to kill them were just a few miles behind was enough to make them pick up their pace. For the next few days, they travelled almost constantly with only short rests to snatch some sleep.

There was one great obstacle to their northern progress. The river took a two-hundred mile loop to the east which brought it back into their path. Their route lay on the other side. They must cross the water or go around the loop and back again.

The river came within sight from the top of a hill in the middle of a starry night. Moving about over its surface Skrimsli could see huge creatures with light on their side and ends, shaped like fish, but *on* the water, not in it.

What are they? he asked the bear.

Human things.

Not alive?

Not alive, except by human power. They carry humans and their things.

Skrimsli couldn't remember if Owl had a word for these things that floated on water. Even in darkness the river was busy with them. If he and Karu tried to swim across the river, they would meet one, for sure. They were very big. Easily big enough to swallow a bear and a tiger. Skrimsli turned away. They would have to walk around the bend and find a place where there was none of this unwelcome activity.

Head east, he told Karu, but the bear went on staring and did not follow.

Too far, he said. *Another way to cross. There.*

Downstream, a dark line divided the gleaming surface of the river. Skrimsli had seen similar things on their train journey to the Sand City. *Bridge* was the word Owl had for them, which meant a dry road that joined the two sides of a river. At each end of this bridge, was a swarm of lights and the shapes of roofs and walls: a human town that they would have to walk through. And the bridge, just like the river underneath it, was alive with humans and their things.

Too many humans! said Skrimsli. *Head east!*

Karu snarled. *NO, too far*, said the bear. *Come. Follow!*

The way Karu said it was not a request. Skrimsli flattened his ears a little, but he followed all the same.

17
Kal

A Map in the Sand

The flood had washed the Palatine's rings from her fingers, but it had left one chain around her neck. Gold didn't buy much in the towns and villages stricken by drought, where flour was more valuable than gold. It had been just enough to provide a couple of wool ponchos, that also served as beds and blankets, a bag of cornmeal for porridge, and oats for the horses. Now and then it had bought them the shelter of a shack or in the corner of a barn.

Kal hoped their deception had worked and that the ghosts and whoever paid them now believed their job was done, that the 'Erem terrorist' and the Palatine were dead. But that wasn't certain, pursuit could be edging closer with every passing day. So Kal kept them moving on a zig-zag, unpredictable path, away from farms and hamlets unless they needed to buy more food. Kal had no bigger plan other than to keep them out of danger, but as danger lay to the south their haphazard path led north, in the direction of Erem.

The land became hilly. The horses picked their way along tracks between rocky outcrops and through sparse, dry forest. Kal guessed how both Luja and Zait must long for the space in which to run, but they carried on, uncomplaining, mostly walking with Kal and the Palatine on their backs.

At first, a day of riding had taken all the energy the Palatine could muster. Now her wound had healed, and she was growing strong again. But she didn't speak. She ate and drank what Kal put before her, got on Zait's back and rode without a word. She communicated only with her eagle. He fell from the sky every few days to visit his mistress and spend a few minutes with her head close to his. Perhaps he was tracking their every move; perhaps, thought Kal, he was ranging far to find food then relying on his incredible sight to find them again; perhaps he would warn them if pursuers came close. Kal didn't ask. The silence that had fallen between them was like a landscape that it was too dangerous to cross.

Tonight they made camp under a rocky overhang, away from the track that they had followed all day. Luja and Zait wandered off, finding what grass they could between the thorny bushes. The Palatine rested her back against the rock, eyes closed, while Kal cooked a pan of cornmeal over the fire. A fire and its tell-tale smoke was a risk, but they hadn't eaten hot food in three days and tonight the clear skies had made the air chilly.

Kal stirred until the cornmeal thickened then placed the pot beside the Palatine and handed her their one wooden spoon. For the first time in days, she spoke.

'Why do you always let me eat first?' she asked softly.

'Because you were ... wounded,' Kal replied.

'But I have survived. I am well enough. I was not *killed*.' Her voice was no more than a whisper, but its edge made Kal look away.

'Look at me, Kal!' Her quiet voice was full of the command of a queen, but underneath was the fear of a child. 'Why did you try to kill me, Kal? Am I a prisoner now?'

'No! *No*,' Kal cried. 'You are not a prisoner! I'm heading north to keep you *safe*.'

'Safe? Firing a bullet that would have *killed* me, is that what you call *safe*?'

The Palatine's anger pierced Kal like a blade, drawing the words out like blood.

'I didn't know it was *you*.'

'You mean you didn't know *I* was the *Palatine*. But you wanted to kill *her*?'

'I didn't *want* to kill anyone,' Kal cried. 'I'm not a killer. I didn't have a choice, Najma.'

'I'm not Najma. I'm the Palatine whom you tried to murder. When you chose to pull the trigger, you killed Tiff.' Her voice quavered. 'My dear, dear, loyal friend is dead because of what you chose. You *chose*.'

Anger sprang up in Kal. What did this privileged aristocrat know about the lives of ordinary people and the decisions they were forced to make?

'Not everyone gets to choose, the way a Palatine does,' Kal snapped.

'You think I get to choose?' the Palatine snapped back. 'I have to think about a whole *nation* before I think about myself!'

Protecting a whole nation from civil war; that's what Kal had failed to do. Instead Kal had run away, then given in to the ghosts' demands and become a murderer. Kal's head hung in shame.

'I was just trying to protect my kin,' Kal whispered. 'They said they'd kill them if I didn't do what they asked.'

'Who said they'd kill your kin?' The Palatine was still angry.

'The assassins, Listig and Spion! Didn't you see their guns?'

The Palatine stared at Kal. Something in her confused memory of the night when Tiff was killed clicked into place.

'The acrobats?'

'Yes,' Kal replied. 'They are assassins, and they started the civil war in Erem.'

The Palatine froze, realisation dawning behind the dark eyes. She spoke at last.

'Forgive me,' she said. 'There is a great deal here I don't understand. I think it's time we shared those secrets we spoke of on the day we met.'

For a moment at least the queen was gone and Najma looked out into Kal's face. Kal nodded, smiled, and they began to talk.

Some things were very hard to share. Kal trembled with the retelling of the murders at Talo, the ghosts' knife in the night and the note stained with Havvity's blood. The Palatine faltered as she spoke about Tiff's loyalty and of her brother's betrayal. It was as hard for Kal to recount the dressing of Tiff's corpse in the Palatine's robes as it was for the Palatine to hear it. They both shook their heads over the evil of the twins, Listig and Spion, and of those who'd sent them.

By the time they were done, they understood each other and the events that had brought them to this odd place far from either of their homes. But there was a bigger picture too and that was harder to piece together.

The Palatine took a stick and began to draw on the firelit ground.

'Here is Erem, a long, long way from Yuderan, here. And this is Rumyc, a long, long way from both, with all of Nordsky in between. Rumyc is where the Automators come from; their greed for power and wealth is the source of all our troubles.'

Kal frowned. 'But aren't they just soldiers the Nordskys pay for? Hired thugs?'

The Palatine shook her head. 'They are much more. I have heard of their rise in Rumyc. They are gathering power for themselves. They want gold from your land so they can get the tar oil from under mine.'

'What will they do with tar oil?'

The Palatine shrugged. 'Burn it to run their horseless veekles? Use it to make lectric? There is no logic to it. Only their desire for wealth and power. The war in your country is to pay for the destruction of mine!'

Kal looked at the map scraped in the bare earth. Mountains blown apart, and people murdering each other. And all because of some men with a red fist on their chests. All because of a witness who was too afraid to tell the truth.

'It's all my fault,' Kal whispered. 'If I'd had the courage to stay…'

The Palatine cut Kal's word's short.

'They would have killed you. You were right to leave. You kept your secret safe. But,' she went on, 'if we go to Erem together, there could be a way to let the truth be known and stop the war.'

The unmistakable snap of a rifle being cocked made them both spin round to look behind. The assassin Listig stepped into the firelight with her sister beside her.

'Well, this is nice!' she said. 'We've enjoyed your little chat, haven't we, Spion?'

'Indeed,' Spion gloated. 'But in our experience truth-telling is quite hard for dead people.' She pointed her weapon at Kal's head and beckoned five Automator thugs from the shadows. They were masked and, covered from head to foot in their dark uniforms.

'Tie them up,' Spion barked.

'And don't try anything, *Queenie*,' Listig snarled at the Palatine. 'I won't miss a second time.'

They bound Kal and the Palatine with their hands behind their backs and put gags around their mouths. One of them bought Luja and Zait to the fireside. Somehow they had managed to put head collars and reins on the two horses, something neither of these independent creatures would ever allow a stranger to do. The two animals stood now, dull eyed, slack jawed and compliant. Kal met the Palatine's eyes thinking the same chilling thought: *their horses had been drugged*. Listig saw the look and grinned.

'Oh, have we tied up your special little friends?' she said 'Oh, dearie dear! Then you'd better behave, or I'll shoot them both.'

Spion gave the Palatine a slap across the head.

'You are foolish to care. It's weakness. You should be hard like us,' Spion said. 'I wouldn't care if someone harmed my twin. Listig wouldn't care if someone harmed me, would you, sister?'

'No!' said Listig. 'Course not.'

The ghosts and their five helpers marched their prisoners back to the track where they had left their own horses and a tiny, closed carriage, little more than a box on wheels. The Palatine and Kal were locked in the 'box', pulled by two of the horses and driven by the twins. The men rode alongside while Luja and Zait were tied behind the carriage.

Kal knew that the twins wouldn't hesitate to kill Luja and Zait. They were only still alive because they were a further way to keep Kal and the Palatine under control. As they bumped along the track, the drugs the horses had been given wore off and they grew anxious. Both Kal and the Palatine could feel it.

Kal chewed the gag until speech was possible.

'Best they get away.'

The Palatine understood at once what Kal meant. Heartbreaking though it was to send their friends away with no idea of how they would find each other again, it was the only way to keep them safe.

The Palatine worked at her own gag. Now they could both talk.

'Distraction?'

Kal nodded and immediately began to scream, kicking the wooden floor as hard as possible with bound feet.

'Get off! Get off me!' Kal spluttered. 'Help! She's trying to kill me. I should have shot you when I had the chance! I'm going to throttle the life out of you!'

They both screamed, rolled around, kicked at the side of the carriage and made it sound like, even with their hands tied, they could fight to the death. After all the weeks of keeping calm, of holding in the horror and deception, it felt wonderful.

The carriage stopped. Voices shouted orders. Luja began to

whinny and kick and Zait joined in. That set off the other horses. Kal could hear now that the Automators were struggling to keep control of their own mounts. The back of the carriage was opened, lantern light showed the angry faces of Listig, Spion and their henchmen. One man was holding Zait and Luja's reins. Luja grew suddenly still and looked intently toward Kal, awaiting instructions.

Smart boy! Kal thought. *Go as soon as you think you can. Just go or they will kill you.*

There was a moment's pause, then Luja replied, not with words but with a pure pulse of love.

Go. Kal told him. *Be safe, my friend!*

The Palatine bought her hysterical screams to a crescendo and Luja took the cue; with one swift, efficient tug, he jerked the reins from the guard's grasp. Zait followed suit. A moment later they were gone, no more than the sound of hooves receding into the darkness.

Listig drew a gun and pointed it at the prisoners.

'Shut. UP!' she yelled.

'What was that about?' Spion demanded. Neither Kal nor the Palatine replied.

'No more noise, no more tricks!' Spion growled. She turned to one of the men. 'Tie them tighter. Replace the gags. Allow them to breathe and no more.'

The guards did what they were told but the extra discomfort of the tightened bonds and suffocating gags was worth it. At least now the horses were out of the clutches of these monsters. The carriage was closed, and they trundled on and on into the night. Kal's heart was wrung: Luja was gone! They might never meet again.

The twins argued constantly. Their seat outside the carriage was only just above Kal's head and every word was clearly audible to Kal and the Palatine. It was like the mindless bickering of children. But when the two voices dropped into that ghost-like whisper, its sinister chill drew Kal's full attention.

'Why don't we just kill them now?' That was Listig. 'It's so much less trouble. Everybody will pay us what they owe: Yalen and the Nordskys, the Automators too!'

'Your thinking is always so childish, sister,' Spion hissed. 'My ransom plan will make us more money than we have ever had. There is no pension for assassins, you know. We have to take care of ourselves.'

'But it might not work,' Listig whined. 'Oh, *please* let me just kill them now. It would be *so* easy.'

'Oh, for goodness' sake! I have already explained the plan!' Spion scolded. 'Itmis has secure cells already in the amphitheatre in Otok.'

'But I don't want to stay in Otok!' Listig whined again.

'Oh, Listig,' Spion snapped. 'Your stupidity is breathtaking. *We* don't stay there. *Itmis* does. *We* go back to the Sand City and…' Here her voice dropped so Kal strained to hear '…tell them the Erem and the Palatine were taken from us by an armed gang…' Spion dropped her voice another notch. 'Who sadly killed all the nice Automator guards we took with us.'

Listig gave a horrible little giggle.

'Meanwhile, Itmis cares for the captives,' Spion continued, 'runs a little show as cover, makes lots of money – which will keep him happy. When we have negotiated our payment, we will send word to Itmis, tell him that he will soon get his cut. Then we return, kill the captives and get evidence that we have done so. We'll kill Itmis too and all the others, obviously. Don't want any loose ends.'

Kal and Najma exchanged a horrified look while Listig giggled again.

'When are we doing the part where the guards get killed?' she breathed.

'Quite soon, I think, don't you?' Spion said, and the two assassins laughed quietly together.

'How much money do you think we could make out of this?' Listig asked.

'A lot,' Spion replied. 'Enough to retire to an estate somewhere.'

'Could I have a dog, Spion?'

'You can have a whole pack of dogs, dear Listig.'

There was an odd sound then, that it took Kal a few moments to identify: the sound of an assassin clapping her hands like a child at a birthday party.

Kal and Najma sat in silence, waiting for the sounds that would signal the twins were putting their murderous plans into action. Surely two slight, skinny assassins would struggle to overcome five burly trained fighters? Kal listened for the sounds of fighting, but there was nothing. Then, close to dawn, the carriage stopped.

'Breakfast, gentlemen?' Listig cried. 'I think your hard work has earned a short rest and some refreshment. I have a loaf of spotted bread from Rumyc! From home!'

The guards sounded pleased. Kal heard the assassins climb down from the carriage and go amongst the men, handing out their breakfast. The poison in the food was fast-acting and effective. The men barely made a sound. A little coughing, a cry or two of alarm, the noise of bodies falling to the ground. Gunshots and the sounds of a knife being drawn followed as the assassins made it look as if the men had been killed in an attack.

Then they drove off their horses and got back on the carriage and set off again. The whole thing had taken less than half an hour. Kal and the Palatine sat in horrified quiet as the hours and the miles rumbled on.

By evening, the unmistakable smell of the river came into the carriage. The wheels rolled over the echoing metal of a bridge and the sounds of a bustling town rose up around them. They had reached Otok. Kal had heard sailors in Turgu talk about the place. 'Two Towns' was the name they gave it because Otok had two parts; Otok East was an important port on the river, where all the fingers of the Shamanow's headwaters finally ran in to one. Otok West was a seaport at the end of a long inlet called the Finger, that lead out into the Belugi Sea. An ancient ridge of rock, the Divider, lay between the two towns, separating the river bend from the Finger of the ocean. From Otok you could sail anywhere! But it was a lawless town, a freeport, where anything, or anyone, could be bought or sold.

Kal managed to squint through the holes between the boards. They moved down streets that grew ever narrower and stank of open sewers. The sisters bickered about directions. At last gates opened and the horses pulled the carriage into a small yard filled with rubbish. Someone with wild hair and a muddy blue coat was closing the gates behind them. When the person turned, Kal saw it was Itmis Majak. He had changed since the night his father had died. No longer merely vain, there was a look in his eye that spoke of madness.

The twins jumped down to stand beside him. He tapped on the carriage.

'You have them?' he asked.

'Of course we do, Itmis,' Listig said.

'Are the cells ready?' Spion said.

'Not yet,' Itmis scowled. 'I've been busy with my own fugitives.'

'Itmis, you were supposed to be ready,' Spion scolded.

Her sister interrupted. 'I'm sure dear Itmis has been doing his best,' she said. 'What news of the tiger?'

Itmis smiled then, a slow horrible smile like a snake about to swallow something. 'He is with that mutinous bear and the freak boy. They are close.' Itmis rubbed his hands together, a gesture that Kal remembered was Kobret's too. 'They will be back in my control very soon.'

18
Owl

Under the Bridge

Owl steered the ochre boat into the narrow path of the moon and drew his story to its end.

'Slowly, so slowly, the forest began to live again. The woman forgave the man for his foolishness and the Owl flew over their heads and the moon shone.'

Owl's small audience, perched on sacks of lentils and rice, clapped. Madam Engedo clapped loudest of all. She came and sat beside him, ready to take her turn at the tiller.

'Sit for a minute, Owl,' she said and offered him half of an apple cake she had wrapped in a cloth. They ate the cake and watched the moon climb.

'You know,' Madam Engedo said, 'you spoke the truth when you said it was a good story. I have heard you tell it many times now, and it is different every time.'

Owl looked at his boots. He still had no idea how to cope with a compliment. He was more used to being mocked for his voice and his appearance. But, Owl reflected, no one seemed to notice those things anymore. Not even himself.

'You have been very useful, Owl,' Madam Engedo continued. 'I would be happy for you to stay aboard. I could pay you, not much, but a little.'

It was tempting for certain. Madame Engedo was as tough and enduring as a rock, but she was fair and kind. He loved the little world of the boat: arriving at some new village or town every day and leaving a few hours later. Blit fitted in, the way she managed to fit in anywhere. That was the business of dogs, Owl thought, to fit in around humans. No one would ever guess who she really was inside.

But the forest called to him more urgently every day. Every day there were bigger rafts of dead trees, freshly cut and headed downstream to build the railway over the Sea of Sand. And almost every day he re-told the story about the dying forest and who it was that saved it.

He told Madam Engedo he would think about it. And he *would* think carefully. A trip or two up and down the river would put a little store of money in his pocket and that was useful. The forest would wait a little longer, surely?

'Don't think too long!' Madam Engedo said. 'Otok is just around the bend. We'll rest under the bridge overnight, but Otok is a wild place. All sorts goes on there. All sorts come there: sailors, smugglers, pirates. I'll be heading downstream again as soon as I've unloaded.'

Owl helped the other passengers to find places to sleep amongst the sacks of lentils and rice. Once they were settled, he stood in the prow with Blit and watched the dark banks slip by on either side. They rose into high cliffs and then, around a long bend; a bridge came into view, high over the gorge. Even now, in the middle of the night, it was crowded with carts and people crossing it in both directions. The river beneath was busy too, with boats arriving and leaving constantly.

As they drew closer, Owl could see that the bridge of Otok had seen better days. The smooth curves of its arches were cracked and the pillars on which they rested no longer stood up straight. A tangled web of beams and girders held the whole thing up.

Madam Engedo steered the ochre boat to the left-hand arch. There was a wharf right beneath the shelter of the bridge, where smaller boats like theirs could tie up for the night. A scruffy pontoon poked out into the river. Owl left Blit on lookout while he jumped to the pontoon with the mooring lines and helped to make the boat fast.

With the ochre boat securely tied up for the night, there was nothing to be done until the markets in the town opened at dawn. There wasn't a great deal of night left for sleeping but Owl settled down with Blit in their favourite spot in the prow of the boat. Tucked down between two sacks, whose contents moulded to his shape, with an empty sack or two for a blanket, Owl was very comfortable. Blit turned round three times, curled up at his feet and was instantly asleep, snoring delicately.

Owl lay for a while staring up into the arch of the bridge above him. Should he do as Madam Engedo suggested and stay with the boat? Or leave as he had planned and get another ride further upstream into one of the tributaries of the river? He fell asleep without a clear decision.

He dreamed, as usual, of Skrimsli. The ache inside his heart had grown no easier to bear or less painful. By day there were enough distractions to hold the hurt at bay, but in his sleep it rose up like a tide. The Skrimsli in his dream tonight was different. Not a small cub, nor a drowned corpse, not snarling in defiance at Kobret, not rolling in the snow with Taze.

This Skrimsli was bigger and bolder, even *oranger*, and he was very definitely telling Owl to *wake up, wake up now!*

Owl opened his eyes. The nest of haphazard metal and wood that supported the cracked arch above him was softly lit by the yellow streetlights on the wharf. Staring from it was a vivid, stripy ghost with eyes of green fire. Owl sat up so quickly his head spun. The face above him did not vanish. He shook his head, looked away, looked back and concluded that he was not dreaming. He looked steadily up into the green eyes and felt the cub's familiar presence bound into his mind, almost knocking him over with purring enthusiasm and joy.

Owl! Owl! Owl!

Get up! Get up! Come come!

Meet end of the bridge. Upstream. Quick. Before light.

With that, the striped apparition vanished. Owl sat down, dazed. Dream or real? There was only one way to find out, but where *was* the end of the bridge exactly? The end of the *underside* of the bridge was a different place from the end of the *upper* side, where the road ran. If he was to make it before light he would have to leave now.

Blit was still asleep. He scooped her into his jacket ignoring her sleepy growls, then grabbed his bag and a small loaf he had been saving for breakfast and climbed up onto the pontoon. He walked back along the side of the boat until he was level with Madam Engedo's little cabin. The curtains were drawn and there was no sign of her. There was no time to wake her or to say goodbye. He whispered a thank you to her window and set off.

The paved surface of the wharf gave way to mud just a few yards back from the water's edge. The downward curve of the bridge's last arch met the ground in deep shadow. It was impossible to see anything. Owl wandered around in the dark and decided that couldn't be where the cub meant. He headed out from under the bridge. There was just a little light in the eastern sky, enough to find a narrow path along the bank, heading upstream. But it led away from the bridge. There seemed to be no other path, just a steep bank covered in brambles and young trees. Owl began to run. Blit, now fully awake, was grumbling about being carried.

Where we go? her wolf-self demanded.

Find cub! Owl told her.

Cub dead, she said and wriggled from his arms to run in front of him along the path. *Stupid Owl.*

Owl hoped the path would loop back, or fork into a path that led back to the top of the bridge. But it only wound down. It was getting light fast.

Quick before light, the cub had said. Was Skrimsli in danger? Was he being chased? Or had Owl just imagined it all? If he couldn't find the right spot on the bridge he'd never know.

He turned and retraced his steps, looking for a path that led in the right direction, that he had somehow missed. Suddenly, out of one of the trees up the bank, a white owl took flight, and swooped silently in front of them. It was so sudden that Owl gasped and looked up to where it had come from. *There* was the path leading to the upper side of the bridge, a narrow slice though the bushes. Another step and he would have passed it by again.

This way, Blit. Quick.

The path was so narrow, the plants so tall, and Owl so short that, once he was running along it, Owl couldn't see more than a few paces ahead or behind. It was no longer *'before light'*. Even if he found the right place, would Skrimsli wait? Short legs working hard, Owl struggled on. Before he expected it, the path popped through a hedge and Owl and Blit found themselves on the roadside. It was very definitely 'the end of the bridge' and this was the upstream side. There was already a river of carts and people on the bridge but absolutely no sign of a tiger.

Owl stood to one side, trying to keep out of the way, as the people and vehicles streamed past. Then a stone hit Owl on the back of the head. He turned to see a group of about a dozen children, barefoot, in dirty ragged clothes. They were smiling smiles that Owl knew so well. He turned away, knowing that in a moment he would have to run. Blit barked and snarled but the children did not see her inner wolf and just threw stones at her too. Owl began to run back towards the entrance to the path but, in his panic, he missed it and found himself running in among trees on the side of the road. The children followed, shouting names and throwing stones. Soon he was surrounded, his back against a tree trunk, Blit snarling at his feet. One of the children, the one who Owl guessed had thrown the first stone, began to chant.

'Freak, freak, freak.'

Gleefully, the others joined in. They picked up sticks and began to close their circle. Owl sank down and wrapped his arms over his head in a feeble effort to protect himself. Blit stopped snarling and wriggled into the shelter of his curled body. Owl shut his eyes.

Without warning the chanting ceased and the children fell deathly quiet. There was a deep growl that at first Owl thought came from Blit's inner wolf. Except that he could hear it with his ears. Then came a long, yowling moan. The children made high sounds of utter terror far beyond the realms of screaming and Owl heard their footsteps pound away. Owl unfolded himself and looked up. There in front of him, not a dream and definitely not dead, was Skrimsli: bigger, bolder and more beautiful than ever. Owl ran towards the tiger and buried himself in his stripes. Blit danced around their feet.

Cat not dead, her thoughts sang delightedly.

It took them both a moment to notice that Skrimsli was not alone. He had a bear companion. A massive creature as big as Kobret's poor slave bear.

'Karu?' Owl exclaimed.

Karu, the bear replied lumbering into Owl's mind, communicating not in words, or pictures but in a feeling whose meaning took shape like a slow paw-print. *Not Kobret's creature now. Alive. Yes.*

He stepped forward and sniffed Owl's face. The eyes that had been like dark holes were warm and friendly, brown flecked with sparks of green.

Owl, I hurt you, Karu said. *Hurt no more! Hurt no more!*

Owl felt the bear's deep sadness. It was hard to communicate anything back to match his odd mixture of image, feeling and thought, but Owl did his best.

Friend now, Owl tried to say. *Friend!* And he felt that Karu had understood.

In the towns Owl had seen along the river, animals, apart from dogs and cats, were rare. There were herds of goats wandering along the riverbanks, and sometimes elephants doing lifting work for humans, but nothing more. The news of a bear and a tiger scaring a gang of children near the bridge would spread fast. People would come after them. They needed to get out of the town and back into wilder country as soon as possible.

They travelled in a line with Karu at the front, then Owl and Blit, and Skrimsli behind. Owl had often seen how good Skrimsli was at moving silently but he was amazed to see that the bear could do so too. When Karu had been under Kobret's command he had crashed about, often bumping into things. You could always hear him coming. But now he moved like a brown shadow, ghosting between the trees, knowing just when to be still to escape attention and when to move fast.

They couldn't go along roads and simply take the fastest route out of town. They had to skim through gardens and vegetable plots and patches of weeds, down alleyways and over abandoned building plots. All in broad daylight because there was nowhere to hide until nightfall. It was slow work, with lots of stopping to hide to avoid being seen. By early afternoon they were still not clear of the town.

Otok bulged out to the north, squeezed between the Divider and the river. The town here was dense with the houses of rich traders, ship owners, smugglers; there were shops and wide streets and no scruffy patches of forgotten greenery to hide in. It was through this difficult terrain that Owl and his friends now tried to move. They crouched in the last patch of weeds they had found at the back of a large stables. Just ahead was a

191

road full of horses, carts, people and lectric veekles. On the other side of the road were shops of all sorts and then more streets.

We'll have to go back the other way through that park, Owl said.

We can't, Skrimsli replied. *They have hounds back there on our trail. Listen!*

Owl's ears picked up the barking and baying of a pack of hounds that Skrimsli's keener ears had heard minutes before.

They were trapped.

On the other side of the wooden wall of the stable, horses were picking up the smell of tiger and bear. Even though they had never actually encountered either of these creatures, they sensed danger. They began to wicker in alarm and kick against their stalls.

Horses don't like bears and cats and wolves, Blit said.

The hounds could be seen now on the far side of a park nearby: a carpet of dogs with armed men on horseback beside them. Inside the stables, human voices sounded alarmed. They would soon start to wonder what was spooking their animals. The traffic on the road clattered and clanked.

On the opposite side of the road from the stables was a bakery. Its large side-door opened onto an alleyway. As Owl watched, a bakery delivery wagon drawn by two horses backed off the road and into the alley, its driver talking quietly to the horses to get them to walk backwards. Then the driver jumped down and went into the bakery. It was a large, closed wagon, easily big enough for a bear, a tiger, and a small wolf. Owl could see the back was not locked.

Quick, Owl said to Skrimsli. *In there.*

If their situation had not been so desperate, there might have been some disagreements about stealing a large wagon. But as it was, there was no choice. Before the man could come back, Karu and Skrimsli darted round the back and got in, while Owl climbed up onto the driver's seat and took the reins although he had no real idea what to do. Blit scrambled up beside him.

Galu Mak and me drove these, Blit the wolf said in Owl's head. *Pull that.*

She pointed her nose at a metal lever at Owl's feet. Owl did as she told him.

Now, giddy-up, horses!

That part Owl could do. He'd ridden in carts travelling between towns with the circus. He slapped the reins and said what the jantevas always said: 'Get on there!'

Rather to Owl's astonishment, the horses began to move, and the van pulled out of the alley and into the throng of traffic along the road. The horses turned north. That was where the last delivery of the day always was. They began to trot. The faster it was done, the sooner they got a nice rest in their stable with a nosebag full of supper.

The wagon was big, and the other traffic seemed happy to get out of its way. Some people even waved, although when they saw little Owl driving and not the usual driver, whose size indicated that he sampled quite a lot of the bakery's deliveries, they looked puzzled. The sound of the hounds faded behind them. They were heading north on the main road out of the town. In no time they would be leaving danger behind.

After a mile or so the horses began to slow and veer to the

left, into the driveway of a large house. Owl steered them straight, and they were soon trotting along the road again. Traffic thinned out; the road narrowed. Owl began to look out for places where he might turn off, and they could leave the van behind. But the road was lined to left and right with smart houses and perfect gardens, shining in the spring sunshine. Owl grew nervous, then more nervous still when up ahead he saw that the road crossed a bridge over a small river and that on either end of the bridge were stern-looking men carrying cudgels and guns. Beside him a butcher's van drew level with Owl and Blit, as all the carts and veekles slowed to a walking pace on the approach to the bridge.

'Where's Sappy, the usual driver?' the butcher's van driver asked Owl.

Owl swallowed and tried to make his voice less squeaky. 'Sappy took sick!'

'Oh yeah?' the woman said. 'When?'

'Sudden!' Owl replied. 'Very sudden.'

'Too many pies!' said the woman and grinned.

Owl looked at what was happening up ahead. The men at the entrance to the bridge were speaking to every driver and even looking inside some of the wagons and carts. Should they jump out now and just run, he wondered? Or was there a chance they could get through?

'What's happening at the bridge?' Owl squeaked, his voice scratchy with anxiety.

The butcher woman rolled her eyes.

'They're collecting tolls. It's not legal but who's gonna stop 'em? Sappy keeps his toll money under the seat, by the way, so you should be fine.'

Blit jumped down and scrabbled around under Owl's feet. When she jumped back up, she held a purse in her jaws.

It was too late to alert Skrimsli and Karu now. They were almost at the bridge. Owl could see the fierce looks on the faces of the men who blocked everyone's way.

'You go first,' the butcher woman said. 'I'm not in a hurry.'

Be quiet. Keep still.

Owl sent a thought to Skrimsli and hoped he'd hear, as one of the men took the reins of the baker's horses.

He stuck his hand up towards Owl. 'Pay up, then!'

He sounded bored. He hardly looked up at Owl. There were no questions about where they were going or who they were. Owl fumbled the money from the purse into the man's hand. He hardly looked at it.

'On you go then, son!'

'Get on there!' Owl told the horses and on they went, slowly clopping over the wood of the bridge. Owl's heart sang. They'd done it! They'd done it! On the other side of the bridge there were no more buildings. Half a mile ahead Owl could see a copse of trees. Perfect cover. They could get out there and leave the road behind.

There were several men milling around at the side of the road on the other end of the bridge. They were different from the ones who had collected the toll. Older, fatter, scruffier, and not doing very much that Owl could make out. They were in conversation with someone. A person standing at the centre of their group waving his arms around, getting very agitated by the looks of things. Owl could even hear him shouting now. The sound of his voice made Owl's blood run cold. His coat was no longer smart, he had no hat, only a mat of uncombed hair, but he was still unmistakable.

The man's back was turned. If he stayed that way, they would get through. Don't turn round, Owl thought. Don't turn round! They were almost past, almost becoming just another bit of traffic vanishing up the road. But the man did turn round, and he saw Owl at once.

'Freak! Freak!' cried Itmis Majak. 'I've got you! I knew I would.'

19

Skrimsli

Back in the Cage

Skrimsli snarled and struggled in the tangle of the net. Blows from clubs wielded by a number of humans rained on his head. He felt Karu's terrible anguish at being recaptured, and it was almost worse than his own.

The men who captured them were big and brutal, but they were slow, so Skrimsli and Karu had at least made them pay a little blood for what they did. Best of all, Blit, the smallest she-wolf, danced away and escaped them entirely. But Owl did not.

Bound with ropes and nets, the three of them were trundled back into the city, through stone gates into a place that smelled of age and dust.

It was dark by now. Skrimsli peered about him to see where they were and saw who was behind this capture. Not just Itmis, Kobret's vile cub, but those two acrobats, who danced on horses' backs and smelled of death. They all smiled and smiled the worst kind of human smiles that made Skrimsli want to bite them.

Skrimsli was furious. He snarled and struggled, even though he knew he couldn't break the nets or stop the beating. Then Itmis held poor Owl by the scruff of the neck and shook him in front of Skrimsli like a rag, just as his father had done.

'Be still now, Stripy, or I will hurt him!'

The man was not smooth as he had once been. His outline was jagged, his hair wild and there was a new smell of decay about him; he was a creature out of control and might kill the boy at the slightest excuse. Skrimsli grew still at once.

Owl came into his mind as he lay helpless in the human's nets.

Sorry, Owl said in his mind. *Sorry.*

Sorry. What a stupid human word that was! What purpose did that serve? None. It changed nothing. Skrimsli could feel how hurt and frightened Owl was, but he was too angry to help. He pushed Owl from his mind.

They dragged him in the net and shoved him through a barred cage door into a space that smelled of wet straw and rats. He paced about in the dark of it with nothing but the white heat of his anger in his head. Anger with himself; anger with humans for the things they did. Skrimsli roared until his throat hurt.

But as the anger receded, he saw that it was no use looking back and snarling about what he could have done. That was something humans did. He must be a tiger and deal with his situation as it was, not as he wished it to be.

He paced about inside his cage and found stone walls, stone roof with a slit of sky, covered in bars. The floor sloped, with a door made of metal at the top and one at the bottom. He wondered what Itmis had done with Owl and reached out with his mind to see if the boy was anywhere close by. But Owl was nowhere near.

Sorry, Owl, Skrimsli thought. *Sorry! Sorry?*

He growled at himself and decided he was too tired and too hungry to endure being awake any longer, so he put the world away and slept.

When he woke, light came through the barred slit above Skrimsli's head and with it the sounds and smells of a busy town waking up. Skrimsli lay still and closed his eyes again. He matched up the sounds and smells in his mind. Behind them was something else. It was a smell he'd never smelled before: not strong but very big, cool and fresh. Salty! Its sound was faint, too, quite far off but like a huge, slow breathing. Long, slow breaths. Skrimsli found he was breathing in time with it.

He liked this smell and its sound. It made him curious. It made his paws tingle. He liked it so much in fact that he didn't hear Owl's small footsteps bringing the boy to the other side of the metal door in the top of the sloping cell.

'Skrimsli! Skrimsli?' Owl called.

He gave a small yowl of greeting and then Owl was in the shared space of their two minds, where Skrimsli could head bump the boy and purr in spite of the door that stood between them.

I'm so sor... Owl began to say that word, but Skrimsli would not listen to it.

No! No! No! Skrimsli insisted. *We are alive. We are together. We are!*

Owl agreed at last.

What is this place? Where are we? Skrimsli asked.

Owl hesitated. *It's like a kind of circus, Cub, made of stone. It's a prison too. Karu is in a cell like you; he's fine. Kal also and her friend are prisoners here. I don't know why yet...*

A prison and a circus! Skrimsli pushed the dread down underneath his paws.

He could feel Owl push it down too. They must think of something else instead.

What is that smell? That salty smell? he asked.

It is the ocean. Otok, this town, is between the river and the ocean.

Skrimsli had never heard that word 'ocean' before. He searched in Owl's mind for the meaning of it and found just a moving, blue vagueness.

It is very big water. As far as you can see.

How could water go as far as you could see?

This ocean is called Finger. Owl told him. Ocean called Finger? Really, humans and their words were impossible. But whatever ocean was, he liked the smell and sound of it.

I can't stay, Owl said. *I have to go with Itmis.*

Owl was fearful. Skrimsli could feel it.

I have to go, he said again. *Be careful, Cub!*

The boy was afraid, for himself and for Skrimsli.

We will escape, he told Owl. *We will escape.*

Itmis' voice snaked through the air, calling, 'Freak! Freak, come at once!'

Owl turned and ran.

We will escape! Skrimsli said to himself. But how? As if in answer there was a sudden scraping and a small slot opened in the bottom of the door. Through it, a tray of meat and a bowl of water appeared. The meat was stale. The cow from which it came had been sad and sick and had died some time ago. But it would fill his belly. To escape, he would have to keep strong, and he would need to mend. His body ached from the beating

200

he had received. For now, the answer to *how to escape* was simply *eat* and *sleep* and wait to see what happened. Skrimsli yawned and curled up on the driest bit of straw he could find.

Hours later, someone banged on the bars over the skylight above Skrimsli's head. It was an angry sound, and he could guess who made it: Itmis. Skrimsli decided he would take his time waking up. Very slowly he stretched; very slowly he opened his eyes and looked up. The sky was sunset bright and silhouetted against it was Itmis. The man's eyes were red and wet, and he smelled even more of something sick. It made Skrimsli want to cover his nose with a paw.

'You are back where you belong! In my control!' Itmis gloated. 'Soon you will begin your repayment for all you have taken from me, you evil monster.'

Skrimsli didn't understand the words very well, but he understood the feeling behind them, the hate and badness. A prickle of fear danced along his spine.

'You will see a door in the lower part of your cage, Stripy. When it opens, you must go through it. At the end of a tunnel, you will fight whatever you find there. If you do not, the Freak boy will be the worse for it.'

Skrimsli turned away. He didn't even want to look at Itmis but he reached out with his mind, testing for a route to the inside of Itmis' head. It was like reaching to touch a cold stone or a body, long dead. Skrimsli shivered and drew back. No, he would find another way to defeat this human.

'You may not look at me, Stripy,' Itmis shouted on, 'but I know you understand. You will fight a gorilla and a red ape, and whoever else I choose. And you will make me a great deal of money.'

Itmis' laughter was like a stink of dung trailing behind him as he walked away. Ugh! Why had he not killed the cub as well as the father? He was a prisoner again, forced to do tricks for humans. He paced the cell, growling to himself. Thinking.

He examined the information that Itmis had given him. He was required to fight to keep Owl safe. But would his opponents – 'gorilla', 'red ape' – whatever *they* were, fight back? And if they did, what would be the outcome? Kill? Be killed? Perhaps there were other outcomes, that would help them all survive and escape from Itmis' power. Skrimsli chewed on the bare bones of the cow and thought and thought until there was the start of a plan in the quiet space inside his head.

Night came and the sounds of a human crowd gathering rained down from above. Many humans, all males, came and looked down at him through the bars, shouting and jeering. Skrimsli snarled at them, showed his teeth and claws and told them clearly how much he would like to kill them all. They laughed at him, even spat or threw things. He could hear them still talking and laughing after they moved away.

The noise of the crowd died down a little and the door slid open as Itmis had said it would. Skrimsli went through the door, which slid shut behind him, and entered a long, dark tunnel, where the voices of the human crowd echoed. He saw a door ahead of him and a space lit by lights like the ones from the circus. He stepped out into it, all his senses on alert, and looked around.

He was in a circular pit with a sand floor. Stone walls stood all around and above them rose tiers of seats packed with noisy humans. High on one side was a raised platform with a rail around it. That's where Itmis stood, in his dirty coat, with poor Owl on a lead beside him, close enough to see but too far away to contact. With a grating scrape, one of the other doors that lined the perimeter of the pit opened, and a huge black creature rushed towards him. It was not a bear, and with fur that colour it could not be a 'red ape'. This was a 'gorilla' then.

Skrimsli had never seen anything like it before. It was a male, and although it lacked the teeth and claws of a hunter, it was bigger than he was. The gorilla could grasp like human hands did and its shoulders were almost as wide as Skrimsli was long. It was incredibly strong. It grabbed him round the neck and shut off his breathing almost at once. Skrimsli had never fought anything apart from Taze. He gagged and gasped and felt his consciousness slipping into blackness. But his deep tiger-self fought to the surface of the dark, and the memory of those long play fights with Taze rushed back. He had 'fought' carefully with Taze, so as not to hurt her. Now, all he had to do was fight with less care. He wrenched himself round, just enough to rake the gorilla's belly with the claws of his back feet. The gorilla released its hold and jumped back. They stood looking at each other, while the crowd yelled and bayed and screamed.

The gorilla rushed at Skrimsli and grabbed his neck again. This time he bound one arm, with its incredible strength, around the cub's throat and started to push a finger into Skrimsli's right eye. Skrimsli sprang the claws on his front paws and dug them into the dark fur of the gorilla's shoulders, until they cut flesh. He pushed at the gorilla's belly with all the strength of his back legs and felt soft skin rip under his claws. The gorilla had to use his hands to fight this assault, so let go of the hold on Skrimsli's neck. That was enough for Skrimsli to get his jaws around the short, thick throat. He felt his canines pop the skin and very slowly, with precise control, began to close his mouth, bit by bit, until he felt the gristly resistance of windpipe. He tasted blood, not much, but enough that his opponent would know how near he was to cutting through vital blood vessels. The creature froze; he understood that he was in the tiger's power.

This was stalemate. If Skrimsli let go even a little, the creature would fight back once more. Then there could be only one of two outcomes. Kill or be killed. Somehow Skrimsli had to communicate an alternative to the mind of this unfamiliar being. With Owl it was easy: a space they had always occupied together. With Kobret, Skrimsli had just followed the path that the man's brutal cruelty had opened. And Karu had always seemed to come into Skrimsli's mind rather than the other way around. But how to reach inside the skull of this wholly unfamiliar being? This stranger? All the cub could do was try. He reached out, as if he were stretching out a paw into darkness, or pushing his nose between blades of grass or...

He had barged into the gorilla's head! It was a place rather similar to Owl's. Right now it was aflame with fear and fury. But it was not the mind of a killer any more than Owl's was. He was equipped with behaviour for defence, not really for attack. There was a lot of bluff in his head.

In their minds they looked at each other. The gorilla did not have any human words. He 'spoke' in pictures and feelings, which Skrimsli understood very well.

What are you doing here? The gorilla challenged.

I don't want to fight. I don't want to kill. I don't want to die.
Skrimsli responded. *Do you?*

There was a pause. *No*, the gorilla replied. *Man will hurt my friend if I don't fight.*

So, Itmis was using the same tactic on everyone here! It wasn't surprising. The gorilla began to fight back again and gripped Skrimsli's throat once more. But the cub simply increased the pressure on its windpipe a little more

You will die first, he told it. *Do you want to die?*

No.

Then do this.

Skrimsli hesitated then. He had thought of a plan but not how to explain it! How would he describe biting, strangling, struggling, but with enough restraint to do no harm? Then he had it. A memory of himself and Taze fighting when he was a cub. He showed it now. The gorilla was smart. He understood at once and answered with a memory of his own: a smaller version of himself and another just like him, rolling over and over, falling out of trees and rolling again on the ground.

Yes, said Skrimsli.

Yes, the gorilla responded. *YES!*

Skrimsli released his grip a little and was immediately wrapped in strong arms and legs that rolled him over and over in the dust; this time they held but did not crush. Skrimsli let the gorilla stand above him and even hold his head and shake it. The cub could feel the strength that his opponent was no longer using but holding in reserve. Then he rolled on top and put his mouth around the gorilla's neck again. The gorilla screamed so convincingly that Skrimsli let go. It pushed him off and ran around the pit, whooping and beating its huge chest with its big flat hands.

And just like that, they were playing. Really playing. For the next few minutes neither of them thought of anything else but the pleasure of wrestling and rolling, ambushing and escaping, until they were both tired and out of breath. Skrimsli remembered what Taze did when she'd had enough and rolled onto his back and played dead. The gorilla stood on its hind legs and beat its chest again. Yes, thought Skrimsli, bluff is what you do best!

The human crowd roared so loud Skrimsli thought his ears would burst.

Then the doors to their respective tunnels slid open with a rasp and they could escape back to the quiet of their cells. Play fighting was exhausting. Skrimsli lapped his water bowl empty and slept.

Over the following nights, Skrimsli met all the other animals who were Itmis' prisoners, one after another. The first night it was Karu, who was easy to communicate with but who had forgotten how to play. In his years under Kobret's control he had got used to dominating small opponents with overwhelming strength, or simply threatening violence and doing nothing. He was stiff and out of condition. Only by *really* scratching him on the nose and getting him *really* angry could Skrimsli elicit a convincing fight. And that was dangerous! Karu eventually understood what was required of him but not before Skrimsli had a torn ear and bruised ribs.

The next night a female gorilla came into the light of the pit. She had been told what to do by her partner, so from the first moment they were playing. She was smaller and not as strong as her companion, but she was quicker and cleverer. She out-smarted Skrimsli several times, poking, tweaking, pinching and leaping out of reach. She taught the cub a whole lot of new things.

The most difficult opponent was the red ape. When Skrimsli tried to reach out to her mind, he felt himself pushed aside by a powerful force, just as if she'd struck him. She would not fight. She paced around and around the pit and stayed out of Skrimsli's way. The crowd booed – a sound that Skrimsli knew from the circus was very bad. Itmis could see that Skrimsli was holding back.

'Fight! Fight, Stripy, or you know what will happen,' he called down. Then in a louder voice he yelled to the booing crowd. 'If she won't fight, kill her. Kill her, kill her.'

The human crowd took up the chant: *kill her kill her kill her.*

Skrimsli could feel the horrible desire for blood which filled the air. Blood for no reason, not for food, not for safety but for some dark human reason that smeared the air with its stink. At that moment, if he could have killed the entire human crowd, he would have.

The chanting grew more and more frenzied and Skrimsli feared that something bad would happen. Perhaps some of the humans had guns and would shoot the ape and himself? He needed to do something.

Skrimsli paced behind the ape for two more circuits of the pit until the movement of her limbs, the way her eye flitted about fearfully, was in his head. He relaxed his body, looked loose, inattentive. Then, he pounced, pinning her on her back, his forepaws on her arms. Underneath her fur her body was skinny, her long, long arms very thin. She didn't struggle but it was *she* who came into *his* mind.

Do it, she said clearly, in human words. *I want to be gone from this world that is not my own. I want my head emptied of their voices and their words.*

Her misery was overwhelming. Skrimsli felt himself drowning in it.

Fight me! he told her. *And you will live to escape!*

Escape to what? she replied. *My forest home is cut down. My family dead. I have never known a life that was not made by humans. Why should I want to live?*

A life made by humans? Was that all that he too had lived? He had never even seen another of his own kind! Why was he was not filled with this blackness? What answer could he offer this poor, sad creature? Only the answer in his own heart, the vision he had seen through the elephant's eye, and the sound and smell that had made his body thrill – ocean. There was still a world to discover.

Because there is a trail in the world to follow, and this is not the end of it, he told the red ape. He felt this thought sink into her, like water into parched ground. The red ape's mind opened softly, and he saw it was a mind for finding and remembering, for mapping in space and time. She understood the meaning of a trail. Slowly her face, which was very close to his, changed. Her eyes lit up.

Perhaps, she said. *Perhaps.*

Then with one hand she reached up and pulled his whiskers very, very hard!

All of the fighters in the pit had been circus animals, kept to perform tricks to keep humans amused. They had lived with humans and had acquired the human habit of naming words, even if there were no other words that they used. The male gorilla was Silverback. His friend, the female, was Leaf; and the red ape was Ray. Every day Skrimsli thought of new ways to outwit Silverback, Leaf, Ray and Karu and when they met to fight, he knew they had been doing the same. Sometimes he fought three of them in one night, sometimes just one, and sometimes they fought each other. He did not see these contests but heard the reaction of the crowd. The fights between the red ape and the female gorilla made the humans scream with laughter. Every night the crowds around the pit grew bigger and louder.

But what the humans thought did not matter. Skrimsli began to realise that what was more important was that every day all the fighters in the pit grew stronger, more wily, more experienced. Grew to know each other better. Grew to trust each other more.

Skrimsli watched the human guards whenever he could and encouraged the others to do the same. He grew certain that he and his opponents in the pit could defeat them if they worked together. But how to work together when they were locked away in separate cages?

20
Kal

Possibility and Uncertainty

 The twins put their photographic equipment away. Listig had taken photographs of both Kal and the Palatine, standing against one of the walls of the dirty courtyard of the amphitheatre. Listig had been very careful that nothing about their surroundings would give away their location. She packed the photographic plates into a box and locked it.

'There,' she said. 'All the proof we need that the Palatine and the Erem terrorist are still alive and dangerous!'

'And in the hands of ruthless kidnappers, whose only thought is money!' Spion added.

The two sisters snickered together.

'Now, we have the photographs, sister. *Please* can we kill them?' Listig asked.

'How many times, Listig!' Spion snapped. 'We may need to offer more proof that they are alive, or no one is going to pay to make sure they *become dead*. Patience, sister!'

Itmis stepped forward from where he had been standing in the shadows.

'Their cells are ready,' he announced. 'I expect to be reimbursed for the new locks I've had to fit and the guards I've had to employ.'

'Oh, you'll get your cut, Itmis, never fear,' said Listig, with mock sweetness. She sidled up to him and kissed his ear. Itmis looked as if he didn't know whether to blush or throw up.

'It will be quite the fortune,' Listig continued, wrapping herself around him like a cat. 'I'm going buy a whole pack of *dear* little dogs, did I tell you?'

Spion sighed in exasperation at her twin's frivolity.

'If everything goes to plan,' Spion told Itmis sternly, 'these photographs will ensure that interested parties will pay a great deal to fund the final elimination of the Palatine and the Erem terrorist. At that stage, we will send you notice of our imminent return, to finalise their demise and the proof thereof.'

'What my sister means,' Listig said, leaning her head onto Itmis' shoulder, 'is that as soon as the Yalen, the Nordskys and the Automators pay up, we'll come back and kill 'em and take some snaps to prove it! And you will get lots of lovely money.'

They'll kill you too, Itmis, you fool, Kal wanted to say, but the gag was in place now and even breathing was a strain.

'In the meantime,' Listig continued, 'all you have to do is make even more money from your new show here! And we all know how much you like money, Itmis, dear.'

Itmis looked like a dark cloud.

'I like money well enough. I need money to rebuild my father's circus. But I like revenge too, and I will take mine on that wretched cat and his friend, and the treacherous bear. They will pay for what they did.'

He strode away barking to his new hired helpers. 'Get these prisoners to their cells!'

Kal didn't remember what had happened next because *get*

211

these prisoners to their cells meant a wad of cloth, steeped in some sharp-smelling chemical was pressed over Kal's face and everything went black. Kal woke inside the walls of a stone cell. One tiny window let in enough pale daylight to show that the cell was empty but for a low bed of wooden slats, a grubby blanket and a tin bucket.

'Palatine?' Kal called. 'Owl?' The words echoed mockingly in the dank air.

There was a sudden scuff of heavy boots outside the door.

'Shuddup. You're not in 'ere to talk. *No talking*, alright?'

Kal had never liked walls of any kind. Walls had always made Kal want to run outside and breath the open air. Inside these walls and the darkness, panic rose like a flood. Kal's heart pounded with one thought:

I'm going to die here.

I'm going to die here.

I'm going to die here.

Kal pushed the thought away, but it kept seeping back.

Several sets of boots scuffed the floor outside and there was the sound of something, *someone*, being dragged along a corridor.

'Palatine?' Kal risked a shout.

'Kal!' came the answer. She was here, close by. It was like reaching the surface after someone tried to drown you. But she was dragged into the next cell and the door banged shut. The panic rose again and Kal wrestled with it. Focus. That was how to get through this. *Do* something: *concentrate*. If the walls are the enemy, then get to know them. Find out if they have weaknesses.

The cell was eight paces long and four wide. Kal measured it twice, keeping the paces even and accurate helped to keep the panic at bay. The ceiling was high, perhaps twelve paces up, with solid roof beams and huge overlapping tiles; there would be no way to lift even one of them to make escape that way possible. The door was heavy wood, with studded metal braces, and hinges that looked like they had lasted for five-hundred years and were ready for another thousand. The lock was huge; the key that opened it must be massive. Perhaps too large to be carried on the belt of the guard. Could it be hanging on the wall outside? There was a sliding panel at the top of the door that covered a grill for the guard to look through, and another at the bottom that Kal guessed was to slide out the bucket and slide in food. High up in the end wall, too high to see out of, was an unglazed window, secured with close-set bars that even Owl could not have squeezed through. It did at least let air in. The cell would be cold at night, but Kal was used to cold.

After inspecting every corner, crack and stone, and finding no obvious possibility for escape, Kal made just one encouraging discovery: a gap between two stones, where mortar had been scraped away high in the shared wall between Kal's cell and the Palatine's. Kal stood on the bed with a strip of wood pulled from one of its slats and poked the hole. Mortar fell out on the other side of the wall; the hole went right through! Kal wiggled the slat again and pushed more loose mortar through, hoping the Palatine would notice, hoping that this could be a way for them to communicate. But there was no response, and then the guard stepped to the door; Kal only just had time to lie on the bed and pretend to be asleep before the panel in the door slid back and the guard scowled through the grill.

Kal lost track of time. At some point the panel in the door slid open again.

'Bucket!' the guard growled.

Kal slid out the full bucket and the guard slid an empty one back. Then a wooden bowl appeared, with a scoop of grey porridge in. There was no spoon. Was the light in the sky fading? Was it dusk or dawn? Why was it so hard to work this out? Kal's heart was racing again. It was impossible to keep still. Pacing the cell, over and over and over was the only way not to scream.

At last, the light did fade. Darkness was a relief; the definite coming of night was a way to hold on to reality. Kal kept pacing; the guard began to snore. A tiny fall of mortar and a 'psssst' sound came from the hole in the wall. At last. At last! The Palatine had found it.

Kal leapt onto the bed and pressed lips to the gap between the stones.

'Are you alright?' Kal asked.

'Yes,' the Palatine whispered. Kal had never been more glad to hear any sound! 'But that porridge is even worse than your cornmeal!'

'At least the beds are comfortable,' Kal replied, 'and the view is very lovely.'

The smallest gasp showed that the Palatine was suppressing a laugh. Kal knew the gesture: the back of her left hand raised to her mouth, her eyes darting. They fell silent for a moment, then both tried to speak at once.

'You first!' the Palatine instructed.

A hundred thoughts crowded Kal's mind in a tangle of confusion but one thing seemed the most important.

'How long do we have before the twins get back?'

The Palatine's voice came firm and quiet between the stones. 'You must stay calm, Kal.'

'How can I stay calm when they might come to kill us at any moment?' Kal hissed back. 'When anything could be happening in Erem? When that man has Owl and the tiger in his grasp?'

'Kal. Kal. Listen to me. *Listen!*'

Kal's forehead pressed to the cold stone of the wall. 'Alright, I'm listening.'

'I have been keeping careful track of the time since we were captured,' the Palatine said. 'The twins will travel downriver to Shamanow, then to Bisque City across the Sand Sea. They must present their report and convince the Nordskys and the Automators that they are telling the truth and then they must do the same with my brother. And only then will they return. It will all take weeks.'

'And what do *we* do? Just wait to die?'

'We do not wait to die. We wait for *opportunity.*'

'What opportunity? Have you looked at this place? There's no way out!'

The Palatine sighed. 'We just haven't found it yet, Kal. We have weeks to find it, perhaps months. And in that time, who knows what will happen. As the twins said, Itmis is very fond of money. He will use the tiger and the bear and whatever else he can lay his hands on to ply his father's filthy trade here in the amphitheatre. He will be distracted from us. *Something* will happen and there will be an opportunity.'

Kal tried to believe what was said but the walls pressed in and panic pushed its way up again.

'We're going to die here!' Kal whispered.

'No, Kal,' said the Palatine, her words hard-edged. 'We are *not*. You *must* have hope. Please, Kal!'

'I'll try. I'll try,' Kal told her.

'Goodnight now. We must sleep,' the Palatine said. 'We will need our strength.'

Kal lay down on the hard, cold bed. Strength had drained out through the damp walls. Hope was something that existed under the stars, not here in this miserable cell. Even so, surprisingly, Kal slept.

Days passed, their slow rhythm set by the sliding open of the metal panels for buckets and food and the changing of the guard. At first, the guards were vigilant, pulling back the grills to peer in at their prisoners every hour. But they grew lazy, and it was possible for Kal and the Palatine to spend longer whispering through the stone gap. The Palatine persuaded Kal that it was necessary to learn to fight.

'When opportunity comes,' she counselled, 'you must be ready, and useful.'

It was comforting to hear her being the bossy Palatine, giving orders, being certain. So Kal agreed to a list of exercises and drills that everyone in Yuderan learned to defend themselves from attack.

'Every morning, every afternoon,' the Palatine ordered. Every night she rehearsed Kal in imaginary combat. They whispered moves and counter-moves in the darkness, like the steps of a complicated dance. Kal grew to like the drills; they became a talisman to drive the fear away. Hope remained elusive but focus, concentration and the whispered fragments spoken through that tiny stone opening made it possible to endure captivity.

Gradually clues about what went on outside the cells seeped in. At nightfall, a few days after their imprisonment began, they heard the familiar sound of an excited human crowd flowing into the amphitheatre. Kal and the Palatine stood at either side of their precious channel of communication listening and trying to make sense of what they heard.

'You were right!' Kal whispered. 'Itmis is putting on a show.'

The man's voice boomed and bellowed, playing the ringmaster, sounding more like his father all the time. The words bounced against the stone walls and blurred but they heard enough. Skrimsli was being made to fight a *monstrous ape from the forest isles.*

'How will a tiger cub fare against a full-grown gorilla?' the Palatine breathed anxiously. Kal didn't know, but one thing was sure, and that was that Itmis was controlling Skrimsli by hurting Owl. Kal was certain of it.

They stood in silence, listening to the shouts of the crowd, wondering what it was they watched. But the tell-tale death roar of the crowd never came, not on that night nor any of the others that followed. Itmis' voice announced each new creature that the tiger faced: a bear, a red ape and another gorilla. Whatever was happening out there, the tiger was surviving and so were his opponents.

Kal and the Palatine began to rely on the noise of the audience to cover more conversations. Every night it grew louder as Itmis' shows grew more popular.

'Itmis must be making money. A lot of money,' Kal

commented one night when the crowd was especially loud. 'He'll want to keep Skrimsli alive.'

'Perhaps,' the Palatine replied. 'But how long can the tiger hold out, fighting every night?'

The crowd suddenly erupted into laughter.

'I don't think there's any killing going on,' Kal said. 'Skrimsli's a tiger not a cub. If he were really *fighting* in that ring, something would be dead and no one would be laughing.' The thought that the tiger might be up to something was the most encouraging thought Kal had had in days.

Information came from the guards too, through their conversation as they changed watch. Mostly this chat showed that Itmis was only paying enough to employ the oldest and stupidest people. The guards' talk gave away that the cell keys were kept hanging just outside the doors, as Kal had imagined, and that the cells were on a passageway. To the left lay the entrance to the amphitheatre itself, but to the right lay a stairway to a back entrance. A map of their prison, even one as vague as that, was helpful.

They got news of Owl. He was being kept in the apartment where Itmis lived above the main entrance. Itmis took him out on a lead like a pet creature. Spanner, one of the chattier guards, did not approve.

'He's a kid, not a creature. That's not right, is it?'

The other guard laughed. 'If you're worried about what's right, mate, you're working for the wrong bloke.'

At least they knew that Owl was safe, for now. But time was ticking. Every day was a day closer to the twins' return. All their lives – not only Kal's and the Palatine's, but Owl's and

Skrimsli's too – were threatened when the twins returned. Kal remembered, with a shiver, how Spion had said that she wanted no loose ends.

They needed an escape plan for everyone, but still neither Kal nor the Palatine had any idea of how they could get out. Then Spanner's chattiness brought some news.

'You heard about the boss' new plan?' he said one evening as he arrived for his shift. 'We might get a bonus.'

The second guard didn't sound impressed; he just wanted to get away. 'Oh, yeah?'

The first man's excitement showed in the way he said the next word: 'Pirates!'

This seemed to irritate the second, whose voice creaked like a rusty hinge.

'Whaddya mean, "pirates"?' said Rusty Hinge. 'There's decent seafarers being called that all the time in this town.'

Spanner sighed. 'Alright then, *decent seafarers* from two ships have been fighting. And one killed the captain of the other and stole her ship. He took the crew prisoner and now he's paying the boss to lock 'em up here. Boss is gonna put them in the pit against Stripy and the gorillas and all.'

Rusty Hinge found this interesting at last. 'Oh,' he creaked, 'haven't seen human against creature fights since I was nipper. Big money to be made betting on those!'

'Well,' said Spanner, sounding very pleased. 'That's what the boss reckons. That's why we might get a raise.'

'When is this all happening, then?' asked Rusty.

'Couple of days? Boss's got posters out all over town already.'

Spanner did nothing while on guard but sleep, no matter

what time he was on watch. They waited until he was snoring then both leapt to the gap between the stones to speak.

'This could be our chance!' the Palatine said. 'Itmis' guards won't be able to stop a crew trained to fight!'

'How will that help us?' Kal replied. 'All it means is that Skrimsli will be killed and then Itmis won't have any reason to keep Owl alive. You heard Itmis say he wanted revenge. This is how he'll take it!'

'The pirate crew will want to escape more than they'll want to fight creatures. There will be chaos, Kal, and chaos is our chance. In uncertainty lies opportunity.'

'Maybe. Maybe not,' Kal said. 'But if the pirates are fighting the guards, Itmis will be afraid and distracted, then Owl could do something to help us get out?'

Spanner had stopped snoring, the scrape of his boots said he was paying attention to his job for a change and would be peering at them through the grill any second. There was no more time to talk. Kal lay on the bed, pretending to be asleep, thinking that they still didn't have much of a plan. If only they could get a message to Owl or to Skrimsli. If only they knew more about the layout of their prison.

Kal was awake early, pacing and worrying. Eight paces one way and eight paces back. It was getting light. Kal looked up at the scrap of sky visible between the bars of the window. Bars and walls, that's all there was in the way. How could it be so hard to get out under the sky again? Kal stared into the sky watching the light slowly take possession of it. Something was moving, high up in the air. It was an eagle, a really big eagle!

Kal sprang up on the bed and pushed bits of mortar

through as fast and hard as possible, whispering wake up as loud as was safe. At last, the Palatine woke.

'I think it's Sayka! In the sky above our window.'

The Palatine gasped. 'I see him. But he's too far for my mind to reach!'

'Try, Palatine. Try.'

Sayka, with his bird's eye view, could tell them what they needed to know, maybe even show them a way to get out. And he might be able to contact Owl, or even Skrimsli.

Kal watched the shape of the eagle wheeling in ever wider circles. The silence in the Palatine's cell was singing with her effort to reach out to the bird. The silhouette grew more distant, veering away. Perhaps he hadn't heard his mistress calling; perhaps it wasn't even Sayka. Then something brought the eagle back. It almost stopped in mid-flight, turned suddenly, then dropped from a thousand feet, shocking and powerful as a thunderbolt. Kal heard the rush of air, saw the flurry of wings, heard the scrabble of claws on stone and heard the thin peeping cry as the bird greeted his mistress.

Their guard was waking; he'd heard the noise. Kal could hear him sleepily lumbering about. Sayka and the Palatine would have just a few more seconds. Would it be enough to explain to the eagle what they needed? To give them a chance of escape?

21
Owl

The Eagle and the Dart

 It was easy to pretend to be stupid with Itmis. The man already believed that Owl was a 'freak', that his short legs and face made him different. So Owl played the part of cringing slave: willing, obedient and afraid. He scuttled about like a terrified ant, the way he'd done before Skrimsli's arrival in his life. It was horrible, but it made Owl realise how much stronger and braver he now was. And it kept Itmis fooled and off-guard. Owl wasn't sure how that helped but he hoped it would.

Owl's days at the amphitheatre were boring. Each day began when Itmis unlocked the door of the tiny room where Owl was imprisoned. Then Owl had to make Itmis his breakfast of coffee and toast and serve him at the big wooden table in the large living room of the apartment. All the time, Owl had to endure being taunted and slapped. Itmis liked to boast, too, about how much money he would make when the twins came back to put an end to Kal and the other prisoner. Owl didn't understand how keeping two people alive and then killing them made anyone money, but he didn't doubt that the twins would come back and that they were murderers. Although when Itmis talked about the Queen of Yuderan, the Palatine, being 'my prisoner', Owl *knew* he was going loopy.

After breakfast Itmis would lock Owl back in his room and leave the flat for a few hours. When he returned in the afternoon, Itmis would go to his own room, where he had a desk. He typed frantically, talked to himself and drank wine. Just as the sun was going down, he would emerge, unlock Owl's room, attach a lead to the collar he forced Owl to wear all the time, and drag him out to watch the 'performance' in the pit.

Owl dreaded those evenings, watching Skrimsli fight. The balcony where Itmis stood was too far above the pit to allow Owl and the cub to communicate. All Owl could do was watch, full of fear. But after the first few nights Owl saw something Itmis and the other human watchers didn't. The fights *looked* real, there was even a little spilt blood from time to time, but they were no more real fights than those that Skrimsli had with Taze when he was a small cub. Skrimsli was keeping himself and all the others safe by pretending. That made Owl so proud and reassured. While that was going on, Skrimsli and all the rest were safe.

Every night Itmis returned to the apartment at the top of the stone steps with a huge bucket of money which he took into his room. Owl was sure he could hear the man counting it far into the night, while Owl was once more locked in his tiny room.

There was no way to escape; Owl had worked that out early on. The windows could not be opened and were made of ancient green glass, thick as a hand's breadth; the front door was closed with two locks and bolted from the outside. There was a large window in the roof of the kitchen through which

Owl could see the sky and birds flying. It could be opened by turning a handle on the wall, but Owl could not work out a way to climb up to the opened window, or even reach the handle on the wall. How would he get down from the roof anyway? There was no way to communicate with Skrimsli or Kal, no way to know what was going on in the world outside.

So the days ticked past. Every one a day when Spion and Listig might come back. Owl knew it would be best *not* to wait to see what happened then. Yet what could he do, stuck in this powerless little bubble?

Then things began to change. Firstly, the crowd had begun to realise that the 'fights' they had paid good money to see were just play. One night they booed and jeered; the next night Itmis' bucket was only half full of money.

Then Itmis began to get even more crazy. He began to laugh and cry for no reason and his afternoons at the typewriter grew noisier; he punched walls, broke bottles and shouted on and on. He talked to his dead father, sometimes angry, sometimes crying. He talked to Kal, Madam Numiko, and to the Yuderan Queen. When his hired thugs came to get orders they looked more and more uncomfortable in the face of Itmis' strange behaviour.

He grew more violent; the slaps Owl received now sent him flying. When, one night, Itmis sat up until first light, his head in his hands, Owl feared what he would do. He hid in his room and was relieved when Itmis finally left the apartment. Itmis was gone almost all day and when he came back his mood had definitely improved. He unlocked Owl's door, calling for coffee and wine, and laughed to himself.

'I have been offered a fine opportunity, Freak,' he gloated, 'that will make a very, very, *very* great deal of money *and* your little stripy friend will finally get what's coming to him!'

He said no more. Owl worried about what Itmis' 'fine opportunity' could be, but that night's performance was the same as always: Skrimsli and the female gorilla fought, then Karu chased the red ape around the pit. There was some laughter but more boos and jeers and an even smaller crowd. Yet Itmis didn't seem to mind. He laughed as he counted the much-reduced amount of money in the bucket at the end of the night.

What was going on? The very next morning a messenger came banging on the door while Itmis drank his morning coffee. Itmis took the message to his room and shut the door. Five minutes later he burst through the door and began to pace about the apartment, running his hands distractedly through his hair and exclaiming things to himself.

'Just when I could make a fortune…' And 'Why now, after all these weeks…'

Owl worked out that something was about to get in the way of Itmis' 'fine opportunity'. But after a while of ranting and raving, he seemed to come to a conclusion and slapped his own head as if in sudden realisation.

'Tonight! Why not tonight? There's just time to make a very, very, very great deal of money before our little show here ends!'

Then he ordered Owl to bring him his coat and went out, so distracted that he forgot to lock anything except the front door.

Careful as a prowling cat, Owl emerged and approached Itmis' door. It was essential that he find out what Itmis had planned, and the clues surely lay behind it. But if he were caught in Itmis' room there would be a painful price to pay. Owl scuttled back to the front door and listened. No sound of footsteps. He would be brave. And quick. With trembling fingers Owl approached the door of Itmis' bedroom.

The curtains were drawn, and the room was dim and deathly cold. The floor was covered in discarded clothes, and the last slice of what had been a large cake lay lopsided on a plate on the bed. Owl's stomach growled. He had not eaten anything since the day before, but Itmis might notice an empty plate. He wouldn't notice a few missing bank notes however, piles of paper money were strewn over the bed and the floor, toppling over into each other in chaos. Owl removed a stack or two and tucked them inside his clothes; if he ever escaped from this place, money might prove useful.

Then he went to Itmis' desk. It too was untidily strewn, but with letters and papers. The floor all round was carpeted with screwed-up sheets. This is what the man must spend his afternoons doing – typing words and throwing them away!

Everything was piled on top of everything else. Owl climbed into a chair so he could look down at the papers without disturbing them. Owl had learned to recognise the written words 'Owl' and 'Freak' through looking at the label over his little booth at the circus, day after day. He'd moved onto the words on the circus advertising posters:

The best horse riders in the world
You will be amazed
Death-defying acrobats
Trained elephants

Returning due to popular demand
Galu Mak and her performing pooches
Tickets on sale now

But the papers on the desk were covered with so *many* words. Owl couldn't see anything he knew. He closed his eyes to make the words stop moving and a memory came back to him, from the green place, his forest home.

You have to know what you're looking for, a voice had said. There had been sunlit water, dappled light shimmering over pebbles, and a shape in his hand: the little fish that he wore now round his neck.

Here now, feel the shape, then you can look for it in the water.

His fingers had run over the smooth wood, learning the outline.

There! There!

Then he'd seen them, baby fishes appearing where just a moment before there had been only sunlight and water.

See? When you know what you're looking for, there they are!

Owl opened his eyes. He didn't need to see *all* the words, just look out for one he recognised and start from there. On the very top of the paper pile was a narrow band of pale-yellow paper. This was the kind that could be rolled into a tiny cylinder for a bird to carry. Neatly handwritten words ran all along it. It was a message. Perhaps the very thing that had put Itmis into such a spin. He decided that would be a good place to start.

The letters were so tiny and so neat they could have been written by a mouse. He scanned the words carefully and saw one that he knew: *Return.*

There! The words around 'return' were harder to read. They were not words Owl knew. He had to spell each one out from its sounds, then say them aloud until he had something that sounded right. The word at the very end was the one he worked out first and it made his blood run cold.

Spion

That's who had sent this message. That was bad.

He worked through all the other words until he had them all even though he didn't know what some of them meant.

Negotiations: that took the longest time of all. It meant bargaining.

Complete: that meant finished.

We return: they were coming back.

Imminently. Owl had no idea what that word was or what it meant.

Assets must be alive.

Although he didn't know what *asset* was he understood what the message must mean: the twins wanted Kal and the Palatine to be alive until *they* came to kill them. But how long would that take? What in the world did IN-IM-ENT…

No EM-NI-NET

No … *that* word, whatever it was, mean? Then he remembered Itmis' agitation this morning.

'There is just time for me to make a very, very, very great deal of money.'

Itmis had hatched a plan for the fights in the amphitheatre, that was the opportunity. But the twins coming back was somehow going to spoil it. Which meant they were coming back very, very soon.

Imminently.

This was information that he had to get to Kal. Even a desperate escape attempt was worth it in the face of this approaching doom. But how? How?

A sudden crashing sound from the scullery made Owl almost jump out of his skin. He thought for a moment it meant that Itmis had crept in and started throwing crockery about. Owl rushed from the bedroom in a panic. But the front door was still locked. The sound was not so much a crashing now as a scraping, confused sound, like something trapped or floundering. Fearfully Owl peeped around the scullery door. A huge silhouette flopped about against the skylight, high up on the ceiling. Vast wings and huge talons scratching on the glass. It was an eagle, and it was trying very hard to get through the skylight! What was it doing?

Its yellow eyes blazed down at him, and it cried out again, its voice almost sharp enough to shatter the glass in the skylight. It wanted to tell him something, Owl was sure. He wished he had that easy ability that Ead and her family had so he could just slip into its mind and understand what it was trying to say. But perhaps he could open his mind so that the bird could get in, the way Skrimsli and Blit and Karu could. Owl stood very, very still and looked back at the bird. It stopped screeching and sat still too. There was a tingling feeling in Owl's head, and then a picture materialised there. The image sparked with the bird's complicated feelings – like a painting drawn and redrawn with more and more detail every second, as the bird's mind fed in all the detail from its eyes. It took Owl a few seconds to adjust to this unfamiliar way of perceiving and then he saw what the bird wanted him to: a pair of windows, high in a wall; windows covered in bars. Owl recognised the building as the amphitheatre. In the dark space behind one of the windows was Kal's face, looking up as if from the bottom of a well, but clearly recognisable.

But it was the face that looked from the other window that really mattered to the eagle. It belonged to the woman Owl had glimpsed on the day he and Skrimsli had been captured. The one Itmis thought was the Yuderan Queen. She was a queen to the bird that was certain; the picture in the eagle's mind was suffused with fierce love. This was his mistress, the force that steered his life: his whole life. It was she who had sent the bird to Owl!

If she had sent the bird to him, then he could send it back with a message! Owl sensed that the eagle had more to communicate to him, but Itmis might get back at any moment, so whatever it had to say to him he had a more important message. Kal must be warned that the twins were on their way.

Tell her the twins are coming, Owl thought. The eagle gave no sign of having seen the picture of the twins that Owl had tried to make in his head. Kal *had* to get this message and it would not get through like this. He had to try something else.

'Wait,' he told the eagle. *'Please wait!'* And hoped that it would.

Owl dived back to Itmis' bedroom. There wasn't time to write anything; in any case he didn't know *how* to write and guessed it was not something you could teach yourself in a panicked half minute. Owl grabbed the yellow note and the least crumpled of the sheets strewn under the desk. Then he gave the rest of the paper pile a small shove and it toppled

230

onto the floor in a storm. He hoped Itmis would assume that the note was somewhere on the floor with the other rubbish.

He ran back into the living room and dragged one of the chairs across the floor into the kitchen. The eagle was still there, showing no sign of taking off. Standing on tiptoe Owl reached the handle that opened the skylight. With his whole weight almost hanging from it, he got it to turn. The skylight opened wide and the eagle poked in its head though the narrow gap. Its yellow eyes blazed again it made a series of high-pitched chittering sounds like the working of a creaky hinge.

Owl spread the yellow message inside the larger sheet of paper and, very carefully, folded them together into one shape.

One summer season when the circus had spent a month in a field outside Pokov City, Kobret had engaged a young man who performed with trained green crickets. He made them paper darts which the crickets piloted all over the Big Top. Owl had loved it, but the audience were not so sure; it was clear that the man was a Listener because how could anyone *train* an insect? In the capital, Listeners were falling out of favour, so at the end of the summer the boy and his insects had vanished. But not before he taught Owl to make very good paper darts.

It was the best dart Owl had ever made; fast and accurate.

Owl stared into the eagle's eyes, like looking straight at the sun, and willed it to understand what he told it.

Take this to your mistress, Owl told it. *Take it now. It's really important.*

Then he aimed the paper dart up at the skylight. It flew true and straight up through the open skylight, sailing past the watching bird into the air beyond. The eagle's foot flashed out and grabbed the dart, then its wings spread, and it flapped away.

22

Skrimsli

The Pirate Princess

 Kobret's cub smelled bad. Skrimsli's nose prickled with the rankness as he looked up to where Itmis stood, at the barred roof light of his cell. There was a new tone in his voice too, like a sinew stretched to breaking. A sickness was in him. Skrimsli hoped it would prove fatal.

'No more play fighting now, Stripy,' the man said. 'You'll be up against a real opponent. Not a stupid beast like you. A human. A pirate princess. And *she'll be the end of you.*'

The cub heard the hate, the triumph, the desire for revenge in the voice but the exact meaning of the words floated past, off into the chilly, night air.

I will kill you, Kobret's cub, Skrimsli thought.

He imagined leaping up, flying though the bars and straight at Itmis' throat.

The satisfaction of it distracted Skrimsli from the thought that, in all this time, he had not found a way to get out of this terrible place.

As he trotted down the tunnel to the pit, he could hear that the crowd was larger than the night before. More noisy too. Skrimsli's nose wrinkled at the smell of them. Blood.

233

Blood. Blood. That's what they wanted. Skrimsli hated them for it.

The gate to the pit slid open and he stepped into the bright, white light. He glanced up. There was Itmis with Owl beside him. The boy was always nervous when Skrimsli entered the pit, but now he was terrified; even at this distance Skrimsli sensed the child's attempt to reach out to him, to warn him. What was going on?

A sudden rush of air, then searing pain! The crowd erupted in a roar that was deafening. Blood. Skrimsli was hurt. A wound to the outside of the left upper leg. His body leapt to high alert, sweeping the pain aside, delivering information and dictating his response. In less than a second, he had taken in this new, unexpected opponent: not the red ape or one of the gorillas or a bear, but a human female. She was square and solid, well-muscled, and her stance showed that her balance was excellent. Like all humans she lacked the inbuilt weaponry of teeth and claws, but she had a metal tooth and she had thrown it at him. The dagger stuck out of Skrimsli's body, he grasped it in his teeth and flung it out of reach. She had another weapon, a long, curved blade that she gripped in her left hand.

There was no time to wonder what it was that made her fight; no time to wonder if she might have a mind that was open to his reaching thoughts; time only for surviving her fierce assault. She rushed towards him, her sword raised, fearless. Her intent was real and obvious: she meant to kill him. Skrimsli felt his body arm itself still further, hardening muscles, sharpening senses, speeding up thoughts and reactions.

Her reach with her sword would be longer than the reach

234

of his paws. If he leapt at her, she would have time to place her sword and make it bite him, fatally. She was fast, as her current pursuit showed, and he could not stay out of reach of her sword indefinitely. He could try to get close, so close that using her sword would be awkward. But humans were clever with their hands, so that was too risky. He needed to separate her from the sword; without it, she was no threat.

To do that, Skrimsli would have to risk being within the perfect striking range. Even only a fraction of a second could prove fatal. First, he needed to know more about this fighter. How fast could she move and turn? Were there any weaknesses he could exploit?

She was close now: still running hard, and roaring. He stood head on, presenting the smallest target, and looked at her. She was well protected; her clothes looked tough and would probably resist his claws once, perhaps twice. Her run was springy, suggesting a good ability to manoeuvre and leap. She was not large for a human but adult he guessed, or nearly so. Perhaps like him, an almost full-grown cub. She held the sword in her left hand so if he came at her from that side, she would have to reposition to make a strike.

Closer still now. Close enough to smell and yet she smelled of very little except – what was that word that Owl had used? *Ocean,* she smelled of *ocean!* How did a human smell of a water that stretched as far as the eye could see?

That was close enough! Deftly, giving no hint in his body or his eyes that he was about to do it, Skrimsli jinked to his right, so the left arm and the sword lunged past him. She was close enough to touch. He tapped her moving left foot with his right paw, and stepped back to give her space to fall, ready to jump on her and pin her to the ground. But she barely stumbled. Her balance was marvellous. She swivelled on her right foot and wheeled around, at the same time thrusting upward with the sword. Skrimsli threw back his head and swatted under her raised arm with his left paw. The leather of her jerkin split into three long slashes, and she gasped. Still, she didn't miss a step and Skrimsli had to leap aside to avoid the downward slice of her weapon.

They stepped back from each other, circling and watching, their breath billowing into the cold air. This was indeed a real fight. The possibility of death stood very, very close. Skrimsli had thought that the weeks of wrestling with the other creatures had taught him how to fight. Now he knew he had not learned nearly enough. But just as he had trusted his instincts to find rabbits in the snowy forest, he felt his deep tiger-self take over. He growled.

The sound of the roaring crowd was somewhere very far away. All that existed in the world was the sharp experience of his own body, the zing of every sense, the awareness of how his shape and size and movement met the ground and air. And this human, intent and purposeful.

She stepped from side to side, transferring her weight from foot to foot. She was bleeding where his claws had reached the skin beneath the leather, but she took no more notice of it than he took of the wound she had inflicted with the throwing dagger. Her hair was pale, her eyes too, and there was a long scar under her chin; a bad cut that would have been. Once more that smell that made his paws tingle: *ocean*. It was distracting him. Or was it something else, something entering a corner of his mind, creeping in?

The millisecond of distraction almost cost his life. She had crossed the space between them, and her sword was moving through the last few inches, its point aimed at his chest. Skrimsli folded close to the ground and pushed himself forward in a low lunge that she clearly had not foreseen he could execute. He hit her legs hard and sent her plunging headfirst onto the ground. She did not lose the grip on her sword but that didn't matter now because Skrimsli had twisted, tail swirling, to stand on her back. His back legs pinned her thighs, and his front legs pressed her upper arms and shoulders into the ground. He turned his head a little so as to be able to get the whole of the back of her neck and base of her skull between his jaws. His canines would cut the vital channels from head to body. She would be dead in moments.

Stop!

She stepped openly into his mind, out from the corner where, he realised, she had been lurking.

No.

He pushed her thought aside and then saw that he too stood in this inside-head space. It was shared, the way he shared a space with Owl! Curious.

Stop, she said again, appearing bigger, brighter, older than the figure prone now beneath his paws.

Why? Skrimsli demanded.

She was surprised.

You have words! she exclaimed.

Irritated, Skrimsli started to close his jaws.

Please. Please, she said.

He let go a little.

Yes. I have words. Many words. What words do you want? he said.

Words that tell me why you want to kill me? she replied.

Because you want to kill me! Skrimsli told her, although that was quite obvious. He knew humans sometimes needed to put obvious things into words.

I do not, she said.

You do!

That was ridiculous. She had thrown a dagger at him before he'd even looked at her. She wriggled underneath him, and he pressed her flat.

Not now I know you have words, she said.

That made Skrimsli angry. She was just like the roaring crowd for whom anything not human had no value.

Because words make me human?

That is not what I meant, she said.

Then use better words, Skrimsli snapped. She lay still, thinking. Skrimsli waited, curious.

We are prisoners, both, yes? she said.

Yes. Skrimsli agreed.

Then let us try to work together to get out.

Skrimsli considered this. It was just the proposition which he had presented to Silverback and the others. And a human collaborator *was* what he needed, what they *all* needed to escape. But could she be trusted, this human that didn't smell like a human?

Why do you smell of ocean? he asked her.

Because I am a seafarer, she replied. But those words meant nothing to the cub.

What is seafarer? Skrimsli did not expect the reply she gave, or how it would tingle and sing in his mind.

238

I live on the ocean, she said. *In a ship … like this.*

And she gave him a ship: its picture glowed in Skrimsli's mind; a shape like half a fish, but with giant white wings moving over endless blue. Like the things he had seen moving upon and down the river but so much bigger, so much more thrilling. Skrimsli's mind fizzed, like the bubbles in the cauldron of a waterfall. His whole being lost itself for a moment in that 'ship', that 'blue'. Then the woman did what Owl did when he was very happy, or playing: she laughed.

You have never seen a ship or the sea and yet I feel you love them. That is strange! You are a strange being, tiger, very strange!

She pushed him off her back and he let her. They sat staring at each other inside and outside.

I am Ekar, she said.

And I am Skrimsli, said Skrimsli.

But their introduction was interrupted. Around them the booing of the crowd rose to a horrible crescendo.

Kill, kill, kill.

Two doors into the pit opened with their unmistakable scrape. Two more humans entered. Two men, not tall but broad and muscled: one old, one young. The younger one carried a short sword and a dagger, like the one the woman had thrown away; the older one carried an axe.

'We have come to kill you, Ekar!' the older one cried. 'We have come to finish the job we began!'

'I should have killed you and thrown you into the sea with your mother,' said the younger one.

'I'm going to have a stripy coat to keep the wind off my back,' the old one added.

They showed their white teeth, in that thing that humans did, that smile thing that could mean something good or something bad.

Quicker than a single thought in either of their minds Skrimsli and Ekar shared useful knowledge.

They would work together to defeat these men. Skrimsli would take the old one, who had a small weakness in his right leg and smelled of great fear in spite of his big voice; Ekar would take the younger one because, of the two, he made her angriest.

The only outcome could be two deaths, their own or the men's.

Once again, Ekar was fearless. In his short life, Skrimsli had smelled human fear often and knew it well, but Ekar carried not the slightest trace of it. Even her anger vanished as she began to fight. Her thoughts lined up, just like the pebble-thoughts that Skrimsli moved around in the stillest place inside himself. She made him curious.

But now, he must fight. *Really* fight. Think fast, move faster and do the greatest damage possible whenever he could. He put Ekar and everything to one side to confront this man, dark-haired, squat, and quick eyed. The right arm better muscled than the left. The right leg also. The axe was heavy. He would swing it with great force. Any blow that struck Skrimsli could be the end.

They wheeled round each other. The man's fear was now a little less. What did this man see? An *animal,* that's what he saw. Something less than himself. An animal not full grown, stupid with inexperience, stupid with *not being human.* A beast, easy to outwit, easy to kill.

Well then, Skrimsli would be what he expected. He loosened his body, took the fire from his eyes. Stared at the man dull, slow. Opened his mouth and panted. Stopped moving and allowed the man to get a little closer. Waited. One heartbeat. Two. The man licked his lips, shifted the grip on his axe. Skrimsli turned his head very slightly, as if his attention had wandered to where Ekar was fighting her battle.

That was all the man needed to trigger his assault. Sure of success, he leapt towards Skrimsli. He swung the axe with terrible force and power. If Skrimsli had allowed it to go where the man intended, it would have all but sliced off his head.

But he did not allow that. At the last possible moment, when the man was completely committed to the move, braced for the impact on the solid body of a tiger, Skrimsli shifted. It was only a small movement, but fast and precisely timed. Just enough to make the man miss. He wasn't light on his feet like Ekar, and he had been so sure that his blow would hit the mark. His entire weight and the force of the leap and missed blow was channelled into his leading leg, his right, where the weakness was. Skrimsli hardly needed to tap him with a heavy paw to bring him down. Sprawled and helpless, he was quick to kill.

Ekar was doing well with the other. But he had struck a blow. She now had a head wound that was pulsing blood down the side of her face. Why did that make Skrimsli so very angry? He didn't stop to think. The man had forgotten there were two opponents in this fight, and Ekar, clever Ekar, didn't let her eyes betray that she had seen his swift approach. Perhaps he saw Skrimsli's reflection in her eyes though because he turned a little, just at the end. It was the last thing that he saw.

Skrimsli and Ekar stood side by side as all the humans in the amphitheatre rose to their feet bellowing and clapping.

Skrimsli looked up. He could just see the twisted expression on Itmis' face. He heard the man roar a command and Owl raised his two small hands to cover his face. Skrimsli looked at Ekar and for the first time he saw she was afraid. Then another door into the pit opened. Four men, dressed in metal armour, with long spears and curved swords ran towards them over the bloodied floor of the amphitheatre.

Now, thought Skrimsli, *I am going to be killed.*

23
Kal

The Bird at the Gate

The arrival of the pirate crew was stretching Itmis' helpers to their limits. Not long after Spanner had come on watch, Rusty had returned to shake the dozing Spanner awake.

'Wake up, you old idiot,' Rusty cried. 'We need help with them pirates!'

'Can't leave these without a guard,' Spanner exclaimed.

'Don't fuss!' Rusty scolded. 'Boss says he'll send someone else up here. Come *on!*'

'Alright, alright,' Spanner grumbled. 'Thought you said they was just "decent seafarers"!'

'Ice-ship crew or pirates? What does it matter?' Rusty snapped back. 'We need help to get their captain into a cell. She fights like four men!'

'Oh, does she now?' Spanner chuckled. 'Then she'll be a match for that tiger.'

'We'll find out soon enough!' Rusty replied. 'They're putting her in the pit with him *tonight.*'

If the pirate crew were going to create chaos as the Palatine hoped, then they might do it tonight. In any case Skrimsli could not be expected to survive a fight with well-armed humans. They needed an escape plan fast.

Itmis had been in no hurry to send a replacement guard. Kal and the Palatine used the time to talk without having to whisper and to come up with a plan. It was a bit vague and still unfinished. And, as it stood, their plan would only get them as far as the corridor outside their cells. They needed information that only Sayka could provide.

'I asked him to look at this building so I can see the layout through his eyes, to watch what the guards do! And I asked him to find Owl,' the Palatine said. 'But he has been living the life of a wild bird for weeks now. His head is full of wind and sky… I hope our bond is still strong enough for him to do what I ask.'

The Palatine looked to the sky; there had been no sign of the bird for hours. Kal decided that a vague plan was better than none at all. With a splinter of wood from the bed slats Kal chipped at the soft mortar between the stones around the door of the cell. It was a soft as pastry and fell away easily to make grooves into which toes and fingers could be fitted: essential for the working of the first part of their plan.

It was already late afternoon. Time was running out. They needed Sayka to come back before the guard returned. Where was he? Where was the Palatine's opportunity in this uncertainty, Kal wondered.

Then, without any warning, there was the shushing of wings against stone, the scraping of talons and the eagle arrived. It must be clinging to the sill of the window, more than fifteen feet above the floor of the cell where the Palatine stood. Close enough for ordinary mind-to-mind communication but not close enough to share the detailed layout of the amphitheatre that they would need for their escape. They needed to be much closer together for that. But before Kal could worry further, the sounds of wood scraping on stone, and the gasps of huge physical exertion showed that the Palatine had found a solution: she had wrenched her bed from its fixings and upended it to provide a ladder to bring her close to where Sayka clung. Only the edge of a folded wing showed through the window of Kal's cell, but Kal could hear the Palatine's voice talking gently to the bird, calming its cries, renewing their bond.

The door at the end of the corridor outside the cells banged open and heavy boots rang on the stone floor. Their guard was back! He would look into the Palatine's cell and see her perched high on the wall talking to an eagle. Who knew what extra security measures *that* might trigger? Plus, the Palatine needed more time to find whatever was in Sayka's mind.

There wasn't time to think of anything clever. The first idea would just have to work. Kal shoved the fallen mortar under the bed and began to sing. It was an Erem song about their troublesome greedy neighbours, the Nordskys. It was bound to make the guard cross. Besides the guards were always telling them to be silent: *no talking, no whispering, no noise of any kind.* Certainly never singing! The guard cursed and slid back the door of the grill with a bang.

'Shuddup, you trash!'

It was the one they called Moley, because of the black mole on the end of his nose. He was especially stupid and free with his fists. But a beating was worth it, if it bought the Palatine a little more time to see the map that they hoped was in the eagle's brain. Kal sang on.

'Shuudup!' Moley snarled. 'Or I'll make yer!'

The key slid in the lock, the bolts were pulled back, Kal was braced for the blows that would follow, but then the Palatine joined in. The eagle must have left! Now Moley couldn't decide who he was going to hit first. Kal heard him slide back the grill on the Palatine's door. At once she fell silent, and Kal followed suit.

Grumbling, Moley sank into the chair outside their doors. It groaned and creaked under his weight. Kal knew what came next. Moley would unpack the meal he always brought with him, spend a long time eating it, making about as much noise as a pig at a trough. And then he would take a little nap. Sleeping on the job was the special talent of Itmis' employees.

The Palatine's voice came through the stone at the lowest possible volume but packed with information.

'Luja and Zait are here. In Otok!' the Palatine told Kal. 'They are living in a field outside the town, waiting to come and get us!'

Kal could hardly believe it. They could only conclude that the eagle had tracked their path even after they were captured and guided the horses here. There had been no need to doubt Sayka's devotion! The bird had been circling the amphitheatre for days searching for a sign of his mistress. What was more, Sayka had seen not only the layout of the amphitheatre, but the routines of Itmis, his guards, and of the spectators and fighters in the pit. Now the Palatine had all that information.

She described it as best she could. As the map of the amphitheatre began to form, so the sense of confinement rolled back. For the first time, real hope lit Kal's mind like a wavering candle.

The amphitheatre was one big, round building. At its centre was the 'pit' where every night Skrimsli and the other creatures had to fight for the amusement of the human audience. Around the pit were tiered circles of seating, reached by two stone staircases which ran from inside the outer walls. Leading from the pit were sloping tunnels, that led to a network of cells in which the animals, and now people, were held. These could be opened and closed to allow different combinations of fighters into the pit. The levers to control these doors were on the wall beside the ringmaster's platform above the pit, where Itmis stood for performances. But there was another door, one that opened from the pit onto a staircase that ran into the seating tiers. The lever that opened it wasn't under Itmis' control during performances. It was set into the wall on the opposite side of the amphitheatre, above the highest tier of the seats.

'It's just the other side of that corridor, outside our cell doors!' the Palatine explained. 'In the open air! Not protected at all. Once we're out of the cells we can get to it and release the tiger and the others. Once they get in among the audience people will panic and rush for the front entrance while we make for the back door!'

'Is there a way we can get a message to Skrimsli?' Kal asked. 'So he knows what's going to happen?'

The Palatine shook her head. 'The doors to those cells are under cover, and their windows are on a walkway that's patrolled by guards.'

Kal frowned. Skrimsli was clever and tough; he'd proved that by surviving this far.

You just have to live long enough for us to get that door open, Tiger, Kal thought.

They already knew about the back door into the street, down the stairs at the other end of the corridor outside their cells. Sayka's eyes showed that was their only route out while the audience flooded out through the front.

'That's where I'll go to defend our exit,' said the Palatine.

'What about Owl?' asked Kal.

'He will be with Itmis, on the platform above the pit. I've told Sayka to snatch him up from there.'

'Did Owl send a message?' Kal asked.

The Palatine paused. 'He did,' she said slowly. 'Here!'

The Palatine poked a strip of yellow paper through the hole. Kal read it and felt an icy hand of fear reaching out.

'He must have found it in Itmis' apartment,' the Palatine said.

'When did it come?'

'I don't know but it must be why Itmis has brought his plans for the tiger-human fight forward to tonight. He wants to make as much money as possible before the twins arrive, and he has to wind things up.'

'Before they kill him,' Kal replied.

'Yes,' agreed the Palatine, 'but he doesn't know that. He still thinks he's a partner.'

'He does,' Kal agreed. 'But the twins won't risk a fight. They'll kill him and the rest of us while we sleep. They'll sneak in at dead of night.'

'Yes, you are right,' the Palatine said. 'Tonight perhaps, after midnight?'

'We'll all be long gone by then,' Kal said.

'Ah,' the Palatine breathed, 'that's the Kal I want to hear!'

There was nothing left to discuss. In any case Moley livened

248

up after his tea-time nap, and was poking his big, spotty nose against the grill to spy on them every few minutes. All they could do was wait. Kal lay on the bed and felt for the loose slat that lay under the sacking. Quiet, patient rubbing on the stone floor had sharpened it to a point, hard enough to be a weapon.

As darkness fell the crowds began to arrive. It was nearly time. Their plan was a series of actions, like steps in a dance one leading on to the next. Kal's was the first step of all. The rehearsal of this step went round and round in Kal's head.

Would it work? Could it work? And if it did, what about the steps that followed? What if Sayka couldn't snatch Owl? What if Skrimsli didn't get out of the pit? What if the pirate princess had already killed him? What if Kal couldn't remember the fighting drills that the Palatine had tried so hard to teach?

Kal's jaw clenched tight. Focus. Concentrate.

I'm coming, Havvity, Kal told the night. *I'm going to do the right thing this time, no matter what, no matter how scared it makes me.*

The sounds from outside signalled that the audience had settled down, ready for the performance to begin. It was time for the first step. Kal tucked the makeshift wooden dagger under one arm and climbed the footholds in the wall, to cling just above the door frame. It was a position that couldn't be sustained for long. Outside Itmis' voice boomed, announcing the fight, the words blurred and distorted to a slur of sound.

Now? Kal thought. *Now!*

Kal began to scream. The sound bounced and echoed off the stone walls so loud that Moley couldn't ignore it. Even so it seemed an age before the guard reacted. Kal's fingers sang with pain as they struggled to maintain their grip on the crumbling stonework. This time Moley didn't shout a threat but opened the door and came barging through. It was clear he didn't think the smaller, slighter of the two inmates could be any trouble to him at all. So when Kal dropped onto his back, and shoved the point of the stick against his fat neck, he squealed like a frightened piglet. His knees simply gave way underneath him, and he hit the floor like a sack of grain, begging, 'Don't hurt me!'

Kal was glad the Palatine couldn't see because all the elegant moves that she had been teaching were gone from Kal's head. Moley was down and he was going to stay down. Kal whacked him on the head with the wooden bed slat. The slat snapped in two, but the man slumped and then lay still. A strip of blanket made a good rope for his hands and Moley's own greasy bandana made a great gag. Kal dragged the heavy body into the corner, put the bucket over his head and covered him with the sacking mattress. He wouldn't be crying for help when he came round.

Trembling slightly, Kal took Moley's keys, the heavy cudgel and the dagger that he carried. His leather jerkin was too big and stank, but with his belt wrapped around twice, and his hat pulled low it made a good enough disguise. Kal locked him in the cell and opened the cell next door. The Palatine stepped through the door. Kal hadn't seen anything of her but the slice of face visible though the stone gap, for weeks. She was thin, gaunt and dirty, but here she stood, every inch a warrior queen. Kal handed her the dagger. 'Here, you'll need this.'

The Palatine was stern and professional. They didn't greet

each other or even touch, and there were no smiles about their first successful step, just a curt, soldierly, 'Well done.'

Kal was glad of it. Any warmth right now would have melted Kal to a jelly. The Palatine's cool calm helped to keep Kal's fears at bay. And the next steps of the plan were much more risky.

Another coat and another, larger dagger hung on a hook on the wall. The Palatine took them and gave Kal back the smaller of the two weapons. Kal recoiled but the Palatine gave a stern look

'Useful and ready,' she reminded Kal. 'Take it!' It wasn't a request.

Now they both looked less like prisoners and more like second-rate guards. They would fit right in with Itmis' workers, Kal thought.

They stood now in the stone corridor outside the two cells, with a heavy door at either end. The door to the left lead out onto the walkway above the top tier of audience seating. Halfway along it was the lever that would release Skrimsli from the pit and let him into the audience. If only there had been a way to warn him. It was too late to think of that now. The other door opened onto a narrow stone staircase, down to the rear exit. Who would go through which door had been the subject of much whispered discussion? The final decision had hinged on size and fighting ability. One door led to a task requiring quickness and stealth, the other to something more uncertain: at best a boring wait, at worst a pitched battle.

There was no way of knowing which of the keys on the ring fitted each door. Kal had to try every one for the door to the staircase until its stiff lock yielded to the last key. The door to the walkway at the other end unlocked easily with the third key they tried.

The Palatine took the keys back.

'Let's hope one of these opens the rear door!' she said. Her hand rested on Kal's for a moment, only the slightest tremor betraying the fear that she too was holding back.

'Throw the lever and get out,' she told Kal. 'Sayka can guide us through the streets once he's snatched Owl.'

They both knew this plan but saying it out loud one more time made it feel more possible. All the same, Kal's voice could not be trusted. Just a short nod marked their parting, then the Palatine was gone down the corridor and through the door.

On the other side of Kal's door the crowd were roaring. There was no more time; a sword could end poor Skrimsli's life at any moment. Now, thought Kal. Now! With a lurch of the heart, Kal pushed the heavy door open.

For the first time the reality of the layout relayed through Sayka's eyes was visible. The four tiers of seats that circled the amphitheatre held hundreds and hundreds of people and, in the very centre of the circle opposite where Kal now stood, Itmis Majak was in his ringmaster's box with Owl cowering beside him. He was not looking at Kal. No one was. The whole crowd were on their feet, screaming, arms in the air. People were throwing money down into the brightly lit pit, as if into a pool, and shouting, *Kill, kill, kill.*

Whatever was going on there was bad. Skrimsli needed an escape route very soon!

Kal stole along in the shadows. Just ahead, a short flight of steps led up to the big lever sticking out of the wall. It was just as Sayka had seen it, just as the Palatine had described, except for one thing: it was guarded by a huge man who carried an enormous, toothed cudgel. He was completely absorbed in peering down into the pit, but he was too close to the lever to give Kal any hope of reaching it without being seen.

Kal thought of the fighting drills and of the guard dropping so obligingly to the floor of the cell after a bit of a slap with a wooden slat. None of that would work on this man, who looked like a cross between a barn door and an ox. Sometimes Kal had got very close to wild birds by moving so slowly and carefully they didn't register the motion. So now Kal edged up the stairs, still in the shadows, inch by inch. The guard stared down into the pit; he hadn't noticed the human shape creeping closer. From this new position on the top of the lever platform the action in the pit was visible: Skrimsli and a woman were trying to fight off four armed men. They were both wounded but they were working together! It was clear they couldn't hold out a moment longer. The door that led from the pit into the audience was behind them. If Kal could open it now, it might just save them. *Now or never*, Kal thought.

One last lurch upwards almost did it. The lever was at Kal's fingertips when the guard finally caught the movement at the edge of his eye. He spun like a spark and pinned Kal against the wall, feet dangling, throat almost crushed by his massive hands.

'What are you doing?'

Kal spluttered and coughed, fighting to breathe. Down in the pit the fighters were closing in; it was all over for Skrimsli and the pirate and there was nothing Kal could do to stop it.

Over on the other side of the pit, on his high perch, Itmis' face was lit with malice and triumph. Like the rest of the audience, he raised his arms above his head to celebrate the bloody victory of the armed men over the tiger and the woman.

And as he did so, he let go of the chain attached to Owl's iron collar. Through the black spots of looming unconsciousness Kal saw Owl dart sideways to reach the panel where a forest of levers controlling the gates from the cells into the pit stood out from the wall. In a second, he had thrown them all! Immediately a huge snow bear and a grizzly – Karu – two gorillas, a red ape and several humans rushed out. The four armed men swung round, dismayed, suddenly outnumbered.

But they were all still trapped in the pit unless Kal could reach *this* lever. Kal struggled but the man was intent on cutting off all life and air.

Then came a rush of air, sudden as a punch, and Sayka's talons thumped into the guard's head, knocking him sideways. He released his grip and Kal slid, gasping, to the floor while man and eagle tumbled from the platform struggling in a tangle of wings and limbs. It took all Kal's weight to move the stiff mechanism of the huge lever but, with a groan and deep clanking, the door from the pit into the audience opened.

The snow bear was the first to run through it up into the first tier of audience seats. For a split second the voice of the crowd died from frenzied bloodlust to stunned silence. Then a wave of panic erupted, and terrified screaming broke out as the audience scrabbled and ran to escape. Every creature – animal or human – that had been caged was now free and running among the fleeing crowd.

This was exactly the chaos that the Palatine had hoped for. Hundreds of people surging in one direction, back towards the main entrance, sweeping all the guards with them, while the captives made their escape.

But what about the plan for Sayka to snatch Owl from Itmis' clutches? Kal looked around. The huge guard lay still in an impressive pool of blood. But the eagle sat beside him making a distressed cheeping, looking at its own left wing which hung limp and broken at its side. Over the top of the screaming crowd Kal could see Itmis dragging Owl up the stairs from the ringmaster's platform to the door of the apartment above the main entrance. A second later and the door had slammed behind them.

Kal scooped up the bird and stood against the wall as the chaos of fleeing audience streamed by. Now what? It might be possible to get into the apartment and rescue Owl but not with a large bird tucked under one arm. Sayka was the Palatine's oldest friend; he could not simply be abandoned.

Skrimsli, followed by a large red ape and the lumbering form of Karu the bear, burst through the fleeing humans and bounded up to where Kal stood, clutching the broken bird.

Skrimsli burst into Kal's mind. *Where is Owl?*

Kal was stunned. A tiger in the mind and speaking! Kal wasn't sure how to reply, but just thinking seemed to work.

But I am not a listener, was all Kal could manage.

No, but I can speak here, Skrimsli responded, a little irritated. *Where is Owl? Where is Owl?*

Skrimsli had grown bigger and stronger since they had been in the circus together. The growl that accompanied the repeat of his question was impressive.

On the other side of the building, Kal answered. *I just saw Itmis take him in there.*

Kal pointed to where the outline of a skylight showed in the roof.

The eagle can get him? Skrimsli asked.

No. Its wing is broken, Kal said.

Then you and I will go to him, said Skrimsli.

Skrimsli was no longer the playful cub. He was serious and his air of command reminded Kal of the Palatine.

Skrimsli, there is a back door, Kal told him. *Through there, past the cells, down the stairs.*

How easy this kind of communication was!

Good. Karu and the ape will go there, the tiger replied.

Skrimsli and the ape looked at each other and something passed between their eyes. Then the ape's long arm reached out and took the eagle from Kal. In a whispery, breathy, smack of lips the ape spoke, not inside Kal's head, but with real words and a soft voice that Kal heard with outside ears.

'Bird safe with me,' she said. Very gently she put the long fingers of one hand over Sayka's head, covering his eyes, just like the hood that the Palatine used. Instantly the bird was at rest.

'There,' she said. 'Sleep!'

She walked away on two legs with the eagle wrapped tenderly in her long arms and Karu lumbering after.

Kal looked towards the apartment where Owl was held. They couldn't reach the staircase that led there from the ringmaster's platform, nor the door that lay on the far side of the main entrance hall. There were still too many people in the way, and perhaps guards unseen in the shadows. The only way in was along the top of the outer wall and through the skylight.

Skrimsli must have had the same thought.

Up, he said. *Up. Now!*

He bunched himself like a coiled spring and in one move was on the parapet. Kal scrambled up behind him and a second later a pair of hands appeared on the top of the wall. A young woman with pale eyes pulled herself up beside them. She was covered in blood but smiling. This must be the pirate princess herself.

'Where are you two going?' she asked.

This is Ekar, Skrimsli said. *She is a good fighter. She comes with us to help.*

Ekar nodded as if she too heard Skrimsli's remark.

'You have weapons!' she commented, glancing at the knife and cudgel in Kal's belt.

'Weapons, yes', Kal replied. 'But skill in using them, not so much.'

'Well, you look useful enough to me!' Ekar said.

They walked in line: Skrimsli in front, then Kal, with Ekar at the rear. The top of the parapet was narrower than a human foot and a fall to either side would be fatal. At least that part was easy. Kal was used to standing on the backs of galloping horses. Up here they were very exposed. Silhouetted against the sky, they would be easy targets for anyone with a rifle or a bow, especially now that the chaos inside the amphitheatre was dying down.

As they drew close to the glass of the skylight, a shot rang out.

Down! Skrimsli warned and Kal dropped, belly to the narrow wall.

Another bullet zipped over their heads and a mad, unmistakable voice boomed out: Itmis Majak.

'Sitting ducks is the expression, I believe,' he yelled. 'I'll pick you off one by one.'

Another shot hissed by.

'He is a terrible shot!' Ekar remarked. Kal glanced round at her. Not *so* terrible, it seemed, Ekar was pressed low on the top of the parapet too!

'With enough bullets he'll still hit us!' Kal said. Now Kal's eyes had adjusted to the low light, Itmis could be seen standing at the open skylight with a rifle. He was balanced on top of something. He didn't look very stable.

One push. He will fall, Skrimsli said.

'I think I can hit him with a knife from here,' said Ekar.

Good. Then I will move with Kal.

Another shot. Far too close this time, spitting shards of stone from the wall just below Kal's chest. Another manic laugh.

'Get ready!' Ekar whispered. 'Now!'

With one spring she was on her feet and had thrown the dagger. Kal, with Skrimsli right behind, sprang forward to follow the dagger with a close attack.

But in the dark, Ekar's throw had gone awry. It smashed the glass next to Itmis. It was enough to distract him for a moment, but not to stop another shot. They could see the grin on the man's face and the gleam of sweat on his brow.

'Die, Stripy! Die!' he yelled as he took aim. Even Itmis' terrible shooting couldn't fail to hit a large orange target at such short range.

Then the light behind the skylight snapped on. Blinded by the brightness, Itmis could no longer see out into the dark to take his shot. He began to wobble, then he shouted and disappeared from the window with a crash. Kal and Skrimsli rushed forward and peered through the shattered window down into the room below. Itmis lay insensible next to a toppled ladder and among a sea of broken plates.

Beside him a small, pale face appeared.

'Hello!' said Owl. 'Hello!'

24
Owl

Leader of the Pack

Kal ran along the top of the wall, dark hair swaying. The pirate princess, Ekar, was in front and already almost at the other side of the amphitheatre.

Skrimsli was right behind. Owl could feel the cub's warm breath on his neck as he placed one faltering foot in front of the other along the top of the wall.

Not look down, Skrimsli counselled. *I am here.*

So Owl did not look down and kept putting one foot in front of the other.

Inside, Owl was shaking. The last few minutes had been an exploded blur of actions and events, ending with Itmis lying on the scullery floor. There was no triumph for Owl in that; pushing the ladder and causing the man to fall had been terrifying.

I had to do it, Owl told himself. *He would have killed the cub.*

It was true, Owl knew, but he did not want to be a murderer, even if the victim was Itmis Majak.

He was still breathing, wasn't he? Owl asked himself.

Skrimsli however was impressed.

You opened the doors to the pit? he asked as they moved along the parapet.

Yes, Owl replied.

And you made Kobret's cub fall?

Yes.

Skrimsli's purr conveyed both praise and pride.

They'd reached the other side of the amphitheatre now and climbed down from the wall. All the lights had gone out and, below where they stood, the pit and the seating tiers were a pool of silent darkness. There were still some shouts from outside where the crowd had dispersed into the street beyond the main door, but otherwise there was an odd quiet. There was no sight or sound from Ekar's crew or any of Skrimsli's fighters.

'I don't like this quiet,' said Ekar.

'Neither do I,' Kal agreed. 'Perhaps they are all waiting at the back door as we planned?'

'Perhaps.'

Skrimsli and Ekar moved forward, with Kal and Owl behind. With a small wring of the heart, Owl realised that Ekar and this new stern and grown-up Skrimsli were communicating in their heads. Owl knew it was not right to be jealous, so he tried not to be. He stood tall and tried to feel stern and grown-up too.

They stole through a door and along a corridor past two cell doors.

'This is where they kept us,' Kal whispered. Kal's shudder told Owl how long that time had seemed, longer even than his own grim service as Itmis' slave.

At the end of this corridor was another door and a stone staircase spiralling down. As quietly as possible, backs to the wall, they moved down the stairs into darkness. With every step, the silence seemed more and more sinister. Owl stared ahead imagining shapes looming in the blackness, a scream sitting in his throat ready to escape. Then came a slight sound, something soft and heavy shifting position slightly on the floor, and the warm hay smell of horse breath. Kal's hand caught Owl's shoulder and squeezed.

'Luja!' Kal whispered. 'Luja!'

A match was struck, and a lantern gleamed to life. Like a magic trick, the space that their minds had filled with threat, was suddenly full of friends: Karu and another brown bear; the two gorillas; the red ape; Ekar's crew – four burly humans, with varying amounts of blood on their clothes and faces; and a huge snow bear, whom Ekar introduced as Beart. Most amazing of all was Luja, standing with another horse.

He stood forehead to forehead with Kal.

'How did you get here, old friend? How?'

'I thought you'd drowned in the flood!' Owl cried and buried his face in the horse's side. Luja snuffled his nose into Owl's hair and immediately Owl was enveloped in the bubble of wellbeing which they had shared briefly on the journey to Shamanow. Owl understood at last that it had been Luja who had made that feeling. After the weeks of misery with Itmis, it was like having sunlight poured straight into his soul.

Luja whinnied softly as another horse stepped from the shadows at the back of the space. Beside him was a tall, stately woman, the one Itmis had called the Palatine of Yuderan. She made her way through the throng of introductions and greetings to Kal's side and for a moment the two of them were speechless, the air singing with unsaid words.

Kal said at last, 'Sayka saved my life! I'm so sorry he was hurt.'

The Palatine's face clouded. 'He may not fly again. But the red ape is caring for him. I must not think of him now.'

Owl saw her put her worry about the eagle aside as surely as if she'd put it in a sack. She turned to him and smiled.

'I have seen and heard much about you, Owl. All very good. I am pleased to meet you, even in these difficult times!'

'Owl, this is the Palatine of Yuderan,' Kal said. 'My friend.'

Owl was speechless. He never imagined he would meet a queen!

'Owl saved Skrimsli and Ekar,' Kal told her. 'He threw the levers that opened all the gates to the pit.'

'So I heard!' said the Palatine, with a small smile. Then she turned to Kal.

'Kal, I must speak to our company. I don't know what waits outside these doors. I fear the twins will be close by. But if there is fighting, stay with Luja and keep Owl close. Be safe!'

With that, she led her horse to the staircase, climbed the steps and stood looking over this strange group. She had a power about her that Owl found fascinating. It seemed to be working on everyone else too. Owl couldn't see how the Palatine had done it, but everyone fell silent and looked towards her.

'Friends, let me introduce myself. I am the Palatine of Yuderan, its rightful ruler, though my brother Yalen sits upon the throne. But I do not seek to be your ruler. We are one band, united by our struggle to be free. So far tonight, Madam

Ekar's crew, and Mr Skrimsli and his fighters have seen that Itmis' thugs will not give us further trouble.'

Smiles and nods passed around the ring of faces. Judging by the cuts and bruises, the battles hadn't been easy. The Palatine went on.

'But our escape is only just beginning. I do not know what will be waiting outside these doors, or where we should go. But whatever fate awaits us, we will face it together.'

Grim nods, grunts and snorts of assent sounded in the lamplit space. The Palatine had spoken with more than words and reached into every mind. Ekar stepped up beside the Palatine and Skrimsli stood beside her. Owl saw that they too both had some of the Palatine's power: they were leaders.

Our cub, Taze, Owl thought proudly. *Our cub.*

'My crew and I go to our ship,' Ekar announced. 'She is anchored in the West Town, beyond the Divider. But many of our shipmates are dead and we will need more crew to sail her. If you will be our crew, she will carry us all to freedom.'

How far would a ship take him from the forest, Owl wondered? There was no help for it; this was their only way out. He gave his agreement along with all the rest. Skrimsli looked at Ekar and his eyes glowed; for now, at least, circus and seafarers were one crew.

Skrimsli and Beart would go first through the rear exit, the stone archway that led out into the streets behind the amphitheatre, with Ekar to guide them.

'We are close to the edge of East Town here,' Ekar explained. 'A few narrow streets to traverse, no more. Then over the Divider, a mile or two. Our ship is anchored on the far side.'

'What is the Divider?' the Palatine asked.

'It is the ridge of rock that separates the river bend from the sea. It's not high but there it is full of deep cracks and fissures, treacherous at night and with plenty of opportunities for ambush. I know the safest path, but we will have to be wary.'

It was time to go. Kal boosted Owl up onto Luja's back. It felt like a very long way down.

'Don't worry, Owl,' said Kal, leaping up behind him. 'Luja and I won't let you fall.'

The lantern was doused and they all they stood in dark and silence. Owl reached for Skrimsli in his mind.

Good luck, take care, he told him. A short buzz of purring came in return and then the tiger was gone. Then they all rushed out through the stone arch into the night.

There was nothing to fight. The street was full of nothing but shadows and a faint misty drizzle. The only light was a faint shine from a distant streetlamp reflecting off the wet cobbles.

'This way,' Ekar said. 'With care!'

They skulked along a narrow alley. The sound of Luja and Zait's hooves and their whispered voices bounced eerily off the high, windowless walls on either side. Their breath made plumes in the cold air. Owl wound his hands nervously into Luja's mane. It seemed too quiet. They reached the end of the street. Voices, laughter and music came from a tavern on the corner. Lights went on in windows, curtains were calmly drawn. It was an ordinary night. No one seemed to care about escaping pirates and tigers on the loose. Perhaps that was just the kind of wildness that happened in Otok freeport every day.

They passed two other taverns, loud with drinkers, before the town petered out. The lights faded behind them and a path rose up the rocky curve of the Divider.

'Stay close,' Ekar called from the front. 'We don't want crew with broken ankles!'

The ragged cloud cleared, and the starlit sky gave enough light to see the landscape around them. The path wound through a maze of small ravines and cracks, perfect for falling into in the dark; some good for breaking ankles others big enough for crouching figures to hide in. Every step was nerve-wracking. Kal spoke quietly to Luja all the way and felt the warm pulse of the horse's kindness flowing back. They came to the top of the Divider and saw the gleam of the sea on the other side. Owl stared, letting the size of it sink into his eyes. He had heard of the ocean, but this was nothing like the vague blue picture in his mind. It was dark and glittering, alive, dangerous and wonderful. What would Skrimsli make of it, Owl wondered.

They couldn't stop to look at the view. They hurried down the final, smoother section of path. It seemed almost miraculous when they left the rocks and ravines behind and stepped out into the grey light of a streetlamp shining on the stone of the harbour. Low warehouses, stacks of crates and barrels covered the wharf, and all manner of craft were tied up, like so many tethered horses.

'There she is!' cried one of Ekar's crew. 'Our *Snow Gull!*'

At the far end of the harbour a large ship stood out against the sea and sky. She was so huge that she made the Ochre seem like a toy. The harbour was deserted. Surely, Owl thought, all the other boats had crew who would be coming and going at all hours of the day and night, just like those of the river boats he had got to know?

'It's too quiet!' whispered Kal. 'Much too quiet!'

The words were barely out of Kal's mouth before they heard fast-moving feet and the clash of metal. A ring of figures surrounded them, springing up from behind all the gear that dotted the harbourside. They were dressed in dark clothes and held weapons that looked like rifles. They looked grim and ready for a fight and they outnumbered the ship's new combined crew three to one. Among them were two more slight figures whose voices, when they spoke, were sharp and horribly familiar.

'There is no escape. You've walked into a trap. *Again*.'

It was Spion, the assassin! Listig's skinny outline appeared beside her sister. The whine in her voice had strengthened so she sounded even more like a grumpy child.

'You've caused us a lot of trouble! A *lot* of trouble. This is really *not* what we had planned. You were all supposed to be behind bars…'

'Shut up, Listig! Shut up!' Spion hissed. 'This is *exactly* what we planned. The capture of the Erem terrorist and the Palatine. We have no quarrel with the rest of you. Just hand them over and we'll let you go on your way!'

The light caught the barrel of her rifle as she lifted it to her shoulder and took aim.

There was a silence. Beart, the snow bear gave a deep cry and looked towards Ekar.

'Yes,' Ekar said quietly, 'we will all fight.'

'Fine talk, Madam!' Spion shouted. 'But if you all fight, we will kill you all!'

267

Kal cursed quietly, then slid from Luja's back.

'What are you doing?' the Palatine hissed.

'Giving them what they want,' Kal said softly. 'No one's going to die to save my skin.'

'Stay!' Ekar exclaimed. 'Fight.'

'I don't want to fight.' Kal turned to stare at Ekar. 'That's the point. And I won't have anyone doing my fighting for me.'

The Palatine held up a hand to Ekar and shook her head.

'They mean what they say,' she said. 'You are close to your ship. Without us, you can sail away in peace.' Then she too slid from her horse's back.

Skrimsli growled and looked at Ekar. What was passing between them? Owl couldn't tell. Were they hatching a plan? What plan could succeed when they were outnumbered by people with guns? Owl couldn't think but he could feel. And he felt that Kal and the Palatine giving themselves up was unbearable.

'Wait,' he called. 'I'm coming too!' and slithered down Luja's side, fell to the ground, picked himself up and began to walk behind them.

Spion laughed.

'We can kill you, little Freak, just as easily as the others,' she said. 'In fact, it would be my special pleasure after all the trouble you have caused.'

There was something even more than usually odd about Spion's laugh, Owl thought. It was as if it didn't even convince the assassin herself. He was closer now to the ring of thugs the assassins had brought with them. It was odd that only two or three of the assassins' force had raised their guns. The rest just stood there. Owl glanced over his shoulder, to see if anyone else had noticed this and saw that Ekar was walking forward, and Luja, in fact the whole company were expanding their circle to challenge the one that the assassins had created.

Listig laughed nervously. 'We are happy to kill as many of you as want to die!'

But the assassins' helpers were stepping backwards, and still showing no sign of raising their guns.

'Stop!' Spion shouted at them. 'Stop! That's far enough! We have them in the light now so we can see our targets better!'

Now that Owl was closer, he saw that many of what had looked like rifles from a distance were in fact just gun-shaped sticks. The dark uniforms were only dark sacks belted with black rope. At least half of the twins 'soldiers' were just a sham. Owl realised what must have happened: Listig and Spion had come to Otok alone, expecting to find an easy job: all their victims behind bars and Itmis fast asleep in bed. Murders they could easily perform unaided. But they'd found a different situation and had to recruit whatever help they could in a hurry and make it look better with pretend guns and uniforms.

Owl could see something else too, between the legs of the twins and their hopeless gang, the flash of eyes. First one pair, then two, then five, then ten, then many, many more. Out of the shadows, from between the barrels and boxes, a hoard of dogs had silently materialised. And at their head was the smallest she-wolf in the world, Blit! In the time since Owl and Skrimsli had been captive she must have been busy gathering this pack of the toughest street dogs she could find, all of them at least five or ten times her size. She stood, with two huge, scarred mastiffs on either side of her, and bared her teeth. Every other dog in the circle did the same. They were ready, all it would take now was for someone to make the first move.

Skrimsli was close to Owl now, and he slipped into their shared mind space.

Go to that building. Take the horse. Hide by the wall. Keep out of this fight, Skrimsli ordered. Owl had no intention of obeying. If Blit could fight, then so could he. But he wasn't given the choice. When Blit's dogs leapt forward to begin the battle, Luja caught Owl's coat in his teeth and carried him off. The circle of attackers had already been breached and Luja took the chance to run through it. Beside them the red ape ran too, clutching the sack with Sayka inside to her chest. They crouched together, as the fight exploded.

It was chaos. Blit's small form had vanished in the sea of bodies, but her pack had already brought down some of the twins' supporters. The twins themselves had been swiftly engulfed from two sides. Spion, ever the professional, kept her calm and used her rifle butt to send the first two dogs flying then turned around and fired multiple shots at another. The bullets struck sparks from the cobbles and skittered away, but one hit its mark and the dog fell. Spion was instantly engulfed in more angry dogs and couldn't reload.

The fighting was close contact. Paw and hand, tooth and claw and knife. It was hard to see exactly what was going on but the terrible sounds – screams, yelps, groans – made it clear just how much blood was being shed and how many bones broken. Luja trembled. Owl reached up to put his hand on the soft nose, and told him, 'It's alright, Luja, it's all right,' even though they both knew it wasn't.

270

The red ape was shaking too, although whether with fear or cold Owl didn't know. He knew these creatures came from warm forests and the loose tunic in which she was dressed could be no protection from the cold of this night.

He unwound the scarf from his neck and offered it to her. He was astonished when she spoke in a real voice – breathy and quiet but definitely not inside his head.

'Thank you,' she said. 'It is the fighting not the cold. Always with humans, this fighting.'

Her eyes were the saddest Owl had ever seen. He didn't know what to say to make excuses for his kind. He put his hand on her back and tried to make her feel its warmth, its comfort, and they stood together looking out at the mayhem that the twins had brought.

The fight surged on, messy and disorganised. Some of the twins' supporters fled at once, but others fought back fiercely, using their wooden 'rifles' as clubs and spears. The dogs were fearless, fast and clever. They tore at legs, ripped at arms and then, when fighters were down, fastened their jaws around necks. The sheer brute force of the bears was hard for anything to resist, their huge strength and size simply threw their opponents to one side or crushed them under foot. Skrimsli shot about like a deadly shadow; he barely seemed even to touch his victims and yet he brought them down. Most he allowed to escape, wounded and screaming, but any that really fought back, he did not. He seemed untouchable. Still Owl's heart was in his mouth, every moment fearing that the cub would be harmed.

Before Spion could use her rifle again, Beart the snow bear swiped at her with his huge paw; she ducked just enough to avoid its full force but was knocked to the ground. Beart leant down to crush her skull in his jaws, but as he did, Listig slipped a knife between the ribs of her human opponent and swirled round to face the bear. Somehow, she had recovered her rifle and reloaded it. At such short range she could not miss. She did not see Kal pop up behind her like a jack in the box. The Palatine's order to keep out of the fight had clearly been completely ignored. Kal leapt as if entertaining the crowd at Shamanow: an impossible front flip that brought Kal's legs down on Listig's shoulders and knocked the rifle from the assassin's grasp. Beart dived off into another knot of fighting, and Owl saw Spion crawl away into the safety of the shadows. She vanished in the mayhem of the fight, but he wondered then just how far she might manage to slither.

Listig and Kal were rolling over and over on the ground. Kal was strong and fierce and fast, but Listig was trained in killing. Owl could see that Listig was getting the upper hand. She was reaching into her boot for another little blade and Kal was too close to see it. Kal would be killed. At the same moment that Owl began to run, without even realising that he had decided to do so, Luja leapt forwards straight into a gallop. The horse was running full pelt to rescue his friend.

But even Luja's speed was not enough to reach Kal before Listig had got her hand around the blade. Luja's hoof made contact with Listig's body as she pushed the knife into Kal's side. Deftly the assassin rolled out from under the horse's hooves and grabbed at the fallen rifle. She spun towards the horse and fired from the ground up into his chest. His legs gave way and he fell beside his friend.

Listig scrambled to her feet, and looked down grinning at the two bodies, too busy gloating to see Owl, legs pounding, still running. He was aflame with horror and an anger so hot he felt he might actually be alight. With a shriek he launched himself at the assassin's legs. His shoulder hit the middle of her left shin. She staggered sideways but she didn't fall. She punched Owl so hard he saw stars and then poked the barrel of her gun hard into his head.

'I am going to enjoy this very, very much, *Freak*!' she gloated.

Out of the mayhem and tangle of the fight came Blit. Like a black spark, with razor-sharp teeth, she flew at Listig. She fastened her jaws around Listig's arm where her clothes were ripped and there was bare skin to be bitten. Blit knew how to make pain count. Listig dropped the rifle.

Run, Blit told Owl. *RUN!*

Her wolf-self stood, bristled and bloodied in his mind. But Blit's body was not that of a wolf. Listig grabbed it with her other hand and ripped Blit's jaws away with brutal force. Listig swung the dog by her back legs and dashed her onto the cobbles with a horrible crunch.

Owl had managed to get to his feet, but he did not run. Instead, he attacked Listig again, but she simply pushed him over and put her foot onto his chest. She reached down to retrieve her rifle and, almost lazily, aimed it at his head.

'No getting away now!'

Did she squeeze the trigger? Owl couldn't tell because Skrimsli came for Listig with heavy paws. There was a scream that slit the night apart and the whole world went dark.

Time bent and twisted then, so Owl couldn't tell if seconds

or hours had passed. The Palatine, her face streaked with blood and tears, was beside him. She scooped Blit and Owl into her arms and began to walk.

'Hold on. You're going to the ship,' she said.

Owl had just enough strength to wrap an arm around Blit's small body. She was crushed and broken, but she still breathed. She opened her eyes, bright as stars even now and rushed into his head, her wolf-self and her dog-self flickering together.

I will run in the forest for you, Owl. I will guard it until you get there.

Her eyes closed and her presence faded from his mind. Fierce little Blit, the last of Galu Mak's companions, was gone.

The Palatine laid Owl on the deck. Above him the clouds had gone and there were a million stars and the salt wind smelled of freedom. Around him, ropes were hauled, and sails set. A foamy wave marked the ships, progress toward the open sea. Owl sighed and slept.

But unseen in the shadows something slithered, seeking a place to hide, waiting for revenge.

25
Skrimsli

All at Sea

 Skrimsli lay in the swaying resting place called 'hammock'. He could neither curl up in its narrow confines, nor stretch out because he shared the space with Owl. Below was a hammock he could have occupied alone but the disturbance in Owl's dreams had leaked into his, so he had climbed up next to the boy to comfort him. Owl now slept peacefully, wandering in that mysterious forest, whose green-ness seeped into the mind space that they shared.

In spite of the discomfort, for the first time in a long time, perhaps since he had slept between Owl and Taze as a small cub, Skrimsli felt safe. Various things hurt, injuries sustained during their fight to reach Ekar's ship: the deep scratch above his left eye; the tear in his ear; the long cut over his ribs. Plus the many bruises on almost every part of him that the last weeks had inflicted. But the hurts didn't matter because the pain was good; it informed him that all was well, that his body was taking care of the business of healing. He would be restored to full power and strength quite soon, without having to do or think anything more about it. That was a deeply pleasurable sensation. Seeing Owl peacefully asleep at last,

Skrimsli trusted that the boy's body also was mending and that the bullet – that evil flying tooth – that had scraped his skull would do no lasting harm.

He listened to the sounds of the ship. Beyond the most obvious – footsteps, voices talking – there wasn't *one* he could identify. None of the sounds were loud; there were various kinds of creakings, raspings, rubbings, slappings and bumpings. The ship was made of wood and canvas, metal and rope, all materials familiar to Skrimsli from his life in the circus, and yet here they worked together very differently. They worked in fact, like the different parts of one body. The ship felt alive, sounded alive. When he listened very attentively, as he did now, he was sure he could hear a heart beating and sense a presence, a consciousness that was in communication with the air above and the water below. He reached out a paw and rested it on the curved wall, the 'hull'. He felt the minute trembling of the water flowing past, echoing through the wood like a conversation. It was wonderful, fascinating, exciting. In fact, so wonderful that he could not lie here any longer. He wanted to see everything and experience every part of this new being that was 'ship'; he wanted to put a name to every one of those sounds.

Very gently he slid his paw out from under Owl's bandaged head and moved as smooth as water down onto the floor. The floor, of course, moved. He stood for a moment taking in that movement through the pads of his paws and all the joints of his legs. He thought he had the measure of it, then the ship moved in a different way, and he had to begin again. At last, he felt confident enough to be able to walk across the floor but only by remembering that the ship behaved like a living thing, and living things were unpredictable.

Skrimsli explored the quiet spaces of the ship silently. It was night; most of the people and creatures were resting. As he travelled along the corridors, faint yellow lights were activated and showed him the snug doors behind which were more hammocks. He picked up the smells and sounds of sleepers both human and creature. Vague wisps of dreams came to him as he passed, too fleeting to identify what they were really about or to whom they belonged. It was so peaceful, as if, in sleep, all the living beings had somehow become part of the whole that was the ship. Only one thing was discordant: a faint, faint smell, coming from a hatch that led down into the deep belly of the vessel. A smell of hiding and of badness that made his fur bristle. He thought he would investigate, and then Karu's snores coming from behind the next door drowned out that thought. A warm buzzing and the taste of sweetness oozed from the bear's mind as he slept.

Why, Skrimsli wondered, could he feel so many dreams tonight, when before he had only ever experienced Owl's? Had something in him changed? Or was it the ship, softening sleeping minds with its whisperings of wood and canvas, rope and metal, so that their contents leaked out? He walked on, that strange, bad smell forgotten, as he wandered, like a shadow, his tiger brain mapping out the anatomy of this new place.

Up, up! Skrimsli felt the need for air. Along a corridor, up one set of wooden stairs and then up another. Towards a square of sky that moved, showing one set of stars then shifting to another. Another fascination! Skrimsli would have stayed still on that companionway, watching the lurching shift of the sky through the hatch if his stomach had not begun to request some stability. He bounded up the last few steps and out into the open, onto the foredeck.

The front of the ship rose and fell as it moved through the ocean, as he'd seen a horse move up and down when it galloped. Above him, the foremast reached up into the sky and sails stretched like white wings, gleaming faintly in the starlight. Little pieces of rope dotted their surface making a tiny pattering. There, that was the meaning of one more of the tiny voices he'd heard, swinging in his hammock!

Skrimsli stood with his front paws on the gunwale and looked out over the dark sea. There was nothing but sea and star-filled sky in every direction. He gazed at it. Before that moment the world had existed for him in a series of scenes, each one extended for a few tens of feet beyond where he stood, each one centered on his own being. Now, for the very first time, he perceived that the world was very much larger than he had thought, and he was not in the centre of anything, but his own, small self. His heart raced with this new understanding of a limitless world and himself as a speck within it. It was terrifying; it was *thrilling!* There was so much more to be known than he had ever realised, more to be explored, to be lived!

He was not alone on the deck. Beart stood on his hind legs, at the narrow, pointed front of the ship, his nose into the breeze, his eyes looking ahead. His front paws wrapped around a thick wire that ran from the prow right up to the top of the mast, and which emitted a faint whine as the wind blew over it. There, another sound labelled! At the back of the boat on the other raised deck Bollovar, one of Ekar's human companions, stood with his hands on a big wheel; it creaked a little as it turned. Above them the white sails were tight with wind, pulling the ship smoothly through the water which rushed and gurgled along the ship's flanks and left a white mark in the sea behind them.

Skrimsli turned at the sound of a footstep on the deck behind him. It was Ekar. She stood beside him and, very gently, she was in his mind, or was he in hers? Just as with Owl, he couldn't tell.

Thank you, she said.

That was a word like *sorry* that Skrimsli found difficult. So he did not reply.

I would not be back on my ship without your help, Ekar added.

Once again Skrimsli did not reply. Why did humans think it necessary to put into words things that were obvious? Instead he found he had a question. He lifted a paw to point.

Where is that? The place where the sky meets the sea?

Ekar smiled.

The sky does not really meet the sea. It just looks that way. What we see is the horizon line.

How could something look like something it was not? Skrimsli doubted Ekar's answer.

There was a long silence then Ekar asked, *Do you like the ship?*

That was easy. *Yes. Yes. How does it move? What does it eat? How can it see?* The questions tumbled from him.

It moves in two ways, Ekar answered. *With the wind in these big white things, the sails. And when there is no wind, we row. You see, down there? Those benches and the oars?* She pointed into the lower deck. *Beart and the other biggest crew members put those in the water and move them, so as to pull the ship through the water. As for eyes, her crew are her eyes and her ears!*

Skrimsli could not quite believe this.

The ship has no ears or eyes of its own? he asked.

The ship was made by human hands, from wood, from dead trees. It was built a hundred years ago, in Danet on the White Sea. It does not eat or hear or see. It is not alive.

Skrimsli couldn't believe this either. He struggled to express how he felt about the way the ship moved and the sounds it made that seemed like conversation.

Feels alive. Moves like a live thing. Belongs to the sea, like a bird belongs to the air, he said.

Ekar shook her head. *It belongs to the sea because humans made it that way. It does not go where it chooses as a bird does. The ship goes only where we steer it. It has no purpose or belonging of its own, only what we give it. It is not alive.*

Was that what alive meant then? To have purpose? To belong?

What is my purpose? Where is my belonging? Skrimsli asked. He dropped all four paws onto the deck. The size of the world, the curiosity about the place where the sky ran into the ocean, all left him. He felt wretched and confused and very, very small. He did not listen to the answer Ekar gave him. He left her standing at the rail and went below.

Her thought hung in the night air, un-received. *You are a strange being, Skrimsli. But you are young, and you will find purpose and belonging.*

Ekar sighed, and went to Beart, to relieve him of his watch.

26
Kal

You Are Yourself

The thin face of Daunt, the ship's surgeon, loomed over Kal like a rising moon.

'There,' he said, 'you are back with us!' He looked over his shoulder. 'Madam? Our patient has come round!'

He vanished and his face was replaced with another, cut, bloody, smeared in dirt, but still most welcome.

'Palatine!' Kal tried to say, but there was just a breathy croak where a voice had been.

'Shh,' the Palatine said softly. 'Don't try to speak. You are safe. You are on Ekar's ship.'

'Luja?' The Palatine's face clouded. Kal could see that she had prepared to dodge this question. 'He is alive … close by. In good hands,' she said.

'Owl?' Kal croaked.

'Is with Skrimsli. All is well.'

'Sayka?'

The Palatine's eyes slid away.

'A broken wing…' She shook her head. 'Enough questions now. Captain Ekar is a wonder, and we are all ordered to rest until we are well enough to be of use.'

Daunt's face appeared again beside the Palatine. 'An order which extends to you also, madam!' he said. 'Go! Rest!'

Kal almost laughed as the Palatine reined in the desire to tell him that she took orders from no one. Instead, she pursed her lips and told him, just a little sharply, 'I will remain here, Daunt.'

One of the man's eyebrows chased briefly up his forehead and, with the slightest shrug and sigh, he was gone.

'Daunt is the ship's doctor and communications officer,' the Palatine explained. 'He is a very clever man. He knows about the insides of radio machines and of bodies. Now,' she went on, 'you must drink!'

The Palatine slipped a strong arm under Kal's shoulder and brought a cup to Kal's lips. Her skin was on Kal's skin; then the water spilled and ran down over more skin. Kal realised that all the careful layers and wrappings that no one but Luja ever saw removed were gone. Kal was naked, but for the band of gauze that bound the wound from Listig's dagger. Kal choked on the water. Swallowed. Swallowed again. Twice.

'You … you undressed me?'

The Palatine's face was very close, but perfectly unreadable and controlled.

'It was necessary,' she replied, 'to see to your wound.'

Kal's throat felt tight. If only it were possible to get up and run away. But it was not.

'Then you know,' Kal whispered. 'You know … *what I am!*' Kal turned to face the pillow, eyes squeezed shut.

'Kal,' the Palatine said softly, 'please, look at me?'

Slowly, fearfully, Kal's eyes opened. The Palatine's face was very close, but the inscrutable expression was gone. Her eyes were open and clear, showing that her words came, straight and true, from the very depths of her being.

'You have always been a who to me,' the Palatine said, 'and never, *never* a *what*. You are yourself, that's all that matters.'

Kal's tears ran then, and, with infinite care, the Palatine brushed them away with her long fingers.

27
Owl

Kin

 Skrimsli had poured himself back into Owl's swaying cot: its ropes and wood groaned under his weight, pulling Owl from the shallows of sleep. The cub sat now, slightly squashed under the ceiling and staring at Owl, his big green eyes wide and full of questions.

Tell me about the green again, Skrimsli demanded.

Owl sat up and a pain stabbed him in the head as he did so. Ah, yes, Listig and her gun.

I have told you about the green many times, Owl grumbled. *Didn't you listen?*

Owl tried to get into a position that didn't hurt too much.

Tell me again. The green in your head. The forest. The place you want to get to.

The cub seemed very agitated.

What is the matter? Owl asked.

Skrimsli snarled. A real snarl. Owl drew back in shock and Skrimsli sat stock still, just as shocked at his own behaviour. There was a long pause in which neither of them moved.

Sorry, Skrimsli said.

I thought you didn't like that word, Owl replied.

Skrimsli looked away and licked a paw. His whiskers drooped and he flopped down to put the top of his head against Owl. Suddenly all his stern grown-up tigerness was gone, and he was a cub again, a cub who needed protecting.

Where do I belong, Owl? The cub's head pressed on Owl's wound. It hurt like mad, but Owl said nothing. He scratched in the soft fur behind the cub's ears.

The green is the forest. The forest in the north. The tiger and the sturgeon and the owl are the keepers of the forest. This is what I learned before I was taken away, Owl told him. *A keeper means a protector. So, we – tiger, owl, sturgeon – are meant to protect the forest.*

Skrimsli raised his head, his green eyes shining into Owl's.

Is the forest my purpose? Is the forest where I belong?

If Skrimsli had asked Owl any time before, on all the many other occasions when Owl had told him about the forest keepers, Owl would have answered 'yes'. He knew for himself that the forest he had been taken from was where *he* belonged and would some day reach. He had always thought that Skrimsli would come too. But now when he thought of Skrimsli, with his power to talk in many kinds of minds, with his ability to fight and lead, he wondered if Skrimsli could live as an ordinary creature in among the trees? Perhaps there were other ways for the tiger to be a keeper of the forest. Owl stroked the cub's ears.

You are my kin, Skrimsli. For now, this is where you belong.

28
Ekar

New Crew, New Name

They sailed from the long narrow channel of the Finger and turned west out into the Belugi Sea. Ekar guided them along the coast to a port called Mott, almost as small as its name, tucked away at the mouth of a modest river. The wind and tides favoured them and, in spite of Ekar's reduced and inexperienced crew, they dropped anchor successfully just half a mile offshore. It wasn't long before the *Snow Gull*'s water tanks were brimming, and her stores full of food. Ekar reflected on the difficulty of catering for such a range of living beings but concluded that, although their stores might not please everyone on board, there was enough variety to keep them all alive.

With provisioning done, it was time to set a course and make a decision. These were things that her lifelong training as a captain had prepared her for, but she had never had to do them alone before. The last time the *Snow Gull* had set a new course, Ekar's mother had been Captain.

Ekar sat down at the chart table and opened the ship's log. Her mother's firm, decisive handwriting looked up at her. The last entries recorded the facts: the position and the speed of the *Snow Gull* and that of their pursuer the *Vallatta Mourir*.

Just two and a half pages told the ghastly story of the chase, played out in the teeth of a storm. They had so nearly got away, and then a sail had split.

We will be overrun within the hour. We will surrender to prevent unnecessary loss of life.

Captain Rabec Ekar Herulf

Her mother had written calmly but signing her full name at the bottom showed that she may have guessed that it could be her last entry.

The surrender had not prevented the loss of life. It hadn't been just an ordinary pirate raid that left crew and captain tied up and the hold stripped bare of anything valuable. The *Vallatta's* captain had slit Ekar's mother's throat himself and thrown her body over the side along with those of Ekar's Aunt Neel and Uncle Omfroy. His son was all set to do the same to all the rest of the crew. When his father stopped him, he had said, 'But what about the orders?'

'Never mind *orders*,' the captain had snarled back at him. 'I can make money selling this lot to fight in the pit.'

'But we've been paid to *sink* her!'

'Sink her? When I can tow her back to Otok and sell her? Shut up, son. You obey *me*, not Lazit.' The captain had slapped him across the head. 'I won't bow down to some Rumyc mercenary in a fancy suit!'

Ekar knew who the Rumyc mercenaries were: the Automators. Their symbol had popped up everywhere on the White Sea coast in recent times. 'They have long, greedy fingers,' Ekar's mother had always said, 'in every evil pie!' But why did they and this Lazit person want Captain Herulf dead? The *Snow*

Gull was no pirate ship. Sure, Captain Herulf's crew knew how to fight. Ships like the *Vallatta* made that essential. But the *Snow Gull* was an ice ship; all she did was pick up bergs from the White Sea and tow them south to sell where people needed ice. A little trading with the ports along the way, the occasional paying passenger, but that was all.

Or at least that's what Ekar had always thought. Had her mother been keeping secrets from her own child? Ekar pushed her hand deeper into the compartment where the logbook had been hidden. There! A folded sheet of the good cream paper that her mother favoured, wax sealed and with her name on it.

Ekar

If you come looking for this, it means the worst has happened, and you are now captain of the Snow Gull. I have raised you well and you are from good seafaring stock; you will be a fine captain, I know it.

There are things you should know. Things that I have shared only with Neel and Omfroy, not the rest of the crew.

For the last few years, we have been trading more than ice and tinned food. We have been carrying weapons to support the rebels on the Rumyc coast of the White Sea. The private army called the Automators has forced the Celeddi – who are kin to our folk in Danet – from their land to take tar, which they call 'black gold', from beneath it. These same villains are at work in Erem now, stoking up a civil war. They, and the Nordskys, will suck Erem dry, I am sure. My plan was to set a berg or two in the path of their supply ships off Turgu. You know how good small bergs are at sinking ships without a hull like ours!

But you are reading this, so my work in the world is done. The Snow Gull is your ship now, Ekar, to do with as you will. The ice business is steady, honourable and will make a good-enough living. You know our ports and you know our contacts as well as I. It is up to you if you want to continue my other work or not. But if you do, I suggest a new name and a new coat of paint, to throw our enemies off the scent. And be wary of the Automator commander called Lazit; he leads their force in Erem and is wickedness made flesh.

Whatever you decide I know you will think and act well. You have my blessing.

Your mother

Rabec Ekar Herulf.

Captain and Seafarer

So that's why the Automators wanted her mother dead. The *Vallatta* and her crew were just the tools they'd used. They, at least, were dead, but their paymasters were still working their evil in the world. Lazit. Ekar would remember that name.

Ekar did not blur the ink with tears; she was her mother's daughter. She closed the logbook and bound it with a good piece of oiled twine. Then she took a new logbook from the store beneath her mother's bunk. The pen paused for a moment over the space on its cover where the ship's name should be written. But only for a moment. She nodded to herself and wrote:

Ice Maiden.

Then she opened the first page and wrote the date, their current position, the names of her remaining crew, and the new people they now had on board. The thick, black ink on the good, cream paper was a comfort.

Yes, mother, Ekar said in her heart. *I will continue your work, but I will not keep it secret from my crew. We will do this work together. If I am a captain now, I will be one in my own way.*

An hour later her cabin was packed as tight as their newly provisioned hold. The Palatine stooped to get her considerable height through the door. Beside her was the slight figure of Kal, who was making a good recovery from the wounds sustained in the battle at Otok. Then came the child Owl, his hand on Skrimsli's back. Silverback, Leaf and Ray, the new apes who, Ekar was sure, would prove useful at the top of the mast. Beart, and the new bear Karu, poked their large heads through the door next to Bollovar; the three of them were already a tight team it seemed.

Ekar was used to a mixed crew of humans and creatures who communicated with each other both with spoken words and though mind connection – the skills the Nordskys and the Rumycs called 'Listening'. But not all her crew were gifted Listeners. Some humans, like Bollovar, could communicate with only one other kind of mind, and others transferred information by mysterious means that Ekar could never understand. Looking around, she decided that spoken words would work well enough for all. Bollovar could relay whatever was required to Beart and Karu, and Skrimsli she knew could understand spoken words well enough. Although creatures were never said to be Listeners, it was Skrimsli who was the most gifted Listener of them all. He had shown that he could speak to every mind aboard the ship. Another very useful new addition to the crew.

Ekar cleared her throat and tried to remember how her mother had done talks like these. She took a breath and tried to speak with that same quiet strength and authority.

'You have had little time to get used to the ship,' she began, 'and some of you are recovering from injuries and griefs. But I

290

have decided on the course of our ship and now you must decide if that is your course also.'

She paused to check that Bollovar wasn't laughing at her behind his hand, and found he wasn't.

'We are an ice ship,' she continued, 'not a pirate ship as perhaps some of you may have heard. Our business is bergs. But we are not only an ice ship...'

There was a sudden gleam in Bollovar's eyes. Did he know what she was about to say? Was the ship's true purpose not quite the secret Captain Herulf had believed?

'Our other purpose is to fight against those who steal the land of our kin and who begin wars for profit. You may know their name perhaps: the Automators. They were behind my mother's murder. And I will continue her work to confound them.'

She paused.

'We sail next to Erem. If any of you do not wish to come with us, you may leave the ship now. Mott is a well-served little port; you will pick up another passage easily enough.'

There were silent conversations all around the room. Between Owl and Skrimsli, Bollovar and the bears; looks were exchanged between the Palatine and Kal. Bollovar was the one to respond first.

'We followed your ma,' he said, 'and we knew what she was up to. We'll follow you, Ekar, just the same.'

The Palatine spoke next. 'I will gladly come to Erem. What happens there affects my land.'

Kal nodded. 'Erem is my homeland. The wickedness of these Automators connects us all.'

Ekar got the feeling that there was more behind these two statements. No matter. She would get to the bottom of that some other time.

A small voice, cracked and squeaky, cried out from the back. It was the child, Owl.

'I have seen their symbol on rafts of dead trees as big as this harbour,' the child said. 'I was born to be a forest guardian, so I must come too.'

Ekar had learned from being part of a mixed crew that appearances told you little. In spite of his small stature this child had a big spirit. Ekar made another mental note to find out more about these dead trees and Owl's role as a forest guardian.

At last, Ekar looked to Skrimsli. How much of this had he really understood? She stepped into his mind to see.

Do you understand what we speak about?

Yes, the tiger snarled, *I understand. It's human business.* He snarled again. *It is bad business with no reason.*

Ekar sighed. Skrimsli was quite right. It was a stupid tangle of the sort humans seemed good at making.

Yes, she replied, *but perhaps we can turn the bad to good? Will you come, Skrimsli? You could help us. Help me.*

He stopped snarling and fixed Ekar with his green-eyed stare inside and out. She could not tell what he was thinking. Perhaps Skrimsli himself did not know. He was, she sensed, divided. There was that same confusion in him that she had discerned on that first night when he had left the deck so suddenly. Ekar reminded herself that in spite of his skills, Skrimsli was still a child.

292

Owl is my kin, Skrimsli said at last. *For now, I go where he goes.*

Good, Ekar replied. *Perhaps,* she added, *you may get to see the place where the sky and water meet.*

Just before he vanished from her mind, Ekar detected something in the tiger's thoughts that felt, to her, rather like a smile.

29
Kal

The Erem Plan

 The battle on the quayside to board the ship had left the new crew bruised and shaken. The wounds from fists and knives, claws and bullets slowly vanished day by day, but the scars of grief and violence were slower to mend. For a while they were all a little haunted. In Kal's dreams the ghost assassins whispered their poison and raised their guns.

'They are dead, dead!' Kal whispered to the darkness. Hadn't they all seen Listig's corpse, pale and bloodless, dropped where Skrimsli had left her? Hadn't Beart knocked the life out of Spion? But no matter how many times Kal replayed the scenes of that night, Spion's dead body was nowhere to be seen. As soon as sleep returned Spion rose from the shadows smiling that awful smile and promising revenge for her dead twin.

Luja was the cure for these nightmares. Kal would slip down to the rowing deck where Daunt had set up a makeshift stable for him. Even though he hated the sea, and was sometimes in pain, the horse exuded calm. Only once, early in his recovery, had he been agitated and stepped from the shadowy edge of Kal's consciousness, to speak.

294

Will I run on the Grass Sea again, my friend? he asked.

I promise it, Kal told him. *With all myself, I promise it.*

I will not die on this water?

You will not.

Kal felt his calm return. He sank into the shadows once more, and Kal slept without nightmares, comforted by comforting.

The routines of shipboard life were comforting too and the rhythms of the sea, even when stormy and cold, were a great healer. There was no way to change the distance to be travelled, no means to rush the wind or the tides. It made time for talking, time for learning, time for listening. At last, Kal began to find some peace even though Listig and Spion still appeared in the dark depths of the night.

Any job on deck was impossible for Kal while the knife wound healed. The galley was the only place to be useful. There the cooking lessons from long ago at Talo emerged from where they were buried deep in Kal's mind. Kal found that to pass these skills on was pleasurable. Especially to someone as interested and intelligent as Ray. The acute sense of taste and smell that would have helped Ray to locate a thousand kinds of rainforest plants made her a natural cook. Her long fingers slapped flatbread into perfect, paper-thin rounds and manipulated knives with a skill and dexterity that Kal could never master.

They talked quietly as they worked together, about Ray's forest, far away on the Bay de Verde islands; about the day her forest burned and she was taken from her mother's arms; Kal talked about Talo and about the terrible day when the assassins had come. They retold these stories many times. One day, after the most recent telling, Ray laid her long fingers over her own scalp, then over Kal's.

'I never had much good for words,' she lisped, 'but these words we speak and speak, they heal my head, my heart. Each time the hurt is less, less, less.' Then she gave a snort of laughter. 'Less, less, less. Yes!'

The Palatine's strength and intelligence made her a very useful crew member and she seemed to be enjoying learning about the ship. She and Ekar swapped their two traditions of navigation, one made for oceans of water the other for an ocean of sand. She was nimble up in the rigging too and spent many hours with Silverback and his partner who had both been raised as trapeze artists in a circus and now were using their skills for setting sails.

Skrimsli padded to the galley several times a day. Sometimes just to stand in the door and purr at the smell of frying fish, the closest there was to meat on board. Ray liked to tease him and, although there wasn't room for the rough and tumble play-fighting they had perfected in the pit, she could still pull his whiskers and he could bat at her rear with a soft paw.

Everyone, even Ekar, at one time or other came to the galley door, to stand and chat and sample little bits of what Ray and Kal made. The crew shared what had brought them to this place: first piecing together the shared histories of Majak's Circus, the flood and what came after, then the wider stories of their own lives and the bigger picture of the world in which they were set.

Trust was built in little steps and put into action out on

deck when storms raged and the strength and courage of everyone on board was needed. Bit by bit, the strange and random selection of beings had become a crew who trusted, accepted and relied on each other. For the first time in Kal's life, other people did not feel like scratchy shirts to be avoided.

But it was Owl's visits to the galley that were the most surprising of all. Owl never scuttled nor cowered now. The sweetness that Kal had always sensed in him was still there, but it burned now like a bright, clear flame and Owl used it to light up those around him. Owl had found a talent; he was a teller of stories. When he came to the galley, others drew near to listen. He was no longer self-conscious about his voice but used it to carry all the tones of his tales. Most were from his first home in the green forest, Bayuk Lazil, but he made up stories about other things too: his history with Skrimsli; even little things that happened every day on board.

Owl was also a receiver of stories. Everyone on board brought him theirs and somehow Owl knew when it was right to share them. So it was Owl who told of Karu's enslavement at the hands of Kobret Majak, of Kal's departure from Erem and of the Palatine's betrayal by her brother. It was through Owl's retellings that the *Maiden* crew understood that the fate of Captain Rabec Ekar Herulf, the railway over the Sand Sea, the 'Civil War' in Erem, and the freak flood that had washed away a circus, were part of one big story, with one big villain – the Automators.

From that understanding grew the 'Erem Plan' as the crew all called it; a plan as strange and various as the mixed crew who hatched it. It had the performing abilities of many of the crew and Owl's storytelling at its heart.

'We will go to Erem to tell a story that will make them see the truth!' Owl declared.

But telling a story of any kind in a country occupied by the Automators and their friends was difficult. The port of Turgu was closed to anything other than military supply ships and Automator troop carriers. It was Ekar who came up with a way to get round that. Which was why they had sailed north to collect the berg that was now moving slowly behind them, tethered to the *Maiden* by long ropes.

Kal had added a final part to the plan. This had caused the most disagreements.

'It's my fault they have been imprisoned, so I should be the one to run the most risk!' Kal had argued. But it was decided that Kal's talents as a stunt rider and performer could be more useful elsewhere.

'Our performance will make the perfect diversion,' Owl said. 'So Skrimsli and Ekar can do their part!'

The plan was finally agreed upon. If it worked, Havvity and Roko would be safe, peace could return to Erem and the flow of gold to the Automators' pockets would end.

'It will shrivel their railway,' the Palatine said, 'like a plant starved of water.'

Such an ambitious plan required a lot of preparation. The *Maiden*'s stores of canvas, wood, rope and paint were raided every day; rehearsals familiar to the ex-circus members of the crew became part of the routine of the ship.

Kal's role in it all required a return to fitness but regaining flexibility after an injury was tough. Kal stood now with one foot on the starboard rail stretching slowly down over the extended leg. The Palatine came and stood close by.

'You're getting better!' she said.

'Good enough to row a boat,' Kal replied, 'but still not up to a back flip or a pirouette on a horse's back!'

'Hmmm,' she replied. 'I think Luja would say the same!'

Kal looked keenly into the Palatine's face. 'Is he worse again?'

'No, no! He's fine! Just much too busy eating to think of anything else!'

The gunshot wound he had sustained had almost killed him. For days after they escaped from Otok, the horse had burned and wasted like a candle. When at last his eyes opened to show a bright awareness once again, Kal had been almost delirious with relief. Zait had not been so lucky. They had left his body on the quayside. Kal shuddered to think of the hole that had left in the Palatine's heart. It was there in her face now, like a shadow under the skin, but she never spoke of it.

'How is Sayka?' Kal asked.

The Palatine sighed. 'Daunt and I have done our best; the bone is mended, the wing is sound, but his concept of time is blocking his recovery. He cannot fly *now* so he can't understand that he *will* fly *tomorrow*. I may just fling him off the top of the mast. That way he'll have no choice!'

Kal knew the Palatine well enough to understand that this was not entirely a joke.

'So, this "Erem Plan" of ours,' the Palatine continued. 'Do you really think it can work?'

Kal did not get a chance to reply because Ekar stepped up and stood between them.

'Of course it will!' she said. 'Of *course* it will!'

Ekar had challenged every bit of the plan at first, as if checking the sea worthiness of a life raft. Now that she was confident it was watertight, her calm was unshakeable.

'You see those cracks in the berg?' she said.

They shaded their eyes against the glare and looked out to where the vast, tethered iceberg ploughed their wake, bright white against the blue of sea and sky.

'Yes, like the lines of an ancient face!' Kal replied.

'Bollovar will place explosives there, there and there.' Ekar narrowed her eyes and pointed. 'It will break apart into several main pieces but countless smaller ones. Those are the ones that will do the damage. They are all but invisible in the dark.'

'We have utter confidence in you, Ekar,' the Palatine smiled. 'I'm sure *your* parts of our plan will work. It's the rest of it I am worried about.'

'Just look around you,' Ekar replied. 'Everyone is working to make sure it will all run as smoothly as one of Daunt's circuits!'

She was right. Owl and Ray were making shadow puppets from sheets of thin wood that Owl had found buried in some secret hidden hole. Owl had a good eye and Ray had clever fingers, so the shapes of human and animal figures were soon covering half the mid-deck. Bollovar and Beart were leaning over the side of the boat with paint pots, changing the colour scheme to something less like an ice ship, and Silverback and Leaf were in the rigging, swinging about and practising their routine. The rest of the human crew, plus Karu, were quietly keeping the ship sailing.

'Even the weather favours us,' Ekar said, raising her arms

towards the skies. 'Clear blue in every direction and wind to fill our sails. And we still have ten more days to prepare! Now,' she added, brisk and businesslike as always, 'if you will excuse me, I have a meeting with Mr Skrimsli. I am fitting him with leather armour. I want him properly protected when he enters the Automators' garrison!'

Owl grinned at Kal as Ekar disappeared below decks.

'He won't wear it!' Owl said, smiling.

'No,' Kal agreed. 'He certainly won't.'

Ekar was right about other things, though. The weather continued to be kind, with calm seas and enough wind to mean that rowing wasn't necessary, so Bollovar, Beart, Karu and Mathan, the grizzly bear, could help with painting the ship. They used whatever paint they could find, odd pots left over from twenty years of the ship's life. Ekar leaned over the side and winced at the patchwork pattern that now covered the ship's sides.

'Well, you have made her look quite unlike herself. A dog's dinner I believe the Rumycs say. I will be painting her a uniform dark blue the moment this is done with.'

Bollovar grinned and pointed to the word *MAIDEN* that he had just painted in bright yellow.

'I remember that yellow from the year you were born, and I was cabin boy.'

Ekar gave him a look that could have frozen a volcano and he went back to work in silence.

They were close to Erem now, just off the northern coast; close enough to smell the grass and see the tops of the mountain

Tamen Haja gathering a little hat of cloud. Luja looked out from his tent where a canvas sling kept him steady on his feet and breathed in the smell of his homeland. Kal felt the glow of pleasure flow from his mind, warm as a summer wind.

Soon, old friend, Kal thought. *As soon as possible we will gallop there again.*

On this side of the peninsula the mountains fell sharply into the sea, with just a few villages crouching at the bottom of the steep green cliffs. Many places could only be reached by boat. It was a beautiful wild land, and the Herring villages were especially friendly, always glad to see a fresh face.

Kal climbed high into the rigging, spending hours scanning the coastline with Ekar's telescope, and saw that the place had changed. Some villages were burnt out and abandoned; others had barricades and watchtowers on their edges. Sections of the green mountain side were blackened.

It was worse as they rounded the end of the Erem peninsula. Here there were even more signs of fighting and destruction. At night, many places were dark that should have shown the happy twinkling lights of homes and inns and markets.

Worst of all was the south coast and the southern slopes of Tamen Haja. More fortifications, look-out towers and signs of war. It was hard to see further inland but great clouds of dust hung about the mountains. Kal could make out the lines of roads leading into the peaks and ravines, roads that had never been there before. Once the sound of a great explosion carried through the water. Kal remembered how the Automator commander had said he would blow their mountains apart to reach the gold.

It looked as if they had already begun.

'Kal!' Bollavar called from the deck. 'Captain needs the telescope. Come down, smart as you like!'

Ekar greeted Kal with a serious face and took a look through the telescope for herself.

'Seems the Automators have wasted no time,' she said. 'I think I'll take us a bit further offshore, out of sight. Then approach Turgu with tide and darkness on our side.'

The *Maiden* floated on the Swan Strait, the body of water that lay between the peninsular of Erem and the northern coast of Nordsky. Her sails were furled, and her rowers held her steady in the water. Cloud, thick and low, shut out the moon and stars. Behind them, the berg loomed no more than a paler patch of darkness in the deep black. The atmosphere on deck was tense; the quiet crackled with it.

'Dark light only on deck!' Ekar ordered.

The Palatine leaned over to Kal, who was sitting on the small rowing boat waiting to be lowered to the water.

'What does that mean?' she whispered.

'The lanterns are turned low,' Kal told her, 'and their beam restricted so the light goes only where it's really needed. You can spot a lantern in dark like this from a very long way away. And we don't want to be spotted by anyone in Turgu harbour.'

The lights of the harbour were subdued, but still visible as faint yellow dots to the north-west. There were other lights on the sea, showing the position of a convoy of ships bringing supplies for the Automators from the Nordsky ports under cover of darkness.

Bollovar swung his legs over the rail and dropped into the skiff beside Kal.

'Those ships won't like what they'll get as the tide comes in!' His wicked grin gleamed in the dark. 'Ready?' he said.

'Ready!' Kal answered.

'Lower away!' Bollovar called. The Palatine and Silverback winched them slowly down the side of the *Maiden* and the skiff splashed lightly into the sea.

'You want me to take an oar?' Bollovar asked.

'No, I grew up rowing boats like this for my father's family!' Kal answered.

'No doubt about your skill, Kal,' Bollovar said. 'I was thinking of the hurt that knife made!'

'All healed. Just a bit stiff so a good row will do me good!'

Bollovar nodded and turned the lantern to light a narrow path across the water.

The ropes tying the berg to the ship had been let out to their full extent so there was a good half mile of sea to row through. They had timed this visit for slack water, the time between the tides when the current flowing in the Swan Strait would be quietest, but still the water sluiced treacherously around the berg's skirt of ice. It took all Kal's skill and strength to keep the skiff steady and avoid being smashed to pieces on the berg's sharp edges.

'There!' cried Bollovar and shone the lantern to light a little ledge of ice at the perfect height to board the berg.

'Alright,' Kal replied. 'I'll take her in on the next swell. You'll have to be ready to jump.'

He shouldered the backpack with the explosives and the rope.

'Go!' he said.

Half-rowing, half-surfing, Kal took the next good swell.

Just as the skiff was heading to smash itself beneath the ledge Kal rowed backwards and held the little boat still for the two seconds Bollovar required to scramble out onto the ice.

'How long will you need?' Kal called.

'Ten minutes? Not much more,' Bollovar replied. 'It's like wet soap here! Shame Beart's no good at setting fuses, eh? His paws stick to ice like glue!'

His smile flashed in the dark and he was gone, up the side of the berg. Bollovar behaved as if blowing up icebergs at dead of night was a game to be enjoyed, not an activity that could prove fatal.

Kal rowed out away from the currents that swirled around the berg, all the time keeping an eye on that landing ledge. Once Bollovar had set the fuse, they would have a very short time to get away before the berg blew up. They couldn't waste even a second looking for each other in the dark.

The lights of the supply ships were closer now. Kal shuddered. If their plan worked there was no way that none of the lives aboard them would be lost. At least the *Maiden* could search hard for survivors; that too was part of the plan. The lantern winked from the berg. Bollovar had worked fast. Kal rowed in and Bollovar, nimble for a man of his size, jumped aboard. It could not have gone more smoothly.

Halfway back to the ship, Kal eased off a little and they looked back, hoping to see the flash of the explosion that would split the berg into deadly pieces, just in time to be carried into the path of the Nordsky convoy by the tide.

But nothing happened.

'Hmm,' said Bollovar. 'I set the explosive so that the bang would be a modest one, that you might miss from the shore, but not that modest. The fuse has gone out. We'll have to go back.'

Kal knew there wasn't a choice. The tide was on the turn; now was the time to catch it as it flowed up the strait. And if they missed *this* tide, they would have to go back down the strait with the berg, well out of sight of Turgu. It would be another two nights before they could return and by that time the tide would be smaller, weaker, less able to deliver the berg shards to their target. That might mean a delay of a week or more.

Kal began to row. Bollovar had spoken as if they were returning to a kitchen to check the oven was lit. But they both knew if the fuse was just being slow, and the berg exploded when they were close, it would be hard to survive. When they had covered half the distance back to the berg, Bollovar called a halt. They sat for a minute, watching and listening: nothing but the sound of the water slapping the side of the boat and the very distant moan of a foghorn somewhere on a Nordsky headland.

Twice more they stopped and listened before Bollovar cursed and said, 'Just take me in. I've got more fuses.'

Once again Kal rode the swell and dropped Bollovar on the ice ledge. There was no flash of smile this time and the wait bobbing in the darkness seemed interminable. When the lantern flash came it was frantic and followed by the sound of Bollovar yelling. Kal rowed in so fast the little skiff almost took off from the water. Bollovar didn't wait for it to be close but threw himself from the ledge and landed half in half out of the boat. He scrambled aboard and snatched one of the oars.

He didn't say a word. He didn't need to. Whether the first

fuse had still been burning or something had gone wrong with the second didn't matter. The result was the same. There were seconds before the berg blew up and they were much, much, much too close. They rowed, muscles screaming, lungs burning, heads pounding, knowing that every pull gave them just a little more chance of survival.

Bollovar had placed the explosive skilfully, deep in the heart of the berg's biggest fissure. When the bang came it was a muffled *wwwwumpf.*

There was a small flash of yellow fire. But the shock wave was sickening. Kal imagined that it would feel the same if your own heart exploded in your body. There was a moment's hesitation, as if the berg itself could not quite believe what had happened, and then it fell apart. Waves radiated in all directions as the pieces fell and found new ways to float. The boat almost capsized, took on water, but kept going. Kal and Bollovar were a fine and skilful rowing team and would perhaps have made it out of the danger zone, but for the huge shards of ice that the berg threw out as it fell to pieces. They showered into the water all around like spears. Kal didn't even see the one that hit them. The boat was suddenly more under water than afloat and then they were swimming in water full of ice, and chilled to freezing.

'Dammit!' Bollovar spluttered. 'I have to kick off these boots and they are the best I have ever had!'

Kal too was struggling out of boots and jacket; filled with water they would be like lead weights. But there was something about Bollovar's irritation that was comical. Something in fact about the whole situation that was ridiculous. Kal began to laugh and Bollovar did too.

'I'm so sorry, Kal,' he giggled. 'This is a very, very stupid way to die!'

There was no doubt in Kal's mind that this was about to happen. The ice had made the already cold water far too cold for anyone but Beart to last in for more than four or five minutes and it was at least a twenty-minute swim back to the *Maiden*.

As the coat slipped off and sank Kal remembered that Roko's little boot was in its pocket. That wasn't so funny. Who would save Roko and Havvity now? Would the Palatine? Would they stick to that part of the plan?

'You're right, Bollovar,' Kal said, through wildly chattering teeth. 'It is a stupid way to die. So we won't do it.'

Kal banged against a plank, wreckage of the skiff. It was large enough for them both to cling to. If they could keep some part of themselves out of the freezing water, they stood a small chance.

'Here,' Kal said. 'Hold onto this. And sing.'

'Sing?'

'Like this.'

Kal sang a rowing song in Erem. It had very rude words in it and a very simple chorus. Kal made Bollovar learn the rudest words and told him what they meant. Every time Bollovar stopped singing, Kal hit him.

'Keep singing!' Kal ordered.

His response each time was an ever-fiercer curse, but Bollovar kept singing even if it came out through chattering teeth. When he began to lose his grip Kal put his hands back on the plank.

They seemed to be afloat kicking their legs in that cold water for a very long time, but they had only sung the song three and a half times before the yowl-growl of a worried snow bear came to them and the blessed beam of a lantern found them.

'No more almost dying, please!' the Palatine said as she pulled Kal into the other skiff.

'I didn't know you could row,' Kal stuttered.

'I just learned,' she replied.

As Kal and Bollovar sat in Daunt's cabin, wrapped in blankets and sipping tea, they heard the first crackling cries of SOS on the ship's radio.

The convoy ships had run into the remains of the berg.

'All ships, all ships. Alert, alert! Supply ship *Glyder* holed below the water line. We are sinking. Request assistance.'

Daunt answered their calls.

'Trader ship *Maiden*, Trader ship *Maiden*, we hear you, *Glyder*. Will proceed to your position at once!'

He turned to Kal and Bollovar with a grin.

'There we go,' he said. 'We'll have a deck full off grateful Nordsky sailors and half-drowned Automator troops. That ought to be enough to get us straight into Turgu harbour.'

Kal sipped the tea and tried to stop shivering. The plan was working. But were Havvity and her little son still alive to benefit from it?

30
Owl

Shapes and Shadows

 Most of the time in Majak's Marvellous Circus, Owl had been frightened and alone. But not *all* the time; even before Skrimsli had come, there had been moments of wonder for Owl. When Zuta and Saldo, the trapeze artists, flew through the air, sparkling and flashing in the spotlights, he flew with them; when Dalz and Tapis stood on tiptoe on the backs of their galloping white horses, he galloped with them; when Galu Mak's dogs leapt through paper rings, he cheered. He had watched the faces of the audience and seen their reactions: rapture, joy, laughter, tears. He had seen people come out of the Big Top, somehow different, a small part of them changed, if only for a few moments.

He had longed to be a part of it – to make people cry and laugh and cheer. But, back then, all he had ever been able to do was to make people feel glad that, however bad their lives were, at least they were not poor freak-boy Owl.

The day Owl had sat with Moss and Nettle and heard Ead's story, something had begun to change in him. He had started to see that everyone and everything *had* a story, *was* a story, and that he could tell them. Stories, even ones that weren't real, could make you see what was true. A story was right at the heart of the Erem plan and Owl had been the one who had worked out just how to tell it.

Ekar's iceberg plan had worked even better than they could have hoped. The ships streaming over the Swan Strait had not expected a flotilla of small icebergs, hard and sharp as iron spikes, to pierce their hulls. The *Ice Maiden*, with her hull built to withstand the sharpest bite of any berg, had spent the last hours of the night on a rescue mission. When they finally came to Turgu at first light, there were more than three hundred grateful, shivering survivors on board and no one could refuse them entry to the harbour.

Other vessels, crowded with survivors, had been arriving since high tide. Damaged ships were tied up at all angles, salvaged cargoes strewn all over the quay. The whole port was in chaos, so it was well into the morning before the harbour mistress, a stern Nordsky woman wearing the red fist of the Automators on her coat, had come aboard to inspect the ship.

The *Ice Maiden*, in her new coat of multicoloured paint, looked very different from the *Snow Gull*. It had been decided not to print her full name on the side, so as not to connect the ship with 'ice' in any way. They didn't want awkward questions about the mystery appearance of an iceberg in the Swan Strait. Keeping Ekar out of the way, just in case anyone in Turgu recognised Captain Herulf's daughter, also seemed like a good idea. Ekar had found it very difficult to hand over even the pretence of command of her ship but she saw the logic of it. So it was the Palatine or 'Captain Najma' who greeted the harbour mistress and her assistant, a timid little man called Nalyk.

Owl stood by with a tray of tea as Mr Nalyk fought the

flapping pages on his clipboard and his boss looked over the *Maiden* suspiciously.

'Quite an unusual colour scheme,' she commented with narrowed eyes.

Captain Najma answered with the imperious command of her Palatine persona.

'It is quite usual in the Eastern Ghats where this vessel is registered.'

Mr Nalyk scribbled this down on his forms.

'And your reason for entering Erem waters?' the mistress asked.

'We had no plan to come so close. But we saw distress flares from sinking ships.'

The harbour mistress could not complain about that. By now everyone in the harbour knew that the patchwork ship had rescued several hundred people who might otherwise have drowned.

The harbour mistress looked up at the gorillas climbing about the rigging.

'You are, I see, a *mixed* crew,' she said, her lip curling in disgust. 'So there must be *Listeners* aboard.'

Owl watched the Palatine's left eyebrow rise into a high arch, eloquently conveying contempt for this question.

'We are, Madam,' Captain Najma replied, 'and we use our *gift* of listening to *communicate*. Essential to the functioning of our ship and to our performances. We are traders only in part. Our real skill as a crew is as renowned performers. We are on our way to perform in the Maralakka Stadium in Angellis. Perhaps you have heard of it?'

Up went that eyebrow again, somehow managing to imply

that the harbour mistress was a very ignorant and uncultured person.

Mr Nalyk was especially impressed, even though the Maralakka Stadium was, Owl was almost certain, a figment of the Palatine's imagination. He dared to put a hand on the harbour mistress' arm and drew her to one side.

'Might I have a small private word, Madam?' he asked.

They took a few steps away to the starboard rail, where the wind threatened to take Mr Nalyk's papers all the way to Nordsky. Their conversation was brief but intense, and when the two officials stepped back to resume their talk with 'the Captain', the harbour mistress was trying to be as charming as possible. Difficult for a person whose natural expression was a scowl, Owl thought.

'Captain Najma,' the harbour mistress began, 'as you know we have to accommodate a large number of survivors from last night's tragic sinkings, together with persons displaced by the civil war into which Erem has been plunged. I wonder if you would be prepared to do one of your performances this evening? It might raise morale a little.'

Owl almost dropped the tea tray. They had taken the bait! The Palatine's face betrayed nothing at all.

'I'm sure that would be possible,' she said graciously.

The harbour mistress nodded stiffly while beside her Nalyk beamed.

'Should we say 7pm?' he suggested.

'Later, at dusk, would be better. For the lighting, Madam,' Najma replied.

'If there's anything you need, anything at all,' Mr Nalyk said. 'I was a great patron of the arts, you know…'

The harbour mistress gave him look that would have turned flesh to stone. Mr Nalyk fell silent. He followed his boss off the ship, head bowed.

The whole thing could not have worked better. The Palatine beamed.

'It's all up to you now, Owl,' she said.

Owl's heart turned over in his chest. It was time to get the show started!

There was a lot to do. The hours before dusk seemed to fly by but as the sun sank they were – miraculously – ready. The *Maiden's* largest, cleanest sail was rigged as a screen. The puppets whose silhouettes would tell the story were ready, and Daunt had finished setting up the lighting. They had enough in their batteries to illuminate the whole performance, he had promised. Beck and Nobo, two members of the human crew, were on the stern deck tuning up their instruments. Kal and a still rather wobbly Luja were beside them. Silverback and Leaf were in the foremast rigging and Ray stood beside Owl on the little platform above the sail screen.

Owl looked down into the mid-deck and caught a flash of orange moving in the shadows. He had hardly seen the cub all day. His and Ekar's part of the plan was the most dangerous. For now, they both needed to keep out of sight. Owl had stopped being jealous of how close Skrimsli and Ekar were becoming. He could see the inner fierceness that they shared. He hoped it would keep them safe tonight. As soon as the performance was creating a distraction, Ekar and Skrimsli would slip like shadows into the town.

In the blue dusk, the quay beside the *Maiden* thronged with people. Most were ordinary Erem citizens. They looked thin, ragged and very unhappy. They were herded by the Automators into two different blocks of seating, one for the Herrings and one for the Horses. A row of Automator guards, armed and masked, kept them separate but they still exchanged black looks. The seafarers stranded by the sinking of their ships formed a crowd at the back. The front row of seats was left empty until the harbour mistress arrived, together with a group of Automator officers and Nordsky officials. Owl shuddered. One of them might be the commander Kal had overheard starting a civil war so he could steal Erem's riches. Would he remember those words when he watched the show, Owl wondered?

The clock in the centre of town struck the hour. It was time to begin. Kal looked up to Owl from the deck. Owl nodded.

Good luck, Kal. Good luck, Ekar. And cub, dear cub, good luck, stay safe! he thought. This night might end in triumph or with them all flung in a cell or shot by Automator bullets. All of these outcomes, Owl reflected, were equally likely.

Captain Najma leapt nimbly onto the quay and stepped into the small pool of yellow light around the microphone. Her tall, imposing figure had a presence which glowed, drawing every eye in the audience like moths to a midnight lamp.

'Dear citizens of Erem, I speak to you in Nordsky, which is native tongue to neither of us. But we understand each other through it. Tonight, my crew presents to you a story, just a story, but like all stories it contains, perhaps, something from which we may learn.'

Daunt turned off every light now, and the Palatine leapt back aboard in darkness. A thin line of melody from Nobo's flute flew up with the sweet thrumming of Beck's guitar beneath it. Daunt's lights illuminated the painted screen that made a backdrop for the rear deck. It showed grassland and a group of low, ancient buildings nestled in the distance. The audience gasped as they recognised Kal's painting of Talo Numikalo.

The backdrop parted to allow Luja to pass through. His spotted coat was hidden by a drape of yellow and green fabric – two of Ekar's coats sewn together. Kal lay along the horse's back, spine to spine, long dark plait falling past the horse's shoulder just as it had on the night of the flood. Owl shivered at the memory.

Luja was still frail, but the rear deck was too confined a space to allow for any but the smallest movements. He stepped a little, side to side, back and forth, with great precision and completely in time to the music. The audience sighed in delight and wonder. Then Kal too began to dance on his back, so that the two of them seemed like different parts of the same melody. Kal's grace was breathtaking and the deep connection with the horse was clear. Now the crowd – even the guards and the dignitaries in the front row – was so deeply engaged with watching that there wasn't a single sound coming from them.

Owl smiled to himself. That was exactly what they needed!

The guitar began to build a rhythm like a galloping horse. Luja's hooves slowly paced on the spot, a strange movement for a horse but with Kal now crouched low over his back, it was clear he was galloping, moving through the great waving grassland of the backdrop. At a strum of the strings, Kal sat upright, Luja like a stone beneath, as if they were both struck down with something they had seen. Daunt plunged them into darkness and lit up the foremast rigging where Silverback and his partner gorilla, Leaf, each hung from one extended arm.

A drum began to beat. Two full grown gorillas performing acrobatic moves in time with its steady beating was something that took the audience completely by surprise. Silverback and Leaf were not light; they did not seem to fly through the air, but their strength, control and balance were amazing. They executed a series of daring swings and drops, taking it in turns to catch each other by the hands or feet. The audience gasped so much that Owl was sure some of them would pass out.

But now came the really risky part of the performance. After their last move, Silverback and Leaf dropped to the deck and each picked up a wooden disk on a ribbon and put them on. Their comic solemnity drew a few titters from the crowd. But when the two gorillas showed the symbol that each disc carried, the red fist around the earth, the laughter died. Instantly the atmosphere on the quayside changed. The silence was different now: charged and tense. Owl saw the Automator chiefs in the front row exchange uncomfortable looks.

The gorillas, with their new Automator necklaces, stole across the deck and vanished as Daunt killed the foredeck illumination. At the same moment the light on the main sail, rigged as the screen, came on. The first of Owl's puppets appeared. Their shapes danced behind the sail, in front of the light, and cast big, clear shadows on the screen. Kal, who had left Luja on the aft deck and climbed up to join Owl and Ray, held their strings. To the audience it appeared that the gorillas had vanished and then reappeared as the silhouetted figures on the screen. Kal made them jiggle about and, once again the audience laughed, releasing some of the tension of the last few moments.

Owl had seen enough puppet shows and puppet makers over his time with Majak's Circus to know that his puppets weren't of the highest quality. But he also knew that they were good enough to tell the story that this audience needed to hear.

Daunt had rigged up two microphones on the platform where Owl, Ray and Kal now stood, so Kal and Owl could speak into them and still have hands free to operate puppets.

Owl began:

'Once there were two assassins…'

His strange squeaky voice shaped the Nordsky words that everyone in the audience would understand.

'They were very, very wicked…'

The assassin puppets jiggled as if gleeful about their own wickedness.

'They crossed the sea, to a distant country…'

Ray's long fingers made the silhouettes of a dolphin and a fish jump from the bottom of the screen and vanish again.

'One assassin said to the other, "What mischief can we do here…?"'

'And the other assassin answered, "There are two people here: one called Bets and the other called Cets. Let's make them fight and while they are fighting we can steal their gold!"'

Now it was Owl's turn to operate his puppets. He had made the shapes of two people, Bets and Cets. They were exactly similar except for the shape on their hats: one with a round hat; the other a pointed one. He made them walk now, side by side, then do a happy little dance to the strumming of the guitar.

Owl continued to narrate the story:

'But Bets and Cets got along just fine. What could the assassins do to make them fight?

"'I know," said the first assassin, "let's make Cets think that Bets has killed his dog. And let's make Bets think that Cets has killed his cat."

"'How will we do that?" said the second assassin.

"'Easy! First we must steal Bets' hat....'"

The assassin puppets and Bets chased around making the audience laugh, if a little nervously, until finally the assassin puppets had the hat. The same operation was performed to get Cets' hat. Beck and Nobo played very jolly music to all of this, keeping the mood as light as possible. In the next scene the assassins chased first the dog and then the cat around the screen, until both animals lay dead with their legs sticking straight up in the air.

When the moment came for the hats to be placed on the heads of the dead animals, Owl found his heart was racing. There was one final modification that had to be made to each hat, a cut-out section that could be removed from each one. It hadn't always worked in rehearsals, and Owl wasn't sure it would now. He glanced to the side and saw Ray manipulating the two plywood 'hats'. There was a long, uncomfortable pause but then Ray managed it and lowered the hats onto the bodies of the dead cat and dog.

The whole scene looked strange and funny. Some people

were laughing but once again the laughter died when the shapes of the two cut-outs were seen: a horse was cut from one hat, and a fish from the other. To the people of Erem the meaning was clear: Bets and Cets represented their two communities – the Horse People and the Herring People – now at war within their own borders.

'Bets found Cets' hat next to his dead cat,' Owl continued, speaking into the microphone. 'And Cets found Bets' hat by his dead dog. They were both very, very angry and they got ready to fight. This pleased the assassins.

'"Very good," said the first assassin.

'"Very, very good," said the second assassin. "When they kill each other, we can take all their gold!"'

This time when the assassin puppets jiggled about in glee no one was laughing.

The Cets and Bets puppets squared up to each other ready to fight. But then a little melody from the flute brought a tiny bird puppet, operated by Ray, flying across the screen. Owl told the audience:

'But a little bird told Bets and Cets the truth and, instead of fighting, they chased those two assassins all the way across the sea…'

The characters chased each other across the screen and back several times, to the accompaniment of fast, jolly music. There was some laughter, but not much. The looks on the faces of the audience showed they were thinking very hard.

While the puppets bowed and left the screen, and the jolly music drew to a close, Owl looked at Kal.

'Ready?' he said. Now was the moment for the real finale of the show. The part that might, indeed, get them all shot.

'Ready! I've been ready ever since I left!'

'Now!' Owl yelled to Daunt.

Ray, Kal and Owl pulled their puppets away from the screen and the screen was bathed in deep red light. Kal's silhoutte fell on the screen. Kal's voice rang out, not in Nordsky but in Erem.

'The story you have heard tonight is the story of your own country. The Automators and the Nordskys want this war, not the citizens of Erem! This war is founded on a lie!'

There was a storm of shouting. Everyone was yelling over everyone else. Some Erem people started to turn on the Automators, jeering at them, even throwing things. For a moment Owl's heart soared. It had worked! Erem had heard the story and now knew the truth.

But not everybody was convinced and the Automator commander, Commander Lazit, knew it. He pushed his way to the microphone and began to speak. The performance was 'a story' nothing more: Kal's words were 'lies, with not a shred of proof'.

The crowd fell quiet.

'These people,' Lazit cried pointing to the *Maiden* and her crew, 'are nothing better than terrorists! Get them under control!'

The Automators turned their guns around to point at the crew. The tide had turned against them.

Owl knew Ekar and the Palatine had a plan to escape the harbour in an emergency; Beart and his rowers were ready in the mid-deck with their oars. They would have to do it right now or be destroyed. But where was Skrimsli? Where was Ekar? How could they leave without them?

31
Skrimsli

Into the Dungeon

Skrimsli sat in the bow of the small wooden boat as Ekar rowed. For a thing that was not alive, Skrimsli reflected, it responded very well to Ekar's every movement. She made the boat keep to the deepest shadows between the many boats that now filled the harbour, out of sight of the dark-uniformed humans that marched on the quay. Human eyes were too weak to see in this kind of night, so Skrimsli was sharing what he saw with Ekar. The overlapping space between their two minds was something that they had very quickly grown used to using.

We will row out of the harbour and land on the beach, Ekar said inside his head. Skrimsli already knew this. They had set out their approach route before they left the ship. He said nothing. He was growing used to this human habit of repeating known things. Besides, this space he shared with Ekar was very comfortable. It was full of words, just as Owl's mind was, but somehow in Ekar's mind they were in a form that he could learn more easily. In the short time he had known Ekar, his store of human words had grown very much. He wondered why this was and decided that the space he shared with Owl's mind had been made when he was small, still helpless, wordless.

In returning there, he went back inside that younger self. Ekar's mind fitted him better now.

Ekar spoke again.

You are calm, Skrimsli. It was a comment not a question.

You also, he replied, *in spite of the hunt we go on.*

Yes, Ekar replied. *I am better on a hunt than watching my ship turned into a circus!*

It was true. The day had been very trying. Owl had tried to explain to Skrimsli the aim of '*puppet show*' and '*music*' and the idea of a '*story*'. But it made no sense to Skrimsli. Both Ray and the gorillas understood and Skrimsli was irritated that he did not. When he had asked Karu about it, the bear had made one of his moaning noises and disappeared with Beart to *find fish.*

Skrimsli had watched Karu manoeuvring a rowing boat across the harbour with his companion on board. How had Karu learned so fast? It looked like he'd found purpose and belonging already.

Are you looking out, Skrimsli?

Ekar brought his attention back to the harbour and their progress through the dark

Yes, he replied. *Yes.*

Skrimsli understood the task that he and Ekar were set to do. The freeing of captives, of Kal's kin especially. Ekar had explained that the black uniforms were keeping people locked up. Skrimsli knew better than to ask why. He knew about imprisonment and what that meant. He liked Kal and he didn't like the black uniforms. And that was all he needed to know for tonight's hunt. All the rest of it – war and witnesses, railways and droughts – was another complicated human knot that made his head buzz.

The sea was calm and just breathing in and out a little. Ekar brought the boat onto the sand on one of those quiet out-breaths, and together they dragged the little craft up the beach and left it covered by a few bits of driftwood.

From the cover of uncomfortably prickly bushes, they looked towards the building that Skrimsli had heard Kal call 'townall'. This was the home place of the 'black uniforms' where they kept people locked up. It stood at the top of a low hill with buildings clustered on three sides and a river gully on the fourth which reached the sea a little further along the beach, where they now stood. They would creep up the stream, climb the gully, then find a way in by whatever means possible. Which meant, they both knew, that if violence was necessary, then it would be used. Ekar was a hunter. That was perhaps another reason why her mind fitted his better than Owl's.

The water in the stream was cold and in places deep enough to reach Skrimsli's belly. The chill did not bother him at all, but he felt Ekar's shock as her skin made contact with the water.

You are cold?

Of course I am cold, Ekar replied.

Skrimsli decided that pointing out that Ekar should have fur instead of clothes was not helpful.

They reached the gully below the building. The side was sheer rock and very steep. There was a narrow path cut into the rock with no trees to offer cover. So it was lucky that the night was dark and that the eyes of any guards at the top would be human and therefore almost useless. They began to climb the path. Skrimsli knew instinctively how to place his weight carefully, so not even a pebble was displaced, but such silent movement took all of Ekar's concentration. Their progress was slow.

Just before the top, they stopped. Most of the guards patrolled on the other three sides but they had to be sure. Skrimsli peered over the top.

One, he reported to Ekar.

Not going away? Ekar asked.

No, Skrimsli replied. They did not have to discuss what to do. The guard had to be removed.

It was a human female. Rather small inside her coat, Skrimsli thought: not much of a threat. He squeezed her throat enough to make her lose consciousness but not enough to break anything. Ekar bound her and gagged her and dragged her out of sight. Then they stole along the wall looking for a way into the building. There were no windows on this side but hidden behind a clump of plants they found a door. It looked as if it had not been opened in many years, but it gave way with very little noise. Skrimsli slipped inside and Ekar followed.

They were in a darkened storeroom, full of human objects. Some of these Skrimsli knew: *'chair,' 'table',* but others he did not. Ekar's mind labelled them *'desk', 'bookshelf,' 'cabinet', 'hatstand'.* They were made of long dead things, covered in dust and smelling of misery.

I do not like this place, he told Ekar.

Then move swiftly through it, and find another, she replied.

The storeroom opened onto a long corridor.

Skrimsli sniffed the air. *Humans to the right,* he informed Ekar.

How many humans? Ekar asked.

325

Skrimsli sniffed again. *More than ten.* Skrimsli thought it was a lot more than ten but at the moment he could not recall the word-name of bigger numbers of things.

Also fear, he added, *a lot of fear.*

Ekar drew her metal tooth. With her back to the wall on one side and Skrimsli pressed to the opposite wall, they moved along the corridor. They turned a corner and yellow light showed through a small glass panel in the door ahead. Skrimsli began to pick up smells and sounds that Ekar couldn't yet discern.

Wait, he told her. He listened, breathed slowly and carefully, analysing the information that the air brought to him. Up ahead, heavy boots were scraping on a hard floor. Someone was crying. Farther off, perhaps behind another door, someone was screaming.

The place where they keep beings imprisoned is close. There are guards, not many. Two beyond that door, then more.

They didn't need more words. They moved a little faster now and reached the door. Skrimsli stayed down while Ekar peered through the grubby glass panel.

Two guards. Four cells, she agreed. *Automators. They don't have guns. Just cudgels.*

They both knew that the first two guards must be overcome in complete silence. Most likely that meant a swift kill.

I will go first. I'll take the bigger of the two, Skrimsli said.

I don't like to kill foot soldiers. They are just taking orders, Ekar said.

Skrimsli didn't understand what Ekar meant by *foot soldiers.* But he felt her reluctance to kill.

I can kill both, he offered.

Ekar shook her head.

I can do what needs doing, she said. *I am ready.*

Ekar was ready! She opened the door in one swift, silent movement and punched out the light, plunging the space into darkness. The guards on the other side of the next door would not be able to see what was going on. The shock of the sudden darkness gave Skrimsli the split second he needed to take the first guard down. Ekar had the other one under control. She knelt on his back, with her dagger to his throat.

'One move, one sound and you are dead,' she hissed. 'Give me information and I may let you live.'

The guard began to whimper. Ekar pulled off his Automator mask, stuffed it in his mouth and told him to be quiet. He was not much more than a cub, Skrimsli noted.

'How many guards in this part of the building?'

'Six?' he spluttered. 'Seven?'

'How many cells?' She pulled out the mask.

'Ten cells, four or five in each.'

That was all they needed to know. Ekar struck him hard on the head and he lay still. She bound him up and shoved him back through the door.

Ekar whistled softly through her teeth. *Fifty prisoners,* she repeated.

Skrimsli could not see how many humans that would be, but he guessed a lot. *How will we remove so many?* he asked.

The same way we got in, Ekar replied. *Unless you want to fight all the Automators round the front?*

Skrimsli did not!

There was no time for further speculation. The guards beyond the door had noticed that the light in this part of the corridor had gone out. One of them was peering through. Ekar held up the keys she'd taken from the fallen guard.

I'll open these cells; you take that next guard.

Skrimsli's paws punched the door so violently that the peeking guard was smashed backwards with great force. He crashed into the other guard, and both fell in a tangle to the floor. They were dazed and slow, as most humans apart from Ekar seemed to be. He knew Ekar didn't like killing so he lifted each of their heads in turn and smashed them against the ground. They lay still but, he thought, still breathed. They had however cried out loud enough to be heard. Another pair was now racing towards him, yelling loudly, probably alerting still more guards. Where was Ekar?

Right here, with help.

Ekar had opened the first four cells. Twenty ragged, weak, but very angry humans now came through the doorway. Many were young or sick but there were a number who looked as if they might be of some use. With Ekar and Skrimsli doing the hard work, they could simply overwhelm the guards.

It was clear that none of the guards had been prepared for an attack. Soon all the cells were open, and their guards were either dead or bound and placed inside the cells. The long corridor was full of people, all of them talking, crying, shouting all at once. Where in this crowd were Kal's kin? Skrimsli didn't know. He ducked behind Ekar to avoid any more people trying to pet him like one of Galu Mak's dogs.

Ekar stood on a chair and spoke to the freed prisoners.

'Quiet. Quiet! There are guards outside. We don't want to alert them.'

'Who are you; why are you letting us go?' a woman at the back called out

'That doesn't matter for now. We just need to get you all out,' Ekar replied.

'Will that tiger eat us?'

'No, he is helping to free you.'

They were very overexcited. Skrimsli could feel their desperation to break out. It threatened to boil over and sweep them all away.

If they burst from the building, we will all be killed, he told Ekar.

I know. Wait. I will try to calm them.

'Quiet!' Ekar barked. It was the voice Skrimsli had heard her use on Beart when she felt he wasn't rowing hard enough. The crowd were instantly silent.

'There is no time for talk,' Ekar told them sternly. 'We must leave quietly, secretly, before the rest of the guards here know you are free. We will go through a back door. It will take time. You must be patient.'

'Why can't we just take their guns and get out through the front?' a young woman called out.

'Look at the children and the sick here,' Ekar replied. 'They will die. Keep your fighting for another day.' Nods of agreement spread, and the wave of panic died down.

Ekar explained their route out. It would be very hard, but it could be done if they kept calm, she told them.

Skrimsli looked around. Were Kal's kin here? He couldn't tell.

Ekar, ask for Kal's kin, he told her.

I had almost forgotten, she said and asked for quiet again.

'Does anyone know of a young woman called Havvity and her child, a boy, Roko?'

There were shaken heads all round, then a woman, very frail – probably, Skrimsli thought, about to die – came forward supported by two others.

'She is my niece,' the woman whispered. 'They are keeping her in the basement.'

'I thought this *was* the basement!' Ekar said.

'No, there is another floor,' the old woman said quietly. 'They are kept there.'

There was a dread in her voice that made Skrimsli shiver.

I will go there, he told Ekar. *I will find them. Then, I will come after.*

Ekar didn't like this, Skrimsli could tell. But he could also tell she understood it was the only plan.

The old woman spoke again. 'There is a lift ... that way...'

But Skrimli didn't listen; he'd already seen where it was in her mind.

The lift was a puzzle that it took him a few minutes to work out. It made a hideous clanking noise and as it went down deeper into the guts of this awful place, he was reminded of the barn with the skins stretched on the wall. But he pushed the fear down, and made the space in his mind clear, ready to think fast.

The lift stopped with a judder and a jolt. He pushed its door open. It folded like insect legs made of metal and he wished he had more time to examine it.

The space before him reeked of blood and fear. It contained just one guard, asleep on a chair, who jolted awake at the sound of the lift. He was slower than the others, but he had a gun. Skrimsli saw him grin and reach for this weapon. He saw the thought, too, of the tiger shot dead: a dumb beast, stupid and in the wrong place. Nothing could cure this man of his foolish belief that being a human with a gun made him better than any creature on the earth. Skrimsli felt the man's utter bewilderment as he was knocked to the ground and quickly extinguished. He never had the chance to take his gun from its holder.

Skrimsli stood by the single cell door. He could not detect any sound from within it, although he smelled that there was someone inside. They were holding their breath! He reached out very cautiously with his mind and touched a wall of pain and terror, from which he recoiled. Then a voice came from the other side of the door, small and fearful, trembling.

'Who's there? Who is it?'

There was a wail then, very faint and tiny, coming from the same cell.

'Shh, shh, shh,' said the first voice. 'Sleep now, Roko, Mummy's here. Shh.'

Roko. Skrimsli recognised these sounds. Yes, these were Kal's kin! But he could not release them! He had forgotten that paws cannot use keys. The keys to the cell door lay right there, sticking out from the figure sprawled on the floor. But they were useless without a human hand to operate them.

Skrimsli growled in frustration. There was a small barred, window in the top of the door. He could pass the keys inside perhaps. He had to communicate with them in some way to

331

work out together how to use the keys and get them both out of this place. But they were already very afraid. A tiger suddenly in their heads might be too much.

He would try the little one at first. As gently as he could, he reached out and found the child's mind. It was bruised, afraid, confused. He slipped inside and began to purr.

'Pussy cat,' said the child out loud, with great pleasure. '*Big pussy cat.*'

'What's that, my love?' the mother said. 'Where's the big pussy cat?'

Here said Skrimsli, inside her mind now. *Do not be afraid. Kal sent me.*

The woman panicked. Skrimsli heard her rush to the back of her cell.

How are you talking? I'm not a Listener? I am going mad.

No, no. You are not. Look through your door.

Wide terrified eyes showed through the little grill.

'You've killed him!' the woman who was Havvity said out loud. She gave a sobbing cry, 'And there's the keys!'

Skrimsli did not have to explain the problem with his paws. The woman, Havvity, saw it at once. Her fear subsided and was replaced by the purpose of the hunt.

I can break the grill. Give you the keys, he told her.

It won't work. You can't unlock this door from the inside.

She fell silent, thinking.

You can use the key, she said at last. *I can tell you which one it is and then you can hold it in your teeth…*

Skrimsli saw what she was thinking. *Yes!* he said. *YES!*

It was the biggest key. The feeling of its metal against his teeth was unpleasant and it took several tries to manipulate it correctly but at last it was in the hole. Skrimsli clamped his incisors round the head of the key, but they kept slipping off. Then he turned his head and slipped a canine into the hole in the centre of the top and twisted. There was a click. He unhooked his tooth and Havvity, with the child in her arms, pushed the door open.

She was very thin and small. Not so very much larger than the child she carried. She had many marks on her body – cuts, burns, scratches – but still she smiled. Skrimsli felt the joy of her release soaring through the awful darkness inside her mind. A word came to him: *Brave.* It was what Owl had been the day he had stood up to Kobret and his thugs.

The lift shuddered, taking them upwards, and the insect-leg doors clanked open. Skrimsli heard the shouts of more guards. They had discovered the escape, but they were still in the most distant cells. They were afraid and angry and, he guessed, now armed with guns. Automators seemed to like guns very much.

Fast, fast! Skrimsli told Havvity. *This way, follow!*

Skrimsli lead them back to the storeroom. There was no sign of the other prisoners apart from the path they had cleared through the piled-up furniture and the open door in the rear wall of the building. Ekar had managed to get all of the prisoners out. But they were not far away, just over the lip of the gully making their way in a line down the path. If they were discovered there, they would be easy targets.

Havvity's fear was rising again. The child, Roko, grizzled. Behind them the guards were moving past the nearest group of cells and down the corridor. Closing in. Skrimsli peered through the door into the night. More black uniforms were coming, around the sides of the building. There was a way to give the other prisoners the best chance of escape and get Havvity and Roko away. It would seem very risky to these frightened humans, but Skrimsli was sure it would work.

Almost sure.

Once more he stole, purring, into Roko's mind and showed him a picture of his own small self, riding on Skrimsli's back. Instantly the grizzling ceased.

'Ride on the pussy cat!' the child cried.

Skrimsli went now into the mother's mind. He used her naming word. That was a thing that humans liked very much, he had noticed.

Havvity, I am very strong and clever and fast. I can get you away from here, but you must do what I say.

He felt her hesitate but only for a moment.

Yes.

Get on my back, put the child in front. Hold my fur. Do not let go.

Havvity was heavier than she looked but not too heavy. The child clung on like a tick and his mother learned by looking and did the same.

Skrimsli stood half out of the door. Through the tangle of vegetation, he could see the guards. They were blundering about, blinding themselves with torch beams. Thank goodness for the incompetence of humans!

Ready? he asked.

Ready.

Hold on.

Skrimsli pushed the door open with a bang. The guards started as if they had been shot. Their torch beams skittered around wildly. By the time they had started towards the door, Skrimsli had cleared the clump of weeds and was heading past them down the side of the building. Another man stood in his way, screamed and dropped his torch; another two fired their guns into the space where Skrimsli had been two seconds earlier.

Skrimsli skirted the edge of the lamplit space around the front door. He showed himself just enough for more guards to shout, shoot wildly and then give chase. None of them would be looking in the gully behind the building now. In ten more paces he was down a dark alley, with the smell of the harbour up ahead and the sound of running boots fading behind.

'Fast, fast, pussy cat!' Roko cried in delight.

32
The Palatine

The Last Assassin

Sayka was still not flying, so the Palatine had climbed into the rigging with him perched on her padded shoulder. It had been hard work and she had been glad that she was clipped onto the foremast with a rope that would save her life if she fell.

The Palatine looked down now at the performance on the deck and the crowd assembled on the quay. It was far from certain that the outcome of the night would be what they hoped. And if it wasn't, it was up to her to protect the ship and the crew in Ekar's absence.

'My ship is my kingdom,' Ekar had told her as she left with Skrimsli. 'Guard her as you would guard your own land. Leave without us if you have to. Skrimsli and I are fighters; we can take care of ourselves.'

So the Palatine was watching everything very carefully. Especially the Automator commander, Lazit, in his seat on the front row. He had accompanied the Nordsky ambassador when the delegation had come to her with their lies about the railway. He had been a silent threatening presence there. He must have got back to Erem only a few days ago. She looked at him now, the dark glitter of his eyes betraying the wheels of his mind turning. Cunning, slippery and wicked.

As the crowd began to grow restless, he whispered something to a junior officer beside him, who got up at once and made her way to the back of the crowd. The Palatine tracked the progress of this figure through Ekar's telescope: along the quay she ran then onto a shadowy network of old pontoons. There was little light at that end of the quay, but the Palatine could just make her out. She boarded an old fishing boat and vanished below deck.

What was on that boat that was so important? She needed to know. She had a feeling that all their fates might depend on knowing. She reached up to Sayka's head and took off his hood.

My dear old friend, she told him. *I need your eyes, your flight. That boat, lost in the dark there?*

She directed him to where she needed him to look but he was reluctant, dull with inactivity. He hunched his shoulders and ruffled his feathers like an old man drawing a coat over his shoulders. There was only one way to do this.

I love you as my life, but if you do not fly you are not alive!

The Palatine pushed him off and into the air. For a split second he was like a stone then, like struck tinder, he sparked to life.

There, she told him. *Over there, show me what you see. Tell me what that boat carries.*

His wings spread, his mind flamed, and he was hers again! Sayka spoke into her mind as he never had before.

I fly! I see! he cried. *I fly, I see for you, my heart, my heart!*

337

The crowd was rumbling like a volcano, about to explode. Anger was building. People jeered and threw stones at the Automators. Herring folk and Horse folk united for a moment against this enemy. But the tide had not quite turned and Lazit was very far from beaten. He leapt up to the microphone to call their performance 'lies and nonsense'.

'My Automator forces are all that stand between the people of Erem and ruin!' he cried.

It was strange how such nonsense would pass for truth in anyone's ears, but she was sure her brother was selling the same deceptions in the same way in her own home city. Perhaps they would indeed have to run from the harbour without Ekar and Skrimsli aboard. Beart and his rowers were standing by at their oars, the fore and aft mooring lines attended to and ready to be released at once. She had only to give the signal and they could be heading from the quayside out of range of Lazit's guns.

Any moment now. She held her breath … and then there was movement in the dark streets that led down to the quay. Ekar and a band of ragged citizens came running, with the noisy pursuit of more Automators close behind. They pushed through the bewildered shipwreck survivors and into the crowd of Horse and Herring. The crowd on the quay cried out as some of them recognised loved ones they'd thought lost to them. Ekar leapt onto a chair and shouted, her voice clear as a trumpet above the hubbub.

'Here is the *welfare* of the Erem people!' she cried. 'Innocent citizens and children imprisoned.'

The Automators who had pursued the escapees through

the town held back, as the Erem crowd enveloped the freed prisoners.

Lazit shouted something about dangerous escaped criminals, but no one was listening because now there was yet another wonder. A tiger came bounding from a side street with a woman and a child upon its back. The crowd parted in astonishment to let them through. The tiger walked slowly right up to the Automator commander whose face at last betrayed emotion; he looked terrified. But his orders to 'shoot this monster' were ignored.

The girl who must be Havvity slipped from Skimsli's back. She staggered a little, but she steadied herself with a hand on the tiger's back, then scooped her child into her arms and stood straight at Skrimsli's side. Her voice was weak, but the crowd were now hungry to listen, and they were very, very quiet so as not to miss a word. Havvity looked straight at Lazit, a gaze as sharp and precise as a needle, pinning him to the spot.

'I have been imprisoned, beaten and tortured by this man,' she spoke slowly, making every word count. 'Separated from my child, threatened with death. All because the witness to the lie that began this war is my friend, Kal Numiko!'

Her voice broke.

Lazit's eyes darted. He could see things were not going in his favour. But he wasn't quite done.

'Where is this witness that you speak of? Or is this just another terrorist lie?'

Don't take the bait, Kal, the Palatine thought. *He just wants to get you in the open!* But it was too late.

Kal appeared on the aft deck and pulled the green covers from Luja's coat, revealing the dark stars on a milk white ground, the very image of the wanted poster *Pale horse with distinctive spotted coat.*

'Look!' Lazit cried. 'Not a witness but the Murderer of East Cove! Let us deliver justice now!' He turned to the Automators standing with their weapons at the ready and ordered them to shoot.

But they did not. Around them, the crowd had become loud and violent. Horses and Herrings jeered at the Automator forces, throwing whatever came to hand. A clod of mud struck Lazit on the cheek and he had to wipe away the mess. Lazit's forces would not spend bullets on Kal and Luja when the shooting would further enrage the crowd, and they might soon need the bullets to defend their own lives!

Kal took the microphone that Daunt had brought hurriedly to the aft deck and shouted over the crowd. The Palatine saw no uncertainty or fear in her friend now, just an inner flame.

'I am no murderer. I am the child of both Herring and Horse,' Kal cried. The crowd grew quiet to listen. 'I saw assassins kill my old friends at Talo Numikalo, then put weapons in the hands of two dead Herring men. The people murdered at East Cove were my kin. Killed by the same assassins. My horse and I fled Erem in fear of our lives because the Automators branded me guilty to keep me silent. I was a coward to run. But I swear to you the truth of what I saw.'

Kal stood up on Luja's back and pointed out at the Automators and their commander. 'These black uniforms are not your protectors. They are here to steal our power and our wealth, to blow apart our sacred mountain for the sake of gold.'

The words landed like a missile and the crowd erupted once again. Lazit began to panic. He stood on a chair and screamed at the jeering crowd, wild eyed.

'Do you believe this freak on horseback? I ask you, where is your proof?'

The Palatine smiled at his words. 'Proof is about to drop from the sky, Commander Lazit!' she whispered to herself. The Palatine had seen it coming in Sayka's mind as he flew back across the bay from that ragged little fishing boat. He had seized a gold bar from the hoard of them stacked beneath greasy canvas on the deck. The boat was heading out to sea now, under Lazit's orders, but the *Maiden* and her crew would soon catch up with it.

Erem gold won't pay for the Sand Sea railway now! the Palatine thought.

But now it was time to meet Lazit's request.

Drop it! the Palatine told Sayka, then shouted her warning to the crowd.

'Look out!'

All eyes saw the gleaming object fall from the eagle's claws and hit the ground with a dull ring. They watched the bird fly back up to the imposing figure at the top of the mast. Daunt, with great presence of mind, shone a spotlight on to the mainmast so she appeared like a goddess high above them.

'There is your proof,' the Palatine shouted. 'Gold, taken from that little fishing boat chugging from your harbour. Carrying a load of gold taken from your sacred mountains.

Horse people, Herring people, you have been deceived. Chase away your real enemy. What more proof do you need?'

As if taking a cue, a figure crawled onto the deck and staggered to a stand. It was Spion, alive as Kal's nightmares had predicted. She must have followed them on to the ship and stowed away in some dark corner on the night they left Otok. She was filthy, ragged, thin as bone, armed and very dangerous. She seemed unaware of anything or anyone but Kal.

'You *Erem terrorist*,' she screamed, her voice full of venom. 'You have caused me pain and trouble. My sister would be living still if not for you!'

Then she pointed her gun to take some last revenge. She was shaky and might well miss, but it was a risk the Palatine was not prepared to take. She gave silent thanks for the rope clipped to the mast and jumped. She hit Spion from behind, knocking her off her feet. The Palatine grabbed her skinny arms and, like the pendulum of a clock, they swung together beyond the *Maiden*'s decks towards the quay. At the farthest extent of the swing the Palatine let go.

The last of the twin assassins dropped at the feet of her employer.

'You want more proof?' cried Kal. 'There it is! One of the assassins that began your war!'

33
Ekar, Kal, Owl

Partings: Ekar

Mr Nalyk, the new harbour master, had delivered the paint in person.

'The very smallest of thank-yous,' he said, 'for all the good you and your ship have done for our country, dear Captain Ekar.'

Ekar was very glad to see the patchwork of colours vanish beneath the neat, dark blue. Not least because it would stop people coming and asking when the circus was doing another show. She had allowed the new name, *Ice Maiden*, to be painted in yellow because it made Bollovar smile.

In the days after 'the show' as the *Maiden* crew called it, Turgu was a dangerous place to be. As the news of the treachery of the Automators and Nordskys spread, armed bands of Horse and Herring fighters united to push them out of Erem and send them back across the Swan Strait. The fighting had been horrible, but peace was slowly returning. The hurts that the Herring folk and the Horse folk had caused each other in their months of fighting could start to heal. Erem people were finding their old unity again. The language of Erem, that people had spoken only at home with their families, was now to be heard in the street and seen on the signs in the shops.

343

That was the idea of the new chief of the Turgu Council, Kal Numiko. It was generally agreed that there was a wise head sitting on those skinny young shoulders. Councillor Numiko had also come up with a plan for the gold Lazit had tried to make off with which had been recovered by the *Maiden* from the old fishing boat. It would pay for the rebuilding of towns and villages destroyed in the war. It had also been Kal's idea to rebuild Talo Numikalo, but in a new place with a new purpose. New Talo would be a centre for the sharing of Horse and Herring culture, and for the young to learn the old traditions and to invent new ones of their own.

Kal had argued eloquently that the gold mines should be closed over. It had been a close vote, Kal had told the *Maiden's* crew, but Kal's supporters had won.

'We in Erem have learned that mountains and the spirit that lives in them matter more than gold,' Kal had said.

'You are more like a politician every day!' Ekar had teased.

'I don't win every argument!' Kal said. 'I wanted Spion to go on trial here, but she's wanted for crimes in Danet. So now she's their problem.'

Things were on the mend in Erem, and Ekar was pleased with the part the *Ice Maiden* and her crew had played. But one thing chafed at her. Lazit had escaped without having to answer for anything, not least being behind her mother's murder.

'I want him fed to the crabs, piece by piece!' Ekar had told the Palatine.

'There are many roads to justice, Ekar,' the Palatine had

counselled. 'Such as helping the rebels fight the Automators in the White Sea!'

Ekar had smiled then. The four gold ingots that hadn't *quite* made it back to Turgu and were now in the secret compartment in Ekar's cabin would help pay for those activities.

They had left Kal and the Palatine behind when they sailed. Kal had a country to rebuild, and the Palatine had one to reclaim. She had found a ship to take her all the way to Bisque City. They both had new paths to follow and Ekar did, too. It was time to set a new course. The hold was full, and she had her crew. Karu, Beart, Mathan and Bollovar were her solid rowers. Silverback and Leaf could handle most things in the rigging now and the new human hands recruited from among the shipwrecked merchant seafarers were shaping up well. Ray was invaluable. The *Maiden* had certainly never had a cook like her before.

But soon Ekar would lose Owl. He couldn't hold an oar or set a sail, but he was vital in so many other ways. He was the glue that had made the *Maiden* crew into a team.

The question that had kept Ekar awake at night was would Skrimsli stay aboard? He was so useful! He could think in three dimensions and actually purred over the puzzle of fitting as many boxes, barrels and crates as possible into the *Maiden's* awkwardly shaped hold. He was good at climbing the rigging and his claws were fine tools for grabbing flapping sails. He was of course an extremely handy fighter. But his greatest talent was his ability to communicate directly with any member of the crew. His big, stripy presence seemed to be welcomed by minds of every sort.

She watched him now, balanced on the bowsprit, his face to the breeze, his eyes full of green fire – a flame of curiosity that matched Ekar's own. He was a creature shaped by generations of forest life, and yet he loved the ocean. Inside him there was fierce wildness, huge and strange and terrifying, but there were also words, through which he spoke with intelligence and humour. In short Skrimsli fascinated her and the thought that quite soon he would be leaving the ship to return to the forest with Owl was hard to bear.

Partings: Kal

It was late. The sun was dissolving into a bank of orange cloud over the sea and a good, sail-filling breeze blew from the south. The harbour buzzed with the restless energy of departure. Many ships would sail on the tide tonight. Kal, the young chief councillor, walked down the quayside beside the tall, imposing figure of the woman everyone knew as the deposed Yuderan queen. People smiled and greeted them as they passed, a little in awe of these two beings whose presence among them still seemed rather like the visitation of deities.

'We will get some privacy when we reach the ship,' the Palatine said. Kal said nothing. Words could not be trusted in this moment of impending separation and pain. The business of boarding the ship took forever. The captain and all the crew wanted to greet their illustrious passenger and her famous companion. By the time they were behind the closed door of the Palatine's cabin, the ship was almost ready to sail.

'I will have to leave soon,' Kal said, without meeting the Palatine's eyes.

'Unless,' the Palatine said with a smile, 'you want to come with me?'

Never in all the days since their separate paths had become clear had the Palatine invited Kal to accompany her. It had hurt Kal deeply. This obviously flippant remark was a new, sharp cut. Kal's eyes flashed up to meet the Palatine's at last.

'Don't you know how it wounds me that you have never asked?'

'Yes, I do,' she replied. 'But don't you know how much it hurts me that I didn't?'

The Palatine took Kal's face in both her hands and lifted it towards her own.

She looked at Kal in wonder: grace born of inner turmoil; courage born of fear; and identity born of confusion. Kal had been forged in the fire of adversity into someone extraordinary.

'I go to reclaim a kingdom,' she said. 'You have a kingdom to repair. You are so much more than the companion of the Palatine. We have more to do than attend to our own happiness. Purpose, Kal. Purpose is the thread of life.'

Kal could feel the tears gathering.

'Not love? Can't love be a thread?'

The Palatine nodded. 'Love is a thread, one that will be unbroken by the distance between us.'

There was no more time. Outside the steward called for all 'non-passengers to leave the ship at once'.

Kal did not stand on the quay waving. The ship's parting from the mooring felt like the wrenching apart of Kal's own body.

Out on deck, the Palatine watched the slight, dear figure stalk away along the quay. With a great effort, she opened the deepest doors of her heart and let Kal out, like an eagle thrown from the fist.

Partings: Owl

Ekar was a fighter and a stern sea captain, but she was also very kind. In spite of all that she had to think about on board the *Maiden*, she had found time to ask Owl about his 'green place', the forest where he was born, and about the rafts and rafts of logs Owl had seen on the Shamanow river. When Owl told her the name of his bit of the Great Northern Forest, Bayuk Lazil, her eyes shone.

'Ah!' she said. 'I think I have seen that name on a map.'

The next day she had called him to her cabin and handed him a magnifying glass.

'There,' she said. 'There is a river with that name. It flows into the Belugi, ten day's sail from Turgu. I'm sure that river will take you to your home place!'

Owl squinted through the glass until he saw the tiny letters. He had never seen the words Bayuk Lazil written down, so it took him a moment to find them. He traced its letters with his finger and made the sounds.

'Bay-ook laaa-zil!' he whispered. There it was, printed in words on a map!

'We'll sail the *Maiden* to the river mouth,' Ekar said. 'The map shows that there is an island just offshore. I'm sure we'll find an anchorage. We can sail north from there and pick up a berg before the season turns against us.'

The forest was real, real at last, and with every hour at sea it was closer. Owl spent all the time he could on deck, unable to rest in peace, willing the *Maiden* to cover the distance swiftly. Skrimsli too was on deck, often in the place that had become his favourite, standing on the bowsprit. Ekar stood close behind him in the prow with her telescope and sextant.

They talked in their heads for hours.

Owl knew his own connection with the forest was deeper, wider, truer than ever. It called to him day and night and he was hungry to be there. But was the forest really the best place for the cub now? Or should he stay with Ekar on the *Maiden*? Karu had already decided not to come. He and Bollovar had made a deep connection. Owl suspected that Bollovar's benign presence in the old bear's mind drove out the dreadful shadow of Kobret. Karu had told Skrimsli, *This my place now. With Bollovar. I'll be a bear with Beart. Sea bears together!*

Yet Skrimsli still said that the forest was where he wanted to go. He would leave the ship behind and come with Owl on his journey. Although he spent almost all the days with Ekar, he sometimes flopped into Owl's swinging wooden cot (whose ropes Owl had reinforced) at night to hear again about the keepers of the forest. Owl conjured up the deep green of the trees, the ancient fish, and all the moments from his own long-lost early life. Skrimsli purred to hear it all again.

Your kin are there, Owl? At this Bayuk Lazil? Skrimsli asked.

Yes, I think so. Though I was so young when I was taken, I don't remember.

And my kin are there? Skrimsli asked.

There are tigers in that forest, yes. Tigers are one of the forest keepers, like the story says.

I want to see my kin, said Skrimsli, *other tigers like me. Very much.*

Owl could feel Skrimsli's longing. He hoped there *would* be tigers but even if there were, would any wild tigers be like Skrimsli? Owl wasn't sure.

The day came for their departure. The *Maiden* anchored by a small island covered in small, sea-blown trees and seabirds. Ekar rowed Owl ashore in the little boat. Skrimsli sat in the bow, very straight, his green eyes facing forward like lanterns. They towed another small boat behind them, Ekar's gift to them.

'I've named her *Lidaya*, after a seabird and a great traveller!' she said.

In the days it had taken the *Ice Maiden* to deliver them to this coast, Ekar had made sure both Owl and Skrimsli could row and sail *Lidaya* well enough to navigate up the river to their destination. Ekar had made modifications that allowed Skrimsli to hold the oars with his front paws and row.

They ran into the shingle shore. Skrimsli jumped into the water, hooked a paw over the boat's prow and pulled her out of the reach of the waves. Then Owl did the same for *Lidaya*. They stood looking at each other and the waves washed around their feet and pearly light danced between the clouds. Ekar broke the silence by stepping forward to lift Owl in her strong arms and hug him close enough to flatten him.

'You know that if you don't like the forest, Owl, if there are simply too many trees, you can come back. There will always be a place for you on my ship.' She put him down.

Owl smiled and he suddenly felt the hole in the bottom of his heart that Ekar was going to leave.

'And if you get tired of the sea,' he said, 'all that boring blue all the time, come and find me!'

In the long, warm look that passed between them, both knew that they would never see each other again.

Owl turned to Skrimsli, expecting him to change his mind at this last moment. Owl braced himself for the awful goodbye that would mean. But instead, Ekar dropped to her knees on the shingle to be head to head with Skrimsli, who rubbed his forehead and his cheeks into hers. They stayed motionless like that for a long moment. Then Ekar rose and stood straight, Captain Ekar once again.

'I have told him, Owl,' she said, 'that I will be back here in the spring. We will anchor here, in the first full moon after the Equinox. I will wait for two nights before and two nights after the full moon. If he finds the forest is not his place, I'll be waiting.'

They helped her push the little boat from the shore and Ekar rowed away. She did not turn round. Without another word between them, Owl and Skrimsli took an oar each and rowed the *Lidaya* into the broad mouth of the river. Wind played in the sparse bushes on either bank and shore birds whirled around, landed and whirled again as they began to move upstream, away from the sea.

Skrimsli was silent for a long time. At last he came into their shared mind space.

Owl, he said, *we are going home. I am going to be a tiger at last.*

Owl didn't answer but reached out his hand to stroke the fur between the big round ears.

You are already a tiger, Skrimsli. A very, very fine tiger.

34
Skrimsli

Tiger

 The sun was up, slanting fingers of light through the trees. Skrimsli lay along the branch and listened. He played the old game that he had played long ago in the circus, tuning in to the sounds around him one by one. High in the layers of green above him was a small voice crying *wee-wee-wee*. Its little mind was too far and faint to pick up more than a spark of agitation.

Another small, feathered being poured out notes, like a bright trickle of water. Then stopped and began again. It was a fierce message full of possession, stating where the boundary of its land lay. There were ten or more other bird voices calling from every part of the tree in which he lay.

Skrimsli's listening plunged through the layers of vegetation around him, into the minds hidden there. The thoughts of birds, mice, squirrels, martens flashed lightly over Skrimsli's mind like sunlight through leaves. Deeper still was the constant commentary of the insect minds, quite different from the high, rasping sounds they made in the air. There were dark glints and chips of thought, full of instinctive purpose, and slow chants made by the ants and bees and wasps who lived in colonies where many minds all thought as one.

He breathed deep, teasing out the many other messages that the smells around him carried. He understood the mammal ones best, the scent marks everywhere that said 'keep out' or left news about who was going where and why. But the scents of insects were much harder to fathom; there were so many tiny signals, piled on top of one another! Plants were scent-speaking too, in conversation with the insects. All of this was a mystery he could only breathe in and wonder at.

The deepest layer of all were the minds of the trees. He caught only the faintest hint of their long thinkings. His own brain still moved too skittishly to pick up more. Perhaps when he had been in the forest for long enough, he would hear them properly.

Three days ago, Owl and he had left the boat behind when the river grew too rocky. They followed the riverbank up towards the summit of the ridge that ran parallel with the coast for many tens of miles. The slope was clothed in trees whose fat trunks had split the rocks they grew through long ago and whose high canopies drew skeins of mist from the sea to deliver moisture to the land.

The river came down from the ridge in a series of waterfalls and pools. One day Skrimsli had seen a bear hooking a fish deftly with a paw. Skrimsli's attempts at fishing lacked the bear's skill and had ended in some unplanned swimming, but he *had* caught some. He ate two on the spot and took another to Owl, who made a fire and burned his before he ate it. Skrimsli had looked on but said nothing. He knew humans had nothing really sensible to say about their habit of burning food.

They were drawing near to Owl's home place now and

every day the forest was bringing about a change in Owl. Skrimsli could see it. The boy was growing on the inside, getting still stronger and more certain.

On the outside too. Skrimsli was certain he had grown taller since the last full moon. Even his voice was less scratchy.

You have got bigger, he told the boy one morning as they left their sleeping spots and began to move.

Have I?

How could someone not know their own size? Skrimsli was aware of the exact proportions of his body and how it fitted into any space he encountered. He knew that he had doubled in size since the dark circus days and his body told him he would get a little larger still. Perhaps the same was happening to Owl.

Look, Skrimsli said, standing close to the boy. *In the circus my back came to your shoulder. Now my back comes only to your chest, and I have grown much larger.*

Oh, Owl had said, surprised. *Then yes, I must have grown.* Owl seemed dismayed.

Don't worry, Skrimsli told him. *You still look very little like a human. More like an owl with no feathers. Your home people will still know you.*

Skrimsli didn't know why Owl had found this so funny.

Skrimsli rose and stretched. He looked down at Owl, packing his small objects into the bag he carried on his back. Owl fitted here, he belonged. Skrimsli could see it. Soon, today even, they would arrive at Owl's home place, where he would find some human kin. Skrimsli wondered what it would be like when he finally met another tiger. But in all their journey

354

from the sea, Skrimsli had never once had the slightest smell of another tiger although he checked the ground, the trees, the air for any sign, constantly. Would he know the scent of another tiger in among all those others? He wasn't sure. More and more, two questions bothered him: what would it be like if he did *not* meet another tiger? And what would it be like if he did?

'Skrimsli! Skrimsli!'

Owl's outside voice called up to him from the bottom of the tree.

'Time to go!'

Skrimsli scrambled down and they set off together comfortably, side by side, climbing up between the trees. Skrimsli was happy to take the journey at the pace Owl's short legs set. Their minds overlapped gently as they walked, like two people holding hands.

I remember things, Skrimsli, Owl said as they walked. *Things I never thought I knew. The words for trees and plants. Which ones are good to eat.*

Owl plucked the top off a tall fleshy-looking plant and bit into it.

Mmm. It's very good, he said, and offered it to Skrimsli.

It *was* good! It crunched pleasantly in Skrimsli's mouth, but he spat it out. He was in his forest. He must behave like a tiger.

Tigers do not eat plants, he said, *only meat.*

Owl tried to hide his smile but failed. But he did not offer Skrimsli any more salad.

They reached the top of the ridge before the sun was high and could look out over the land beyond – an ocean of hills, hazy in the early autumn light, falling away into the far distance with the glint of lakes and snaking loops of river at their feet.

This is the land where the great river that flows past the Sand City is born, Owl said. *This is the land where the great fishes come from the ocean, the ones I saw on the night of the flood.*

'Fishes bigger than you, Skrimsli,' Owl had said, 'with knobbly backs and turned-up noses.'

Skrimsli had seen the memory of them in Owl's head. But there were a lot of things in Owl's head and Skrimsli had never quite believed in fishes bigger than himself. He said nothing.

Owl shaded his eyes and looked intently into the distance. He caught his breath.

'Look, look,' he cried. 'Those three rocks! I know them. I *know* them.'

At the summit of a hill, perhaps two or three hours walk away, there was a clearing in the trees where three tall rocks stood together like a group of humans.

That's it, Skrimsli. That's my place.

And with that, Owl began to run.

Skrimsli had never known Owl move so fast. Down the side of one hill, up the next. His legs didn't stop, although the ground was humped with the fallen trunks of dead trees and deep with soft moss. Skrimsli bounded beside him, delighting in the faster movement and in the utter joy that spilled from Owl's mind. It was like chasing Taze through the snow! Skrimsli felt that there might be a whole group of tigers waiting to welcome him, too.

Down the hill below the three rocks, between thin, silver-skinned trees with crowns that shimmered in the light, and then onto a path worn by human feet. It led into a grove of huge trees – their trunks so big that the circus elephants could hide behind one. The trees' skins were like those of elephants too, deeply wrinkled. High above, their sighing voices called into the air from their wild, green heads.

Village, that was the word-name for it. But the village into which Owl led him was not like any of the villages that Skrimsli had seen on his journey north or on the coast of Erem. The houses were domed pods, woven from strands of plant, covered in bark, so like nests that Skrimsli could not think of another word for them. They hung from the great trees not far off the mossy ground but out of reach of bear paws and of rising water. Nearby Skrimsli's ears picked up the slow sluice and gurgle of a river.

Owl stopped running and looked around him. Skrimsli felt the boy's heart pounding and the rush of images that flooded through his head.

This was my home. This is where I was born.

Owl walked forward into the grove of trees and their human nests. Out of the nests came human cubs and Skrimsli felt Owl's thoughts rush to meet them. But Skrimsli hung back. There was something here that was not right. Where were the adults? Hunting perhaps. *What* were the adults out hunting? Were there striped skins hanging on the inside walls of those nests? A terrible thought suddenly came to him that, here in the forest, it might no longer be possible for Owl and he to be kin!

Skrimsli took another step backward, sliding instinctively into the sun-streaked shadows. As he did so he crossed a strand of scent in the air: faint, fragile but unmistakable. Tiger! *A tiger that wasn't him.* Owl had found kin, now it was time for Skrimsli to find his. He would come back and explain, but now he must not lose this trail. It was already fading and breaking up in the breeze; if he waited, he would lose it. Skrimsli turned from the village, keeping the precious thread in his nose.

It led west, along the river that flowed by the village clearing. It ran upstream and floated in the air like a stem of grass caught in the wind. Sometimes it dropped onto the mossy ground at Skrimsli's feet in a little pool that he could pause at and breathe in. He followed it through the wet meadows and beside bending trees, up a hill among boulders and silver-skinned birches.

As he followed, Skrimsli thought about the scent, teasing apart the signals it contained. He was used to reading human, dog, and bear smells. He could tell when Owl was tired, or ill or hungry, or when Karu wanted to go to sleep. But the only tiger smell he knew was his own and he never had to read that. Some of the strands in this smell were like his own smell. But others were very different. He noticed that if he paused the smell would then grow stronger. Almost as if it were telling him to 'hurry up'. It was puzzling.

He followed the scent across the foot of a rocky, south-facing slope, where the heat in the stones almost burned his pads, then followed it back again. When he had walked three times around the same stand of trees, he stopped. He was being played with. Whoever was leaving the scent was watching him. He sat down and licked his paws and looked around. He had never had to spot a live tiger. What were the tell-tale signs? He took a deep, careful breath and thought about the information the scent contained. The tiger was very, very close indeed.

In fact…

Skrimsli looked up and, for the first time in his life, looked into the face of another live tiger. It was like and unlike his own. The stripes were delicate crescents, and the paleness below the eyes was brighter. It struck Skrimsli that this was a better tiger face than the one he had. Suddenly, all the mystifying differences between his own familiar tiger smell and the scent of the tiger he had been following made sense. This tiger was a female, and she had *wanted* him to follow her. She leapt down from the tree. Her movement made Skrimsli feel dull and clumsy. She flowed, like water or light, effortless and precise. She looked at him, ears forward, nose searching. He must smell of humans, and of the sea too, perhaps, which would seem strange to her. But she was not afraid. Skrimsli kept very still, while she inspected him with her nose, her ears back. She sniffed at his cheeks on both sides, looking at him intently with her big light eyes. She gave a small in-breath and pulled back her whiskers. Skrimsli thought she was going to snarl, but her ears flipped forward, and she butted his cheek very gently with her forehead!

Skrimsli fizzed inside. In his excitement, he rushed into her mind. And then she *did* snarl at him, hit out with a paw and drew blood from his nose in at least two places. He stepped back, with his body and his mind, and sat looking at her. She snarled again. Skrimsli waited.

Waiting was hard.

But it did allow him to look. She was smaller than he was, but older. Full grown. She was well fed and sleek, so she must be a good hunter. After a while she licked her nose, then rolled around on her back in the sunshine. She lifted her head and looked at him. He didn't dare try to reach into her mind again. Was she pleased or not? He couldn't tell. Skrimsli got the feeling that she was playing a game that he didn't know anything about. But when she walked off, tail slowly swaying, Skrimsli decided that it was safe to follow.

The tigress knew where she was going. She had a destination in her mind. Soon Skrimsli smelled it too. A dead thing: a deer, he thought, although he'd never eaten one. Dead for a while, but still perfectly good. She was going to share her kill! Skrimsli was very pleased. He hadn't eaten anything but fish for weeks.

But the deer was not her kill. Skrimsli saw at once that humans had killed it with a wire round its neck. It had been dragged to where it lay by two humans. Skrimsli sniffed at the ground around the dead deer carefully. The humans who had dragged it were not like the ones in Owl's village. They smelled of tar, and machines, not of bark and leaves. Their horrid smell was all over the deer. They had swished a pine branch over their tracks too. Why would they do that? It made Skrimsli suspicious. He sniffed the deer all over once again. The female sniffed it too; she licked her lips then invited him to eat, with a warm *chuff, chuff, chuff* sound.

But Skrimsli didn't want to eat the deer. Behind the tar smell of humans and the piney resin of the branch they had waved about was another smell, one he didn't like. He concentrated hard trying to work out what it was. The tigress was cross that he didn't start to feed; she was hungry, she didn't want to wait, so she settled down to feast. As she opened her jaws ready to bite into the carcass, Skrimsli finally recognised the smell; it was that bitter stuff that Kobret's men had used to send him into long, dark sleeps. The deer was poisoned!

Skrimsli thought of the skins on the barn wall. Cold horror filled him at the thought of losing the only other tiger he had ever met, almost as soon as he had found her. There was no time to explain to her, he had to stop her eating the poisoned deer. His superior size and the fact that she didn't expect him to do it, helped; he slapped her head with a paw and sent her rolling over. She didn't miss a beat. She leapt straight at him, claws out, snarling. It reminded him of his first meeting with Ekar. But this female was a lot better equipped than any armed human. His greater size and strength could keep her at bay for a while, but they would end up really hurting each other. He had to make her see why the deer was dangerous.

There was nothing for it but to get inside her mind. This time she was already snarling, so there was no point in drawing back. Of course there were no words, but feelings were kept in the same places as his own brain and he could put pictures in her mind that she could understand. If their conversation had been in words, it would have looked like this:

Tigress: *Get out! Get out! Get out!*
Skrimsli: *Danger! Food is danger!*
Tigress: *Food is mine!*

Skrimsli: *Food is danger. Humans put poison in it. Poison! It will kill you.*

Tigress: *How do you know?*

Skrimsli: *Smell it. I know this smell is poison. This smell is death. Learn it. You smell it again, keep away.*

The tigress was very shocked and afraid. She snarled at the deer, hit it with her paws and then set off at a fast pace to a place where she felt safe. Skrimsli followed to a rocky ledge high on a hillside, protected by an overhang. She lay down, panting, and Skrimsli lay close, but not too close. Gradually her breathing slowed, and she became calm. When Skrimsli came into her mind now, she didn't snarl. They rested together in the dappled shade.

Skrimsli thought about the deer. It meant that tigers were not safe in Owl's green place. But it was not Owl's kin that had killed the deer and poisoned it. There were other humans at work here. He wanted to find out more. He would, but right now the sun was delicious, and he was with another tiger for the first time. He closed his eyes and slept.

The tigress woke him.

Hunt, her mind said. *Hunt now.*

She jumped down from the ledge and was about to vanish down the hillside. All Skrimsli could do was follow. It was hard to keep up with her! She knew every leaf and twig and rock. Skrimsli was sure she could have followed the same path with her eyes closed, her nose blocked, and her whiskers clipped. She knew her territory the way Owl knew the words about the forest keepers.

Deer, she told him. *Deer soon.*

She knew they would be there even before their scent gave them away. Three of them. Two females and a half-grown fawn, grazing nervously in a small clearing.

You, there! the tigress commanded.

She wanted him to stalk around the clearing and drive the deer into her path. Like flushing rabbits from the cover of the snowy forest for Taze to catch, Skrimsli thought. But it was much more difficult to move silently through a weft of undergrowth where every tiny twig was ready to snap, every fallen leaf ready to crunch. Skrimsli advanced very slowly and even from the across the clearing he could feel the tigress growing impatient. The deer were very close now. He saw the shine of their big dark eyes, and the pattern of their spotted sides. The females were alert and wary, but the fawn was not. It was too hungry, too taken up with the next green mouthful. Another two body lengths and he would be in the right position to spring from cover and send them straight into the tigress' jaws.

Then one of his hind paws cracked a twig. He felt it give beneath his paw, too late. The sound seemed loud as a gunshot. The deer leapt away too soon and in the wrong direction. The tigress would be angry. But perhaps he could still snatch the fawn and appease her. Skrimsli gave chase.

The deer panicked. They fled through the forest without care for silence, their only thoughts *away away away.*

Skrimsli leapt and ran and ducked and slithered through the maze of trees and branches. The fawn, less experienced and more afraid than its adults, had become separated from the other two and ran uphill. A foolish mistake which allowed

Skrimsli to gain on the creature. He was almost on it. The movement of its hind legs, the smell of its fear, filled his whole attention. He reached out a paw to trip it, and with a sudden scramble it was gone and Skrimsli had slammed into a fence of metal mesh, just like the ones that had divided the circus like a prison compound.

He stood, panting, and stared through the fence and the tiny opening through which the deer had fled. The hillside beyond was bare. Bare in the way a skinned dead body is bare. It was utterly silent. All the voices of the forest gone. The fence ran far in each direction and, within it, was this horrible nothing. It stretched down one hillside and over the next, where a human road had been carved into the land like a wound. Human huts, square and ugly, stood in a group at the top of the opposite hill. Great machines squared beside them. They trailed a stink of tar. This was where the humans who had killed the deer and poisoned it had come from.

Two more hills met at the end of the valley and here a huge wall had been built on each bank of the river. Between it the water still flowed, but through and over a great pile of rubble, blocking the passage of any creature up or down the stream. Downstream of this was a deep pool beneath a tall cliff of sheer rock that stretched to the summit of a third hill. It was strange. Skrimsli didn't like it. It was steeped in fear and dread.

The tigress came and stood beside him. She felt the fear too.

Go. Leave. Now, she said. *Danger. Danger!*

She was right. It wasn't a smell, or a sound; there was nothing to see and yet a terrible alarm seeped into Skrimsli and made him want to run.

364

But he didn't. Because fear did not know everything and there was more here to know. He pushed the fear down under all his paws and climbed the fence into the starlit emptiness of the hillside. To Skrimsli's surprise, the tigress followed.

The ground stank of death. Even the starlight that came between the clouds seemed tainted with it. But somewhere here there was life. Skrimsli sensed it. Life that cried out the warning that he now felt in every nerve. As they made their way down the hillside, it grew stronger. The tigress snarled; she felt it too. It was coming from the river, from the pool below the walls and the rubble barrier.

The only way to get close to it was to swim. The water was cool and still sweet, but sad. Skrimsli reached the gap between the high walls and climbed up onto the rubble through which the water still flowed. He stood with the broken river pushing its way around his paws and peered downstream into the dark water of the pool. Huge, dark shapes moved there, older, darker even that the shadows. Sturgeon! The fish in Owl's words.

The tiger and the sturgeon and the owl are the keepers of the forest. Each must speak to each to keep the forest whole.

Was that why Skrimsli felt them calling out in fear and warning? Not a sound he could hear with his ears, but a cry of another sort, born from a mind as old as the rocks. Skrimsli shut his eyes and listened with his mind to those strange voices. There was information in their chanting that he could just discern.

If the fish had used human words they would have said, over and over:

365

Rock. Rock will break the river. Rock.

What did that mean? Skrimsli looked down at his paws, on the dam of rubble and boulders. Hadn't the rocks already broken the river?

Then he examined the rock face that rose from under the pool, where the fish swam, in an unbroken surface to the top of the hill. Perhaps the fish could sense things that happened above their watery world through that rock. Skrimsli looked more closely and saw the cliff was pock marked with lines of neat round holes, filled with sticks of some material that smelled of fire.

Was this why the fish had raised an alarm that must be ringing through the whole forest. What were the holes and the sticks that smelled of fire?

'Woouff! Woouff!'

The tigress' low voice called from the other bank, sounding another, more urgent alarm. Up the hill, by the human huts, there was movement. It wasn't safe here, near those humans with snares and guns. Skrimsli swam back upstream and climbed from the water next to the waiting tigress.

Humans, said the tigress. *Run now!*

But when Skrimsli looked up the hill the only human he could see was a small figure that he knew at once was Owl. For a moment he was alarmed to see Owl in the place from which the poisoned deer had come. Then Skrimsli saw how alone and afraid Owl was. He was not part of that place; he was looking for something: on a hunt of his own.

Owl was still his friend! He had been foolish to think it was otherwise.

Whatever bad business went on here – the fence, the empty hillside, the poisoned deer, the broken river and the sturgeons' cry – Owl and tiger were the forest keepers, they would understand it together.

So when the tigress said, *Run away, Run away,* Skrimsli told her, *No, this human is my kin!* And he began to run up the slope. Confused and afraid as she was, the tigress followed. Like Skrimsli, she was a curious creature.

35
Owl

Home at Last

 As Owl ran down the hill towards the treehouses, he felt he was running into the past. Memories rushed up from where they had been sleeping and wrapped him like a wind, threatening to carry away his whole being. Faces, voices, tastes and sounds. But when he stopped running, and stood in the space between the home trees, the reality was very different from his memories. The treehouses were ragged, roofless, torn. There were no vegetable gardens in the sunlit clearings between the trees, no birds roosting on the roofs, no songs sung over cooking fires, no voices calling from the river. Even the trees looked less green. It was too quiet. He had finally returned to the green inside, only to find it broken. He was too late after all. For a moment, he felt his heart might break too.

Then the children appeared. Around twelve of them, of various sizes but most very small. They surrounded him, without coming too close, and stared at him. But it was not the kind of staring that he had experienced sitting under the sign that said 'Freak' in the circus. This was different. These children were a little afraid of him, in the same way they might be of a powerful animal. Like a tiger! Owl glanced over his shoulder but could not see Skrimsli.

'Are you … real?' one of the smallest ones asked. She spoke in a language that Owl had not heard anywhere but inside his dreams. Owl nodded.

'Yes, I'm real!' he answered. The children were skinny, dirty and obviously miserable. Owl felt sorry for them.

'Are you the keeper of the forest?'

Owl looked around at the little faces. He took a deep breath. 'Yes, I am.'

The children smiled at each other. Then a boy, a little older than the rest, pushed forward from the back. The other children looked to him. He was their leader. Perhaps the nearest thing they had to an adult, Owl wondered. The boy did not smile.

'I'm Nopea,' he said. 'I'm the biggest kid here so I'm the boss. Aren't I?'

The other children nodded, a bit reluctantly, Owl thought.

'If you are the keeper,' he challenged, 'then where's the tiger? Where's the big fish?'

Owl met the boy's eyes. 'The tiger is with me. Somewhere,' he said. 'But I saw the big fish start their journey from the sea. They could be in the deep pools of your river already.'

Owl pulled out the wooden sturgeon that he wore around his neck. Nopea stepped forward and snatched at it.

'Where did you get that?' he cried.

Gently, Owl took the fish back. 'I got it here, in the place where I was born. It was given to me. Because I am a forest keeper.'

'You aren't a real keeper. Cos keepers aren't real,' Nopea jeered. 'It's a story. You're just some *freak* with a stupid face and short legs.'

The children began to chant. 'Freak, freak, freak.'

That word that meant misery and never, ever belonging anywhere. Owl backed away. The children were fighting their own fear with this word, he knew, but still it was hard to hear it, here, now. The children advanced, a wall of hard eyes and shouting mouths.

'Skrimsli!' he called out loud and reached out with his mind. But the cub wasn't there! He'd vanished.

Owl turned, ready to run, but hands touched him on the shoulder and turned him round to face the jeering children. A woman now stood close behind him, her warm presence holding him steady.

'You stand right there, Owl,' she said.

The children stopped chanting. They stood, frozen to the spot.

'So,' the woman said slowly, 'freak, is it? That's the word you chose, eh?'

She looked at each one of them in turn. They, in turn, looked down at their feet. The woman was small, not much taller than Owl and wrinkled as the bark of a tree. But in her eyes was the life of a whole forest! Strength flowed into Owl through the hands that still rested on each of his shoulders.

'Have you lot grown as foolish as your parents?' the woman scolded. 'Don't you know a forest keeper when it's standing right in front of you?'

Only Nopea had the courage to look up and meet her eye.

'What can a forest keeper do now?' he cried. 'All your talk is just nonsense!'

The old woman's eyes flashed, but she spoke softly. 'I hear you, Nopea,' she said kindly. 'I hear your fear!'

Owl could see that the boy was close to tears.

'I'm not afraid,' he said.

'Of course you are,' the woman said quietly. 'We all are. When something frightening is happening, then people are afraid. But fear isn't the whole story.'

Nopea held her eye for a moment, then looked away and wiped his nose on the back of his hand. The tension went from the air and the woman smiled, bright and bustling. She took her hands from Owl's shoulder and put them on her hips.

'Right, you lot,' she cried. 'Get cleaned up and I might just have something for you all to eat.'

She pulled a fat bag off her shoulders and waved it about allowing the delicious smell of something just baked to escape from it.

'Get to it!'

The children, including Nopea, ran off in all directions, up into the nests, towards the river, released from her disapproval and clearly very keen to make amends. She turned to Owl and to his utter astonishment she bowed her head respectfully to him.

'Owl, forest keeper,' she said. 'You came back. I'm glad you came, even if it is too late for us.'

Owl stared at her.

'I think,' he stuttered, 'there's a lot that I don't know. A lot that I don't remember.'

The woman nodded. 'It's not surprising. But I can tell you what you need to know. I can tell you the story that you don't remember.'

The woman led Owl to a fallen log, worn smooth with sitting, and drew him down beside her.

'First,' she said, 'tell me what you do know.'

'I was born here,' Owl began. 'I remember being told about the forest keepers. I remember being carried into the water with the sturgeon. I remember the green, the trees. I know I was taken away, and I ended up in a circus, but I don't want to talk about that.'

The woman took his hand.

'My name is Teva,' she said. 'I remember your birth, Owl. Back then, we were strong. We knew other forests had been felled, but we would never let it happen to ours. We trusted in ourselves and in the forest keepers. When the village saw you, a human child who was also an owl, we felt stronger than ever. You were the symbol of our strength. So, when the Nordskys came saying they would buy our land, cut our trees, and fill our valleys with water to feed their cities, we said no. We fought back. We would not lose.'

Teva sighed.

'Then things began to vanish. Tigers first, bears too. Cubs stolen from murdered mothers. Then sturgeon. They pulled the great fish from their spawning places with their nets, took their eggs and threw the fish away. One fish would have fed a village for a winter, but they took hundreds of them. And worst, worst, worst of all, you vanished. We guessed you'd been taken by the ones who took the bear and tiger cubs. Your father went to find you. He never came back.'

Owl looked at his feet. He wished the cub were here. Or Taze. Or someone.

'And my mother?' Owl asked, his voice smaller and squeakier than it had ever been.

Teva shook her head. 'I haven't seen her in a long while.'

She was being kind, Owl knew; she didn't want to tell him that she was dead too.

'I don't remember them anyway,' Owl said, so Teva would know it didn't matter. But it did. He'd hidden his hope for a mother or a father from himself but now it came out into the open, only to shrivel to nothing at once.

'When you vanished, we lost. We gave up fighting,' Teva said. 'We gave up hope.'

The children returned, a little cleaner, eager for what Teva had to give them. Owl sat apart, absorbing all he had been told. The hurt of it sank into him as he watched Teva and the children sharing the bread from her bag.

Nopea handed out wooden beakers and poured water from a jug into them. He came to Owl and handed him a beaker.

'I'm sorry I called you freak,' he said quietly. Owl couldn't manage a smile, but he did manage a shrug, as if being an orphan, being called a freak, and coming home to find it broken didn't matter at all.

Teva returned to Owl's side and offered bread pieces to him and to Nopea.

'You are a good boy really, Nopea,' she said and turned to Owl. 'It's hard for these children. Some of their parents are dead or missing, and the others are forced to work on the dam because the forest doesn't feed us any more.'

'What's the dam?' Owl asked.

Nopea looked at Teva. 'Can I show him?'

Teva nodded. 'You can. But be careful. Very careful.'

It was hard keeping up with Nopea. He had been raised in the forest and moved easily and quickly over the fallen branches, moss-covered rocks and tangled undergrowth. Owl was only a beginner. And a beginner with short legs. Finally, at the top of a hill, they came to a line of fencing beyond which there were no trees, just an ugly ravaged landscape, grey and dead. Several long huts stood on the top of the barren hill opposite. There were bars on the windows. Owl was familiar with bars. He knew what they meant. People who slept in barred huts had very few choices.

Nopea pointed to the far end of the valley. Huge walls had been built on either side of the river just where it ran between two hills. Beyond the walls the river turned around the bottom of the steep rock face of a third hill. Uniformed figures stood around, shouting orders to workers who swarmed over the two walls and on ropes up the face of the rock.

'Some of our mums and dads work there,' Nopea said. 'They aren't allowed to come home until the dam is finished. If they try to, or we try to visit, they get beaten. They've been building it for years.'

Nopea pointed to the figures climbing on the rock.

'One of those is my dad. He used to be the best in the village at climbing trees to get bee honey. The Nordskys taught him how to work blowing things up. That's what they're doing now. See that rock face?'

Owl nodded. How could you not see it? It was the biggest thing in the landscape.

'Tomorrow,' Nopea went on, 'they are gonna blow it up. It'll fill up the space between hills and the walls, then they'll pour stuff in to close up the gaps. Then that's it. The river will stop flowing. It'll fill this valley and ours, and the forest will be drowned. Our home will be underwater.'

'Can't we stop it?' Owl asked.

Nopea shook his head. 'Nothing can stop it now. Unless you really *are* a forest keeper, we haven't got a hope!'

Owl said nothing, but all the way back to the village he thought about the other times when there had been no hope, when everything looked lost. This was just another of those times.

It was almost dark and starting to rain when they got back to the village. Teva had made a fire under the canopy of the trees and the children sat around the fire, toasting whatever they had managed to find to eat – small fish, crayfish, roots – in the lights of their little solar lanterns.

Teva was cooking flatbread on a rock heated by the flames. Everyone was quiet. Nopea took some bread and went to his nest and one by one, the children finished the foraged dinners and took themselves off to their beds. Their sadness and hopelessness filled the air.

Teva handed Owl a beaker of some kind of steaming liquid. Owl didn't care what was in it; it was hot. He gulped it down and shuffled closer to the fire, where Teva sat staring into the flames.

'You know what you said about people losing hope, giving up?' Owl asked.

Teva nodded.

'What if they got some hope back?' Owl asked. 'Would they fight for their forest again?'

Teva shook her head.

'It's too late, Owl,' she said. 'At dawn tomorrow they will blow that hill apart. The river will no longer flow downstream. Our forest will vanish under the water. I haven't seen a sturgeon in a decade. The tigers are gone. You are the last keeper and you're just a boy. Go to bed. The parents will return here tomorrow. They'll have food. They will be paid. We will pack up and move away and take the old stories with us.'

She got up from the fire and climbed slowly to her nest.

Owl wandered from the dying fire, between the trees to the bank of the river. The rain had stopped but only the faintest light managed to get through the cloud and the treetops. It didn't matter; Owl's eyes had always been good at night. The sound that the river made was soothing, a low murmur like someone trying to tell you something nice. Just here it swirled into a pool as round as the moon, then flowed away again downstream, to where the dam lay.

Owl thought about the river. While he stood still on the bank, the water before him changed every second. Bubbling up from the rocks under the hills and gathering to this one fat vein flowing, flowing towards the sea, far, far away. A road of water joining the forest and the ocean in one ever-changing story. When the dam was built all that would be gone. And there was nothing he could do.

The tiger and the sturgeon and the owl are the keepers of the forest. Each must speak to each to keep the forest whole.

He was alone. Skrimsli had gone. The sturgeon had probably swum straight back to the sea. The words were just words, the stories were just stories, they had no power to move stones or stop things being blown up. Owl wanted to throw the words into the river and watch them sink. He was just a freak child, who looked like an owl. He pulled the wooden sturgeon from his neck, drew back his arm to throw it into the water, and froze. There was a sudden rush of air, and the thistledown brush of a wingtip against his raised arm: a fishing owl dropped from the tree beside the pool. It carried silence with it like a heavy cloak. There was the slightest splash, just a breaking of the surface, and the dark curve of talons gripped the silver of the fish. Its huge wings seemed to stretch from bank to bank as it swooped over Owl's head. As silently as it had arrived, it was gone, leaving only the gleam of two big, yellow eyes in Owl's mind.

The greatest keeper is the owl who speaks both to the trees and to the river.

Owl put the sturgeon back around his neck. If the owl was the greatest keeper, then Owl would have to try to be enough on his own.

It took much longer in the dark to find his way to the vantage point where he had stood with Nopea. Everything was quiet. Horribly quiet. But there were lights still showing in the huts. He waited. At last the lights went out and he walked along the wire fence until he found a place where some animal had wriggled underneath. He wriggled too and moved out onto the bare hillside. He felt as obvious as a red bug on a white rock, but he willed himself not to be afraid and to keep moving.

He reached the door of the first hut with barred windows. It was locked of course. He walked round to the window on the end farthest from the next hut, reached between the bars and tapped on the shutters.

Nothing. He tapped again. And again. Still nothing. He tried the next hut, tapping harder and harder on the glass, more and more afraid that one of the uniformed guards would wake and come to find him, but their hut was quite a distance away and he guessed they slept soundly.

He walked back to the first hut. A little solar light shone over the door. Owl took a good look at the lock. The door was half rotten, and the lock looked as if it was about to fall out. This was a lock that could only keep you imprisoned if you wanted to be locked up.

Owl looked around and found a rusty spade leaning against a wall. He swung it with all his might and smashed the lock, then prised it out of the door and walked in. The noise had woken the sleepers in the hut. As Owl walked through the door, a lamp was lit and showed twenty or thirty people huddled together at the end of the hut. As he appeared they gasped and fell quite silent.

No one said a word for a long time. Then one of the adults reached out a hand and beckoned to Owl. He came close and allowed himself to be touched by one set of fingertips after another.

'He's real,' said someone. 'Real as you or me.'

They stared at him and talked about him as if he couldn't hear.

'Should we wake her?'

'Is it really him?'

'We should wake her.'

'Yes, wake her, go on!'

One of the men spoke to him very slowly, in Nordsky. 'How did you get here?' he asked as if speaking to a baby.

Owl replied in their own language. 'I came with my friend the tiger, up the river from the Belugi Sea and then over these hills.'

They all gasped; one man became faint and had to sit down; then everyone began to talk at once.

Another lantern was lit inside the hut, so Owl could see into the rows of beds. Someone that he had not noticed on his way in was being helped from one of them. It was a woman who could not walk without the help of a friend, yet she hurried as fast as she could across the room to where Owl stood. She stared at him in the half light of the yellow lamp, then reached her thin arms toward him. Her eyes were huge like his own, and full of tears. As her hand touched his cheek Owl noticed he had been holding his breath. Perhaps, he thought, he had been holding it since he had been taken from her so very, very long ago.

'It's you!' she whispered. 'It's you, my Owl, my lovely boy! Where have you been?'

It was a question that would take Owl a long, long time to answer. But now, there wasn't time.

'Mama,' he whispered to her, the word strange in his mouth

379

as the idea was in his head. 'Mama, I've come to give you back your hope, your fight. There is still time to save our forest and our river. Will you help me?'

She looked into his face.

'Oh, my dear, what life have you lived that your eyes are so deep, so old?' she breathed. 'Perhaps you *are* the one to make the stories real.'

She stood clear of the two sets of arms that had supported her. She seemed to grow a little taller and when she spoke, her quiet voice was firm.

'Once my son was a symbol of our strength,' she said. 'Comrades, can he be that once again? Can we be strong enough to fight again?'

Owl looked around the room. Some faces were lit up, alive to his mother's words, but others looked away. One man, almost as thin as his mother, shook his head sadly.

'We've lost, Kussi,' he said. 'We lost years ago. All we can do is take the money they give us tomorrow and leave.'

Another woman spoke. 'Your son is back. Well, good for you.' Her voice was hard and flat. 'But my sons will never come back. I was beaten the day they died.'

The voices were growing louder now. One young man was angrier than all the rest. He stood next to Owl and turned to the others.

'Are you lot mad?' he cried. 'We were fools to believe those stories, to believe they made us strong. We were fools to believe that when this kid was born it *meant* anything. He's just a *freak*! Look at him! He's not the keeper of anything!'

The word, *that* word; Owl saw his mother take a breath,

draw herself tall to fight for him. She looked at the young man with fire in her eyes.

'Don't you speak to my son like that, Keel!' she said. Owl's heart swelled with all the missed years of love and protection, but he could fight for himself now. He laid a hand on Kussi's arm.

'It's alright, Ma. I can speak up for myself.'

She looked at him with wonder in her face, then nodded and stepped aside.

Owl came right up to Keel and looked up into the young man's face. He was twice Owl's height, handsome, strong; everything that Owl would never, ever be. But Owl knew that he was stronger still.

'You are in this hut, Keel...' Owl told him, '...in your broken forest, because you stopped listening to stories. Stories show you what you can be if you are brave enough. I am not like you, and you are not like me, but tonight we can choose to make a new story, together, and to stop living inside this old, sad tale.'

The silence in the hut was as profound as the one the fishing owl carried under her wings. It was Skrimsli who broke it, stepping up suddenly beside Owl as if formed in that moment from the air. There were gasps, cries of fear and disbelief and wonder. Skrimsli, of course, ignored them all and greeted Owl with a head bump as he came into their shared mind space.

Kin! he said.

Kin, Owl replied. *Where have you been, Skrimsli?*

Finding more kin! Skrimsli answered him. *See?*

Owl turned to follow Skrimsli's gaze and saw another tiger

lurking in the grey dark beyond the door. Owl sunk his fingers in to the cub's deep fur. His heart turned with joy for his friend and pain for the loss that he knew it would mean.

You will go with her? Owl asked.

Yes, Skrimsli replied, but not yet, *I have found your big fish also. They are in the pool below the rocks. They are very afraid. They know a bad thing will happen here and their warning filled my head, like stings. They said rocks will break the river. What does it mean? I knew you would know.*

Skrimsli's green eyes shone into Owl's own with a new kind of light and trust. A new shared understanding and respect. We've both grown up, Owl said inside himself.

I do know, Owl told Skrimsli, *and it does mean a bad thing, very bad. But we're going to stop it. All of us together, right now!*

Owl stood by his friend, Skrimsli, and turned to look at the people he had lost for so long. This was belonging, this was what it felt like not to be a freak!

'We are the keepers of the forest!' Owl cried. 'And we've come back!'

'The Owl-child and a tiger!' someone exclaimed in awe. 'It's a sign!'

'It's a sign, right enough,' said another.

'It is a sign, that's true,' said Owl's mother, 'but it only means something if we act now. Who is ready to change our story at last?'

Nods and smiles spread through the group. Then Owl and Skrimsli lead them out of the hut into the blue night.

They are afraid of me, Skrimsli said.

Of course they are, Owl replied. *You are a tiger.*

382

If there were any doubts left that the forest keepers had returned, they were dispelled when Skrimsli's tigress appeared, hanging back in the shadows. An Owl-child and *two* tigers was enough to make anyone admit that there was something in the stories after all.

The first job was to make sure the guards didn't get in the way. They did not expect their miserable workforce to resist them, so it wasn't hard. It didn't take long to nail their door closed and two tigers prowling in the dark was enough to keep them inside. Everyone disliked guns, so all the guards' weapons were taken from their store and dropped into the river. Then the workers from the second hut were freed.

Everyone knew what needed to be done. It didn't take long to decide. Nopea's dad, Fetlar, said, 'We'll take the explosives out of the cliff then reset them in the walls. Should be enough to bring the lot down and blast a path for the river.'

The young man who had called Owl a freak volunteered to set light to all the tree-felling equipment and machines.

'I'll leave one tractor,' he said. 'The guards can use that to get out of here when we're done!'

They got to work at once, shining the lanterns from the guards' hut onto the cliff face so that Fetlar and his workmate Giga could get the tricky work of moving the explosives done. Fetlar said it would take a few hours. No one wanted to wait until light because who knew what other forces might come in the morning when it had been expected that the cliff would be blown sky high.

We must speak to the fish, Skrimsli, Owl told the cub. *When the rocks are blown apart, they need to be safe out of the way.*

Owl and the cub turned to head down the hill together.

'Where are you going, son?' Kussi exclaimed.

'We need to speak to the other keeper, Ma, before we blow the dam up.'

There wasn't time to say more. Owl and Skrimsli headed down the bare hillside with the tigress trailing them in the shadows.

Owl found he remembered how to swim and side by side he and the cub crossed the pool above the rubble barricade. They climbed out onto it to look down into the water below. The sky showed the first faint grey of dawn and both Owl and Tiger had eyes that could see in the dimness.

There they are, said Owl in wonder, as the huge shapes cruised back and forth in the pool below. *But how do we speak to them?*

I can hear their fear, but you are the one who speaks to tree and to river, Skrimsli replied. *Perhaps you already know.*

Owl wrapped his fingers around the little sturgeon round his neck and stared into the water. He thought of the green of the forest that had sustained him in his long exile; he thought of the bright day when, as a tiny baby, he had been put in the water to welcome the fish back into the river, and he thought of the night of the flood, and of the huge, ancient bodies that surrounded him and surged away on their old journey.

Their minds were so different from his, their awareness and experience utterly unlike his own, but Owl felt himself slip into connection with the sturgeon as easily as slipping into a pool to swim. Sturgeon, trees, tigers, wolves, bears, birds, insects, they were all ever-changing parts of the big pattern of the forest. He felt it and knew it. In that moment of connection, it was easy to let the sturgeon know that the river was to be unbroken and for a little while they must swim to safety.

Skrimsli, orange and warm as flame, materialised out of the green glow that the fish left in Owl's mind.

My tiger kin calls me, he said. *She will not like the big noise that you're going to make.*

Owl agreed. *She will not.*

We will leave now, Skrimsli said, *and go far. And then a little further.*

Owl leaned his forehead onto the stripes between the cub's eyes. They both knew they might not see each other for a while. They said nothing but thought the same thought.

Kin, my kin.

They swam to the bank together, then Owl watched two tigers walk up the barren slope, over the fence and vanish at the forest edge.

His mother, Kussi, and the others were waving to him from the huts. Owl climbed the hill to his human kin as the eastern sky blushed yellow. Everything was ready. The villagers were used to working as a team.

'We did a good job setting those explosives,' said Giga.

'Yes!' Fetlar agreed. 'The river's path will clear with a nice big bang!'

'We should have fetched the children!' Owl's mother said. 'They should be here to see it!'

But the children were coming anyway, with Teva. A line of lanterns was snaking down the hillside from a new hole in the fence. The adults and children ran into each other in a tide of tears and laughter.

385

'I saw you go,' Nopea told Owl, from the circle of his father's arms. 'I followed you. When I saw you smash the door of the hut and the tigers came up from the river, I went and fetched everybody!'

Now everyone was here, it really was time. The whole village made a ring holding hands around the two men and the detonator.

'Why didn't we do this before?' Fetlar said sadly.

'Better now than never,' Giga said.

'Should we say some words?' the young man, Keel, asked. 'Something from the stories?'

'What do you say, Teva?' Kussi said.

Teva turned to Owl. 'What do you say, forest keeper?'

Owl shook his head. 'Words can come afterwards. Just do it!' he said. 'Just do it. Now!'

The explosion was massive. It lit up the sky to rival the dawn and shook the hills to their core. Rock spat down on the ground and a dust cloud billowed up, enveloping the place where the dam would have stood and blocked the river's way for a thousand years or more. The river rushed free, gushing and joyful, ready to carry its story all the way to the sea.

As the sun came up, they were all still standing looking at the valley below.

Kussi leant against her son.

'It was so beautiful this world of hills, this great forest!' she said sadly. 'Why did we let this happen? Why didn't we fight back sooner?'

'That's the past,' Owl said. 'You can't re-write that story. But we've just begun to write our future.'

Below them in the valley, the dust cloud from the destruction of the dam finally cleared. The newly flowing river cleared the debris from its path itself and, as the sun rose higher like dull bronze, the backs of sturgeon glinted at the surface as they plunged upstream. They would spawn in the pools. Their countless fry would feed a hoard of mouths; when at last the oldest fish made their last spawning journeys, their bodies would nourish the roots of the trees, in one final conversation between the river and the forest.

36
Skrimsli

The Monster

The tigress taught Skrimsli a great deal. He learned about hunting and he learned about territory. It was necessary to know your own territory so well that you would notice if a single rock was out of place. That was how you found prey, by learning the places where they went and what they did and didn't do. Through the autumn they hunted together and shared their kills. Deer of several kinds, wild pigs too, with wicked tusks and quick minds. The tigress' territory was big. It ran far along the riverbank and then right over the ridge and down to the coast.

When the snows came, they hunted on beaches where the deer came to eat the washed-up seaweed. Skrimsli liked it there, close to the sea. He sometimes stood in the waves to feel their power and breathe in the salty spray. When the winter storms threw ice onto the beaches, they sheltered deep in a cave beneath the roots of an ancient tree, dry and warm, even if they were hungry.

When the ice began to melt, they made their way inland again, picking off creatures weakened by the long winter as they went. Skrimsli could hunt alone by then. He hunted for the tigress too. She was extra hungry now because her cubs would come when spring turned to summer.

But sharing was not part of tiger life. It was remarkable that the tigress had put up with Skrimsli in her territory for so long. He'd found that there were other tigers too. Females related to the tigress, whose territories were next door to hers, and a male tiger whose territory was vast and included those of several females. Skrimsli and the tigress had avoided him for months but, as the first green shoots began to show, he found a trace of Skrimsli's scent and he was not pleased. Only Skrimsli's strange un-tiger-like behaviour saved him from a fight that would almost certainly have ended in his death.

The day after that difficult encounter, consisting mostly of snarls and growls, the tigress said, *Go now. Go now and live.*

Skrimsli knew what she meant: go and find your own territory, your own place where you know every rock and tree and look at it every day and know if even a leaf is out of place. But Skrimsli knew that life was not for him. It saddened him greatly, but he did not want the same place, always and forever. He had been growing restless as the days had got longer. Now the light and dark were almost equal, and he watched the moon, counting up the time until it would be full. He had been thinking of the sea, the constant motion and the endless, ever-changing journey to that place where earth and sky meet. There was no sadness or regret between him and the tigress. He walked from her life as easily as he had walked into it and headed for the village, to see his other kin.

Owl was very, very pleased to see him and understood at once what he had come for. There wasn't any need to talk much. They sat together in the weak sun for a long while, watching the village, listening to the birds, Skrimsli playing his old game with every strand of sound and scent, laying it down inside himself, like a woven rug on which his life would rest. At last, they stood, forehead to forehead.

Your cubs will be forest keepers, Owl said. *And you will be keeping the forest wherever you are.*

Skrimsli could not find words of his own after so long without using them, so he said Owl's words back to him; the words that had brought them so far, on so many adventures.

The tiger and the sturgeon and the owl are the keepers of the forest. Each must speak to each to keep the forest whole. But the owl, who speaks both to the river and the trees, is the greatest keeper of them all.

The little boat was exactly where they had left it, but for the family of mice who had decided it would make an excellent winter home and had stored their hoard of nuts and seeds and grasses underneath. Skrimsli dragged some branches over what remained of their granary, to replace the nice roof the boat had provided. Then he jumped in and began to float. Why was floating so wonderful? Immediately it happened, he always began to purr. Today he didn't question it but enjoyed the feeling and the speed of movement down the river. The little river was nicely swollen with the melting snow, and it carried Skrimsli swiftly downstream. As night fell, swarms of baby eels, elvers, shivered in the depths like leaves made of shredded moonlight. He sensed in their tiny bodies the story of a long, long journey. Where had they come from, Skrimsli wondered. Did Ekar know? Did anyone?

The full moon had come and gone. Skrimsli was anxious. But when the river carried him out into the little bay at its mouth, there was the *Ice Maiden*, anchored off the island that Ekar had named 'Hope'. There was enough of a breeze to sail if he could remember how. The modifications Ekar had kindly made to mast and sheets and tiller made it possible and he recalled enough to manage the boat without too much difficulty.

He steered from the green shore over sea whose surface had been newly stretched and polished. From the little rocky island, seabirds were setting out, of a kind he had not paid attention to before. Their wings were long and narrow, dark as earth, their bellies neatly white, their beaks tipped with a little downward hook. They flew with very little flapping, extremely close to the water, as if they wished to be fish and not birds or had not quite decided which to be. Thousands of them fanned out across the sea, criss-crossing in complex codes and patterns in the air. As they flashed past, he caught their big dark eyes, so serious and thoughtful. He caught, too, glimpses of their minds and that was most thrilling of all. They were the greatest voyagers, their heads filled with endless travelling, the whole world traversed in a constant, life-long journey. All round in sea and air were journeys, bird and fish and whales travelling, discovering. Spring was a season for it.

Everyone was pleased to see him, but Ekar knew that a tiger fresh from the forest should not be crowded. She asked the crew to save their welcome for another day. She led Skrimsli to his favourite spot at the ship's prow and gave the order to weigh anchor and set a course. Skrimsli felt the ship stir beneath him, and the salt air rush around him. He stepped easily into the old, shared mind space as Ekar came to stand beside him, looking out across the landscape of the ocean.

I have missed this, Ekar, he said. *I could not be a tiger in the forest. Territory didn't suit me. I couldn't always be saying this rock is mine. I did not like to be bound to one place.*

You are a natural seafarer, Skrimsli, Ekar answered.

Skrimsli lifted one of his paws and sprung its claws.

I don't know what I am! A killer? A wild thing bound in words? Am I some kind of monster, Ekar? Skrimsli asked.

Ekar smiled again and Skrimsli noted how Ekar's smiles, like Owl's, always told the truth.

Skrimsli, she said, *let me show you something. Let me show you you, as I see you. Look*, she said. *Look.*

Skrimsli gasped. Ekar had made a picture in his head of a creature with stripes just like him but the wrong colour entirely!

I am not that colour! he exclaimed. To his eyes, tigers were more the colour of the long grass.

Not in your eyes, no, but in the eye of humans you are that colour. Orange it is called. With my eyes I see things in you that you cannot see or know. That is the nature of existing, Skrimsli. We cannot know all that we are in the world or see the reasons we are loved. We must just live!

How can I live without knowing what I am? Skrimsli asked.

I will tell you what you are, Ekar replied. *You are yourself. You are Skrimsli, and that should be enough for any creature in this world. It is enough for me.*

392

37
Owl

Nettle's Seed

Autumn was the time for planting. All through the time of the Lost Hope, as the village called it now, Teva had made the children collect tree seeds and plant them. Now, at last the little trees would have a real home. All together children and adults carried the trees to the valley where the dam had been. Each small tree had with it a little store of soil from the old forest so it would bring with it the right fungi so it would be able to talk to all the trees around it.

Scrambling plants had already made their bid to reclaim the valley and the slope. Thorn and berry bushes had sprouted and even put out fruits.

'Bear poo,' shouted one of the younger children. 'I found bear poo, still warm!'

That was a great discovery. Bears would help with the work of tree seed planting, carrying the seeds of trees in their bellies and planting it in their poo, digging roots out of the ground and burying seeds in the process.

Owl was learning all kinds of new stories to tell.

His mother could walk short distances now. She was getting stronger. She had walked all the way today, but she sat down to rest while Owl dug a hole. He drew the small cloth bag from his backpack and emptied the seed, big and round as an egg, into his hand. The voice of the river family's youngest child, little Nettle, so much sweeter than her name, came back to him.

'It's magic!' she'd told him. It seemed so long ago now. Was the seed even alive enough to sprout?

'A little girl called Nettle gave me this,' Owl told his mother. 'Her family were very kind to me. She said she found it on the riverbank, but I don't know what it is!'

'Hold it to the light, Owl, so I can see it.'

Owl held it up and immediately Kussi was calling all the others over.

'Look what Owl's got.'

Owl laughed. 'Are you going to tell me what my seed is?'

'Well, I'll be jiggered!' said Giga.

'Haven't seen one of those since I was a kid,' said Fetlar.

Teve reached out a hand to touch it.

'There was a whole grove of these right here when I was very small,' she said. 'It's a nacep, Owl. A real nacep. It was the ancient food tree of our people. And now, it can be again.'

'They need a good deep hole, Owl. Keep digging!' Giga said.

Carefully Owl placed the seed in the big hole, remembering the kindness of that family, and all they'd taught him. Remembering Kal, and the Palatine, and Ekar, Taze and Galu Mak, Karu and poor Blit. But most of all, Skrimsli, dearest Skrimsli. Perhaps one day he'd visit and see the nacep tree grown tall.

'Let's all plant this tree,' Owl said. 'Come on, everyone, get a handful of soil, and drop it in. And make a wish when you do.'

When they'd finished, everyone seemed a bit solemn. The little trees looked so vulnerable in all that space and the nacep tree was still underground. Who knew if it would even grow? But it wasn't right to be solemn. Planting, even planting in a place that should never have needed planting, should be happy, because it was all about hope and making the world better.

So Owl began to dance. A silly, throwing himself around sort of dance, and pretty soon everyone else was dancing too, and laughing and crying, watering the seed with their tears of sorrow and joy.

38

The Palatine

The Throne Restored

Yalen had not been as popular as he had hoped. So, by the time the Palatine arrived back in Bisque City to announce that she had definitely not been assassinated, things were already going quite badly for him. He had never grasped the meaning of work and certainly never imagined in his worst nightmares that being the ruler of Yuderan was anything other than one long party.

The Palatine was reinstated, to general rejoicing apart from among those ministers and officials whom she sacked for misconduct. The materials to build the railway had already been moved over the border into Yuderan. The Palatine seized them from Nordsky ownership and conducted a nationwide poll about where the railways should be built. Most people agreed that railway lines that joined Yuderan's many far-flung towns and cities were more useful than a line across the Nordsky border. No one wanted to go *there*, for goodness' sake!

All agreed that the Palatine had returned from her travels and ordeals very much changed and for the better. She smiled more and she had lots of great ideas. She still deftly sidestepped all attempts to get her to marry. It was said that she had a secret lover, but if she did, it was a very, very well-kept secret.

If anyone had ever managed to follow her on one of her midnight walks into the desert, they might have had some clue. They might have heard her talking to the stars or setting her eagle off on one of his delivery missions, carrying letters a long, long way north and returning with messages so precious, that she carried the latest of them next to her heart.

39
Kal

The Grass Ocean

 Kal thought of the Palatine's words often. Hard as it was to admit, the Palatine had been right. Purpose was the most important thing, the thread of life. And Kal's life was very, very full of purpose, all the time: the New Talo programme to oversee; the plans to build new schools to educate Herring and Horse children together; the constant fight against more gold mining that would blow Tamen Haja into bits.

Sometimes, that thread of purpose got itself around Kal's neck: that's when escape was absolutely necessary. That's when the grasslands and the hidden ravines of the mountains called and Kal answered.

Today was beautiful. A sky of palest duck-egg blue, and the first hints of spring greens pulsing through the grass. The slopes of Tamen Haja faded from deep indigo to purple as the light came up. Kal crouched low over the horse's back, his mane streaming. Go Luja, Kal told him, and he went, changing from that loping canter into a gallop that most horses could still not catch.

Luja slowed when they got close. All the remains of the old place had been removed, along with all the bodies. Now Old

Talo was just as it had been for centuries, before humans built here: grass and flowers. Kal had been determined that this place would not become a place of horror, because it had been such a place of joy and freedom. It was where Luja had become a friend. It was where all those lives had been lived with purpose *and* with love. The manner of their ending was not what mattered. The assassins could not assassinate what they had been. So Kal came often, to remember the good things and erase the bad.

There was another reason for the visit. A reason now dropping from the sky, tired after his long journey. Kal pulled out the gauntlet and the goat meat, and while Sayka feasted, Kal undid the little package from his foot and replaced it with another, so neatly bound that Sayka could rest and hunt on his way home without impediment. Kal had come to love this ritual, of waiting at the allotted date and time for the appearance of the Palatine's noble friend. It wasn't just the contents of the letters and packages they exchanged, it was this moment, looking to the same sky and knowing that it was also over her head. The Palatine had been right about that, too: love was a thread that neither distance nor time could break.

Epilogue

At last, they had left the ice behind, and the wind blew steady. The sails were taut and full, and the ship cut the swells with a creamy wave at her breast. Skrimsli felt the *Ice Maiden*'s conversation with the water and the wind thrum through his paws and sing in his whiskers.

I am sure she is alive, Ekar, Skrimsli said.

Ekar smiled. *Perhaps you make her so, Skrimsli!* she replied. *Perhaps you and she are a new kind of being entirely!*

Perhaps, said Skrimsli. *I am not a tiger like my ancestors, that's certain.*

And I am not a captain like my mother, Ekar told him.

Skrimsli turned to look at her. *Are you certain of that, Ekar?*

I am. I have had many months to watch you and to think, Ekar replied. *We will share my ship, Skrimsli. I will be her guide and yours, we will command her course and crew together, but you will be her captain.*

Skrimsli held her in his green fire gaze. At last, he nodded.

Together then, he said, *we will sail to the place where the sky and ocean meet.*

Ekar smiled and they both turned back to look at the sea. For a thousand miles in all directions there was nothing but blue and themselves, one speck of green and one of orange, travelling endlessly towards the horizon.

Fun Facts

Skrimsli was not a character I planned. He happened without me having to think about him first. And then he almost took over *The Song that Sings Us*, so it seemed a good idea to give him a story of his own, and to tell the history of how a tiger becomes a talking sea captain!

The character of **Owl** is based on a very special kind of owl – the Blakiston Fish Owl. This is the largest kind of owl in the world with a two-metre wingspan. It lives in the forest of northeast Asia and shares it's habitat with Amur tigers (the kind that Skrimsli is), black bears and leopards. It needs big ancient trees for nesting and wide slow rivers full of fish to catch its food.

I did lots of research into **circuses** and I found how they travelled around the country by train and then would parade all the animals around town when they arrived. Trick riding acts were very popular and many circuses began with just horses and rider doing daring tricks like balancing on galloping horses. These kind of acts are still popular in some parts of the world today. I'm really hopeless at riding! But I would love to be a brilliant rider. It was great fun imagining the scenes where Kal and the horse Luja are working together as a team with Kal standing on Luja's back as he gallops at full speed - pretty much my dream!

The forest in the book is based on a real forest that surrounds the banks of the Amur River in northeast Asia. It is one of the most remote and beautiful forests in the world, covered in snow in winter and steamy hot in summer. I've read lots about it and I would love to visit it one day.

The Song that Sings Us
hardback edition
by Nicola Davies

cover and internal illustrations by Jackie Morris

Nominated for the Yoto Carnegie Medals
for Writing and Illustration

£14.99 (Firefly Press, 2021)
ISBN 978-1-913102-77-7